ANNE SAT DOWN IN A CHAIR AND WATCHED MARK'S HANDS MOVE OVER THE WOOD.

His fingers were long and supple; the skin very tanned.

Anne stared, fascinated by the movement of one hand, while the other steadily gripped the block of wood. When he ran his fingers over his work, he seemed almost to caress it, moving with a competence and care that reminded Anne of a lover's touch. An ache Anne had thought long dead was rising. It had been so long since she had felt even a spark of desire. . . .

"Kristin James fans will take great pleasure in her latest powerful romance HEARTWOOD. . . . Several eloquent sequences will leave your heart in tatters. . . . HEARTWOOD is special reading that will win a reserved spot on your bookshelf."

—*Romantic Times*

Heart-wood

Kristin James

PUBLISHED BY POCKET BOOKS NEW YORK

This novel is a work of fiction. Names, characters, places and incidents are either the product of the author's imagination or are used fictitiously. Any resemblance to actual events or locales or persons, living or dead, is entirely coincidental.

Another *Original* publication of POCKET BOOKS

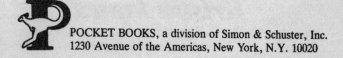

POCKET BOOKS, a division of Simon & Schuster, Inc.
1230 Avenue of the Americas, New York, N.Y. 10020

ISBN: 0-671-52778-9

First Pocket Books printing May, 1986

10 9 8 7 6 5 4 3 2 1

POCKET and colophon are registered trademarks
of Simon & Schuster, Inc.

Printed in the U.S.A.

Prologue

THE HOUSE LAY AT THE FOOT OF THE MOUNTAIN, FLANKED BY pines and aspens, like a perfect jewel in its mounting. It stood at the edge of Iron Creek just far enough back from the highway that it could be viewed in all its magnificence and yet remain private. The rocky, tumbling creek from which the town took its name swept in front of the house and curved around one side on its tortuous way back into the mountains, so that one had to cross a narrow wooden bridge to reach the house.

It was named Heartwood for the hard, long-lasting center of the tree, and it was built of Colorado red granite, a stone the color of rust and as enduring as time. It was a monument to a miner's wealth and love for his bride, neither of which had lived as long as the house.

Sophia Reynolds Kerr stood in the formal front room, still referred to as the parlor, and gazed out across the gently sloping land to the highway and the mountains beyond. This was her house, and she loved it beyond measure; she thought the worst thing was knowing she would soon have to leave it forever. She turned and inspected the room with a critical eye. The front parlor and the music room she kept almost as museum pieces, the windows shrouded by heavy velvet curtains, the furniture ornately Victorian. Intricate plaster moulding ran around the edges of the ceiling and encircled the crystal chandelier in the center. She crossed the room, her steps muffled by the thick Oriental rug, and walked into the hall. All but the entrance and kitchen were floored in the original hardwood, its surface protected by area rugs and runners. The entryway was laid in a diamond pattern of black and white Italian marble; Sophia loved its coolness beneath her feet even in winter.

She drifted down the hall past the paneled study and dining room and the more modern den. Beyond her she could hear Linda clattering pots and utensils as she prepared dinner. Sophia went down the narrow back hall and up the servants' stairs to the floor above. Most of the rooms here were furnished but unused, their doors closed, so that the corridor seemed dark and small. Sophia paused at the door to her sitting room.

It was where she spent most of her time, partly an office and partly a place to relax, where she was rarely intruded upon even by her housekeeper. A door in the north wall connected to her corner bedroom, which had two large windows with a view of the mountains. This room held only a single window, but Sophia loved to sit there on the recessed seat and look out at the towering lodgepole pines interspersed with narrow white aspens, trembling in the wind. Through the trees she could glimpse the sparkle of the rushing, twisting creek that curved around Heartwood and wriggled back into the mountains. And towering above everything were the ever-present mountains, blue-tinged, barren above the timberline, and topped with snow. The patches on the highest peaks never melted, even in the middle of summer.

Sophia glanced out the window at the familiar view, then sat down facing the room. Strangely, it seemed as if she were seeing it for the first time. Or perhaps looking at it with new eyes, eyes that knew the future. For the first time she saw it as a collection of furniture: several chairs, a desk, a sofa, and some lamps. She noted the scratches on the side of the delicate French writing desk, the black marks on the wall where the door handle had touched too often, the lack of light in the room. People nowadays seemed to love light streaming into their houses, fading the furniture and rugs; it didn't make sense to her.

Another person would own this house. The attorneys would sell the furniture and then the house, or perhaps someone would buy them all together. Probably not. They'd want to put their own things in here, repaint the walls, take down the drapes. Sophia pressed her lips together; it was almost a physical pain to think of others here, meddling, changing. This was the room where she had last seen Gary alive. It was here that he had faced her, defiant and angry, his black hair raked back by fingers that trembled, his blue eyes blazing at her. He'd argued and raged, begged her to change her mind, and when she refused, he had charged out of the house, leaving her coldly furious. They'd parted with nothing but harsh words between them. The next time she saw him Gary was lying in the hospital on a cold metal table, lifeless and white.

There wasn't a room in this house she hadn't cried in. Not a room that didn't hold a memory. How could she let strangers have it? But she was alone; she had no family. She turned, curling her legs up on the cushion of the window seat; at 74, she was still that supple, and even now the thought pleased her. She stared out the window at the trees.

Of course, there was the girl. Anne. Beverly's daughter. She'd sworn never to see or speak to Beverly again, after what she'd done to Gary, and Sophia had never yielded to the temptation to seek out the girl. But now it was too late for pride and bitterness. She wanted to see her. What color was her hair? Her eyes? Was there a dimple beside her mouth; did she have that way of quirking her lips when she smiled that made you smile back? She wanted to see her in this house, to hear her voice, to watch her laugh.

Sophia swung out of the casement seat and strode to the phone. Picking up the receiver, she punched out the number of her attorney and waited impatiently for his secretary to put her through. "Charles? Sophia Kerr. I need to see you this afternoon. I have some legal business I want cleared up right away." She grimaced, and her voice turned imperious. "Well, move something. I need to see you now. Good. Two-thirty, then."

She lowered the receiver and stood for a moment with her hand resting on it. She'd never contacted Beverly, but she had made it a point to keep track of her. She knew her husband's name and her daughter's name, even knew when her daughter had gotten divorced. Unconsciously Sophia wet her lips and picked up the receiver. Flipping open the telephone book beside it, she ran a finger down the list of area codes and pushed the numbers for information. When the operator answered, inquiring, "What city, please?" Sophia answered, "Dallas. I'd like the number of William Mitchell."

Chapter One

ANNE HAMILTON SMILED REASSURINGLY AT THE YOUNG WOMAN before her and motioned toward the high-tech sofa on the other side of the waiting room. "Have a seat, and Dr. Crenshaw will be with you in a moment."

Anne was good at putting the clients at ease; it was a necessary skill in a receptionist for a group of psychologists. Her smile was friendly and catching, her voice well-modulated. She was pretty without being threatening; her face was soft and almost square rather than classic, with the slightest indentation in the bottom of her chin that added to her air of vulnerability. Her eyes were large and a dark blue under narrow brown brows. Her mouth was generous, with a full lower lip. She was dressed neatly in a crisp white suit with a wide white leather belt around her waist. To anyone with an eye for clothes, it was an obviously expensive designer dress, but any intimidation the perfect suit carried was offset by the warm disorder of Anne's dark red-brown hair, put up in a pristine knot this morning, but now loosening and trailing a few strands down her neck. Her frequent attempts to brush it back and tidy it only worsened the problem, until now the knot hung heavily at the nape of her neck, threatening to fall apart altogether.

The phone buzzed and she picked it up. "Family Counseling." She smiled. "Hello, Dan. No, she's with a client right now. You want me to have her call you back?" She chuckled, a warm, throaty sound. "I'm not going to tell her that! Okay. I'll have her call you. 'Bye."

Anne set down the receiver and scribbled a note on a pad, ripped off the page, and stuck it on one of the three spikes on the left side of her desk. Then she turned, put the dictaphone headset in her ears, the top curving under her chin, and resumed typing a letter. She liked the work she did, at least most of the time. Although it had been years since she had typed and she had never used a phone system like the one this office had, she had caught on to the skills quickly. Anne enjoyed keeping the office organized and running smoothly. She even liked making the coffee and keeping the workroom and reception area tidy. All her life she'd tended to be in the background, not a trailblazer like her sister. She was a helper, and keeping everyone in the office on schedule and prepared was far easier than keeping her own house and family in order had been when she had been only a housewife.

Only a housewife. That was too prosaic-sounding for the wife of a successful plastic surgeon. It didn't encompass planning and putting on a dinner party for the hospital staff and their wives or attending the charity parties and hospital auxiliary coffees or manning the hospital gift shop one afternoon a week. Fund-raising and social gatherings—they were something she certainly hadn't missed since her divorce! Though she liked people, Anne preferred them one on one, not in masses at parties. Nor did she like asking for handouts, even if it was in the name of a worthy cause—or, rather, pressuring people for donations, because that was usually what it had been, not simply asking. But Bryan had loved parties; he'd thrived on the political jockeying. And he had firmly believed that his wife must belong to the right charitable associations, the ones frequented by the wealthiest and most social of Dallas's women, from which would come an endless demand for nose jobs, tummy tucks, and eyelid lifts.

Bryan. Well, he must be the happiest of men now. He was marrying into one of those elite families; his position would be secured among the face-lift set.

Anne made a mistake and sighed, ripping the sheet of stationery from the typewriter and sliding in another. Why was she letting her mind wander onto Bryan? You'd think she was still in love with him, when really any affection between them had died years before the divorce. She remembered when he came to her, frowning solemnly, carefully picking out his words, and told her he wanted a divorce. Her first thought had been pure rage that after all the times she had wanted to leave and instead had stuck it out, had tried again for the sake of the children, now here *he* was, asking for a divorce! As if he were the injured party! She had wanted to cry out that it was unfair.

But of course she hadn't. Instead she'd burst into tears, and ever since she had regretted giving Bryan the satisfaction of seeing her cry over him. Worse, it was to him another proof of her instability, her rampant emotionalism, one of her many failings which he cited as driving him away.

Thank heavens he hadn't seen her in the first few months after he left! She'd been on a real emotional roller coaster then. Even her younger sister, Bit, usually Anne's mainstay in any crisis, had flung up her hands in despair. "I don't understand you!" she had exclaimed in exasperation. "I would think you'd be happy the jerk was gone. He's cold and selfish; surely you can't still love him."

No, she didn't still love him, not really. But she couldn't explain it to Bit—the despair over failing again, the trembling terror at suddenly facing the world alone, the crushing responsibility of raising two children by herself. She had failed in the most basic thing in the world. She couldn't please a man; she couldn't hold her husband. Her sense of feminine worth was shaken to the core. And with her self-esteem at its lowest, she had to tackle the world all by herself. She, who had never lived alone, who had gone from her mother's home into her husband's, who hadn't worked at a real job in almost seven years, must now compete in the job market with much younger, more experienced, better educated women; must take care of every problem with the car, house, and children all by herself; and, moreover, must begin a single social life again.

The whole prospect had been crushing. But she couldn't have expected Bit to understand. Bit, three years younger than she, was many years Anne's superior in confidence. She marched through life with brisk competence, independent, single, and career-oriented. She couldn't have understood standing before the open freezer, gazing at the frozen dinners, exhausted by a hard day's work, with two hungry children whining behind her, and bursting into tears because she couldn't decide which packaged dinners to warm up.

The telephone rang, and Anne started, surprised to find that she had been staring at a blank page, typing nothing. She removed the earphones and reached for the telephone. "Family Counseling."

The voice on the other end was brisk, male, and very familiar. "Anne? I haven't much time. I'm due in surgery in ten minutes."

"Hello, Bryan." He hadn't changed. She couldn't count the number of times she'd heard the same words from him.

"I just wanted to remind you to have Nicole ready earlier this evening."

"You told me that last week when you dropped her off."

"I wanted to make sure you remembered."

"I'm not an idiot, Bryan."

"Come on. You have a memory like a sieve, and we both know it." His voice cut off sharply, and he drew in a breath. Anne knew the expression on his face—slightly martyred and determinedly seeking patience. "Anne, let's not fight."

"That's fine with me." He treated her with the same faint contempt he always had. The fact that she had managed to stand on her own two feet after he left, hold down a job, and keep family and house in order hadn't increased his respect for her one bit. His attitude still managed to make her blood boil, but at least it no longer wounded her.

"The wedding's at seven, and I need to pick her up by six-fifteen."

"I understand. I'm getting off work a little early tonight, so I can pick her up and get her fed and dressed in time."

"Good. I'll see you then. Gotta go." It was his usual

good-bye. He hung up abruptly and Anne set the phone down with a sigh.

A client came down the hall from the psychologists' private offices and walked out the front door. Anne smiled at him automatically, then glanced at the woman sitting on the couch across the reception room. Dr. Crenshaw was running late this afternoon. Anne gave the waiting woman a reassuring smile and turned back to her typing.

The phone buzzed, and Anne grimaced slightly, pulling out her earphones to answer it. It was Susan Crenshaw, her voice a little flat and tired. "Anne, is my four o'clock out there?"

"Yes, she is."

Dr. Crenshaw sighed. "All right. Send her in. Oh, and did you type that letter to Jeff Henderson?"

"Yes, it's right here in your box."

"Good. Thank you. Bring it when you show the client in, please."

"All right." Anne hung up the phone and took the letter and envelope from the out box labeled "Crenshaw." "Mrs. Danacek?" Anne rose and came around from behind her desk. "Dr. Crenshaw can see you now. If you'll come with me . . ."

Just as Anne returned from Dr. Crenshaw's office, the glass doors opened, and Anne's sister walked in. Her sister's office was three flights up in the same building, and she often dropped by on her way in or out of the office. It was she who had heard of the position open in the psychologists' office and urged Anne to apply for it.

"Bit! How are you?"

"Don't ask. Geez, I'm tired. I spent half the afternoon trying to corner a judge." Bit plumped her briefcase down on the floor and perched on the edge of Anne's desk. Dressed in a tan suit and with her large, serviceable briefcase, she looked the soul of efficiency.

"And did you?"

"No, he left by a private door in his office." Her eyes gleamed predatorily. "But I'll get him tomorrow; there's no way he can avoid me two days in a row." She lit a cigarette and took a deep pull. Anne automatically moved the heavy glass ashtray closer to her. "So what have you been up to?"

"Nothing special. I just finished talking to Bryan. He was his usual condescending self. He wanted to make sure I had Nicole ready to leave at six-fifteen."

Bit rolled her eyes. "Only Bryan Hamilton would expect his ex-wife to get their daughter dolled up for his second wedding." She glanced pointedly at her sister. "And only you would be patsy enough to agree."

"That's probably true," Anne agreed. "But it's important to Nicole to look good tonight and impress her father."

"It's important for you to have some self-respect. Bryan's mother or sister could have helped Nicole dress. In fact, Bryan could have picked Nicole up from day care if it was so all-fired necessary for her to be there early."

"Oh, you know him. He'll be in surgery until almost six."

"So what? It's his wedding. If he's late, that's his problem."

Bit was right, of course. She shouldn't continue to conform to Bryan's wishes. But it meant a lot to her daughter that she look good tonight, and Nicole didn't really like Bryan's mother. She wanted Anne to help her dress and fix her hair. Frankly, with the way things had been between her and Nicole since the divorce, it warmed Anne's heart for Nicole to request her assistance and support. Anne knew she was being a doormat again, but Nicole needed something extra from her now; she'd been very hurt by the upheaval in her life this past year. Anne couldn't bear to deny her daughter what she asked simply for the sake of her own pride.

Anne looked up to find Bit frowning down at her again. "I know you think you're doing this for Nicole. But, damn it, Annie, you've got to show her you have a spine. Keep it up, and you'll have another Bryan for your daughter."

"Bit! How can you say that! Nicole would never—"

Bit raised her hands as if to ward off an attack. "Okay, okay. I know better than to argue with Supermom. I love Nicole, you know that. I'm just saying, be careful; she'll be a teen-ager pretty soon, and if you don't watch out she'll walk all over you."

"Like you did with Mother?"

Bit laughed, her eyes lighting mischievously. "How do you think I know? I speak from experience as one who is a walk*er*, not a walk*ee*." She leaned over and ground out her cigarette. "I have to run. I just stopped by to say hello. There's a stack of work this high on my desk that I have to finish tonight. I'll be lucky if I get out of the building by ten o'clock. So long." Bit gave her a brief wave and lifted her heavy briefcase.

"'Bye." Disappointment flickered through Anne. She had been thinking about taking the baby and going over to visit Bit this evening while Nicole was at the wedding. The evening of her husband's second wedding wasn't one when she wanted to be alone. "'Bye."

Anne watched Bit back out of the glass-and-chrome doors and stride off in the direction of the elevators. She was soon out of Anne's sight. Funny. All the books Anne had read on the subject said the first child was supposed to be the achiever, the go-getter, imbued with all his parents' hopes and pride, and the second child was the one who lagged behind. But Anne couldn't remember a time when Bit hadn't been smarter, faster, more aggressive, and more popular than she. Bit had been one of those golden children who seemed to have been blessed with all the attributes. She had walked at eight months, learned to read when she was four by listening to their mother work with Anne on her lessons, was on the girls' all-star softball team three years in a row in elementary school, topped the charts on all the school's achievement tests, and could have been one of the best track runners in the state if she hadn't opted to be a cheerleader instead. Her real name was Elizabeth, but Anne at three had had difficulty with her name and called her Bit; the name stuck, varied sometimes by calling her "Little Bit." It had seemed appropriate for her angelic face framed by soft, pale hair. Somehow she had never shed the name, though as she grew older the diminutive nickname became incongruous for all of her achievements.

Bit had natural ability. Sometimes Anne joked that Bit had inherited all the talent of their athletic father, leaving her none. But it was more than that. Bit had a gritty determination that never admitted defeat. If she was unable to do something on the first try, she kept at it doggedly until she accomplished it. Anne could still remember her younger sister wobbling around the driveway on Anne's bicycle when she was only five years old. It was too large for her; she had to stand up to pedal it. She fell off it again and again, but each time she got back on, heedless of scrapes and bruises and the blood that dotted one knee, until at last she made it up and down the driveway in one continuous circuit. Anne, eight years old at the time, had watched her with a creeping sense of defeat. Two years earlier Anne had learned to ride on a bike equipped with training wheels, and after her first spill, her mother had rushed out to help her up, saying with some asperity to her husband, "I told you she was too young to ride." It had been almost a month before Anne had tried again.

When Bit learned to ride, their mother had opened the front door, having watched the trial through the window, and tossed out casually, "Congratulations, honey! I knew you could do it. Come here and let me wash off that knee."

Anne sighed at the memory and turned back to her typing. She had accepted Bit's superior abilities long ago; at least she hadn't tried to hide from the truth. And given Bit's zest for life and natural friendliness, it wasn't hard to see why their mother preferred Bit. There had always been a separation between Anne and her mother, a sort of coldness in Beverly Mitchell's attitude toward her daughter, as if the hugs and kisses she bestowed on her were forced and false. But with Bit she had been spontaneously affectionate. Once Anne realized her sister's superiority, she understood: Bit satisfied her mother; Anne had consistently failed to achieve.

Without conscious thought or effort, Anne had retreated from all things competitive and shielded herself with a sweet, generous, helpful personality. She didn't seek the limelight, but neither was she cast out to the farthest, coldest corners. In class, in friendships, in romance, she was accepted because she never caused problems; she could be counted on to do more, work harder, and smooth over all the rough spots.

Anne gave herself a mental shake and set to work on the letter. She had asked to take off fifteen minutes early tonight in order to get Nicole ready in time, and she wanted to make sure all her work was in order before she left. A client for another of the psychologists came in, and Anne greeted him with a smile. He had been seeing Dr. Kleinschmidt for a long time and headed straight for the couch, merely giving a half-hearted wave in Anne's direction.

Anne finished the letter and walked down the short hall to the workroom to run off a copy. Fastening copy, original, and addressed, stamped envelope together with a paper clip, she left the set in Dr. Brown's plastic tray and turned to clean off her desk. Pencils and papers were quickly swept into drawers; files were placed in the filing cabinet in the workroom, and the cabinet was locked. All the business here was so confidential that Anne had learned long ago to hide everything out of sight and lock it up. No client wanted to think that anything pertaining to him might be left out where anyone could see it. With her desk clean and the drawers locked, Anne whisked the plastic cover over her typewriter, grabbed her purse, and headed for the elevators.

The office building where she worked was located on Preston Road in the prestigious area of Dallas north of the LBJ Expressway. Fortunately, the day-care center which kept John Peter and picked up Nicole after school was also located in the north Dallas/Richardson area, as was their home. Even so, it was still a ride of fifteen minutes to get to the day-care center and another twenty minute trip home in evening traffic.

Anne had asked the center to have the children ready fifteen minutes early, so the two of them were waiting for her in the anteroom. Nicole was slumped down on a bench in front of the receptionist's window, watching disgustedly as her young brother rolled across the floor. When John Peter saw Anne, he scrambled to his feet, crying, "Mommy!" and pelted toward her like a runaway freight train. He flung himself against her knees, and Anne laughed, picking him up to squeeze him.

"How's my boy?"

"My fine." He was just beginning to string words together to form two- and three-word phrases and used the word *my* for every reference to himself. "Woh," he said enthusiastically, pointing to the floor. "My woh."

"Yes, you roll very well." She gave him another squeeze and settled him on her hip, then turned to her daughter. "Hello, Nicole."

"Hi." Nicole had risen, her blue parachute-cloth knapsack thrown carelessly over one shoulder. At ten she was slender and not yet gawky, hovering on the edge of adolescence. Anne knew Nicole resembled herself when she was a child because she had compared her daughter to old pictures of herself. The hair was thick and unruly, clustering around her face. Its color was darker than Anne's had been at that age, a medium brown, but touched with red highlights; her eyes were blue. There was the same slightly indented chin, like a heart turned upside down; the same squarish shape to her face, and large, thick-lashed eyes. Anne smiled at her, feeling a familiar, bittersweet lump in her throat. What a mixture of pride and anxiety it was to have a child who looked so much like oneself. Except that Anne had never had that upward tilt of her chin or the unswerving gaze.

As always, Nicole was neat and fashionable. She wore designer jeans and a soft knit shirt with an alligator on it; even her feet were adorned in tennis shoes with a highly visible, fashionable name on the side. Her hair was pulled back from her face by a plastic bandeau in a bright color to match one of the sets of stripes in her shirt. Anne doubted that she had ever looked so fresh and presentable after a day at school. Moreover, she didn't think she'd known the brand name of a single thing she wore until she was in high school. It astounded her every time she was around Nicole and her friends to hear them discussing their clothes and everyone else's, throwing out "Izod," "Calvin Klein," "Jordache," and "Polo" as if they were magic incantations.

Nicole glanced at her eighteen-month-old brother contemptuously. "He's a real mess. He got dirt on your suit."

"It'll come off," Anne replied with a shrug. "And you haven't got any room to talk; you were just as grubby and grimy when you were a baby."

Anne glanced down affectionately at her son. Splotches and stains were dotted over his clothes from top to bottom, and over all was a layer of dust he'd picked up rolling on the floor. She turned her smiling gaze to Nicole and reached out to ruffle her hair as she'd done since Nicole was a baby. Now Nicole jerked away from her touch, her hands flying up to hold the headband in place. "Mother! Don't. You'll mess up my hair."

They walked out to the car, and Nicole hopped into the front seat while Anne strapped John Peter into his car seat in back. "I hate this car," Nicole said plaintively, as Anne finished with the baby and slid in under the wheel. "I wish you hadn't sold the Mercedes."

"This is a perfectly nice car, and it wasn't exactly inexpensive, either," Anne argued and turned the key. "At least it's paid for." The Mercedes hadn't been, and the monthly payments had been more than she could bear. After she had sold the car and paid off the remainder of the note, there had been barely enough left to buy this small Nissan Sentra.

"I wish I'd gone to live with Daddy."

Pain sliced through Anne, and her fingers clenched around the steering wheel. Children hurt their parents with impunity; they seemed to think that parents were robots, mechanical and without feelings. She struggled to remain calm and reasonable, to find the right words. "I'm sure your father would love to have you live with him, if you'd like." That was a fabrication, of course; Bryan would be appalled at the idea of having a ten-year-old girl thrust upon him and his new bride. The beginnings of a wicked grin touched the corners of Anne's mouth at the thought of his dismay. "However, you'll have to talk to him about it. Newlyweds generally like to have some time alone."

Nicole shrugged. "I don't like Gwen, anyway." Her voice sneered over the name.

"Oh? Why not? Have you talked to your father about it?"

"Why don't you ever say his name anymore? Why do you always say 'your father,' as if he was somebody you didn't know?"

Anne glanced at her, nonplussed. "I hadn't realized I did."

"Well, you do." Nicole turned her head to gaze out the window.

"You side-stepped that pretty neatly. I'll ask again: why don't you like Gwen?" Nicole shrugged, but Anne persisted. "Is she mean to you?"

"Ah, she yells at me sometimes. Like the other day, when I was trying on that dress for the millionth time. I told her it was a real bore, and I didn't see why I had to try it on again, just because all the bridesmaids were. She started cussing and held out my dress and shook it like this . . ." Nicole demonstrated vigorously. "And she said, 'You *will* try this on.'"

"Brides tend to be nervous, honey. I doubt she meant anything by it. And when you don't have any children, it's hard to understand how they feel."

"Why are you standing up for her? I'd have thought you'd hate her. After all, she took Daddy away from you, didn't she?"

Anne frowned. How could one explain it to a child? How could she tell Nicole that she'd love to say a thousand catty things about Bryan's new wife, that she resented to the core that the children would spend weekends with them as a family? But she had promised herself from the beginning that she would not use the children in her split-up with Bryan, that she would not try to influence Nicole, putting herself in the right and Bryan in the wrong. He was Nicole's father, and that was an important relationship; for Nicole's sake, she must not try to turn the girl against him. And that meant not turning her against his new wife, either. It was pointless to encourage Nicole to resent her father's bride; it would do no one any good and could do Nicole great harm. Nicole had to learn to get along with and accept Gwen, for that was whom Bryan had chosen to spend his life with. If Nicole tried to fight Gwen, she would lose.

Anne couldn't allow Nicole's relationship with her father to fall apart. Besides, it hadn't been all Gwen's fault, much as her bruised soul would like to lay the blame there. It was she and Bryan who had wrecked their marriage; it had been in trouble long before he ever met Gwen Willingham.

"It isn't quite that simple," Anne said slowly. "Of course, I'd love to have someone to blame. But I'm afraid the problem was that your father and I weren't suited for each other."

"Why did it take you so long to find out?" Nicole retorted.

"I knew long before that; I just hated to admit it." She gave Nicole a little smile. "Please, honey, try to get along with Gwen. She's very important to your father, and you'll be around her a lot over the next few years. Remember that she doesn't have any experience with children, and sometimes she'll probably be a little harsher or less understanding than someone who has children of her own."

"Daddy's right. You're weak. I'll never be like you. Never!"

Tears sprang into Anne's eyes, and she kept her gaze on the road so Nicole wouldn't see. She was aware of a fierce desire to reach over and slap her daughter as hard as she could. How could this have happened to her and Nicole? They had always been so close before the divorce! From the moment she was born, Anne had adored Nicole. She had played with her, dressed her, fed her, lavished care and attention on her, and Nicole had responded with a warm love. Nicole had whispered her secrets to Anne, confided her accomplishments and despairs. They had giggled together, gone shopping, snuggled up in bed and read bedtime stories. Nicole had been Anne's solace in an increasingly unhappy marriage.

Then Anne had had the baby. Even though Nicole loved John Peter and usually treated him like a little mother, she had resented the attention Anne gave him. She had begun to withdraw. Less than six months later, Bryan had left the house and filed for divorce. Since then Nicole had become an angry stranger. Bryan had never spent much time with his children, but Nicole loved him, and there had been the special bond of a father and daughter. Nicole bitterly regretted his disappearance from their lives, and she had blamed the whole miserable mess on Anne.

It had hurt Anne worse than anything else about the divorce to hear Nicole's voice turn bitter and resentful, to listen to her lash out at Anne. It was hard to take Nicole's anger calmly, maintaining a sure, steady love for her daughter. What she really wanted to do was lash back at Nicole, to scream that it wasn't *her* fault but Bryan's. She wasn't the one who had filed for divorce; she had stuck out lots of bad times simply for Nicole's sake. And Nicole's father didn't do things for her, didn't love her a third as much as Anne did. But those were things she couldn't say to Nicole; she couldn't wound her daughter like that.

Instead, she tried to ignore Nicole's bad temper, as she did now. Nicole glared out the window, and Anne drove on in silence. In the back seat John Peter, hungry and sensing the turbulent emotions between the other two, began to bounce up and down in his car seat and unleashed his powerful cry. Anne felt a severe pain beginning behind one eye. "Johnny, hush!" she snapped, changing lanes and almost scraping the front bumper of another car. This kind of emotional turmoil made her careless, and she shuddered to think of what might happen sometime while she and Nicole sniped at each other.

She turned right at the next street. "How would you like a hamburger for supper?" she asked with an assumed brightness. Nicole shrugged, but John Peter ceased his crying and began to accompany his energetic bouncing with babyish claps.

"Fwies!" he bellowed triumphantly, knowing what went with hamburgers and what he particularly loved. "Fwies!"

Anne pulled into the drive-up window lane at the fast-food restaurant. It was a typically long Friday evening line. Nicole glanced nervously at the car clock.

"Will we have time? Daddy's picking me up at six-fifteen."

"I know." Anne's voice was curt, and she instantly regretted it; after all, Nicole wasn't to blame for her father's annoying reminder this afternoon. "This will be faster than cooking something, and you have to eat or you'll be sick with nerves. We'll have you ready on time. Don't worry."

The line moved quickly, and a few minutes later they were speeding home with sacks of hamburgers, cokes, and fries between Nicole and Anne. When they pulled into the short, quiet street leading to the cul-de-sac where their home lay,

18

they still had thirty minutes before Bryan was due to arrive. Anne turned into the driveway, not stopping to retrieve the mail from its box or the evening newspaper from the lawn. After all the times she'd seen it, her eyes didn't even flicker toward the bright yellow real estate sign in the front yard with the word "Sold" slapped across it in bright red letters. But Nicole's eyes went to the sign and quickly away. For an instant, unshed tears sparkled in her eyes.

Anne parked in the detached garage beside the French Provincial–style house. She unbuckled John Peter from his seat and pulled him out, gathered up the sacks of food, and followed Nicole to the back door, touching the button of the automatic garage door opener on her way out. She fumbled through her keys and awkwardly opened the door, still carrying the sacks of hamburgers. Nicole raced through, stumbling over John Peter, who went down with a thud and set up a wail. Anne stepped around him and dumped the sacks on the kitchen table. John Peter followed her, his tears and bruises forgotten in his quest for "fwies."

Anne swung him up into his chair, tore part of her burger into bits on the tray before him, and dropped a few fries beside it. Nicole was gulping down her hamburger between swigs of cola, and Anne frowned. "Chew it up, please."

"Oh, Mother."

"You don't want to throw up at the altar, do you?"

"Mom! How gross!"

"There's no need to get excited. We have plenty of time."

"I wanted to roll my hair!"

"We will. We will." Anne started a conversation to slow her daughter's eating. "How was school today?"

Nicole rolled her eyes. "Moth-er! It was nothing. It was the last day. You know that."

A little shimmer of guilt passed through Anne. The last day of school for the year, and she hadn't even remembered. In the past she would have known, would have been there for the class parties, handing out refreshments, but now . . . everything was so hectic, she had forgotten it entirely. Nicole would be home for the rest of the summer, and Anne could imagine how she would react to spending all day every day at the day-care center. Inwardly Anne sighed at the thought of another long-running battle to be faced.

"I'm glad it's over," Nicole said as she stuffed another fry in her mouth. "At least I won't have to ride in that stupid van anymore!"

"The van from the day-care place?" Nicole nodded. "What's wrong with it? Don't they drive well?"

"Of course. That's not it. But I hate having to go out and get in it. It's got its name plastered all over the side. I'm the only kid that gets picked up by a day-care center."

"Surely not."

"It's the truth! Everybody else gets picked up by their mothers or a maid or a car pool or something. Nobody but me has to get in a bus and go to a day-care center. It's embarrassing."

"You know something, Nicole Hamilton? You are turning into a proper little snob."

Nicole shrugged and set down the uneaten portion of her hamburger. "I gotta get dressed." She slid out of her seat and dashed down the hall and up the stairs.

What she had said was the truth. Nicole was rapidly becoming a snob. It was the private school she went to that was doing it, Anne was sure. It was a very expensive and exclusive school attended only by girls from the best and wealthiest families. They'd had to be on a waiting list three years before Nicole got in. There were times when Anne fumed over it and vowed she wouldn't let her daughter remain in such an isolated, hothouse atmosphere. How could she let her grow up thinking nothing was as important as the name on the seat of her jeans? But Nicole had gone there since the second grade; she knew it and was secure there. Anne hated to tear her away from any form of security after she had been so unsettled by the divorce. Moreover, Bryan paid the outlandish tuition, not she, so she couldn't claim it was too large a burden financially. And whenever Anne thought of leaving the school, she balked at the idea of taking her daughter out of the most advanced educational system in the city and plunking her down in an overcrowded, under-staffed public school.

Anne sighed and glanced sideways at John Peter. He was still happily chewing his way through his fries, catsup smeared all over his cheeks and fingertips. She wondered if she dared leave him in his high chair by himself while he finished. She needed to help Nicole dress if she hoped to have her ready on time. But John Peter would yell bloody murder if she yanked him away from his food, and she couldn't let him take the messy stuff upstairs with them. On the other hand, left alone in the chair he might choke and there would be no one there to save him. Anne took another bite of her burger, then set it down. It seemed more than usually tasteless tonight.

How many times had they had take-out hamburgers this week? At least twice. They'd dashed by McDonald's the other night on their way to Nicole's dance lesson. She really had to stop feeding the kids so much junk. She should get back to cooking them good basic food as she had done in the past. Their systems must have undergone nutritional shock this past year. But by the time she and the children made it home, it was usually six o'clock, and all three of them were starving. She couldn't expect two hungry children to wait another hour while she whipped up a well-balanced meal—even longer if she had to stop by the grocery to buy some of the ingredients.

Perhaps if she was organized enough, she could plan her meals for a week in advance, make out a grocery list, and buy it all on the weekend. She knew working women who even cooked all weekend and froze the food, then whipped each night's dinner out of the freezer and into the microwave to warm up. Anne couldn't imagine it. She never managed to get caught up, let alone be able to prepare for the week ahead.

Anne decided to risk John Peter alone in the high chair and hurried after Nicole. Nicole had already plugged in the steam curlers on her bathroom counter and had wriggled out of her clothes and dumped them on the floor. Normally Anne would have remonstrated, but she was too tired and in a hurry. She jerked a plastic-wrapped pink silk dress from the closet and pulled off the plastic bag, unfastened the dress from the hanger, and laid it on the bed while Nicole ran her bath. With the skill of long years of practice, Anne rolled up her daughter's shoulder-length hair on hot electric curlers, then Nicole jumped into the tub for a quick scrub.

While Nicole bathed, Anne pulled out the lacy white tights bought especially for the occasion and the white patent leather slippers with the barest suggestion of a raised heel, which had sent Nicole into ecstasy. She set them and clean underwear outside the door of the bathroom just as the doorbell rang downstairs. Anne pushed back her sleeve to look at her watch and groaned in frustration. The wretch was five minutes early!

"Daddy's here, honey. Better hop out of the tub and dry off."

There was a muffled shriek inside the closed bathroom door. Anne hurried down the stairs to open the door. John Peter was yelling in the kitchen at the top of his lungs. Well, at least he hadn't choked.

Anne jerked open the front door. Bryan stood outside, already dressed in his tuxedo, dark hair stylishly blown dry, a perpetual slight frown between his eyes. He held out the newspaper, which had been lying on the front lawn.

Anne snatched it from him ungraciously and tossed it aside. "You're early!" she accused, before she ran into the kitchen to free John Peter from his imprisoning chair.

She set the baby on the floor and cleaned the catsup from his hands and mouth. Bryan followed her into the kitchen. His eyes swept the room expressively, taking in the jumble of papers, bags, and half-eaten hamburgers on the table and the breakfast dishes piled in the sink. Before he could say anything, Anne jumped in, "Take care of John Peter for a minute. I have to help Nicole with her hair."

John Peter, grinning, ran at Bryan's knees, his fine hair flying out around his face. Anne left Bryan warily inspecting the baby's hands and his own flawlessly clean trouser legs. Anne smiled to herself as she bolted up the stairs and hoped secretly that she hadn't cleaned off quite all the catsup from John Peter's hands.

Upstairs Nicole was in a state of anxiety, dressed in tights, shoes, and slip, her hair still up in rollers. "Oh, Mama! I'll never make it!"

Anne gave her a quick hug; suddenly she seemed to have reverted to the little girl who had once been so close to her. "Of course you will. Daddy'll just have to wait. They can't start without you."

"He'll be furious."

Anne took out the pins and rollers, tossing them hurriedly onto the counter. "Worse things have happened to him, believe me. He'll be okay. Don't you dare start crying. You don't want your eyes to look red when you go down the aisle, do you?"

Anne brushed out Nicole's hair, and it curled softly around her face. Anne formed bangs with a flick of her wrist and brushed the hair back on either side, securing it with small, pale pink bows edged in white lace. "Gorgeous." She grabbed the dress and held it out for Nicole to step into. "We're almost on time, and if I know Bryan, he allowed several extra minutes when he told us what time to be ready."

Anne zipped up the back of the dress and shook out the skirt, pulling out the puffs at the shoulders to their full measure. Nicole stared at herself in the mirror. "Oh, Mama, it's beautiful!"

Nicole had professed to hate the dress from the very beginning, calling it a baby pink, but even she had to admit that Bryan's fiancée had chosen well. It was made of pale pink moiré silk with a small Peter Pan collar and below that a triangular bib of white lace. The same white lace peeped an inch below the hem and circled the cuffs of the short, puffed sleeves. Nicole was a pretty girl, and in the elegant, feminine, and yet appropriately childish dress, she looked beautiful. Anne's eyes stung with tears.

"Okay, let's go." Anne trotted down the stairs, leaving her daughter to the full glory of descending by herself before her father's eyes. There was nothing Bryan loved like beauty, and

Anne knew he would be impressed by their daughter. "Bryan! She's ready!"

Bryan emerged from the living room, John Peter toddling at his heels. "Where's the living room furniture? And the dining table? And that huge thing you put the china in?"

"I sold them," Anne replied shortly.

"Sold them! I bet you got nothing for them."

"Of course I got something for them. I wouldn't have sold them otherwise. Look. Here she comes."

Bryan looked up, and a smile crept across his tight lips. Seeing it, Nicole burst into a wide smile and pelted down the last few steps to fling herself into his arms. "Hold it. Hold it." He lowered her to the floor. "No rowdiness tonight. You're going to be a little lady, right?"

"Sure."

Anne glared at him. If he didn't say something nice to Nicole about how she looked . . . "Bryan, how does Nicole look?" she prompted.

He smiled down at his daughter. "Absolutely perfect. I'll have to fight off all the men."

Nicole giggled. "Oh, Daddy."

"Okay, let's go." Bryan neatly side-stepped John Peter, who was dancing at his feet, squealing, wanting to be picked up. "We're late."

He shot a quick glance at the steps down into the empty sunken living room. That was where Anne had chased down John Peter this morning in her daily struggle to put on his clothes. His pajamas were still draped across the steps. Anne thought of the messy kitchen and the den, where John Peter had raked all the magazines off the coffee table and onto the floor this morning before they left. She had no doubt but what Bryan's observant eye had noted every instance of disarray. Bryan opened the front door, and Nicole went out. He looked back at Anne. "Honestly. Don't you have more pride than this? How can you let the house get into such a mess?"

"Bryan, for heaven's sake, I haven't had time to clean up today. I have a job now, you know."

"So do lots of other women, but they don't turn slovenly. You're simply disorganized and inefficient. If you'd only plan in advance, you wouldn't have this kind of harum-scarum, last-minute rush all the time."

White-hot rage surged through Anne. How dare he criticize her! It was easy for him to talk of organization and efficiency. All he had to take care of was himself. He had a part-time maid at home and a nurse and office worker at work to take care of everything for him. He didn't have to get up at six-thirty to see that the kids were dressed and fed, then make a mad dash to get them to school and the day-care center in time to get to work. He didn't have a lively, exploring baby at home or a rebellious daughter. He didn't have laundry and cleaning and food preparation for three people. Anne was always behind, always battling to keep her head above water, squeezing out money, worrying about bills, struggling to make the children's environment as secure and homey as possible, swamped with loneliness and depression, facing daily a new world where all the women seemed to be younger, smarter, and far more skilled than she. Yet Bryan sneered at her for a few dirty dishes and a messy floor!

Anne would have liked to jump at him, screaming and scratching, but she forced down her anger. What purpose would it serve? She didn't want to spoil Nicole's moment of triumph with an ugly scene between her parents. And she certainly didn't want her ex-husband to know he could still push her buttons like that. She forced a smile onto her face. "I'm sure you're right."

Bryan looked startled, and Anne followed up her advantage by inquiring sweetly, "Don't you want to take John Peter with you? I can have him dressed in a second."

Bryan's mouth dropped open and he stared, appalled. He began to stammer. "Uh, no. I—that is, really, Anne. It's not the kind of place for a kid his age."

"Of course not. I should have realized."

She looked Bryan steadily in the eye, and he had the good grace to flush. Bryan hadn't liked John Peter from the moment he was born. He showed him little affection, rarely picking him up or even talking to him. Since the divorce he hadn't taken John Peter with him when he picked up Nicole for her weekend visits, saying that the baby was too young to be separated from his mother for two days. He almost pretended that their son didn't exist.

Anne couldn't understand Bryan's attitude toward John Peter, and it had hurt her deeply. Bryan had not been a particularly warm or attentive father to Nicole, especially when she was a baby; he didn't like the mess of young children. But he had played with her and called her affectionate names; he had never avoided her as he did John Peter. What did he have against the child? She knew that Bryan couldn't abide ugliness or ill temper, but John Peter was a beautiful, sunny baby. Anne would have thought he would have been pleased to have a son—didn't every man want one?—and would have been planning already for John Peter to enter medical school.

Whenever he turned away from the boy or ignored John Peter's outstretched arms, it twisted Anne's heart. How could he be so cruel? So thoughtless? Couldn't he see how John Peter hungered after his father's affection?

Bryan lifted his hand in a wave of sorts and closed the door. Anne reached out to grab the baby, who was trying to toddle out the closing door right after Bryan. She locked the dead bolt lock and picked up the newspaper, then trailed back into the kitchen. Now that the rush was over, she felt drained. She looked at the half of a hamburger she had left on the table. It would be all right if she warmed it up in the microwave, but somehow it didn't seem worth the effort. She wasn't hungry, anyway.

Anne knew she ought to tackle the dishes in the sink. She could get the downstairs rooms squared away and looking presentable in a few minutes. But the very thought of it increased her lassitude. Besides, she didn't want to jump at Bryan's command as she had when they were married. He no longer ruled her life, thank heavens.

She left the kitchen, the baby lurching along behind her and squatting down now and then to investigate something interesting on the floor, and went into the den. This was the only room in the vast house that seemed homey to her, for the furniture here had been chosen more for durability and comfort than for looks. Anne flopped down on the sofa and stretched out her legs, flinging an arm across her eyes.

She thought about Nicole and Bryan. They would be arriving at the church soon. In less than an hour Bryan would be married again, this time to a wife that suited him. Someone young and glamourous and social. Well, Gwen Willingham was welcome to him. Devastated as Anne had been by the divorce, she had always known she was better off without Bryan. Now she could be herself; she no longer had to struggle to live up to his notions of perfection. Now she could wear her hair in braids if she felt like it or cut it off short, and there would be no one to tell her she looked foolish. There was no one to criticize her faded, patched jeans or to frowningly inspect the tiny crow's feet beginning to emerge at the edge of her eyes. No one to harp at her about exercise or losing five pounds so she would be model-thin.

But she couldn't help thinking about their marriage tonight. Ten wasted years. And at the end of it, the knowledge that she had failed at being a wife. Was failing, even, at being divorced. She watched John Peter cheerfully rip a cover from a magazine and crush it between his hands, twisting and tearing, as he emitted little crows of glee. Tears filled her eyes and coursed down her cheeks, and she turned her face into the couch and sobbed.

Chapter Two

BEVERLY TOOK A LAST DRAG ON HER CIGARETTE AND CRUSHED IT out in the ashtray with quick, nervous motions. She had to make up her mind tonight. She'd gotten the phone call Monday, and she had put off a decision as long as she could. The reservation for Denver was for tomorrow.

She glanced across the room at her husband. Bill sat with his feet up on the hassock and his face buried in the afternoon newspaper. He was fifty and a bald spot on his crown was growing more and more visible, but the rest of his hair was a crisp salt-and-pepper. Years of sitting behind a desk had drained his body of much of its firmness, but he wasn't pot-bellied or sagging. She couldn't see his face, still pleasant-looking but with the added dignity of years, only his blunt, capable hands curled around the newspaper edges. The plain gold band she had given him almost thirty-two years ago shone quietly on his left hand.

They had been married a long time. Beverly had loved Bill as much as she was capable, but their relationship had always been lopsided. He had brushed aside the inequity, saying she'd given him enough by simply marrying him and allowing him the opportunity to love her as he'd longed to. However, Beverly knew that she owed him more. Surely she at least owed him the continued love of his daughter without doubts or divided loyalties.

She owed the old woman nothing. Beverly didn't want Anne to see her, didn't want Anne to know. It had all been dead and gone for years, and Anne had never known a thing about it. Why bring it up now? Why unsettle Anne's life any more than it already was? Beverly feared the news would make her relationship with her daughter even worse; Anne might actively hate her now for having lied to her all her life.

Beverly sighed and ran a distracted hand through her usually immaculate hair. It would be much better not to tell her about Sophia Kerr. And yet . . .

"How can you deny Anne the opportunity?" Her husband's voice echoed her own thoughts so unexpectedly that Beverly jumped and turned to stare at him.

"What?"

Bill lowered a corner of the paper to look at her. "You heard me. How can you not give Anne the chance to choose whether she wants to see Sophia?"

"How did you know I was thinking about that?"

He quirked an eyebrow at her pointedly. It was a stupid question, and she knew it. She'd been thinking about nothing else all week, ever since Sophia's telephone call Monday afternoon. She had told Bill about the call, just as she'd always told him everything. They had been friends forever, and they never lied to each other. Even when they got married, she hadn't lied to him.

"I don't know what to do. If I tell her what Sophia wants, she'll want to know who Sophia is and what it's all about. I'll have to wind up telling her the whole story. Then we'll all be hurt."

"Maybe we should have told her long ago."

"Maybe. But we didn't, and if I tell her now—who knows what she'll think? She's standoffish with me enough as it is. Still . . . I almost felt sorry for the old lady. She must be terribly lonely or scared or something to stoop to calling me and asking to see Anne. Can I hold back something like that from Anne? What if Sophia wanted to help her? What if she wanted to give her something or leave something to her in her will? I couldn't deny Anne that; she's in such bad financial straits."

"There may be personal benefit to her, too."

Beverly glanced at him. "Are you willing to risk it?"

Bill sighed. "I'd hate to have her feelings for me change. You know that. But it seems unfair to let her remain in ignorance of her background."

"You worship fairness too much. Being fair isn't necessarily the best thing in every situation. Sometimes it's better to be kind than fair."

"And is this kind?"

"She won't be hurt."

"That's true. But she might lose something that would be a tremendous help to her. Something valuable. If you don't tell her, it's awfully irrevocable."

"And awfully selfish." Beverly leaned her head back against the couch and closed her eyes. That was what she really feared; that was why she delayed telling Anne. She couldn't bear to think what Anne would feel for her after she learned the truth. She was scared to risk losing her daughter entirely.

"Why carry the burden? Tell her; let her decide. Then you won't have the turmoil and guilt. She's not a child anymore, Bev. Do you think you have the right to decide for her?"

"I suppose not." She rose and walked to the mantel, looked aimlessly at the things atop it, and wandered away. Bill watched her, his newspaper forgotten in his lap. His wife was a beauty, even though the sparkle in her had died long ago. And he still considered himself lucky to have married her.

Beverly walked with a natural grace that contained a certain aloofness. Her eyes were large and green, highlighted by carefully trimmed brows and thick lashes. Her hair, now graying, was tinted its original blond and cut into a short, soft style that parted on one side and curled under just below the earline. Her taste in clothes was excellent, and she bought not for fashion, but to enhance her looks. There was a quiet elegance about her, a calm so rigidly maintained she seemed unshakable.

She had been a perfect executive's wife—lovely, charming, unflappable in the face of panic. Beverly had kept her face and figure with exercise, diets, and careful attention to her skin. She met people without complaint and was adept at engaging even the shyest or least attentive in conversation. She organized and arranged and worked hard and never exploded. No one could fault her looks and competence, though there were those who thought her cold and distant and even Bill sometimes remembered wistfully the dazzling girl she had once been.

Beverly wandered out of the room and up the stairs to their bedroom. She moved to her dresser and opened the jewelry box that lay upon it. Reaching inside, she tugged at a tiny satin ribbon on the bottom of the box, and a small square of the velvet lining lifted to reveal a shallow hidden drawer. Beverly pulled out an ancient black-and-white photograph and held it up. It was small and glossy, creased across the bottom, and with one corner missing. A young man smiled out of the picture, leaning negligently against a '48 Ford, arms folded across his lean chest. His dark hair was ruffled, and he squinted against the sun, grinning. Even in an old snapshot his vitality blazed forth; one wanted to laugh with him.

Beverly hadn't touched the picture in years. Her fingers trembled against it as she gazed into the young man's face. She rarely thought of him now, but she hadn't forgotten a feature. Lightly her thumb brushed his face. She replaced the picture in its cubbyhole and shut the little trap door. Funny, how looking at it still made her ache inside. She sat down in a chair and rested her elbows on her knees, her chin on her interlaced fingers. She felt weary and every bit her forty-nine years.

Finally she sighed and rose, smoothing her expensive trouser and blouse ensemble into place. She knew what she had to do, had known it all along, of course. She'd just been putting it off. She automatically went to her bathroom mirror to comb her hair and refresh her lipstick; she noticed that her fingers trembled slightly as she applied the lipstick. But her steps down the stairs were firm and even, and when she picked up her handbag and paused in the doorway to the den, there was no trace of anxiety in her voice. "Dear, I'm going over to Anne's now."

Bill lowered his newspaper again and studied her. "Want me to come along?"

"No." Beverly smiled and shook her head a little regretfully. "No, I'd better do this myself."

"All right. Drive carefully."

"I will."

She went down the side hall and into the garage. Bill did not pick up his newspaper again. He listened to her steps and the sound of the door closing behind her, then the low roar of the car starting. Still he sat, gazing at the doorway, the paper spread over his knees, forgotten.

Anne had just gotten the baby to bed when the doorbell rang. She frowned and glanced at her watch as she started down the stairs. Surely Nicole couldn't be back from the wedding already. She went up on tiptoe to peek out the small peephole in the door. Her eyebrows went up in surprise when she recognized the slender form of her mother through the distorting glass. She swung the door open. "Hi. I didn't expect to see you tonight."

Beverly's smile was narrow and forced. "I guess I should have called in case you were gone or had company."

"Now what company would I have? For that matter, where would I go?" She grinned to cover up the sting of the words and stepped back. "Come on in. Would you like something to drink?"

"A diet soft drink would be nice, if you have one."

"Sure." She led her back to the kitchen. Beverly glanced into the empty rooms as they passed down the hall.

"Have you sold all your furniture?"

"Everything I don't need."

Beverly sighed. "To think of you having to peddle your furniture."

"Mother, really. You make it sound as if I went around the

32

neighborhood hawking my wares. I merely put it on consignment with an auction company."

"Well, it makes the house look like a mausoleum."

Anne shrugged. "I try to keep all the doors closed and the air conditioning off in those rooms; it saves money." She pulled a can out of the refrigerator, pulled off the tab, and handed it to her mother. Beverly glanced at it with surprise. "Oh, sorry." Anne reached into one of the cabinets and brought out a glass, which she filled with ice and poured the can of soft drink into. "There. Come on, let's sit in the den."

"Is there anyplace else *to* sit?" her mother inquired, and Anne grinned.

"Only the kitchen. Face it, Mother; I am now among the poverty stricken."

"It's such a shame you and Bryan got divorced."

"I'm afraid I didn't have much choice. But I've gotten over the worst of it. Now I'm glad he did it. I was a constant disappointment to him, and he drove me crazy, always bugging me to be something I wasn't. I'm happier now, even with the money problems and Nicole blaming me for everything."

"I saw the 'Sold' sign out front."

"Yeah. A couple have signed a contract on it. We should close the deal in a few weeks."

"It's so sad. It's a lovely house."

"It's too big. I never really liked this house." Anne had spent more miserable days here than anywhere else in her life. If she hadn't hoped it would offer the children some security and stability in their suddenly uprooted lives, she would have sold it as soon as the divorce was final. "Nicole loves the place; she has lots of friends in the neighborhood. That's the only reason I tried to keep it. But the payments were huge! We had only about a third equity in it. There was no way I could keep up the payments on my salary and Bryan's child support."

"I don't understand why you didn't get a better settlement."

"I got the house, the car, the furniture, half the cash, and an irrevocable life insurance policy on Bryan's life for the kids. But we didn't have solid, paid-for assets. We lived on Bryan's income, making enormous payments on everything. There wasn't much cash, and the attorney's bills took a lot of that. The house ate up the rest. But when the sale goes through, I'll get about a hundred thousand in equity. I can buy a nice little townhouse with that. We'll be okay then." At least financially. She'd still be plagued with doubts and regrets about having the children in a day-care center instead of being with them. There would still be tussles with Bryan and all the problems of raising two children by herself. Not enough time, not enough energy, simply not enough of herself to go around.

"How's Nicole taking it?" Beverly knew she was talking to keep from getting to the reason she'd come here, but she needed some time to gather her courage again.

"Poorly." Tears sparkled in Anne's eyes. "She hates me for selling the house. She doesn't want to leave the neighborhood. She says she'll be embarrassed to bring her school friends home when we're living in a dinky little townhouse. She makes me so angry sometimes I could throttle her. But I know how important peers are at her age, and, going to that school, most of her friends are filthy rich. She told me today she's embarrassed getting into the day-care van when it picks her up at school. I told her she was turning into a snob. But it's more than that. The divorce shattered almost everything in her world, and she blames me for it. Every problem is caused by me."

"And I imagine you're letting her get away with it. Why don't you stand up for yourself?"

Anne frowned. "It's not that easy." It was ironic that her mother should now be urging her to stand up for herself. All her life Beverly had made decisions for her and Anne had let her. She had wanted so badly to please her mother, and she hated to fight; it was so much easier to give in.

It was Beverly who had introduced Anne to Bryan, and she had encouraged their romance and marriage even though it meant Anne's giving up college to work while Bryan did his internship and residency. After they were married, Bryan had stepped into her mother's place, making decisions for

Anne, telling her what to do, guiding her along the path he thought best. The difference had been that Bryan had expected far more from her than Beverly ever had. What Anne couldn't understand was why her mother, who knew what her ex-husband was like and who before that had engineered Anne's life, would think that Anne could suddenly sprout a sense of independence. When and where did Beverly think she had learned to stand up for herself?

"The kind of stability Nicole needs in her life is not a house," Beverly pursued her point. "What she needs is a mother who is firm, even when she goes against Nicole's wishes. The things she wants aren't nearly as important as knowing she has a parent who's a rock. She needs structure and order, a parent she can depend on, not one who'll change her mind if Nicole wheedles enough. Not one who begs her for forgiveness or makes excuses."

"Oh, Mama, how can I be like that?" Anne wailed. "It's not in my make-up. I don't have an ounce of firmness. It's taken every bit of courage and stubbornness I possess just to get a job and survive after the divorce. Most of the time I felt like giving up and lying down and crying for weeks. I didn't have the energy or the desire to be forceful with Nicole. I still don't, for that matter. I don't know how."

She couldn't expect her mother to understand the closeness she and Nicole had shared before the divorce because it hadn't existed between Beverly and Anne. Anne didn't think Beverly had known it even with Bit. Anne and her daughter had loved and enjoyed each other; they had been friends. Nicole had been a pleasant, open, generous child, and Anne had rarely scolded or corrected her. Anne remembered with quiet joy the last thirty minutes before Nicole had gone to bed each night, when Anne had read to her. They had progressed to some of Anne's favorite books from childhood—*Little Women, Hans Brinker and the Silver Skates, The Five Little Peppers and How They Grew*—when the divorce came. Since then Nicole had scorned the bedtime ritual, informing her mother that she was too old for that kind of thing anymore; she could read the books herself.

It was just one example out of many. Sometimes Anne

cried with despair over the lost friendship with her daughter. She could be firm until doomsday with Nicole, and it wouldn't bring back their happy closeness. It seemed to her as if she no longer had anyone except the baby. Thank heavens for John Peter.

Beverly sighed. "Well, enough lecturing. I'm sure it doesn't help you any, and it isn't why I came." She rose and walked across the room, her fingers twisting her wedding ring.

Anne watched the other woman's nervous gesture with a growing dread. Beverly was rarely nervous or unsure of herself. There must be something terribly wrong. "Why did you come?" Anne sat up straighter, fear suddenly clenching around her heart. "Is something the matter with Daddy? Is he sick?"

"No! Goodness, no; it's nothing like that." Beverly wet her lips and turned to face her daughter, but her eyes went past Anne and focused on the wall beyond. "I, uh, got a call last Monday from a woman I know in Colorado. Her name is Sophia Kerr. She has a house in a little town called Iron Creek, up in the mountains. It's a beautiful place. Anyway, she would like . . . for you to visit her."

Anne stared, completely bewildered. "What?"

"She'd like to meet you. She's paid for the airline ticket, and made a reservation on a flight tomorrow."

"Mother, have you flipped? Why should I fly up to see some lady I've never met?"

"It would be a nice little vacation. The Rockies are beautiful in the summer. You could take a couple of days rest, get away from the kids."

Anne's eyes narrowed suspiciously. "What is going on? Why should this woman invite me? And why do you want me to go?" She stood up and walked toward Beverly. "Mother, why won't you look at me?"

Beverly turned to gaze straight at Anne. Her eyes were dark and unhappy. "I never wanted to tell you any of this. It seemed to me at the time that you would be better off not knowing. I hope you won't—" She stopped, her face more vulnerable than Anne had ever seen it.

"Won't what?"

"Won't hate me for not telling you before. Really, I thought it was for the best, but now that Mrs. Kerr wants you to come, well, I guess you have to know." Beverly turned away and sat down on the edge of a chair, her elbows on her knees, leaning forward, huddled into herself as if for protection.

Anne watched her, troubled and completely awash. She couldn't imagine what her mother was hinting at, but it sounded dreadful. Beverly wasn't one who exaggerated or embellished for dramatic effect.

Beverly wet her lips. "You know I came from a little town in the Panhandle. Bill and I had been friends all our lives. He was my best girlfriend's brother."

Anne nodded, wondering what Beverly was getting at. She'd heard this story a million times. "I know. Daddy said he'd loved you for years, and he was the happiest man alive when you married him right out of high school."

"It wasn't exactly right out of high school. First I went to Colorado for the summer. Pop loved the mountains and fishing, and we had a cabin up there where we'd spend the summers. Pop'd come up for two weeks at the beginning and a week at the end of summer, and Mom and Jimmy and I stayed there the whole season. Jimmy and I used to run wild all over the place, having fun. We loved it. We got to know a bunch of the kids around there, other summer kids and some who lived there all year round. Our cabin was near a small town named Iron Creek. It's in the mountains, about 70 or 80 miles west of Denver."

"Is that where you knew Mrs. Kerr?"

"Yes. She and her family lived on a ranch in southern Colorado most of the time, but she was from Iron Creek, and she and her son would come to visit her family every summer. They lived in a grand old house named Heartwood. Anyway, I'd seen her son there every summer. He was in college by then, a couple of years older than I, and he was so handsome." Her voice roughened, and she frowned. "Sorry, I—" She cleared her throat. "I still hate to remember. His name was Gary. He had dark brown hair with red highlights in it, and his eyes were blue. He, well, we fell in love that summer.

37

I'd never felt that way in my life. We wanted to get married. I didn't care about college or anything except marrying him, and he felt the same way."

Beverly paused and laced her fingers together, studying them. Anne thought she was struggling to retain control over her voice. Imagine, after all these years, her old love still hurt so much. "What happened?"

Beverly shook her head. "He was under twenty-one, and he needed at least one of his parents' permission to get married. So he went to his mother and told her we wanted to get married. Mrs. Kerr flatly refused. He begged and argued, but she was adamant. She said our love could wait until he was out of college if it was that strong. She didn't really like me; she felt I was trying to steal him away from her. Gary called me and told me what she'd said; he was furious. He said he was going to drive down to their ranch to get his father's permission. So he left the house and started driving through the mountains. He lost control of his car and went off the side. He was killed instantly."

Anne drew in a sharp breath. "How awful!"

"There was something he didn't know, though. I hadn't told him because I didn't want him to think he had to marry me. I probably should have. Maybe the old lady would have let him get married if she'd known." She gripped her hands together tightly and said in a rush, "I was pregnant."

It took a moment for what Beverly had said to sink in. Then it seemed to Anne as if all breath had left her body. Finally she whispered, "You mean—"

Beverly faced her squarely. "You're Gary's child. I didn't tell Mrs. Kerr about it; I hated her for killing Gary, and I didn't want her even to know about his child. I went home and took my problem to Bill. He was a little older and my good friend. As soon as he heard, he asked me to marry him." Beverly's eyes glimmered with unshed tears. "I hadn't known it until then, but he had been in love with me for several years. I protested, but I let him talk me into it. It was the easiest thing, and at the time I was pretty lost and didn't much care what happened."

She paused, seeming to wait for her daughter to say

something, but Anne couldn't think of a thing. She was too stunned by her mother's revelation. In an instant her life had turned upside down. One of the most basic, unquestioned premises of her life, of her very being, was false. "I'm not—I'm not Bill's daughter?" Her words ended on a wistful, pitifully childish note of question.

Beverly shook her head. She hadn't expected this. She had feared that Anne would leap up and accuse her of lying to her for years, that she would despise her mother for withholding the truth. But Anne's main concern seemed to be that she was not Bill's flesh-and-blood. She should have known. Bill had delighted in the baby girl Beverly had given him without the slightest hint of jealousy because she was the child of another man, and Anne had reciprocated his affection. In many ways, they'd had an easier, closer relationship than she and Anne had—probably even better than the one Bill had with his natural daughter, Bit. "Honey, I'm sorry I had to tell you. But now Sophia Kerr wants to meet you. I didn't feel it would be right to keep that chance from you."

"What chance? To meet a woman who didn't consider my mother good enough to marry her son? Who ignored her son's only child all these years? Why in the world would I want to meet her?"

"I haven't any fondness for her. She killed the boy I loved." Beverly's face hardened with bitter memory. "But that doesn't change the fact that she's your grandmother."

"My grandmother died three years ago," Anne retorted, referring to Bill's mother.

"I don't expect you to love her like a grandmother. I'm just saying that perhaps you should meet her. Give her a chance."

"Why? She's never acknowledged me before, has she? Why now?"

Beverly shrugged. "That wasn't entirely her fault. I didn't give her a chance. I never wrote or spoke to her after Gary's death. She didn't know you were alive."

"Obviously she found out sometime."

"It could have been recently. I don't know how she knew; she didn't say. But whether she ignored you before or not, the fact remains that she wants to see you now."

"And you think I should go? Doesn't it bother you?"

"Of course it does. I started not even to tell you. But Bill and I talked it over, and we agreed that you might lose some opportunity by not going. She's a wealthy woman, and she's getting old; perhaps she wants to give you some kind of legacy."

"I wouldn't want anything from her! I'm not going to brown-nose some autocratic old lady so I can get some money when she dies."

"Nonsense. I'm not asking you to put on a phony mask of friendliness. Just meet her; see what she wants. Besides, Gary was her only son. If he had lived, everything she had would have gone to him, and you're his child. You deserve to have anything she might leave you."

"But what would I do with the kids? Bryan's leaving on his honeymoon this evening; he won't be here to keep them."

"That's no excuse, and you know it. Either Bit or I would be glad to keep the children."

Anne sighed and smoothed her hands across her face. "This is so sudden. I can hardly take it in, let alone decide whether I want to see a grandmother I never knew I had."

"I know it is. I'm sorry. I should have told you as soon as Sophia called me. Then you would have had time to think it over. But I didn't have the courage. I kept putting it off and putting it off until I couldn't wait any longer." Beverly rose and crossed to the sofa to sit down beside her daughter. She picked up Anne's hands and held them in her own. "Look. At first I didn't want you to go; I didn't want you to know, and I certainly didn't want you to meet *her*. But after thinking about it for several days, I changed my mind. That's why I came and told you all this tonight. I think you ought to go."

"Why?"

"Because you never knew your father. Because I never told you anything about him. I feel bad about that. Guilty. I thought I was doing the right thing, but now I wonder. You have no knowledge of the man who fathered you, and he was a wonderful person. Bill is a very good man, and I know you love him, but it wouldn't mean you loved him less if you wanted to find out more about your natural father. Nor will he be hurt by it; he urged me to tell you tonight. He wants what's best for you. I want you to see Iron Creek. I want you to visit that magnificent house where they lived. I want you to know the country where Gary lived and where we fell in love. It's part of your heritage. So is Sophia. She could tell you things about Gary, stuff I never knew. Show you his pictures. She could open up a whole past that you had no idea belonged to you. I want you to go, honey. Learn about your real father. Please. Don't cut yourself off from that. I wronged you when I did that; it wasn't fair to you or Mrs. Kerr. I didn't give her a chance. Please, don't make me feel even guiltier by rejecting Gary and his life and his family now."

Anne cast a sideways glance at her mother. She didn't really want to meet this old woman. She sounded like a real dragon lady. And why should she care about Iron Creek, Colorado, or the house where Gary Kerr grew up? She didn't know him; it was nothing to her. Yet there was the faintest stirring of curiosity inside her shock-numbed mind. What had he looked like? Did she resemble him? How did his mother look, and was she as fierce and domineering as she sounded? And why was she interested in seeing Anne all of a sudden?

Her mother wanted it. It wouldn't do Anne any harm and it would please Beverly. It would help assuage her guilt for keeping the knowledge of Anne's birth from her. Perhaps she shouldn't care whether Beverly's guilt was lessened, considering the way Beverly had lied to her all these years. But she did care. As always, she wanted to make her mother happier, perhaps to reach a better, happier level of relationship with her. Anne had never been able to withstand a direct appeal from Beverly.

"All right," she sighed. "I'll go see Mrs. Kerr."

Chapter Three

BIT ARRIVED EARLY THE NEXT MORNING TO STAY WITH THE KIDS and take Anne to the airport. Anne greeted her with something less than enthusiasm. She'd had a long, almost sleepless night after her mother left. It had taken her hours to get over the shock; in fact, she wasn't sure she had yet recovered. For a long time, she had paced the house, alternating between anger with her mother for marrying Bill when she didn't love him, only wanted a name for her baby, and anger with Sophia Kerr for ignoring her all these years, then suddenly summoning her and expecting her to obey. She had felt confused and disturbed, unsure of who she was now that she was no longer Bill's daughter. Her whole life had been built on a lie. She had never been Anne Mitchell; Bill's relatives weren't hers. Some of her traits which she had presumed came from Bill had come from somewhere else entirely—from a man she'd never known. A man she'd never even known existed.

Nicole had come home from Bryan's wedding, bursting with details, but Anne, who earlier would have tried to glean every morsel of information from her daughter, listened with only part of her attention. Bryan's wedding was insignificant compared to what she had learned tonight.

After she calmed down Nicole and put her to bed, Anne went to bed herself. She was weary to the bone, but she found she couldn't sleep. Her restless mind and emotions wouldn't allow it. The shock had begun to wear off, and even the anger and doubt were less forceful, but as they receded, her curiosity grew. She began to wonder about her father and his mother. Her growing interest in Sophia Kerr and Iron Creek, Colorado, amazed her. But as the night passed by, she began to look forward to her trip this morning.

However, after only four hours sleep, she had lost the eagerness of the middle of the night. Now she felt only drained and exhausted, and she wished she had never agreed to go on this trip for her mother. She smiled thinly now at Bit and moved away from the door to let her in.

"Come on in. I hope this isn't a terrible inconvenience for you."

"Nonsense. You know I love Nicole and John Peter. Where are they?"

"In the den watching cartoons. Where else? It's Saturday morning."

Bit groaned and set down her suitcase. "I figured it would be easier for me to move in than to move them out to my apartment. I have to work this afternoon, but I'll drop them by Mom's on my way to the office. I'll be here tonight and tomorrow."

"Thanks. I really appreciate it."

"No trouble. Do you have any coffee?"

"In the kitchen." They walked together down the hall toward the kitchen.

"Why are you going to Colorado?" Bit asked, glancing at her sister curiously. "I was surprised when Mom called and said you needed me to take care of the kids."

"Didn't Mother tell you?" Anne hedged, uncertain what to say. She felt sure Bit thought it was odd. Bit knew she didn't know anyone in Colorado and didn't have the money to waste on an airplane ticket. But if Beverly hadn't explained it all to Bit, perhaps she wanted to continue to keep it a secret. There was no reason why Bit shouldn't know, really, but . . .

"I'm going to visit someone Mother knows."

Bit stared. Anne shifted uncomfortably.

"Look. It's a long story. I have to run upstairs and pack;

I'm late, as always. I'll tell you all about it when I get back. Okay? Maybe I'll understand it all better then."

Bit cast Anne a puzzled look. "All right," she agreed reluctantly. "But you've really got my curiosity up now."

"Sorry." Anne smiled. "But if I don't hurry and pack we'll be late."

"Sure. When does the plane leave?"

"Ten-oh-six. We need to leave here in about fifteen minutes."

"Okay. Call if you need help. I'll be down here reading the newspaper."

Anne hurried back upstairs to throw in the last of her clothes and slip into the outfit she had decided to wear to meet her grandmother, a simple white knit dress, slim and elegant, its only decoration a fragile gold butterfly on the clasp of the belt. It had taken her ages to decide what to wear and even longer to decide what to include in her suitcase. Wasn't it cooler in the mountains, even in the summer? Should she take a sweater? She wondered if slacks would be too casual. Mrs. Kerr sounded like something of a tyrant, and Anne suspected she would prefer conservative clothes. But surely the woman couldn't expect her to stay dressed up the whole time. And should she take something in case she decided to tramp around on the mountains or walk through the town? Jeans and sneakers? Or would she have to risk her expensive slacks on the nature trail?

Of course, she had so many clothes that she could dress for any occasion, anywhere. Her closet was still that of a well-to-do doctor's wife. She had thought about selling some of her fashionable, expensive clothing to one of the ritzy secondhand stores around town, but the amount of money it would bring in had seemed paltry compared to what she needed. Besides, nice clothes were an asset at work. A couple of times she had sold a few evening gowns or hostess pajamas to raise enough cash to get her through to the end of the month or to pay a towering electric bill, but she still had most of the suits, slacks, jeans, blouses, and dresses she had bought during the last few years of her marriage. Bryan had been generous with her clothing allowance; more than that, he had expected her to look pretty, wealthy, and pampered.

Anne closed the suitcase with a sigh and checked her image in the mirror. She looked better than she felt, that was for sure. She grabbed her handbag and suitcase and walked back down the stairs. She set the bags down by the front door and headed back to the den. "Okay, kids, time to leave. Turn off the TV. Bit?" She stuck her head inside the kitchen door. "You ready?"

"Sure." Bit slid her feet back into their shoes and stood up, setting aside her coffee cup.

John Peter trotted into the kitchen, Nicole trailing behind him sulkily. The baby, seeing his aunt, threw his arms out and ran to her, barking out her name. "Bit! Bit!"

"Hi there, tiger." Bit swept him up in her arms. "Hey, sweetheart, why the long face?" She shifted the baby onto one hip and circled Nicole's shoulders with her other arm.

"I don't want to go to the airport," Nicole complained. "Why can't I stay here by myself? I'm old enough."

"Because you and John Peter and I are going to eat lunch out and then I'm taking you to Gee-Gee's for the afternoon while I go work."

"Oh. All right," Nicole agreed. She found it hard to resist Bit. Anne sometimes thought with despair that Bit would make a far better mother than she; the children sensed strength in her and obeyed her almost without question, just as they sensed weakness in herself and jumped to take advantage of it.

They piled into Bit's car and drove to the airport. Nicole maintained a determined silence throughout. Anne was too tired to try to find out what was the matter. She would just get on the plane and leave it for Bit to deal with. Finally, however, when her silence brought no response, Nicole spoke up, "Why are you going? Why can't I go along?"

"I'm going to see a friend of Gee-Gee's. I told you that." Anne turned to look at Nicole in the back seat, a frown creasing her face. "And you can't come along because she's paid for my ticket, and there's just one."

Nicole scowled. "I don't know why you want to go up there, anyway, just to see some old lady."

"Nicole, just because someone is old doesn't mean they aren't interesting or worth meeting," Anne began, then stopped abruptly and looked closely at her daughter. There was something in the blue eyes that wasn't anger or annoyance. Fear—that was it. Nicole looked scared and was trying to cover it up with a gruff, angry manner. "What's the matter, honey? Do you not want me to go? Why?"

"I don't care if you go," Nicole protested, and gave an elaborate shrug.

"Are you afraid I might not come back?" Anne asked softly.

"What would I care?" Nicole's eyes were stormy; her chin went up defensively. Then, out of nowhere she added, "Daddy left last night."

Suddenly Anne understood. First Bryan had left the house, and now he had remarried and walked out with his bride into a new life that didn't include Nicole. His wedding had rung the death knell for the hopes Nicole had probably harbored that her parents might remarry. The very next day her mother was flying off without her. "Honey, Dad's not gone for good. He just went on his honeymoon. He'll be back in a couple of weeks, and you'll continue going to his house on the weekends like you have for the past year."

"It won't be the same."

"Of course not. But he's not about to desert you. And neither am I. This is only a trip. I'll be back tomorrow night. I'm not leaving you, sweetheart."

"I wasn't worried," Nicole retorted scornfully, but Anne saw the troubled fear in her eyes recede.

"Besides," Bit added cheerfully. "We'll be too busy having fun to miss Mom, right?"

Nicole made no reply, but Anne shot her sister a grateful glance. Funny, she thought with a start. Bit was really only her half sister, wasn't she? Last night had changed everything.

* * *

The airplane ride was short and pleasant, except for a slight bumpiness in the clouds over Colorado. They landed in Denver a little over an hour later. Anne gazed eagerly out the window, but she found the view a disappointment. There were no mountains, only flat, scrubby land stretching away from the runway, and, beyond that, buildings. She could have been in Texas still. Anne unhooked her seat belt slowly and let many of the other passengers leave before her, delaying the moment of meeting as long as possible. Finally she joined the last trickle of passengers from the plane and walked through the hot metal corridor into the terminal. Her steps slowed even more as she glanced around the waiting area, searching for a white-haired woman. She must be in her seventies or eighties, not hard to spot, Anne thought. But she saw no one that fit that age group.

She came to a stop and waited, making another search of the area. Perhaps Mrs. Kerr had stepped into the bathroom or was late. She ought to wait here for a few minutes, just in case. Again Anne turned slowly, her eyes sweeping over every person around. She stopped on a man who was staring at her intently. He was dark, with thick, slightly shaggy black hair, black eyes, and skin that looked as if it had been browned and weathered by hours in the sun. He was dressed in faded blue jeans, scuffed boots, and a blue work shirt, its sleeves rolled up to reveal corded forearms. Strength was obvious in his arms and hands, but he was whipcord thin, as if any spare flesh had been burned away long ago.

Anne glanced away, then sneaked another look at him. He was staring at her in a disconcerting way, gazing at her too long for a normal look, even from an admiring male. And there was something too intense in his gaze, as if he were studying her. Anne turned aside and looked down the hall, trying to ignore him. But out of the corner of her eye, she saw him move away from the post against which he had been leaning and start toward her, and her head automatically turned in his direction.

For the first time she noticed that he held a wooden cane in his left hand, and as he walked, he leaned upon it. His left leg moved stiffly, giving him a hobbled gait. The infirmity was incongruous with his lean, healthy frame and deep tan. He stopped about three feet away from her. Anne didn't know what to do. It had been years since a man had tried to pick her up. She had never been good at turning them down; she tended to blush and get confused and embarrassed, as if it were her fault he'd decided to try it. Anne wished she were a million miles from here. She wanted to turn and run, get away from him and the situation as quickly as she could. However, she forced herself to look into his face, attempting an icy stare.

"Excuse me." His voice was low and gravelly, harsh, yet curiously intriguing, as well. "Are you Mrs. Hamilton? Anne Hamilton?"

"What?" Anne gaped. "Yes. Yes, I am, but how—"

He didn't smile or even attempt to be friendly. "Mrs. Kerr sent me to get you." He extended a piece of paper to her. "She gave me this to identify you, but I wasn't sure if that was you."

Anne glanced at the piece of paper; it was her wedding picture, clipped from a Dallas newspaper years ago. She looked impossibly young and excited. Her hair was long and straight, and clouds of white net billowed around her face, thinner then and rather unformed. It hardly looked like she did now, and the newsprint had yellowed with time, blurring her features. Anne couldn't keep from grinning. "No wonder you had trouble recognizing me. That was eleven years ago."

Her grin won a faint smile in return from him, but it vanished quickly. "My name is Mark Pascal. I do a little work now and then for Mrs. Kerr. I quite often drive her or run errands for her. She doesn't drive well any more."

"I understand. It was silly of me to expect her to pick me up. I didn't think about her age."

"The baggage return is this way." He started off down the hall in his slow, jerky gait, and Anne followed. She wondered what had happened to his leg, but of course it would have been impolite to ask. It might be something he was terribly sensitive about. Besides, he didn't exactly invite conversation of any kind, let alone personal questions.

Anne slowed her steps to walk with him; she was used to it from walking with a toddler. It made the walk seem endless, though, particularly since Mark never opened his mouth the whole way. Anne was able to converse with someone who talked easily, but with people who were shy or silent, her brain went blank.

"I hope Mrs. Kerr is feeling all right," she began. Her voice sounded strange and tinny to her ears.

Pascal shrugged.

Anne wet her lips and tried again, "Is it a long drive to Iron Creek?"

"Couple of hours." He didn't even glance at her as he spoke.

"I'm sure it must be a lovely drive, though." He said nothing. Anne flushed a little; she felt thoroughly ignored and unwanted. She decided she'd be better off if she didn't even attempt a conversation with this man. He obviously didn't relish her company. In fact, she got the impression that Mark resented her, though she couldn't imagine why.

Maybe he didn't like being asked to run errands for her grandmother. He might think it wasn't part of his job. Anne wondered what he did for her grandmother. Something outdoors, she supposed. Perhaps he cared for the lawn and trees. Or did odd jobs around the house, whatever needed to be done. She sneaked a sideways glance at him. There was a grim set to his face, almost bitter, but there was a certain sensitivity to his mouth and hands, something rather aesthetic, and his dark eyes were bright with intelligence. He didn't seem the kind of man who would be content doing menial work. But then, nothing said he was content. Perhaps he resented everything, not just her.

They reached the baggage carousels and waited in silence for the luggage to appear. When Anne's bag came down the ramp and onto the moving belt, Anne started toward it, saying, "There it is."

With astonishing quickness, Mark reached the piece of luggage before she did and swung it off the carousel. "This one?"

"Yes, that's it."

Mark weaved through the waiting throng and out through the gate. "We need to take the elevator; the car's on the fourth floor of the parking garage."

He led the way to the elevator, and they rode up to the fourth floor. There they started down a long walkway across the street below into the parking garage. Anne looked at the bag Mark carried in his right hand, banging against his leg with each ungainly step. "Here, let me carry that," she said, reaching out to take the handle of the suitcase.

Mark shot her a fierce glance. "I'll carry it. There's nothing wrong with my arm." He laid heavy emphasis on the last word, and Anne shriveled inside. She had meant only to help him, but obviously her offer had wounded his pride. She had offended him, which made her feel small and clumsy.

He led her to a large, four-wheel-drive vehicle and tossed her bag in the back. They got in and drove down a dizzying succession of ramps. At the bottom he pulled onto the street and took his place in one of the long lines stretching back from the toll booths. They waited at the toll booth forever, it seemed. Anne was uncomfortable. She wished she could think of something to say. She looked at his hands on the wheel, large and supple; she looked at the hard muscle in his arms, the curls of black hair against his brown skin. It was hard to keep her eyes from turning that way. Mark Pascal seemed a very physical man, not at all the professional type she was used to being around. He looked hard and more than a little angry. Strangely, that wasn't unappealing.

Finally, they emerged onto a street and soon entered an expressway. And finally Anne saw the mountains which set Denver apart from other cities. They stretched across the western horizon, jagged and blue and farther away than she had imagined.

But it was only a matter of minutes before they were in the western part of the city, then they were climbing into the mountains. For a long time the slope was gradual, but then the hills closed around them, scrubby piles of dirt dotted with pine trees and covered with rocks. The divided highway sliced right through some of the hills, revealing stripes of dirt and rock colored yellow and ochre and gray. Here and there on the hillsides among the trees Anne saw small openings that looked like caves. Invariably, below these caves was a sweep of stained rock and earth spreading out down the mountain in a triangular shape. Inside the triangle, the earth was barren of all growth.

"What are those?" she asked, pointing, too interested to be inhibited by Mark's silence.

He glanced in the direction she pointed. "What? Those holes?"

"Yeah. And the stripped-looking land below them."

"Mine entrances."

Anne waited for Mark to go on, but he didn't. She grimaced a little and prodded, "Mines? For coal?"

"Gold and silver. In the late 1800s they mined all around here. Iron Creek was a boom town back then."

"What about those barren triangles?" Anne questioned when he stopped again.

"I don't know." He shrugged. "Where they dumped what they hauled out or strip-mined the land or something, I guess."

"Oh. I see."

The road began to climb steeply, and they drove through several tunnels built through the mountains. Anne was fascinated by the view and the drive. They drove through the Eisenhower Tunnel, the longest and grandest of the tunnels, and after that a magnificent vista spread before them. The mountains were on all sides and in the distance stood purplish peaks capped with white. Anne stared, enthralled. All the words she had ever heard to describe the Rockies applied—majestic, rugged, enormous, awe-inspiring—yet none of them were enough. Nothing could describe the breathtaking beauty before her.

She leaned forward intently. "It's beautiful! What's that white across the tops? Surely that can't be snow."

"That's what it is."

"In June?"

He nodded. "Snow stays on the tops of those mountains all year round."

"But how?"

"The earth beneath the snow is frozen several feet down. It's called blackfrost."

"You're joking."

He shook his head. "No. Those are some of the highest peaks in the Rockies. Fourteen thousand feet."

"My heavens!"

"We're about nine thousand feet right now."

They left the major highway and headed south on one of the state roads. It was two-laned and far less traveled, but the scenery was even more beautiful. White-skinned aspens, tall and fragile, shimmered in the breeze, and around them grew lodgepole pines, incredibly tall and straight, ponderosa pines, scrubby juniper bushes, and delicate flowers on tall stems. For a time a twisting stream rushed beside the road, but they soon left it behind as they climbed higher up into the mountains. Now and then Anne saw a narrow waterfall running down the side of the sheer rocks like a silver ribbon.

"I never realized how beautiful it would be." Anne stared in fascination out the side window, gazing up at the peaks around them, treeless and covered with a verdant green. "Why are there no trees there? Did something happen?"

"It's above the timberline. Trees can't grow there. Pines' roots grow to tremendous depths to find water; it's the only way they survive. The lodgepole pines' roots can go down 100 feet through rock. But they can't go through solidly frozen ground. So up there they die. Only the low shrubs and alpine flowers can grow. This is bighorn sheep country. One of the largest herds in the country."

"Really? Might I see one?"

"It's possible." He shrugged. "I've seen one or two on this road." He shot her a sidelong glance. "But I wouldn't get my hopes up."

"How far is Iron Creek?"

"Not far. Twenty minutes, maybe."

Anne nodded and looked out the window. Without her effort, the conversation died, but she was content simply to sit and look at the scenery.

After a few minutes, they began to go down the mountain

and soon were in a narrow valley. Again they followed the course of a narrow stream as it wound in and out around the mountains. When they were close to the stream, it was clear and the rocks in the bed were clearly visible; yet, when they moved away from it, the water took on a strangely dark look, almost a charcoal gray. "Is this the same stream as the one we passed back there?" she asked.

"What? Oh. No. This is Iron Creek. See the rocks beside the stream and in it? The sort of rust-colored streaks on them? That's why they named it Iron Creek. There never was any iron here, though; at least, not to speak of. It was silver that made them rich here."

They rounded the base of a mountain, and beyond the curve lay the outskirts of a town. "This is it," Mark told her. "Iron Creek."

Narrow wooden and stone buildings lined the shallow valley on either side of the road, curving up onto the base of the hills on either side. Some of the storefronts were plain, others had Victorian "gingerbread" trim; all had raised, wooden sidewalks. The town was quaint, but still ramshackle enough that it hadn't an air of phoniness. Side streets ran off and up the hillsides; nothing in the town seemed either straight or level. Anne could see small frame houses lining the streets, one above the other, like a terraced farm. One little house boasted a miniature tower. Downhill to the left and in front of them sat an old-fashioned, plain white church, its short steeple graced with a white cross.

It could have been a movie set for a western except for the people walking through the downtown area and the number of thriving shops. Anne glimpsed signs for jewelry stores, restaurants, souvenir shops, and ice cream parlors as they drove past. The car slowed almost to a crawl in the center of town because of tourists strolling across the streets, and Anne saw a bank with wrought iron bars decorating the windows and roofline, a stone-built opera house, and a saloon with swinging doors from which issued a burst of noise and laughter.

Mrs. Kerr's house was actually outside of town, Anne

found. They left the buildings behind and drove for another few minutes before Mark stepped on the brake and turned left onto a gravel driveway.

Heartwood stood on a rise, looking down on the highway across a cleared field. Built of dark red Colorado granite, it was an imposing Victorian-style house. Gothic arches curved over the windows and front door. A porch encompassed two sides of the house, its roofline imitating the peaks and arches of the house's roof. One front corner was rounded into a turret, and from the center of the roof rose a squared cupola. It was so grandiose and ornate that it was absurd, yet there was a certain dignity and appeal to it as well, as if its excesses were excused by the enormity of its setting.

Anne drew in her breath sharply when she saw it, and a fleeting smile touched Mark Pascal's mouth. "Something, isn't it?"

"I never imagined . . ." She raised her eyebrows and laughed a little at herself. "Everything today's been more than I expected." She paused, studying the house as the car went up the driveway, rattling across a narrow wooden bridge over the churning waters of Iron Creek. "Amazing. Does Mrs. Kerr live here alone?"

He nodded. "Except for her housekeeper during the day."

Anne shook her head. "Imagine. Only two women in that huge house."

Mark pulled to a stop in front of the porch, and Anne stepped out. He took her bag from the back and limped up the stairs. Anne followed him, having no trouble this time slowing her gait to match his, for she was busy staring at the house.

Double front doors opened into the house, each made of thick wood inset with an oval of leaded glass. Mark rang the doorbell to the right of the doors, and after a long moment the right door opened inward. A woman in her seventies stood framed in the doorway. She was short and stocky and dressed in a lurid green pants suit with a dish towel tied around her waist. Her hair was iron gray, short and wispy, and her eyes were a bright, curious brown. Her gaze went immediately to Anne, and Anne felt as if she had been put under a microscope.

"Here she is," Mark announced unnecessarily, and set Anne's bag inside. "I'll go on now."

"Sure. Thanks, Mark." The woman wiped her hands off on the dish-towel apron and extended one hand to Anne. "Hi. I'm Linda Whitton. I'm Mrs. Kerr's housekeeper."

"Oh. Hello." For a moment Anne had wondered if this was her grandmother, though she had seemed several years too young and not at all as Anne had imagined Sophia Kerr.

When she met Sophia Kerr a few minutes later, she was still not at all as Anne had pictured her. Anne had alternated between her grandmother's being a frail invalid of advanced years and her being an aristocratic old lady dressed in an Edwardian dress, with her white hair drawn up into a bun atop her head. Instead, the woman who had come down the stairs in answer to Linda Whitton's summons was a short, wiry woman with skin tanned to a leathery brown. Her hair was pure white, but she wore it cropped short, and she was dressed in a pair of faded blue jeans, moccasins, and a long-sleeved Western shirt. A gigantic turquoise ring weighed down her right hand, and a squash blossom necklace hung around her neck. Like her house, she appeared rather overdone, yet curiously appealing.

She stopped on the bottom step and studied Anne for a moment, then came forward, her hand extended to shake Anne's. "Hello. I'm Sophia Kerr."

"How do you do? I'm Anne Hamilton."

Sophia kept her hand for an extra moment, her eyes searching the younger woman's face. "Yes. I can see. Come into the den, why don't you? I'm afraid these front rooms are all for show." She gestured toward the closed wooden doors on either side of the hall, each double-width. She walked down the hallway, and Anne followed. The entryway of black and white Italian marble gave way to a central hall running the width of the house. Anne stared at the floor of the second hall, fascinated by the beautiful parquet patterns.

They went into the den and sat down on heavy, leather

furnishings, and a few minutes later Linda Whitton bustled in, carrying a large silver tray. Mrs. Kerr solemnly poured coffee from the curlicued silver pot into paper-thin cups that Anne was sure must be the best of chinaware.

Anne took the cup Sophia offered and sipped at it, uncomfortable beneath the other woman's gaze. Finally Sophia said, "You resemble Gary somewhat. Did you know?"

Anne shook her head silently.

"Well, you do. Have you ever seen a picture of my son?"

"No. Frankly, I didn't know he existed until yesterday."

"Here." Sophia rose and walked to the carved walnut mantel to take down a silver-framed photograph. She came back to Anne and held it out for her to see. "There he is. Not the best picture, of course. It was his high school senior picture. I have some snapshots of him upstairs that look more like him. I'll show you after dinner."

Anne unclenched her hand and reached out to grasp the frame. "May I?" Sophia inclined her head, and Anne brought the picture closer to study it.

A young man gazed out solemnly, but there was a certain lilt to his mouth that told you that he was far more used to smiling and laughing. The photograph was black-and-white, so that she could not tell his coloring. But even so, she could see that his mouth and chin were the same as those she saw in her mirror daily. Her eyebrows were her mother's, but she realized that her rounded eyes, which she had always attributed to Beverly, were really more like this young man's. His hair was cropped too short to tell what its natural texture and shape were. He was a handsome youth, and even in the flat picture anticipation and a joy for life quivered in him. Anne felt a stab of sadness to think that such a life as this had ended so unnaturally soon. He should have lived a long life, she thought, and felt suddenly morbid at holding the picture of the long-dead man.

"Thank you." She handed the picture back to his mother.

Sophia replaced it on the mantel and resumed her seat across the low coffee table from Anne. Anne drank her coffee and looked at Sophia, searching for similarities in her face.

Could she possibly be related to this woman? Despite her casual attire and hair style, every inch of Sophia Kerr bespoke breeding. Every word and gesture set her in a class of people that had long known money, family, and poise.

"I'm sorry I didn't come with Mark to meet you, but I take a nap every day about that time. I hope you weren't inconvenienced."

"Not at all. Mr. Pascal took care of everything."

"Mark's usually very competent." She paused. "No doubt you're tired from your trip."

"The ride from the airport was a little long," Anne admitted. Suddenly she wanted very much to be alone.

The other woman smiled. "Why don't I show you to your room? After dinner, I thought you might enjoy a tour of the house. It has a nice history."

"Yes. I'd like that very much."

The staircase was the same heavy walnut as the floors, and was polished and waxed until it gleamed. Anne couldn't resist running her hand over it as she followed her grandmother up the stairs; the wood invited the touch. On the second floor lay a rather dark hallway lined with closed doors. At the end of the hall a wood-encased window provided the only light. Sophia opened the nearest door and showed Anne into a large room. It was in one of the back corners, and windows looked out on two sides of the house. The room was light and airy, furnished sparingly but in exquisite antiques. It had obviously been redone in the past few years. Wallpaper in an old-fashioned rose pattern matched the thick, down comforter on the bed and the light curtains at the windows.

Sophia left her here alone, and Anne walked to the windows. From the back one, she could see the mountain towering behind the house, covered with pines and aspens. The side window looked out onto more trees and also onto the creek curving away into the distant woods. Set almost out of sight was a small house that looked almost a miniature of this house, though constructed of wood rather than granite. Too large to have been a playhouse, she wondered if it had served as a guest house or perhaps as a carriage house or garage.

She turned back to the room. The excitement and emotions of the day had taken their toll, and she felt exhausted. Anne kicked off her shoes and stretched out across the polished cotton spread, luxuriating in its cool softness. She felt a little like Alice in Wonderland, caught in a world both fascinating and scary. She had expected to dislike Mrs. Kerr and to regret coming here, but instead she found herself curious, eager, and halfway in love with the location and the house. She wanted to see the house and hear its history; she wanted to learn about Gary Kerr, to see all the pictures of him Mrs. Kerr could find.

Anne closed her eyes, thinking about Mark Pascal and Linda Whitton and Mrs. Kerr. And her father. Later she would ask a million questions. But now—she drifted into sleep.

Mark backed around and headed down the driveway. Though his cabin was not far from the main house, it was approached by a separate dirt road farther down the highway. His Blazer roared across the bridge and onto the highway, going around a curve and out of sight of Heartwood before he turned off again onto a rougher dirt road. The four-wheel-drive vehicle rattled up the rutted road and took the final steep incline to his house. He stopped beside the small log house, where the road itself stopped, and killed the engine.

Damn, but she was beautiful!

Mark hadn't particularly wanted to pick up Sophia's guest at Stapleton Airport; he was uncomfortable around strangers. But when he'd seen Anne Hamilton, he'd been stunned. She was lovely and warm, almost earthy, with a smile that could light up your heart. Her hair was the color of autumn leaves—no, darker, richer. Her eyes, dark blue, were wide and vulnerable. Her looks hadn't matched the sophistication of the pristine white dress she wore, and the puzzle had intrigued him.

Who was she to Sophia? Why had she come for a visit? As far as he knew, Sophia had no relatives. Most of her friends were either dead or far older than this woman. Sophia had been tense and almost excited when she handed Mark the newspaper clipping this morning and sent him to the airport. It wasn't like Sophia, usually the most serene and self-possessed of women. Anne Hamilton was important to her in some way.

Mark walked around to the back of the cabin and stepped up onto the screened porch that served as his workroom. The smell of wood permeated the room, sharp and familiar and soothing. He settled down on the chair in front of the table and ran his thumb across the smooth, pale wood he was working with.

No doubt he'd made an idiot of himself before Anne. He was unused to small talk and uncomfortable sitting so close to a beautiful woman. It had been too long; too much had happened. After all those years spent locked away, he no longer had any ease with anyone, let alone an attractive woman. A woman he'd like to touch. A woman whose mouth lured him.

He thought about the way her skirt had stretched over her thighs as she sat beside him in the car. The well-shaped calves beneath her hem. The fullness of her breasts. Her hair would curl around his finger, he knew, soft and clinging; it had that look. He could picture her beneath him, taking him in, her blue eyes dark and a little clouded with desire.

Mark shook his head in exasperation. It was silly thinking about her this way. She was nothing to him, just a house guest of Sophia's. She'd leave tomorrow, and he'd never see her again. Even if she had stayed, she was far beyond his reach. Once, long ago, he might have flirted with her, let her know that his body had responded to her immediately. But that was in another lifetime; it was another Mark Pascal. Before the war, before the operations. Before the years in the hospital.

It drove some men crazy—the memories, the pain, the isolation, the fear of returning to the real world. There were those who couldn't cope, who chose to remain in the sheltered world of V.A. hospitals for the rest of their lives. Mark wasn't one of them. He'd gotten out and been happy to, despite his fear. He had found a place to live and work that suited him. He could get by up here in the mountains, essentially alone. But with strangers he felt his difference acutely.

He was an outsider. He didn't belong with people like her. He was a Vietnam vet with a smashed leg, a man who'd known more horror than she could even imagine, who'd seen his best friend die next to him, half his face blown away. He was a person who had spent most of the ten years following his return from Vietnam in army hospitals, then V.A. hospitals, going through surgery and rehabilitation time and again. He had lived for ten years with amputees, the terminally ill, men recovering from yet another operation, drug addicts, and crazies. And he'd spent the last two and a half years in virtual seclusion in the mountains. He was a recluse, a social misfit, whereas Anne was . . .

Well, he wasn't quite sure what she was except a lovely woman in an expensive dress. But one thing was obvious: she wasn't for him. So what did it matter if she thought he was rude and unmannerly? And what did it matter if, for the first time in years, he'd experienced a stab of longing and loneliness so sharp he'd had to face it? Tomorrow he would take her back to the airport, and she'd be gone. Riding beside her in the car would be as close as he'd ever get to her. Mark knew from bitter experience that it didn't do any good to pine over what you didn't have. You took what life handed you and ignored the rest.

He picked up a chisel and hammer from the array of tools scattered on the table and determinedly set to work.

Chapter Four

ANNE TOOK A SHORT NAP IN HER ROOM AND RETURNED DOWN-
stairs well before supper. She found Sophia Kerr in the den
idly flipping through a magazine. Sophia looked up and a
brilliant smile flashed across her face. "Why, Anne. You're
here earlier than I expected. How nice. Are you rested?"

"Yes. I feel very refreshed. I'm ready for the tour now if
you are."

The older woman came forward almost eagerly. "Of
course. I love showing off this house. Let's start in the front
parlor, shall we?"

They spent the rest of the afternoon exploring the main
rooms downstairs and the bedrooms upstairs, even going to
the empty, closed-off top floor and up the narrow, winding
staircase into the cupola atop the house. Anne was awed by
the beauty of the wood and the extent to which it was used.
Dark, almost black walnut framed the windows and doors,
including the double-width opening between the parlor and
dining room, where heavy pocket doors slid back into the wall
itself. The shallow bay window in the front was framed with
walnut, and an elegant pattern of chestnut and walnut
resembling a mantelpiece ran across the top of the set of three
windows. In the library/study one wall was covered with rich,
built-in bookcases fronted with glass. An ornate chestnut

sideboard built into one wall dominated the dining room. The parlor and dining room were floored with the alternating patterns of chestnut and walnut, while the rest of the house was laid with heart pine. Heart pine ran in mouldings around the baseboards and ceilings. There were walnut sconces, mantels, and panels.

The ceilings were at least fourteen feet high. Sparkling, teardrop chandeliers cascaded from the ceilings in the parlor and dining room. Heavy velvet curtains hung at most of the windows, and the rooms were furnished largely with antiques. Only the kitchen sported modern cabinetry, counters, appliances, and wallpaper. Anne followed her grandmother in awe, thinking that she had never been in a house so beautiful.

When she expressed the thought to Sophia, the woman smiled. "It was meant to be gorgeous and rich. It was built by a miner who became a wealthy man overnight. He built this house for his bride, and everything in it had to be perfect. He named it Heartwood for the hard, enduring wood in the center of the tree, which he felt described the enduring love in their hearts. Romantic, isn't it?"

"Very. Were they happy?"

Sophia snorted and shook her head. "For a few months, I guess. Joseph Pemberton's bride, Evie, was a beautiful woman several years his junior. She was reputed to be a real beauty—blond hair, blue eyes, a Gibson girl figure. Two years after the wedding, she ran off with one of Pemberton's financial partners from San Francisco. She became the man's mistress, but Joseph Pemberton never divorced her. He lived alone in the house until his death. Most of it was closed up, and he lived in only a few rooms. The mines in this area played out, and Pemberton lost his money in worthless mining ventures. By the time he died, this house was his only valuable asset."

"How sad."

"Oh, there's more. He died without a will. His cousins would have inherited the house, being his nearest relatives, but Evie showed up and claimed it for herself. She was still legally his wife, you see, and she wanted the money from the house. Her lover had left her by then. There was a long, vicious battle in the courts over the ownership of the house."

"What happened?"

Sophia shrugged. "The house was sold. The judge ruled that since Evie was legally his wife, under the laws of intestacy she was entitled to part of the money. But no one really got much except the lawyers. My father bought Heartwood; he was the local banker and had always loved the house. I grew up in it, and I loved it even more than my father had. Every corner of it is precious to me. Even after I married Wendall and moved south to his ranch, I came back here as often as I could. I always brought Gary. He loved it, too."

Sophia fell abruptly silent and turned her face away. Anne thought she saw a glimmer of tears in the other woman's eyes, and her heart contracted with pity. She wasn't feeling about Sophia at all as she had expected to. Quickly she changed the subject. "What's that little house out in back? The one that looks like this one?"

"The guest house. Isn't it clever? It has two bedrooms and a small sitting room. It's been boarded up for years, though. I've never used it, and neither did my parents. We were always such a small family. There was plenty of room for our guests inside the house. Would you like to see it?"

"Yes, that would be nice."

They went downstairs and onto the front porch. Anne sighed her appreciation of the view before her. There was a stretch of grass in front of the house and then the curiously dark, clear creek cut across the land. Beyond the road there was a gap between the near hills and mountains, so that she could see the towering, snow-capped peaks in the distance. The sun was low in the sky, seeming to touch the distant mountains and casting a yellow-red glow over them.

"It's gorgeous," she breathed. "It must be heavenly to live here and see that every day."

Sophia smiled. "Unfortunately, it's often snow and grayness I see out there."

"I'm sure the mountains are lovely covered with snow, too."

"They are. You seem to like the mountains." Her tone made it more a question than a statement.

"I've discovered I do," Anne responded. "Before today I'd never been in the Rockies. You know, it's funny. I've been to Mexico and the Caribbean, but there are lots of places in the U.S. I haven't seen. We never vacationed in the mountains. Bryan and I always went to the beach. And Mother and Dad—I mean—" She stopped, flustered, and finished lamely, "I understand why now, I guess."

Sophia's mouth drew into a narrow line. "Yes." She went down the steps and turned away from the house. Anne followed, wishing she hadn't mentioned her mother. Sophia appeared to dislike Beverly as heartily as Beverly disliked her. Anne guessed it was because each was a reminder to the other of the painful wound of Gary Kerr's death. Anne had the feeling that Sophia had never recovered from his death. But surely over the years her mother must have. Wouldn't home, husband, and children have eventually wiped out the memory of a bittersweet first love?

She circled the quaint little guest house and peered through the cracks in the boarded-up windows. Then Sophia turned and circled around the back of the house, passing a small detached garage. "I had that built," she explained, pointing to the little building. "Before that there was a carriage house down by the stables, but it fell down long ago."

"The stables?"

"Yes. Over there." Sophia pointed in the direction of the town, on the opposite side of the house from Anne's bedroom. There was a clump of aspen and pines and beyond that, at the foot of the slope, lay a corral and a low, wooden building. Several horses stood in the corral, and there was hay heaped up beside the building.

"You keep horses still?"

Sophia laughed. "Even I'm not crazy enough to ride at my age. No, I lease the stables and corral to a man who rents out horses to tourists. The fences and building were badly in need of repair, and Jim fixed them up. He leases a meadow from me, too, back there." She gestured vaguely in the other direction. "Mark runs his horses up there and brings them down twice a week to exchange. Keeps them fresher."

"So Mark has another job, too?"

"Sure. He doesn't do much for me, just a little trimming and cutting and some odd jobs around the yard and house. He tries to keep the place looking decent and running fairly well, and in return I let him live in a cabin I own."

"I see. It seems like—" Anne hesitated.

"Like he'd want more out of life?" Sophia supplied.

"Yes. I guess so."

Sophia shrugged. "Sometimes it's asking enough out of life just to survive."

Supper was served in the formal dining room. Anne felt foolish sitting at Sophia's right at the end of the long, burled walnut table, a crystal chandelier shimmering above them. "Do you usually eat in here?"

Sophia chuckled. "No. Normally I eat at the kitchen table or take a tray to my sitting room. But tonight is special; you're my guest."

Anne frowned down at her plate of delicately fried trout. It was hard to think of a tactful way to approach the subject. Impossible, really. She'd better either say it or forget it. "Mrs. Kerr—"

"Sophia, please."

"Sophia. Why did you invite me here?" She blurted it out and then looked up, searching the other woman's face as if she hoped it would give her an answer if Sophia's words did not.

For a moment Sophia simply stared back at her. Then her gaze fell, and she traced the rim of her glass. "That's difficult to sum up in a few words. It's an accumulation of feelings over the years. Curiosity. A . . . a desire to know Gary's daughter, to have something of him in this house again. Age. Loneliness."

Anne's face knotted in frustration. "Then why haven't you ever shown the slightest interest in me over the years? Why wait until now?"

Sophia sighed, and suddenly she appeared every bit her age, and more. Anne almost wished she'd left the subject alone.

"After Gary's—accident, I wanted nothing to do with Beverly. I didn't care where she went or what she did. She caused the rift between Gary and me. It was she whom he and I fought over that last day of his life. He died with bad feelings between us, and I couldn't forget that she was the cause of those feelings. I couldn't forgive. Several years later I heard in town that she had married and had a child. Your grandparents, you see, still owned a cabin not far from here and came up in the summers, though Beverly didn't. When I heard the age of the child, a bell rang in my head. I wondered exactly when the child was born. It kept nagging at me—why had she married so quickly after Gary died? Could the baby have been Gary's?

"So I hired an investigator, someone to search the records. When he told me the date of your birth, I realized that you must be Gary's. I wasn't fond of your mother, but I was sure there had been no other man in her life during that summer. The baby had to be Gary's. I was—torn. I wanted to see you. You were Gary's child, and I wanted to have at least that little part of him. But I had hard feelings about Beverly, and I knew she felt the same way about me. At Gary's funeral she practically spit in my eye."

"So you decided not to try to see me?"

Sophia nodded. "It seemed the best idea at the time. After all, she had married, and I presumed that you and maybe even Bill Mitchell believed that he was your real father. I knew your mother would resent my intruding and wanting to know you; I knew she would have fought me. It wouldn't have done you any good. It would have only caused a split in your family and unsettled you. You already had four grandparents; you didn't need another. Your family had enough money; you weren't in need. I thought it would be selfish to try to see you, even if Beverly had let me."

Anne put her elbows on the table and propped her chin on her interlaced fingers. It made sense. Perhaps her grandmother had tried to do what was best for her, not simply neglected or ignored her son's child. "But what about when I was older?"

"I had grown used to things as they were. I thought I could live well enough without knowing you. It still would not have been pleasant for you to discover that your father was not really your father."

"No. It wasn't," Anne admitted. "Then why did you decide to bring me up here now?"

Sophia's smile was brittle. "I told you. Age and loneliness. An old woman's desire to see her grandchild at least once. Sometimes things happen that make you realize there are very few really important things in life. Your family is one of them. I had an idea, and I wanted to meet you—to decide whether the idea was feasible. And I—longed to see Gary's daughter."

There was a long pause. Then Sophia asked softly, "Why did you come?"

Anne glanced up, surprised. "Because Mother wanted me to," she replied honestly.

Mrs. Kerr's mouth twisted into a smile. "Strange, that I should have Beverly to thank for it."

"Maybe she feels guilty, too."

"Too?" Now Anne could see the aristocratic arrogance she'd expected to find in Sophia Kerr. It wasn't how one dressed or looked, really. It was a certain condescending tone in the voice, a particular freezing of the features. "If you think I feel guilty over not seeking you out all these years, you're quite wrong. I did what I thought best, and I'm satisfied with it."

Anne didn't know where she found the courage. Usually the kind of look in Sophia's eyes would have riveted her to the spot, frozen and tongue-tied. But now she responded levelly, "What about guilt over my father's death?"

If possible, Sophia's eyes grew icier. "It was an accident."

"Of course. I didn't mean that it wasn't. But most people would feel guilty if someone died in a car wreck right after a fight with them. Especially someone they cared for very much."

"I regret that Gary died with angry words between us."

Sophia stood up, shoving back her chair. Her eyes were shards of glass. "If anyone is responsible for his death, it's *her*. She should feel guilty. She trapped him. When she told Gary she was pregnant, he felt he had to marry her. God knows why he didn't tell me; no doubt he was too embarrassed. But knowing I'd never sanction such a foolish marriage and knowing she was pregnant and demanding that he marry her—it's no wonder he was distraught."

Anne jumped up to face her. She was trembling slightly all over, and she wasn't sure whether it was out of fear or anger, or both. "That's unfair. You're dead wrong. Mother didn't tell your son she was pregnant. She didn't want him to feel obliged to marry her. She told me that yesterday when she explained who and what you are to me. She said she bitterly regretted not telling him, for perhaps then you wouldn't have refused, and he wouldn't have lost control of his car because he was angry and inattentive. Maybe you did what you thought was best. Maybe it was right not to allow them to marry so young. I don't know. I don't presume to be able to judge what's best for everyone. But I do know that you were selfish and unjust to turn your back on the eighteen-year-old girl your son loved, to blame her for your son's death. I don't know how you had the gall to call Mother and tell her you wanted to meet me after all these years. But I'll tell you this: she has a more generous spirit than you. She asked me to come as a favor to her!"

For a long moment, the two women stared at each other unblinkingly. Then Anne turned and hurried from the room, blindly turning down the hall and rushing out the front door. She had no idea where she was going as she raced down the steps and along the dirt path leading into the trees. She was simply awash in anger and resentment and had to get away before she exploded. For the first few minutes, she charged along the path without seeing anything to either side of her, fuming and letting her mind run wild with all the things she should have said, would have said if she'd had the nerve—and hadn't cared how much she wounded an old lady.

Her steps slowed, and remorse seeped in, as it always did after a flood of anger. What she had said to Sophia Kerr was true, of course, but it hadn't been kind of her to say it. Sophia was an old woman. No doubt deep down she did feel guilty about her son's death; otherwise she wouldn't have blamed it on Beverly, which was illogical. It was a cover-up to a truth she couldn't face. So Anne's question about guilt must have touched a very sore spot with her. It wasn't surprising that Sophia had reacted defensively. It really wasn't any of Anne's business how Mrs. Kerr felt about her mother; she hardly knew the woman. Why had she lashed out like that? She should have let it slide, and the visit could have remained pleasant. Then tomorrow she could have flown away, and Sophia would have gotten what she wanted.

Anne sighed and continued along the trail, preoccupied with the way she had messed up the evening and the visit. Strangely enough, she had found herself liking Mrs. Kerr. She was intelligent and far livelier than Anne would have thought for her seventy-some-odd years. Her conversation was bright and often amusing, and she could be quite charming. Anne had thoroughly enjoyed the time they had spent touring the house. She had felt a curious sense of connection to the woman, as if her instincts responded to the physical fact of their kinship. The day had been unexpectedly pleasant—until she'd blown up.

And why blow up over her mother? It wasn't as if she and Beverly were close.

There was a boulder just off the path, and Anne sat down upon it. For the first time she looked around her and realized how late it had grown. The sun had been setting behind the mountains when she left the house, but now it was almost completely dark. Anne had no desire to be trapped in the woods at night. The path she had come up was already difficult to see. Little as she liked going back to Heartwood after the scene between her and her grandmother, she would have to.

She started off down the track at a brisk pace and was glad to find that she had little trouble following it. Before many minutes had passed, she could glimpse the house through the trees. When she started across the clearing toward the house, a dark figure rose out of the gloom of the porch and came across to the steps. Anne's stomach tightened. It was Mrs. Kerr, waiting for her. She hoped there wouldn't be another fight. Maybe the old lady would just quietly tell her that it would be best if Anne left early in the morning.

"Anne! I'm glad you're back. I was beginning to worry about you." Mrs. Kerr stepped down onto the top step.

Anne came up the steps. This close, she could see Sophia's face clearly, and there was no sign of anger in it, nor any of the cold arrogance that had been there before. Instead, Sophia wore a slight frown that quickly faded.

"I'm sorry. I hadn't realized it was so late."

"I understand. When you're in a temper, you don't see anything at all. That's the way I am." Sophia sighed and shook her head. "The way Gary was." She paused, then went on. "I shouldn't have criticized your mother to you. I'm sorry. It was wrong of me. Whatever feelings Beverly and I have toward each other have nothing to do with you, and I don't want the . . . bad blood between us to spoil my time with you."

"I'm sorry, too. I shouldn't have blown up like that."

Sophia shrugged. "People aren't always pleasant. I know that I can be—somewhat overbearing at times." She smiled wryly. "Wendall—that was my husband—always told me it came from being the banker's daughter in a poor town. Maybe so. He and I had some real doozies of fights. Gary and I did, too."

Anne couldn't understand Sophia's easy acceptance of arguments and fights. Personally, she couldn't bear them; she hated being the receiver of someone else's anger, and she hated being angry just as much. She guessed it was why, in the end, she had always knuckled under to Bryan's wishes, no matter how little she wanted to. It hadn't made for a good marriage, although it had surprised her to find out that Bryan hadn't enjoyed the situation either.

Anne started for the door, but Sophia's quiet voice stopped her. "Do you dislike me because of what I said about your mother?"

Anne turned. "No. I—I didn't like what you said. I think you're unfair to her. But it didn't make me dislike you. I felt bad about getting mad because, well, I like you, and I didn't want a rift between us."

"Good. Neither do I. Would you like to see those pictures of Gary now?"

"Yes. I'd like them very much."

It was odd looking at the old photographs of a boy she had never met, knowing that he was her father. She thought of the years Bill Mitchell had given her, so much more unselfishly than she had ever realized, and all the ways in which he had been a father to her. She loved Bill; she would always love him. Yet she was gripped by a strange fascination as she pored over the black-and-white snapshots of a boy growing into adolescence and then to young manhood. There was Gary Kerr on his first pony, going on his first trail ride, holding up a string of fish he'd caught, perched on the trunk of his car. Anne felt an eerie shiver down her spine—had that been the car in which he died?

She searched for some resemblance to her, for evidence that he was truly her father. Yet she could see little but a happy young man, laughing and handsome. He looked as if he had loved life, as if he'd met it head on. Could there possibly be anything of that boy in her?

As if she had sensed her thought, Sophia mused, "You know, tonight when you were angry with me, you reminded me of Gary. His eyes would grow bright and unbelievably blue like yours did when he was mad. I wish they'd made color pictures back then. You can't see the similarity in your coloring. Your eyes are the exact color his were, and, when he was a child, Gary's hair had a lot of red in it."

There were studio portraits of him, too, and though the spontaneity was missing in them, his features were clearer. Anne studied them carefully. Wasn't her mouth a little like that? And wasn't that the hint of an indentation in his chin, like she had? There was something familiar about him, though she couldn't pinpoint it. Or was it merely her imagination at work, creating resemblances because she knew he was her father?

She wished she had known him, Anne thought, and was

71

aware of a small, fierce ache in her chest. She set the photo album aside and glanced over at Sophia. The older woman was studying Anne as intently as Anne had been gazing at the pictures. Anne felt uneasy, unsettled. She liked Sophia; she loved the house, its atmosphere and story; she even felt some quirk of feeling for the boy in the photographs. Yet she felt as if Sophia had taken her life and shaken it, like a snow scene in a glass ball, and everything was floating around in pieces, with no telling where it would settle.

"At supper you said you had an idea, and you wanted to see me first. What did you mean?" Anne asked.

Sophia didn't answer. Instead she asked, "Do you like this house?"

"Yes, of course I like it. It's beautiful."

"I'm giving most of my estate to charity when I die. I have no relatives, you see. Except you. I don't mind the ranch going to people I've never met; it was Wendall's, anyway. And the money—well, who can have sentimental attachment to bonds and stocks and money market certificates?" She smiled, and again Anne saw a flash of that wealth and breeding that was disguised by her ordinary looks and clothes. But this time it showed up as charm.

Anne said nothing. She had no idea what response could be appropriate to Sophia's non sequitur.

"But I don't like the thought of strangers in this house," Sophia continued. "I hate to have that little man from the trust department in Denver scuttling about my house, appraising furniture and counting bedsheets. I don't want Heartwood to be sold to someone I never saw, never knew. So I'm giving the house to you."

For a long moment after Sophia's amazing announcement, Anne simply stared at her, too stunned to speak. Finally, however, Sophia's words sank in. "You're giving me this house?" she repeated stupidly.

"Yes. And the land around it, of course. The furniture and accessories."

"But—but that's impossible!"

"Not at all. I've already done it." Sophia reached into the top desk drawer and pulled out a legal document, which she extended to Anne. Dazedly Anne glanced over it and realized that it was a deed to Heartwood and its land. Dated the Tuesday before, it gave Anne Mitchell Hamilton title to the house!

"But you can't. No, I couldn't possibly accept. You hardly know me. In fact you hadn't even met me when this deed was drawn up."

"That's true. If you had turned out to be unacceptable, I wouldn't have told you and would have quietly torn up the deed. As you can see, it hasn't been recorded yet. I'll have my attorney do that Monday."

"Please, no. Really, I can't accept your house. It's far too expensive."

"Don't be coy with me, Anne. I'm your grandmother, even though we haven't known each other long. And I'm a realist. If there's one thing you need, it's a valuable asset. I told you I'd kept up with you through the years. I know about your divorce. I know you sold your car and your house. I'm giving you this house with no strings attached other than the right for me to live in it until I die. After that you can do whatever you want with it. Live here. Turn it into a store or a restaurant or a quaint little hotel. You can even sell it. I just want to know that my father's house came to me and was passed on to Gary's daughter. There's a rightness to it, a sense of family."

The house, the land, and the furniture! Anne couldn't imagine how much it would sell for. Enough that she could buy a nice house and put the rest away in investments to earn interest so she wouldn't have to work to maintain her family. She could be a full-time mother to John Peter and Nicole again. No more mad rushing from job to day-care to home, no more guilt about not spending enough time with her kids and not giving them adequate meals. Maybe she could even return to some kind of decent relationship with Nicole.

But not until after Sophia died. She had retained the right to live in it until her death. "I don't want to sit around like a ghoul waiting for you to die."

"Well, thank you. But you needn't think of it that way. The house will be yours. You're welcome to come and visit whenever you wish. Bring your children."

"Have you thought this thing through? I mean, are you certain it's what you want?"

Sophia's eyes lighted with amusement. "You mean, have I gotten senile and don't know what I'm doing?" She chuckled. "No. Not yet. I'm in full possession of my faculties. Just ask my attorney. He tried to talk me out of it. But after a while he realized that my mind was made up and that I wasn't in any way coerced or pressured—or feebleminded."

"But why give it to me now? Why not just leave it to me when you die?"

"I told you. I want you to think of it as yours now, not just after my death. I want you to own it, no strings attached. There must be no taint of your having to placate me or do me favors so you can have the house when I die. There are no conditions."

"But it doesn't seem right."

"What's right about leaving it to a distant cousin in Chicago? What's right about leaving it to a college or a hospital or a fund for the study of some disease? I told you. You're the closest person to me in blood. You're all there is of my family, of my son. I want you to have it. Period."

They sat silently gazing at each other, seemingly measuring the other's determination. Finally Sophia added, "Remember. You don't have a choice. I've given it to you. It's yours."

After that, there seemed little to say. At least, Anne was able to think of nothing. She rose and went to bed, where she spent most the night debating the problem. The idea of accepting the magnificent old house didn't seem quite fair; she felt guilty, as if she had somehow persuaded her grandmother to give it to her. It was ridiculous, because she hadn't done or said anything to influence Sophia to give her the house—why, just before Sophia had given it to her, Anne had rushed out of the house in anger. There was nothing wrong with Sophia's giving her the house; she was, after all, Sophia's granddaughter, her only close relative. People usually left their children and grandchildren bequests; it wasn't her fault that her grandmother was wealthy and the inheritance was a large one. Certainly she could use the money from selling it. So why was she resisting?

Probably because she wanted the house. From the moment she'd stepped into Heartwood, Anne had loved it. The gleaming wood, the sparkling crystal, the leaded glass insets in the doors—all of it wrapped around her and warmed her. She had felt an immediate, passionate, and possessive love for the house. Perversely, the fact that she wanted it made her getting it seem somehow illegitimate. One shouldn't desire an object obtained through another's death, especially a grandmother she knew and liked. If she had never met Sophia Kerr and had received this valuable house after her death, Anne imagined she would have been delighted at the windfall.

It was silly reasoning, she knew, and every time she thought of the house being hers, she felt an upsurge of joy. Why not accept it and be happy? It wouldn't hasten her grandmother's death. Besides, she didn't have any say in the matter, as Sophia had pointed out. Sophia had already given her the title; it would be recorded Monday.

Anne rose early the next morning and showered, hoping that would clear her mind of some of its cobwebs, then dressed and padded softly down the stairs. No one was around, so she fixed a bowl of cereal and ate it standing on the side porch, looking out at the path she had taken last night. The stream was chillingly dark, even with the purling white foam and the sparkles the early morning sun cast upon its surface. In the absolute stillness, it rushed along its path with a muffled roar. Anne heard a bird call and the rustle of leaves as a breeze stirred them. It was a scene of utter peace, and Anne couldn't resist its lure.

Setting the empty bowl back in the kitchen, she started out, taking the same path she had walked last evening. This time, however, her mind was on the beauty around her, and her troublesome thoughts were pushed to the background. She immersed herself in the utter serenity and the clean, crisp feel of the air around her. It was slightly chilly when she entered the trees, and she huddled in her arms, but didn't go back. The thick odor of pine was everywhere. Pine needles cushioned the ground and silenced the sound of her footsteps. It was a strange but pleasant feeling for one used to the city, as if she were completely alone in the world.

Anne paused on a narrow wooden bridge and leaned over its log railing to peer down into the stream. Straight down, the water was perfectly clear, and she could see the tan rocks pebbling its bed. Here and there a larger rock or a sudden drop in the bed sent the water bubbling and splashing. Anne wandered deeper into the woods. The path was easy to follow in the daylight, with no confusing branches. She crossed the creek again, this time on a more makeshift bridge of two wide planks running from bank to bank. She eyed the wooden walkway a little warily, but she tested the planks' strength with one foot and found it stable, so she hurried across it.

Now the path moved away from the stream, gradually climbing. Soon Anne realized that she could no longer hear the roar of the creek. She also noticed that the air was far too thin for her. Although she had come farther than she had last night, it certainly hadn't been an excessive amount of exercise. Yet she was already winded, and she had to sit down on a rock to recapture her breath. She had heard people say that the thin air of the mountains made it difficult to breathe, but she had never experienced it herself. Her breathing was as labored as if she had run.

As she sat and looked about her, Anne caught a glimpse of something through the trees ahead, a wooden structure. A house? As soon as she recovered her breath, she started toward it. The trail led right to it. As she came closer she could make out that it was a small, low, wooden cabin. The trees thinned, and she stepped into a clearing. The house lay in front of her. Made of rough-hewn logs, with a stone chimney at one end, it was small, probably not more than a couple of rooms, but sturdy, with an air of being more cozy than cramped.

Intrigued, Anne moved across the clearing, her footfalls silenced by the pervasive pine needles. She circled to the rear of the house. A screened-in porch jutted out from the back, and two shallow steps went up to the door. The quaint cabin hidden in the midst of the pine forest intrigued Anne, and she drew nearer, wondering who lived there and what it looked like inside. A figure moved on the porch, and she stopped. Though her vision was somewhat obscured by the mesh of the screens, she could see that the figure was that of a man standing bent over a table. She remained still for a moment. She was being nosy and intrusive, Anne reminded herself. She couldn't coolly walk up to someone's house and peer in.

She took a step backward, starting to turn, and her foot came down on a dry branch. It cracked loudly in the quiet, and the man on the porch whirled around, eyes searching, his arm flinging outward. And there, pointing straight at Anne, a knife glittered in his hand.

Chapter Five

ANNE GASPED, ONE HAND FLYING UP TO HER THROAT IN AN instinctive gesture of protection, and she stumbled back another step. Then she recognized the man as Mark Pascal, and in almost the same instant his hand dropped down to his side.

"Jesus!" His breath rushed out in an explosive sigh. "Sorry. You startled me."

"Yes, I see. I—I'm sorry." What was he doing standing around with a knife in his hand, anyway, Anne wondered. And why had a sudden, sharp noise made him whirl and prepare to defend himself? It seemed a rather excessive response to the crunch of a branch breaking.

"Did you need something?" Mark opened the screen door and stepped onto the top step, propping the door open with his shoulder. His hair was tangled, and there was a dark shadow along his jaw that indicated he hadn't shaved. His feet were bare, and he was dressed in ancient army fatigue pants and a white T-shirt.

"What?" Anne stared stupidly. There was a stretched look to his skin that bespoke tiredness and lack of sleep. Anne wondered if he had just gotten out of bed. She thought of him asleep, sprawled across a bed, his spare, tensile strength relaxed, his face smooth and unguarded. The idea stirred an unaccustomed heat deep in her gut. Her reaction embarrassed her, and she wished she weren't here.

"Did Sophia send you?"

"Oh. No. I was, uh, wandering around. I got up early and thought I'd explore a little. Sorry I startled you. I didn't realize anyone was here. I was interested in the house." She glanced beyond him onto the porch and glimpsed a sturdy wooden table on which sat several tools and a curiously shaped block of wood. She narrowed her eyes. It was a figure, or, rather, a partial figure carved in wood. Her eyebrows went up in surprise and understanding. "Oh! You carve things out of wood."

"Yeah." She would have liked to have seen the statue at closer range, but Mark didn't move aside or ask her in.

"Well, uh . . . I guess I'll go back."

Mark shifted and said reluctantly, "You want a cup of coffee?"

"That sounds delicious." She suspected he had hoped she would refuse, but Anne wasn't about to leave if her curiosity could be satisfied. She started toward the steps and he stepped down awkwardly to let her pass. "Do you mind if I look at your work? I didn't realize you were an artist."

He shrugged. "I work with wood. I don't know if that qualifies me as an artist."

Mark used the door and the frame to help himself up and onto the porch. He lurched across the room to the cane leaning against the table, and Anne wondered if he had been so grim and inhospitable because he had been embarrassed at walking in front of her without his cane.

"Oh, how lovely!" Anne exclaimed as she bent to examine the piece Mark had been working on. The figure of a powerfully muscled horse rearing was still rough and unfinished, but the grace and energy of the animal were obvious. Anne ran a forefinger along the animal's back. So he was an artist. Perhaps that explained his moody silences and the grim lines around his mouth and eyes. Artists were entitled to temperament, she supposed.

"It's not nearly finished." Mark clumped into the room, carrying a mug of coffee.

"Yes, I can see that, but it's quite good, nevertheless. You're very talented."

Mark shrugged and set Anne's mug on the corner of the table. "I didn't know whether you wanted milk and sugar."

"This is fine," Anne lied and took a sip. She wasn't about to send him back to the kitchen for a little milk in her coffee; she'd rather drink it black. She felt uneasy standing here with Mark. He didn't smile or speak or seem in any way glad to have her with him, yet for some reason, she wanted to stay. Anne wandered across the porch, finding little but pieces of wood and empty boxes.

"The finished stuff's inside," Mark said and jerked his head toward the door.

"Would you mind if I looked at it?"

"Feel free."

Anne opened the back door and stepped inside. She was in a small room lined with shelves and containing only another table and chair. Statues of animals and people and abstract things she could put no name to lined the shelves. Anne sucked in her breath. Mark's work was vibrant and filled with life, not pretty in a conventional sense, but beautiful in its fierce strength. It was impossible to look away, and Anne couldn't keep from reaching out to touch the pieces.

She walked slowly from piece to piece. One carving in particular intrigued her, and she returned to it more than once, drawn by a bittersweet longing. It was a large head of an American Indian, strong and handsome, yet lined with pain and an infinite sadness. Anne traced his features with one finger, loving the feel of the cool, smooth wood even as her chest knotted with a longing to cry. She felt almost as if she touched his skin, knew his heart. Her own heart beat a little faster. The Indian reminded her of Mark.

She turned away hastily and went over to the table. There lay vases, bowls, and boxes in various sizes and shapes. Most were made of a pale tan and cream wood that looked satin smooth. Intrigued, she picked up a bowl. It was amazingly light. She turned back to Mark who had followed her as far as the doorway.

"What is this made of? It's so light!"

"Aspen wood. I sell those through one of the shops in Iron Creek. Phyllis sells my art work, too, but these are what make money. Tourists love things made out of aspen. Souvenir of Colorado."

"They're beautiful, too."

He shrugged. "They're elementally satisfying. So are the boxes. They require skill and precision; they have to be done perfectly or they aren't salable. But they don't require any creativity."

Anne picked up one of the smaller boxes. It was made of a darker wood than the aspen, and its lid was inlaid with bits of different woods in a design. "I don't know. This mosaic on top looks pretty creative to me."

"The original pattern was, I guess, but I repeat about six of them over and over. It's a craft, not art."

She saw no point in arguing. Mark seemed determined to downplay what he did. She didn't know if it was insecurity or sheer contrariness. He seemed to oppose things on general principles. Anne side-stepped the subject. "These are lovely woods." She ran her index finger over the pieces of wood in all shades of tan and brown and even pink. She thought of his supple fingers on the box, carving, sanding, fitting the pieces together. She imagined the wood warm from his hands, felt his concentration and pleasure. "What are they?"

For the first time, a genuine grin split his face, showing even, white teeth and lifting the lines of his face. "A bunch of things you've never heard of, I imagine. I put a list in the box, so people can identify them. The box is walnut." He pointed to the darkest strip. "Wenge. English walnut. This dark reddish brown is mesua." He glanced up at her; the wood was almost the color of her hair, streaked as it was with brown, but he didn't say so. "Shedua." He pointed again. "Mozambique. Black bean. The pale pinkish-orange is mahogany. Koa. This very lightest is maple, and the satiny-looking one is hickory."

"Well, at least I've heard of two or three of them," Anne joked back at him. He had leaned forward, closer to her, as he pointed out the different woods. He smelled of wood shavings, a tangy, somehow comforting scent. Up close his eyes were a dark brown, not black, but shadowed by the thick brush of straight black lashes lining his lids. His hair fell shaggily around his ears, and Anne felt a sudden, inexplicable urge to brush it back with her fingers. She curled her fingers into her palm and moved away. The feeling disquieted her.

Mark watched her as she trailed in front of the shelves, examining his works. He liked the way she walked, stopping to peer at something, bending down to get a better glimpse. When she bent forward, the khaki material of her slacks pulled tightly over her tight, rounded bottom, and the male in him couldn't help but respond. She brushed her fingers over his work, and Mark felt as if she touched him, so connected was he to the wood. As if each piece were a surrogate that could take her warmth, where he could not.

In slacks, a short-sleeved blouse, and a sleeveless pullover sweater, she looked more casual than she had yesterday, though still a trifle sharp to suit the thick, unruly hair and womanly figure. She was meant to be lush, he thought, and down-to-earth, the kind of woman that made a man want to come home and bury himself in her warmth. She could burn away the chill of the world.

But she disturbed him, too. He knew the anxiety of the artist as another inspected the work that was a piece of his soul. What if she turned with a frown and asked what something was supposed to be? What if she gave him a phony smile, assuring him vaguely that it was "lovely" or "interesting"?

But it was more than that. Anne Hamilton challenged him in a way he hadn't been challenged in years and years. She made him want to be with her, want to try to interest or impress her. She aroused a physical hunger in him and something far, far more, something a hooker in Denver couldn't assuage. He wanted to sit with her and talk and laugh, to listen to her voice and watch the shifting expressions on her face, to tease and seduce and entrance each other. But all that was as far away as the world he'd left behind when he went to Nam. He didn't belong there, just as he didn't belong with Anne Hamilton.

The only place he did belong was right here in the niche he'd created, this life alone here in the mountains. Her presence angered him because suddenly his niche no longer seemed enough anymore. "What are you doing here?" he asked abruptly, almost challengingly.

"What?" She looked at him, puzzled. "I told you, I was out for an early morning walk. It was so lovely and peaceful, I couldn't resist."

"No. I mean in Iron Creek. At Heartwood."

"Oh. I'm visiting Mrs. Kerr."

"You're a little young to be a friend of hers."

Anne's brows drew together. There was no understanding this man. A moment ago he'd appeared to be warming up, had even smiled. And now he was interrogating her, as if he were trying to ferret out some wrongdoing she was engaged in. "I'm not a friend of hers. I'm her granddaughter."

His face hardened. "Ah, so the vultures are already circling."

He turned and stepped back onto the porch, walking to the table as if she were no longer there. Anne followed, puzzled and hurt by his words. "What do you mean?"

He glanced at her, contempt in his eyes. "What else would you call it when relatives who never bothered to visit Mrs. Kerr before all of a sudden start coming now that she's dying?"

Anne stopped, rooted to the floor. "What?"

"You heard me."

"Dying? Mrs. Kerr—Sophia is dying?"

"You know she is."

"I know nothing of the sort! Look, I don't know if you're just rude or quick to jump to conclusions, or what. But I came here to visit because Sophia asked me to. I didn't even know who she was or that she was my grandmother until a couple of days ago!" Anne paused and drew in a sharp breath. "Why am I saying this? I don't have to justify myself to you. Just because you have a warped mind—" Anne stopped and wrapped her arms tightly across her chest. She whirled and strode across the porch to the outside door.

At the doorway she paused and turned back uncertainly. "Is that true? Is she dying?"

Mark nodded. In his unease and defensiveness, he'd jumped at the opportunity to believe something bad about Anne. Obviously, he had revealed a secret of Sophia's. But he could see no way to reverse what he'd said; Anne wouldn't believe a denial now. And there was no point in apologizing; he needed to keep her at a distance.

"How do you know?" Anne asked.

"I drove her to the doctor's office Monday. When she came out, she was shaken. I asked what was wrong, and she told me."

"I see." Anne laid a palm against the doorjamb and leaned against it. "That's why she's giving me the house."

"Sophia is giving you Heartwood?" Mark's eyebrows shot up in amazement, then he returned to his former mocking tone. "Well, congratulations. You'll get it sooner than you expected."

"I didn't ask for it!" Anne blazed. "She'd already signed over the deed to me before I came up here. I told her I didn't want the damn thing!"

He shrugged cynically. "Why turn it down? It's a gold mine."

Anne's eyes flashed. "I don't know what your problem is, but you're a real bastard, you know?"

She slammed out of the door and let it bang satisfyingly behind her. What a sanctimonious, bad-tempered creep! He seemed to think his lame leg gave him the right to look down on everyone else. Or maybe he thought he had too much talent to be expected to extend normal courtesy to others. Well, she had too much to think about now to let him prey on her mind.

The walk back passed much more quickly than the one coming up. Within twenty minutes she was at Heartwood and charging up the stairs to Sophia's sitting room. She banged loudly on the door, then opened it before Sophia could give her permission to enter.

Sophia looked up at her in mild questioning, and suddenly Anne didn't know what to say. She'd rushed in here ready to accuse Sophia of playing games and lying to her, but, facing her, Anne's throat closed over her angry words. She sighed. "Why didn't you tell me?"

"Tell you what?"

"That you're dying."

Sophia scowled. "Did Linda tell you that? I'll have her hide."

"No. It was your driver. Mark Pascal. He's a real charmer, that guy."

"You've talked to Mark this morning?" Sophia's voice rose in surprise.

"Yes. I took a walk and came upon his cabin. He was there working on a statue, and we talked a little. He was nice enough to tell me that I was a vulture coming here to get your property because you were dying."

Sophia sighed. "I never thought to warn Mark not to tell you. I figured, knowing him, he probably wouldn't say two words to you the whole time you were here."

"Why were you trying to hide it from me? Did you think I was a vulture, too?"

"Calm down, for heaven's sake. Why are you so angry that I didn't tell you? What difference does it make?"

Anne stared at her, nonplussed. "I—I'd have just gone home today and not even thought of coming back here to visit for months, a year, probably. I'd have been around you only two days out of my whole life." Sophia continued to gaze at her, unblinking, and Anne sagged into a chair. "Oh, hell! I'm mad because I don't want you to die."

Sophia snorted softly. "Well, it's not something I'm really wild about, either. But there's not much I can do about it." She paused. "I hadn't planned to bring this up until after breakfast. I wanted to see how you felt about our conversation last night. But since Mark's already started it, I guess we might as well go ahead. I told you yesterday that I had a plan. Giving you Heartwood wasn't all of it."

"What's the rest?"

"I'd like you to come live here for the rest of the summer."

Anne stared. "What?"

"You're my closest relative. Most of my friends have already died. I'm facing death with no one I love around me, no one whose blood is mine or who cares about me. I realized a lot of things Monday after my doctor told me what was wrong with me. One of them was that I wanted to see you. I wanted to give this house to Gary's daughter. And I didn't want to die alone."

"I—I don't know what to say."

"Don't say anything for a while. Think about it. I didn't tell you yesterday because I didn't want it to mar our first day together. I wanted to give you Heartwood freely so you wouldn't think you had to stay with me in order to get the house; there's no obligation attached to Heartwood. That's one reason why I deeded it to you instead of leaving it to you in my will. I wanted you to understand that it wasn't conditional on your doing me this favor."

"I see." She did see. Anne didn't know if it was intentional or not, but Sophia had trapped her much more effectively than if she had held out Heartwood as a reward for staying with her. Anne would have rejected that immediately, refusing to be bought. But, having already been given the house, Anne couldn't help but feel grateful and therefore guilty if she didn't do what Sophia wanted. *(After all she's given you, what's this one little favor?)* "But my children, my job . . ."

Sophia waved a dismissing hand. "Your job is nothing special. You can leave it and find another just like it any time you want. Besides, when I die, you'll have Heartwood without any encumbrances. If you live here, you'll have to leave Dallas anyway. And if you sell the house, you certainly won't need that little job anymore."

"No. That's true. But I can't leave John Peter and Nicole for—however long."

"It won't be that long. I have acute leukemia. The chronic kind can go on for years and can be treated fairly effectively. But the acute is quick and sharp. I will probably die within a month or two." Anne looked away, uneasy at discussing Sophia's death so coolly. "Still too long to be away from your children, I expect. But you can bring them with you. A vacation in the mountains would be good for them. You could spend your time with them instead of having to work. And I'd like to see them."

"Oh, but they're so noisy and active. I'm sure it would disturb you."

"Dr. Kressel gives me pills for the pain, and he tells me I won't be utterly feeble until the last. Hopefully, for a few weeks I'll be able to live somewhat normally. This is a big house. They can play outside or in another part of the house, and I won't even hear it. We should also be able to keep them separated from my illness; no use putting the burden of seeing someone die on children."

Anne stared at Sophia, her reasons dying even before they left her brain. Her home was no problem; in a few weeks she would have had to move anyway. She could probably move the signing up or fly back to Dallas for it. What furniture she had left could be put in storage. Sophia was right; her job was of little importance. She could always find another, and perhaps she wouldn't need to. There was no problem with school for Nicole since it was summer. And it would give her the opportunity to be with her children full time instead of carting them off to a day-care center all day, then being too exhausted at night to pay any quality attention to them. It really wouldn't be a hardship on her; in many ways it would be an advantage. It would be nice to spend some time here in the mountains, which had already enchanted her.

No, the real problem was herself. It terrified Anne to think of spending the last weeks with a dying person. She knew she couldn't handle it. She didn't have the kind of emotional strength that would be required. How many times had she buckled under pressure from Bryan or her mother or Nicole? She wouldn't be much support to Sophia. Sophia needed someone strong like Bit, someone who could take charge, not a woman who dithered about decisions. Not someone who went queasy at the sight of another's pain. Why, it had taken all Anne's fortitude just to hold Nicole and John Peter when their pediatrician had given them shots! She had wanted desperately to run away and not have to endure their screams and tears; only the fact that she could not desert her children when they needed her had kept her rooted to the spot.

And now Sophia was asking her to see her through a fatal illness. It was absurd. She couldn't do it. "I—I don't know. I'm not very good at things like that."

"I wouldn't expect you to help nurse me; I'll hire someone if that becomes necessary. I just want a companion, a member of my own family to be here with me. Someone to talk to and laugh with." Sophia paused and turned away. "I've done very well all these years by myself. I never dreamed that at the end I'd be so—scared of dying alone."

Anne's heart went out to her grandmother. How awful it would be to be old and sick and alone in the world. Sophia's money couldn't buy love and kinship. Anne thought of being in her position—no children, no sister, not even an ex-husband to be with her as she faced death. How could she refuse her request? "It's not that. It's just that I'm—a little stunned. I don't know what to think."

"I don't expect an immediate answer, of course." Sophia turned back briskly to face her, only the faint sheen of moisture in her eyes hinting at the emotions she'd just revealed. "Go home and think about it. Call and let me know." Unspoken between them, but deeply realized was the fact that Anne could not wait very long to decide.

"I need to talk to my children, or rather, Nicole. The baby doesn't care where he is."

"I would very much like to see them. Even if you decide not to come for the whole summer, I hope you'll bring them to visit for a few days."

"Yes. Of course."

"Well." Sophia shrugged off the topic and continued brightly, "Have you had breakfast yet?"

"Yes. I ate some cereal before I went for my walk."

"Cereal? Is that all? You stay here long, and Linda'll have you putting down a ranch hand's breakfast every morning."

Anne groaned comically and made a gesture with her hands as if her figure were ballooning. "No, thanks."

"Well, come down and at least have a cup of coffee with me while I eat mine."

"Sure." Anne smiled, and her grandmother linked arms with her and led her from the room, smiling and chatting as if they had been discussing the pleasantest of topics a few minutes before.

In the middle of the afternoon, Mark Pascal came by to take Anne to the airport in Denver. Anne said good-bye to Sophia as Mark loaded her bag into the rear of the truck. Impulsively she reached out and gave her grandmother a final hug. Sophia patted her on the back, and when Anne stepped back she saw that the older woman was smiling. Sophia Kerr was not a demonstrative person and probably not very emotional, either, Anne surmised, but she needed Anne. Anne had the suspicion that somehow she needed Sophia, too.

She rushed down the steps and hopped into the front seat of the car, turning back for a last wave to Sophia. Then she closed her door, and Mark put the car in gear. It leaped forward, and they jolted down the dirt road to the highway.

Mark said nothing to her and kept his eyes determinedly on the road. Anne matched his silence; she wasn't about to try to start a conversation with a man who had insulted her this morning. But the silence unnerved her; it was so uncomfortable sitting in this small, enclosed space and ignoring each other. She wondered what had made him so rude and suspicious. If she did decide to move into Heartwood this summer, she hoped she wouldn't have to be around Mark often. Anne crossed her arms and stared out the window at the scenery.

All the way home—in the car, at the airport, in the airplane—she thought about Heartwood and Sophia Kerr. She thought about the father she'd never known, the grandmother who needed her now, the dignified old house that had claimed her the instant she saw it. Her mother and Sophia disliked each other intensely; each blamed the other for Gary's death. If she moved to Iron Creek, would her mother feel hurt? Would she think that Anne had gone over to the enemy's camp? Yet could Anne ever feel comfortable accepting Sophia's largesse if she did not help the woman when she needed it? What did she, herself, want to do?

That was always the hardest thing for her to figure out amid a welter of obligations, fears, and sympathies. Bit told her (frequently) that she ought to think less about what others wanted and more about what she wanted. But Anne found it a difficult thing to do.

She thought about the house and living there for a few months. She thought about her children being with her and enjoying the beauty and clean air of the mountains. She thought about Sophia dying alone if she didn't come. By the time her plane landed she had made up her mind to return to Heartwood.

Bit met her at the airport, the kids in tow. John Peter squealed with delight when he saw her and squirmed down from Bit's arms to race to Anne. Nicole surprised her by throwing her arms around Anne and giving her a hard squeeze. Bit, smiling, waited in line for a quick hug. "How was Colorado?"

"Beautiful! I loved it. In fact, we're going to go back there, all three of us."

"Yeah?" Nicole's eyes lighted. "For vacation? Hey, that's great! Shelly Clark's family goes up there every winter to ski. They go to Steamboat Springs. Is that where we're going? When?"

Anne smiled, pleased by Nicole's enthusiasm. "As soon as I can arrange it. And, no, it's not Steamboat Springs. It's a lovely little town named Iron Creek."

"Iron Creek? That's a weird name."

"You think Steamboat Springs is normal?" They chuckled, and Anne was elated. She put her arms around Nicole's shoulders, balancing John Peter on the opposite hip. It seemed like old times again, she and Nicole happy together.

Everything was so congenial that when they got into the car, Anne decided to reveal the whole story. "What I'm thinking about doing," she began, as Bit pulled out of the parking lot and headed toward the exit, "is spending most of the summer there."

Bit shot her a surprised glance before she returned her eyes to the road. Nicole's jaw sagged. "The whole summer? Why? I don't want to be gone the whole time!"

"Why not? You'd really like it. There's a stable right next door, and you could go riding often. It's a great place for hiking and exploring. The town is quaint and full of neat little shops."

Nicole continued to stare at her. "But what about Cathy's birthday party? It's in two weeks, and her mom's going to take us to Six Flags. And what about Dad?" Her voice rose in pitch and volume, as if in fear. "When'll I see him if I'm way off in Colorado? I don't want to go to some hole-in-the-wall for three months!"

"It's not a hole-in-the-wall. We'd be living in the most beautiful house I've ever seen."

That caught Nicole's interest and arrested her mushrooming hysteria. "Bigger than Angela Selby's?"

"No, it's not that big, but it's far lovelier. It's exquisitely done—beautiful old hardwood floors laid out in a pattern, chandeliers, antiques, plaster mouldings on the ceilings. The most gorgeous wooden bookcases and sideboards!"

"Does it have a pool?"

"No. It's much too cool there—"

Nicole dismissed it as inadequate. "Then it couldn't be as nice as Angela's house."

Anne gritted her teeth. "You're confusing money with beauty, Nicole. It's not the same thing. Angela's house may have cost more, but it lacks the taste and elegance Heartwood has."

"Heartwood?" Bit interrupted.

"That's the name of the house. You should see it. It's lovely. It was built by a silver miner for his bride."

"Ah, a romantic history." Bit smoothly took over the

conversation, robbing Nicole of a chance to continue the argument. "But who is this lady you went to visit? Are you going to spend the summer with her?"

"Yes. Hang onto the wheel, Bit. Sophia Kerr is my grandmother."

Bit's head snapped around to look at her, then swung back to the road ahead. "What? Annie, have you lost your mind? You already have two grandmothers: Grandmama and Gran. How could you have three?"

"Gran wasn't really my grandmother. Bill isn't my father." Anne related the story Beverly had told her as delicately as possible, mindful of Nicole's curious young ears in the back seat.

When she finished, Bit was too astounded to say anything. It was Nicole who spoke up. "That sounds like a soap opera. Mom, you're making this up."

"No. I'll admit it's strange, but it's the truth. Mrs. Kerr showed me pictures of my father; in fact, his baby pictures reminded me a lot of yours, Nicki."

"What was his name?" Bit asked. Even stunned, she had to know the details.

"Gary."

"Well, I don't want to go!" Nicole snapped.

Anne sighed inwardly. It certainly hadn't taken very long for the enthusiasm and togetherness to vanish. "Sweetheart . . ."

"Don't call me that! I'm not a baby anymore."

Anne's hands clenched in her lap. "All right, then, Nicole. This is something I'm sure you'll enjoy, even though you may not think so now. But when you see Iron Creek and the house, you'll change your mind."

"I will not. I don't want to go there. I won't be able to swim, and I'll miss Cathy's party. And I won't see Dad at all. That's why you're doing this, isn't it? Just to keep me from seeing Dad!"

"Of course not! That has nothing to do with it. And you will see your father. You could probably fly down here and spend a whole week with him later in the summer."

Nicole made a sour face. "I wouldn't see him during the

week; he's always at the office or the hospital. You know that. I'd only get to see him on the weekend, and the rest of the time I'd have to spend with Gwen." Her voice dripped scorn. "It is, too, why you want to go. You hate for me to be with Daddy. You're jealous."

Anne paled. Such arguments with her daughter always drained her. Nicole could be vicious in the things she said. "I am not jealous. What would I have to be jealous of? I'm glad you and your father have a good relationship." She ignored Bit's rolled eyes and quirked lips. "And I think you should spend time with Bryan. But this won't keep you from ever being together."

"I won't be with him every weekend."

"That's true."

"I'm not going."

"Yes, you are." Now that Nicole was arguing against going, Anne realized how desperately she wanted to spend the summer at Heartwood.

"I'll stay here."

"With Bryan? You just said you didn't want to spend a week with Gwen. Think how many weeks you'd be spending alone with her if you stayed the whole summer."

"I'll live with Dee Ann."

"You can't stay with a friend's family the whole summer."

"Her parents like me!"

"I'm sure they do, but you still can't impose on them that long. Besides, I want you to come with me."

"Why? You don't care about me!"

Bit pulled into their driveway and stopped, and Nicole jerked open the car door. "You're always making me do awful things like this! I don't want to go off and spend the summer with some old lady I don't even know! You hate for me to have any fun or do anything I want."

Anne closed her eyes wearily. "That's not true."

"It is true! It is! You're hateful and selfish, and I'd rather run away than live with you. You drove Daddy away, and now you're trying to drive me away. I hate you! I hate you!"

Sobbing, Nicole ran toward the house, but Bit was out of the car in a single, fluid motion. Her voice cracked across the yard in her best courtroom manner. "Stop right there, young lady!"

Nicole couldn't disobey her. It was a talent Bit and Bryan had. Their sharp tones, even if not loud, could bring anyone in line. Anne had never acquired it; she had no idea how one obtained it, even. It certainly wasn't experience or maturity; she had more of those than Bit. But Bit had an air of authority born of a natural confidence in herself. Nicole turned back to face her, arms crossed over her chest, face turned down sullenly.

"I don't ever want to hear you talk that way to your mother again. She's been ten times more patient and loving with you than you deserve. Let me tell you a few home truths. You try running away, and you'll find out what real misery is. You won't see any more swimming pools or fancy schools or Izod shirts and Calvin Klein jeans. If you're lucky, you'll be hungry, thirsty, dirty, and unhappy. If you aren't lucky, you'll be raped or dead or both. As for your mother driving your father away, that's a lie, and we all know it. Your father left of his own free will. And you haven't been deprived of his attention; he's seen you a lot more since the divorce than he ever did when he was living here."

Nicole cast her aunt a fulminating glance, and tears spilled out of her eyes and down her cheeks. Anne's heart squeezed in her chest, and she, too, climbed out of the car. "Bit, please . . ."

Bit sighed and glanced back at her sister. "All right, honey, I'm sorry." She turned back to Nicole. "You're not my responsibility, and you better be glad, 'cause I wouldn't let you get away with the junk your mother does. But I want to say one last thing. If your mother wants to go to Colorado for the summer, you're going, even if I have to personally stuff you into the car. Is that understood?"

Nicole's lips drew down, and Anne knew she was desperately fighting her tears. "Yes!"

"Okay, then I suggest you go to your room and rethink your position."

Nicole whirled and stormed away, but her grand gesture was spoiled by having to stand at the door and wait for the others to come with the key to unlock it. Anne lifted John Peter from his car seat and carried him to the door, Bit bringing up the rear with Anne's suitcase. Anne opened the door and Nicole bolted inside. Anne set the baby down on the floor with a sigh, and Bit dropped the bag.

"Sorry I blew off my mouth," Bit admitted. "She's your kid, and I shouldn't butt in. But it makes me furious to hear her talk that way. She couldn't ask for a kinder, more generous mother than you, and she talks like you're a prison matron."

Anne smiled wryly. "No. A prison matron wouldn't let her get away with it. I know I should have better control over her, but I don't know how. She's been upset since Bryan left. It shook her up far more than I ever dreamed it would. She's clung to him ever since."

"Don't let her step all over you like that. She won't respect you for it, and it doesn't help her any."

"I know. But I had a hard enough time being a good mother. Now that I have to be a mother and a father—oh, Bit, I'm way out of my league."

"Nonsense. You simply need more self-respect." Bit leaned closer. "Let me tell you something. Do you know who Nicole's major role model is? You. You're the female she's around the most and knows best. Do you want her to grow up thinking she ought to let everyone walk on her so they'll like her? She may sound feisty as hell, but once she gets past adolescence, she'll lose a lot of that fire. Remember what she used to be like? That's more her real personality, and someday she'll return to it, only with the notion that mothers and women are meant to be doormats and patsies. Is that what you want?"

"Of course not! But you're crazy. She's not going to be like me."

"Think not?"

Anne grimaced. "Oh, Lord, I hope not."

"See? That's what I mean. Act the way you want her to act when she's a grown woman. Stand up for yourself. And the first way you can do it is by not letting her bully you out of going to Colorado. Or Bryan either."

"Bryan's on his honeymoon. I won't hear anything from him until after I've gone." A grin sneaked across Anne's face. "But his not wanting me to go would make me more determined. I'd love to see his face when he gets back and finds out where we've gone."

Bit chuckled. "There's an evil little creature living inside there somewhere, you know?"

"I know."

"You ought to let her out more often. Now promise me you won't back out of going to Colorado because of Nicole."

"I promise."

Bit studied Anne, her head tilted slightly to one side. "Do you realize that we're really half sisters?" Anne nodded; she had thought of it, and it made her feel uneasy. "Isn't that odd? Talk about your whole life being turned upside down."

"I know." Anne hesitated a moment. "Bit . . ."

"Yeah?"

"I didn't want to say anything in front of Nicole. I never know how things are going to affect her anymore. Sophia Kerr is giving me the house."

"You're joking. The big, gorgeous house you were telling us about?"

"Yes. She's dying. She has leukemia. That's why she wants us to come up there. Do you think I'd be wrong to go? I mean, do you think it would hurt the kids?"

"I don't know." A frown creased Bit's forehead.

"They wouldn't be subjected to a lot of illness or death scenes. Right now Sophia looks fine. And after she gets bad—well, it's a big house. They wouldn't be forced to see her."

"I imagine it wouldn't affect John Peter. I don't know about Nicole."

"I know. She's the one I worry about."

"I think you'd have to tell her that Sophia is dying. It wouldn't be fair to deceive her."

"I was planning to do that as we drove up there. But I don't want to tell her about the house being ours. Her emotions have been so unstable recently, I don't know what it might unleash. She might think we're going to have to live there permanently—or she might become so attached to it she would be heartbroken if we had to sell it. I even cautioned Sophia about telling her. I just want Nicole to enjoy the house without any pressure of any kind on her."

"That's probably a good idea. I wish I could tell you what to do. Death's a natural part of life; I don't think Nicole can be insulated from it. And it might be good for you two to be together more again."

"That's what I thought. Still, it seems a morbid situation to expose a child to."

"I think it could be done without any damage to Nicole. It might even help her. And if you want to go, then I'd say go. It's something Nicole will simply have to deal with."

"I hope you're right."

"What will Mom say about your going?"

Anne shrugged. "I don't know. She wanted me to see Sophia, but she doesn't yet know about our spending the summer in Colorado."

"Don't let her talk you out of it, either." Bit put an arm around her sister's shoulders and squeezed her. "I love you, Annie. Don't let 'em push you around."

"I'll try not to."

"Don't give me that 'I'll try' stuff. You do it. If you need any help, call me."

"I will." But she knew that, no matter how easy it was, she simply could not rely on Bit to discipline her daughter. That was something she must do herself.

After Bit left, Anne fed John Peter and spent the better part of an hour playing with him. Finally she dressed him for bed and put him down for the night. As she left his room, she glanced at Nicole's closed door, mute testimony to her daughter's anger. Anne looked at her watch. It was almost eight o'clock, and still Nicole hadn't come down for supper. Considering her healthy ten-year-old girl's appetite, that said a lot for the firmness of her anger. Anne thought of knocking at the door and trying to persuade Nicole to talk to her, but she made herself walk away. Bit was probably right; she usually was. She must not be so weak-kneed with Nicole; it created a bad example for her. It wasn't what Nicole needed, or really wanted, deep down inside. All the child-rearing books she'd read lately agreed on that; children, no matter how much they fought and argued, actually wanted discipline and structure. She had to be firm and consistent.

She walked down the hall and into the kitchen, stopping beside her purse to dig out a scrap of paper. She looked at the phone number written there and her mind skittered to Nicole in her bedroom upstairs, then to her mother. What would Beverly say about this? She hated to think. Perhaps she ought to call her first and tell her what she was thinking about doing.

No! Damn it, she was tired of waffling around. She had made up her mind what she was going to do, and now she would stick to it. No matter what Beverly or Nicole said. She'd deal with them somehow. Anne picked up the receiver and dialed the number on the paper. A woman's voice answered at the other end, curiously familiar and yet strange to her, as well. "Sophia?"

"Yes?"

"This is Anne. I wanted to let you know—we're coming up to Heartwood for the summer."

Chapter Six

IT WAS SIX DAYS LATER THAT ANNE PILED THE KIDS AND THEIR
suitcases in the car and started for Colorado. With Bit's help,
things had cleared away faster than she had thought possible.
Their remaining furniture and trunks of extra clothes were
packed in a self-storage garage. They stuffed summer clothes
and a few sweaters and trousers for the cool mountain
mornings and evenings into boxes and suitcases. The closing
on the house could not be speeded up, but Anne agreed to fly
back for it later. Anne arranged to cut off her telephone
service and utilities and filled out change-of-address forms for
her mail. After she explained the situation to her employers,
they agreed to terminate her employment with only a week's
notice and promised to write her a letter of recommendation
when she returned to Dallas to seek another job. Even Nicole
packed her things and was content to show her displeasure
with only a few sulks and evenings of silence.

Anne wrote Bryan a letter and mailed it to his townhouse,
explaining what she was doing. He would read it when he
came back from his honeymoon in a week. It gave Anne a
secret upsurge of pleasure to think of his frustration and
anger when he read the letter. It was time Bryan found out
that now that they were divorced, he could no longer control
her movements and actions.

On Saturday morning they set out, with Nicole curled up against the door in a ball of disapproval and John Peter bouncing in his car seat in the back, surrounded by boxes and luggage. They drove northwest across the vast, barren reaches of Texas and into New Mexico, finally turning due north and running parallel to the spine of mountains stretching up New Mexico and into Colorado. It was a long journey, and they had to stop often to let the children stretch out the kinks. They spent the night in Amarillo, huddled together in one bed, John Peter wailing, as a summer thunderstorm poured down outside. The wind howled, and it sounded as if a locomotive pounded across above their heads. Lightning lit up their room bright as day in flashes, each flash followed by an ear-splitting boom of thunder. Fat, hard drops of rain pelted against the windows, sounding like hailstones. The electricity went out, and they were left in the dark, suffocating heat. It seemed like a terrible omen.

But when they awoke the next morning, the electricity was on, and the world outside looked washed-clean and incredibly peaceful. Anne piled the kids and bags into the car and started out with renewed energy.

Soon mountains loomed in the northwest, and they turned northward, taking I-25 into Colorado, running parallel to the ridge of mountains. Anne didn't take time for sightseeing, promising herself that on their way back at the end of the summer they would stop to see the Royal Gorge, the pueblos, the artists' community of Taos. But now she felt a sense of urgency, a compulsion to reach Sophia Kerr as soon as possible. Her grandmother, she knew, was probably measuring her life in terms of days.

They turned off at Colorado Springs, again without sightseeing, and tackled the mountains. As they headed west, climbing continuously, even Nicole, who had long since gotten bored of looking out the window, suddenly tossed aside the book she had been reading and straightened to stare at the magnificent scenery unfolding around them. "Wow," she breathed, peering down and up and all around, twisting and craning to take in all the peaks and trees and coldly rushing water. "Is that *snow?*" She pointed to a distant peak.

Anne smiled. "Yeah. Hard to believe, huh? They tell me it never melts up there."

"Who's they?"

"A man who works for Sophia." A handsome, mysterious, inexplicably rude man, she added in her mind, wondering for the umpteenth time why her grandmother let him stay. She would have thought that someone like Sophia Kerr would have clashed with Mark long ago. Heavens, she had done it herself a couple of times already, and everyone knew she was a marshmallow.

"Is Iron Creek like this?"

"Pretty much. It's mountainous, if that's what you mean."

"It's beautiful." Nicole stretched out the word into an impossible number of syllables.

Anne refrained from pointing out that she had told Nicole she would like it and concentrated on her driving. She was discovering that it was much easier to enjoy the scenery when you didn't have to concentrate on the hairpin turns and sharp cutbacks.

They approached Iron Creek from the opposite direction from the way she and Mark had driven the first time, so that they came upon Heartwood before they reached the town. Anne missed it at first, realized that she had passed it, and made a U-turn to come back. Nicole stared up at the house sitting on the rise as they slowly bounced up the long drive. Her jaw dropped open as she took in the turret and cupola and intricate carved trim.

"It looks like a castle!"

Anne grinned. "Sort of."

"Gee! And we're going to live there?"

"That's right."

"What do I call her?"

"Who?"

"You know—the lady we're staying with. I mean, I don't have to call her Grandma or something, do I?"

"No, I wouldn't think you'd call her that. Mrs. Kerr sounds too formal, though. I guess you could call her Sophia." But that seemed a rather casual name for a child of ten to call her great-grandmother, a woman in her seventies. "Why don't we ask her what she'd like you to call her?"

"What's my bedroom like?"

"I don't know. I don't know which one Sophia will put you in. But they're all lovely."

She pulled the car to a stop in front of the mansion. As Nicole bounded from the car, stretching her cramped muscles, and Anne unfastened the baby from his car seat, Sophia opened the door and stepped onto the porch. A smile lit her face. "Anne!"

"Hello, Sophia." She set down the wriggling John Peter and let him steam across the grass and up the steps. Sophia must have been eager to see them; she had to have been waiting at a window for their arrival. "These are the kids. Nicole and John Peter."

"Hello, Nicole." Sophia greeted her gravely, shaking her hand. "Welcome to Heartwood."

"Hello, ma'am." Anne felt a rush of pride at Nicole's well-mannered greeting. Well, if nothing else, you could say that for her school. It had given her poise in social situations; she wasn't tongue-tied and ill at ease as Anne had been at her age.

Sophia squatted down to eye level with John Peter, beaming. "And hello to you, too, young man."

He stopped at the sight of a stranger so close, and his thumb automatically popped into his mouth, but then he gave a wide grin around it and chuckled. Sophia almost glowed at his response. Anne smiled. Seeing how happy and eager Sophia was to meet the children, Anne told herself again that she had done the right thing.

Anne awoke to the sound of John Peter's voice. The heavy curtains on the windows kept the room in Stygian darkness, but when she peered between them, she saw that it was light outside. She slipped on shoes and a robe and padded down the hall to John Peter's room. The baby wasn't crying, but was standing up, holding onto the railing of his baby bed and rattling it heartily as he dipped and bounced. All the while he jabbered loudly in a tongue known only to himself. He beamed at the sight of Anne and bounced all the harder, setting the whole bed to shaking.

"Come on, tiger, before you tear the place down." Anne swung him out of bed and expertly changed his soaking diaper. He caught his toes and chuckled. "Bobba, bobba!"

"You want a bottle of milk?" Anne interpreted, standing up and stretching out her hand. "Let's go find some, shall we?"

He scrambled up and headed for the door, ignoring her helping hand, as usual.

Anne smiled, watching him. "Independent cuss, aren't you?"

She followed him down the hall and walked beside him as he navigated the stairs in his own way, bumping from step to step on his bottom. She found Nicole already in the kitchen, devouring a plate of eggs and bacon and chatting merrily with Linda Whitton. Linda turned, her face crinkled into a smile. "Hello, Mrs. Hamilton. How are you this morning? Oh, and there's that fine young gentleman." She bent over to address John Peter. "And how are you doing this morning? You look just fine."

"Just fine," John Peter repeated happily, treating her to another sunny smile.

"I bet you'd like some eggs, wouldn't you? Well, sit yourself down, and you'll have some. They're coming right up." She pointed toward the wooden high chair set up beside the table.

"Did Mrs. Kerr buy these for John Peter?" Anne asked. She had been amazed when they arrived to find a high chair at the dinner table and a baby bed in his room. Their presence confirmed Sophia's eager anticipation of their arrival.

"Lord, no," Linda replied emphatically. "They're much more special than that. Miz Sophie had Mark haul them down from the attic. They were Gary's when he was a baby."

"Oh." Anne went over to examine the chair. There were, on closer examination, nicks and scratches that indicated it had been used before, but the fine wood and craftsmanship made it a far lovelier piece of furniture than anything that could be bought today. She ran a finger over the carving at the top. How strange to think that her father, the man she had never known, had once sat in this chair, years and years ago. It was a tangible link to her father; he had sat where she touched. He had banged and spilled food on it with all the zest of a baby. She recalled the baby pictures Sophia had shown her. Somehow the pictures, despite the exact image they had given her, had not had the touch of reality that this special chair had. It gave her father life in her mind.

"Mom, can we go riding this morning?" Nicole asked. "Linda says that Mama Sophia"—she gave her the name Sophia herself had requested—"arranged with the stables so we could go riding any time we want. Can we? Please . . ."

"I don't see why not." Anne stirred from her entrancement with the chair and plunked the baby down in it. "But you'll have to run up and change out of those shorts and into some jeans if you want to go riding."

"Oh, great!" Nicole bestowed a dazzling smile on her and shoved in a last swallow of eggs. She bounced up from the table and set her dirty plate in the sink, then darted from the room and up the stairs.

Amazing, Anne thought, what being in a different place did for her child's manners. It had been months since Nicole carried her dirty dishes to the sink without a fuss.

"What would you like for breakfast, Mrs. Hamilton?"

"Oh, please, call me Anne. And you don't need to fix me breakfast."

Linda shrugged. "I don't mind. Already got the bacon done. Just a matter of whipping up some eggs and toast."

"Well, uh, scrambled eggs will be fine for John Peter and me both." She smiled. "If you feed me like that every morning, though, I'll have to find a lot of work to do, or I'll be as wide as a barn."

Linda snorted. "No point in being anemic. I never can see what's so attractive about those models, all looking like they been in a concentration camp or something." She cracked a few eggs into a bowl, added milk, and whisked them vigorously. Though she wasn't old, her knuckles were enlarged and her fingers somewhat curled, as if gnarled by arthritis, but that fact didn't impede her swift, efficient movements.

"When does Sophia usually come down?"

The older woman shook her head, her face tinged with sorrow. "Not till nine or so. You go on and go riding with your little girl. A couple of years ago, Miz Sophie would have gone with you. That woman always loved to ride. But now it jars her bones too much." She sighed. "It's a sad, sad thing." Her hands never stopped as she talked—scrambling the eggs, toasting the bread, buttering it, pouring out orange juice—as if disconnected from her thoughts and words. "I came to work here when I was twenty-six. It was about a year or so before Gary died. Miz Sophie and him used to come stay here in the summer, though usually he broke away before the end of the summer and went back to the ranch to work. I thought Miz Sophie was the grandest, most sophisticated lady I'd ever seen. She was about forty then, and she wore clothes like we'd never seen around here—that was before the ski resort opened and the ladies from Dallas and Chicago started coming here. She looked like something out of a dream to me." Linda shook her head. "I guess I thought somebody like that could never die."

"It's hard to believe it about people you know and—and care about." This was what she had dreaded, Anne thought: the grief and impending death, the sorrow, the pain, watching someone die day by day. And knowing that she looked to you for help and solace. Knowing that you didn't know how to help, didn't even know how to begin. That you didn't have the emotional strength or courage she needed. Anne feared that all she'd be able to do was mutter a few platitudinous words that would sound too slick and pat to her even as she said them.

Linda made a dismissive gesture with one hand, obviously not paying much heed to general theories of grief. "Maybe. I don't know. I saw my parents die, but it wasn't the same. They suffered a long time, and at the end I was happy for them to go, so they wouldn't be in pain. They'd had long, full lives—fifty years married, five kids and ten grandkids. They'd got what they wanted out of life, even if they never had a lot of money. But Miz Sophie now—it seems like such a waste. No family. Her friends all gone. All she had was this house, and a house isn't much company, if you'll pardon me for saying so. She's been a lonely, lonely woman ever since Gary died, and that's been over thirty years. The past few years, with her parents gone and Mr. Wendall, too . . . well, she's been as lonely as a person can be."

"I'm sorry. I wish I'd known about her before."

Linda shrugged and slapped two pieces of toast down on plates, neatly quartering the piece for John Peter. "No way *you* could have known about it. Miz Sophie brought it on herself." She spooned out the eggs and set the plates down before Anne and the baby. John Peter happily dug in with his fingers, shoving a fistful of eggs into his mouth.

Anne toyed with her fork, pushing the eggs around. "Why do you think she didn't get in touch with me before?"

"Pride," Linda replied with a fierce jerk of her head. "Just blame ole pride. Plus, if you ask me, I think she always felt responsible for Gary's death, you know. She won't admit it, but I've seen this look in her eyes sometimes and—well, I think she torments herself about it. Maybe she was punishing herself all this time, not letting her see her own granddaughter as retribution for that fight with Gary."

"But she doesn't say anything like that. She told me she blames my mother."

"Heavens, no, she wouldn't say it! But that doesn't mean she doesn't feel it. Pride again, I guess." Linda turned away to put the skillet in the sink. "Anyway, I'm glad she finally asked you up, and I'm glad you brought those two kids with you. Nothing could cheer her up like them." With a grin, she went over to John Peter and tousled his hair. "I'll take care of this little fella. You run on out with your girl and have some fun. She's a darling, too."

"Thank you. I think so." Anne smiled and quickly downed her breakfast. It sounded delightful, a morning ride with Nicole acting as she had in the past, warm and bright and loving. Anne couldn't wait to get upstairs and jump into her jeans and a shirt.

They spent the morning riding and returned sweaty, slightly sunburned, sore, and very happy. Sophia was standing on the front porch as they strolled up the path from the stables, and she raised a hand in greeting. As they got closer, Anne saw that Linda was at the opposite end of the porch, and John Peter was keeping both women occupied holding the twigs, rocks, and other treasures he found as he roamed across the porch and up and down the steps. Nicole bounded up the steps, calling, "Mama Sophie! I went riding! And the man let me ride this great big horse that was kind of an orange color. And he said I did real well!"

"Wonderful! I bet you're ready for some lunch now."

"Oh, boy, am I!"

"Good, let's go inside. Linda's got it all fixed."

Anne followed Nicole and Sophia into the house, smiling. She and Nicole had had a wonderful time that morning, the best they'd spent together in ages. Perhaps this summer really would be a time for her to reestablish her relationship with her daughter.

The next day Anne drove her grandmother to see her doctor in Fitch, a town about twenty miles away from Iron Creek. Fitch was several thousand people larger than Iron Creek and boasted four doctors and a small regional hospital. Sophia's doctor was a genial man, small and sharp-featured, and when Sophia introduced Anne to him, he suggested Anne sit down in his office while the nurse wheeled Sophia down the hall to the adjoining hospital for a lab work-up. Anne sat down in one of the leather chairs in his office, and Dr. Kressel followed her into the room, shutting the door and perching on the edge of his desk, one foot still on the floor.

"Mrs. Kerr is a remarkable woman," he began. "A real old-timer. There aren't many of them left anymore. Seems like most people round here now are ski enthusiasts, like me, who move here for our winter weekends." He paused, and Anne wondered why he had ushered her into his office. Surely not to chat about his skiing interests or Sophia's place in Colorado's make-up. He sighed. "I hate to lose her."

"So do I."

"I'm sure you do." His small, bright eyes flickered over her. "I'm no specialist. I'll be the first to admit it. Most of my work here is skiing falls in the winter and hiking injuries in the summer. But I was able to diagnose Mrs. Kerr's illness; there's no question that it's leukemia. I can give her medication for the pain, which will get worse as the disease progresses, and I can monitor her progress. But, frankly, that's what I'm limited to."

"I understand. It's a hopeless disease."

"No," he responded quickly. "Not necessarily. I will grant you that there hasn't been the kind of success with acute granulocytic leukemia—what Mrs. Kerr has—that there has been with chronic or acute lymphocytic leukemia. Research has made real strides in those areas. Still, there is hope that Mrs. Kerr's illness could be slowed down, though not arrested. She could live for months longer, perhaps even a year or more."

Anne glanced at him sharply. "But Sophia—I understood her to say she has only a few weeks to live."

"She does, as long as she refuses to get any treatment for it. I want her to go to Denver to a specialist and a major hospital where she can receive the kind of care she needs. She could take chemotherapy treatments there, but she refuses to go. That's why I wanted to speak with you privately. If you have any influence with her, Mrs. Hamilton, I hope you'll use it. Persuade her to go to a hospital in Denver. Convince her that she needs to take the treatments."

"Me?" Anne blinked in surprise. "But I don't have any influence with her. I mean, well, it's a long story, but we've never been close even if we are related."

A slight smile touched his mouth. "I suspect it's hard to get close to Sophia Kerr. But you do have influence with her. When I saw her last week, she was extremely excited about your moving to Iron Creek for the summer; it meant a great deal to her. Believe me, you have more chance of persuading her than anyone else. I've talked to her housekeeper, a Mrs., uh . . ."

"Whitton. Linda Whitton."

"Yes. And to the man who works for her, Pascal, I think his name is. Neither of them was much help. Mrs. Whitton is so used to being Mrs. Kerr's servant that she can't imagine advising Mrs. Kerr to do anything, and Pascal is a great believer in laissez-faire—it's her life, let her do with it as she pleases."

Anne caught at her underlip with her teeth. "I'm not sure I disagree with him."

"A good theory, but I'm afraid it's not so hot in practice. Many patients refuse things that are in their own best interests—just out of fear. Fear of pain, fear of the unknown. People hate to lose something they have, even if it's killing them. Or they think that if they deny the disease, pretend it isn't there or that it doesn't need treatment or special precautions, then it will go away. Let me tell you, it doesn't. There's nothing wrong with giving a person support and encouragement to face those fears, is there? To face reality instead of hiding?"

"No, I guess not. I—I'll talk to Sophia about it."

He beamed at her. "Good. If nothing else, I'm glad Mrs. Kerr has someone with her who cares. It might make her think she's got something to live for."

Later, as they were driving home, Anne tentatively broached the subject, "Dr. Kressel told me today that he wanted you to go to Denver for treatments."

Sophia snorted. "I figured that was why he hustled me off to the lab while he talked to you in his office. He's been after me about chemotherapy since he told me what I had."

"He seemed concerned about you."

"George Kressel's just not used to losing patients. All he ever gets are broken legs."

"Surely there's more to it than that."

"Yes, there is. He's one of those doctors who is so committed to making people well that he can't bear to accept the idea that sometimes it's better to die."

"Is it?"

"Yes, I think so—when your alternative is living out the rest of your life in a hospital, surrounded by strangers, in an unspeakably sterile, uniform environment, so sick from the chemotherapy that you wish you *could* die! When Dr. Kressel told me what I had and recommended treatments in Denver, I went straight to the library and the bookstore and got everything I could find on the subject. There's no cure for what I have. They can only delay it. The treatments usually have to be repeated. The drugs are harsh. Their success in halting the disease for a short while is eighty per cent, but the chemotherapy doesn't delay it long. The optimum time is twenty months. That's the best; more likely it's only a few weeks or months. And during that time you're miserable, in a hospital, sick, away from everything you know and love."

"It sounds awful."

"It is. That's why I don't intend to have the treatments. I thought about it a long time, and I decided I'd rather live out my remaining time in the house I love, where I can look at the mountains every morning when I get up and sit on the porch and breathe the pines and the fresh summer air. I wanted to see you, get to know you; I wanted to meet your children. It seems a far nicer way to spend the rest of my life."

Tears sprang into Anne's eyes. She understood her grand-mother's reasoning. She suspected she might want to do the same thing herself. Yet how sad it was to know that the days Sophia had left to enjoy those things were so limited. There must be an intensity of feeling to this time for Sophia: a sharpness and impact to each beauty, each enjoyment in daily life, yet an equally strong tug of sorrow and loss, knowing that soon all this would be lost to one forever. By some sort of emotional osmosis, that intensity touched Anne, too; life seemed suddenly coalesced, unbelievably bright and pre-cious. Like carbon compressed into a diamond—small and sparkling and far more beautiful than in its original state. So lovely and yet bought at such a price.

They returned in time for lunch with the children and Linda. Though Linda announced that the morning had gone splendidly, Nicole flashed her mother a surly look that bespoke a different opinion. After they ate, she trailed Anne upstairs to Anne's room. This was not the time, Anne thought; her emotions were too raw after this morning. Couldn't Nicole sense that and realize it was better to tackle her about whatever she wanted at another time? But, no, she probably did sense it. Nicole regularly chose the moments when Anne's nerves were most frazzled.

Anne went into the bathroom and locked the door, hoping that her daughter would have gone by the time she opened the door again. She had no such luck. Nicole lounged against the poster of Anne's bed, waiting for her return. Anne drew a deep breath and made an effort to appear normal and cheerful.

"What did you do this morning?"

"Tried to keep John Peter from breaking all the antiques. He didn't like your being gone."

"He'll get over it."

"I want to go riding again this afternoon."

"No!" Anne answered sharply. She didn't want to do anything right now. She wanted only to be by herself. "Not now. I have to put John Peter down for his nap, and then I promised Sophia I'd play a game of Scrabble with her."

"What am I supposed to do? It's boring here."

"I'm sure you can think of something."

"There's nobody to play with."

"Then play by yourself."

Nicole grimaced. "What am I supposed to do? I haven't got anything to play with."

"For Pete's sake, Nicole, use your imagination! Go play outside. Climb a tree, go for a walk. I don't know! Just do something by yourself."

"Oh, all right!" Nicole stomped out of the room, her back ramrod straight.

Anne sighed and sat down on the edge of her bed. Almost immediately she was overcome by guilt. She shouldn't have snapped at Nicole; her nerves had nothing to do with the child. It wasn't Nicole's fault Anne's morning had been stressful. Anne gnawed at her lower lip. She shouldn't have given Nicole such vague instructions either. She might take it into her head to go a long way from the house.

Anne rose to find Nicole and call her back, but then she forced herself to sit back down. Maybe she shouldn't have been so irritable, but there was no need to restrict Nicole to playing in the yard, either. They weren't in the city anymore, where you had to worry about your child's being kidnapped if she left the house. This was the country; there was no one around. So what if Nicole wandered into the trees and explored a little? Wasn't that what she had wanted for Nicole? A chance to explore and walk and play in beautiful, natural surroundings? It wasn't as if there were wild animals around.

Anne stretched out on the bed. She wondered if she had been right to uproot the kids and move them up here. It probably wouldn't do John Peter any harm; he seemed basically secure wherever she was. But how would it affect Nicole to be taken from her home and friends, even for a couple of months? It had seemed like a good idea, a chance for Nicole to play and run freely, to see the mountains and new places, to expand her horizons. But now she wasn't sure . . . It was so hard raising kids by yourself! There wasn't even another person around to ask his opinion or get his help.

Anne pushed her fingers into her hair and closed her eyes. Well, she'd better get used to it. That was the way it was going to be from now on.

Anne was surprised to awaken almost thirty minutes later and realize that she had slept. She yawned, groggy from her unaccustomed nap, and slipped out of bed. Following the noise, she found John Peter downstairs engaged in a fine game with Linda and Sophia. He was hiding from them by throwing his favorite blanket over his head, then giggling as the women wondered where he had gone, and finally shrieking with glee as he pulled off the blanket and revealed his whereabouts.

Anne put him to bed and afterward played a long game of Scrabble with her grandmother. When they finished, she glanced out the window and wondered where Nicole was. But just then John Peter called from his bed upstairs to let her know he was awake, and she went upstairs to get him. While she was there she decided it was a good time to give him his bath, since the evenings and mornings were both cool here. As usual, he spent a long time in his bath, and by the time she'd powdered, diapered, and dressed him, another hour had passed. It was almost four-thirty.

Again Anne glanced out the window, then settled John

Peter on her hip and went downstairs and out the front door. She circled the house, scanning the outlying area. She saw nothing but trees on three sides and the rushing creek and the road in front. She let the baby slide down to the ground to walk and took the path to the nearby stables, slowed by John Peter's ambling pace.

There were a few horses in the corral, and a teen-aged boy lounged in the shade cast by the stable wall. He informed Anne that the owner, Jim Mueller, had gone on an escorted trail ride with several customers. When Anne described Nicole and asked whether he'd seen her there this afternoon, he replied that there'd been no one there but himself. Anne suspected that Nicole could have come and gone without this boy seeing her, but it was obvious that she wasn't there now. Anne retraced her steps to the house. Again she made a loop around the house. Still no sign of Nicole.

She took John Peter inside and went into the kitchen. "Has Nicole come in?"

Linda turned. "Why, no, I don't think so. I haven't seen her all afternoon."

Anne swallowed the sick feeling rising in her throat and crossed the kitchen to help Linda with her preparations for supper. She must not worry about Nicole. Nothing was wrong. The girl was probably having fun, or she had decided to punish her mother by staying away from the house. She'd come home when she got hungry.

But it was hard to keep the gloomy thoughts from closing in. It grew dark here earlier than at home. What if Nicole stayed out too long and got caught by dusk? What if she'd wandered off a path and gotten lost? What if she'd gone down to the road and someone driving by had stopped and taken her away? By the time Anne had peeled and cut up the potatoes into the boiling pan of water, her stomach was a knot.

"I think I'll have a look around and see if I can find Nicole," she told Linda. "If you don't mind, could you keep an eye on the baby?"

"Certainly."

She walked around the house again, then headed down the

road toward the highway, her pace increasing until she was almost running. It was past five-thirty now. Hunger already should have made Nicole return, unless she couldn't get back. The sun was dipping low in the sky. Twilight would start to set in within another hour. And here there wasn't a long dusk. She cupped her hands around her mouth and called Nicole's name.

There was no answer. Suddenly the hush of the mountains was no longer tranquil, but ominous. Anne called again. She heard nothing in return but the rush of the stream beyond her. She ran to the wooden bridge and came to a sliding halt, grabbing the single wood rail. She stared up the stream, then down, and thought of Nicole slipping off a bridge or a bank into the swift water. Even though it was summer, the water was chilly from the mountain snows that bred it. What if Nicole was wet and cold somewhere? Or what if her head had struck one of the many rocks lining the stream bed? Worse yet, the water could have knocked her down and pulled her with it on its course. Nicole could swim and the creek wasn't deep, but its force was great; it could easily suck her feet out from under her and send her tumbling helplessly along the stony bottom.

Anne shivered in the pale sunshine. Wrapping her arms around her, she searched the cleared area to the road with her eyes. There was no sign of Nicole. She revolved slowly, helplessly, taking in the trees on two sides and behind the house. Nicole could be anywhere! The place was so covered with trees that Nicole could be quite near and still not be seen. Where should she start? Nicole might be in any direction, and Anne's voice wouldn't carry far, particularly when she was near the noisy stream.

One thing was sure, she thought; the way she was going about looking for Nicole now was wrong. It was aimless and too chancy. Walking in a straight line left a huge area unsearched and out of voice range, and even if she walked from the center out in many directions, like the spokes of a hub, there would be gaps in between where Nicole might be. The enormity of it struck her; it seemed hopeless. Why had she let Nicole play outside today? Why hadn't she accompanied her? Why hadn't she realized that Nicole might wander off the paths and get lost in the trees? Obviously, with tall trees all around her Nicole wouldn't be able to spot any familiar landmarks or get a grasp of her directions. She had been an idiot not to realize that!

It was because she hadn't been thinking. She'd been too anxious to get rid of Nicole for a few hours. Anne had wanted to be by herself without her daughter's chatter or problems or fights. Guilt churned in her stomach, turning it sour. How could she have done that? How could she have been so selfish, so unthinking?

Anne started back toward the house, tortured by her thoughts. She felt utterly helpless. She didn't know this place any better than Nicole did. At least back in the city, she would have had some idea how to search for her. She would call neighbors and friends and then get in the car and slowly tour the area. But here! There were no neighbors, no friends, nowhere to drive. She hated to tell Sophia that Nicole might be lost; a sick woman hardly needed that kind of news. Not enough time had passed for law enforcement officials to get involved in it—besides, her fears might be quite groundless; they so often turned out to be. Jim Mueller, who ran the stables, would be the most logical person to ask for help, but he was gone, and Anne didn't think the boy subbing for him would be any use at all. The only other person she knew whom she could ask for help was Mark Pascal, and he had been anything but helpful or friendly in the past! She felt at a complete loss, and she wanted to burst into tears. Why in the world had she moved up here?

Chapter Seven

ANNE CLENCHED HER TEETH AND BATTLED BACK THE SOBS RISING in her throat. She had to stop this; there was no one here to rely on except herself. She must be calm and rational for Nicole's sake.

The first thing to do was to look for Nicole, this time in a more practical way. She could move out from Heartwood in concentric circles, spiraling into an ever-widening area. She'd have to take a flashlight and a sweater with her because it would soon grow dark and chilly. Better carry a wrap for Nicole, too, for by the time she found her, the child might be quite cold. And if she reached Pascal's cabin without finding Nicole, she would ask him to help her. Surely he wouldn't refuse, no matter how churlishly he'd acted toward her earlier, and since he lived out there, he was bound to know the area better than she did.

Making concrete plans calmed and cheered her somewhat, so that she was able to present a fairly normal face to Linda and John Peter when she entered the kitchen. "Did Nicole come back while I was out?"

"No. It's getting rather late." Linda frowned. "How long has she been gone?"

"Almost the whole afternoon, I'm afraid. I've decided to go look for her. Do you have a flashlight here?"

"Sure. In the pantry closet, top shelf."

Anne went where Linda directed and pulled down a large, heavy-duty flashlight. She flicked it on, and it spread a wide, bright beam of light. Thank goodness. Whenever she needed a flashlight at home, its batteries had always run down. "If she returns while I'm gone, tell her to wait here for me."

"All right. If you don't find her shortly, go ask Mark for help."

"I will."

Anne dashed upstairs and grabbed light sweaters for herself and Nicole, then trotted back downstairs and out the kitchen door. She started briskly up the path into the woods toward Mark Pascal's house. After she'd gone deep enough into the trees that she could no longer see the house, she plunged off the path into the trees, traveling in a semicircle to where the trees ended in the clearing on the other side of the house. Then she walked farther up and made the semicircular sweep back. It was rougher walking than on the path, and she had to watch her step carefully. It was already quite gloomy in the trees, and she hated to think what her footing would be like when it really got dark. She went as quickly as she could, stumbling over tree roots and rocks, ducking low-hanging branches, brushing aside spider webs and the entangling little branches of small bushes, and calling Nicole's name over and over.

It was a mammoth proposition to cover the area in this manner. Anne had no idea how long she had walked, but the twilight grew so dense she had to switch on the flashlight to see clearly. Her voice grew hoarse, and her feet had acquired sore spots in several places. It was too much to do by herself. She could never cover this much ground in time. Anne realized that she'd better abandon her search for the moment and go to Mark's cabin to enlist his help. They could divide the area in two, and it would go much more quickly.

The next time she emerged onto the path to Mark's house—or what appeared to be the path to Mark's house (sometimes she was afraid that she would soon be lost herself), she started off as quickly as she could. She saw a light flash in the distance and disappear. Then she saw it again, bobbing eerily closer to her. Anne stopped short, her heart pounding, gripped by fear. As it came closer, she realized that it was someone carrying a flashlight, just as she did. She let out her pent-up breath and moved forward. Thank heavens! Mark must be coming to the house for some reason. Or maybe it was another person, a hiker or someone who would also help her look for Nicole. She rushed forward, focusing her own light on the approaching beam.

A figure moved into the dim edge of the circle of light, curiously misshapen, its gait uneven. Anne sucked in her breath, fear returning, and her steps slowed. Then she realized that it was a man carrying something on his back. Mark, from the way he walked. No, it was not an object on his back, but a child, her dark head lying on his shoulder. Nicole!

She ran forward. "Nicole!"

The head snapped up. Anne's light was bobbing wildly as she ran, and she could no longer see Mark clearly, but she knew the high voice that pierced the darkness. "Mommy!"

Nicole slid down from Mark's back, and he beamed his light on the path in front of him so that Anne could see her way. Nicole flung herself into Anne's arms, and Anne lifted Nicole up to hug her as she hadn't been able to in more than a year, fear and relief lending her an unknown strength. Nicole clung to her mother, gripping her around the waist with her legs as she had when she was a child. They were both crying, and Anne murmured unintelligible words of love and joy and relief.

"Oh, Mommy, I was so scared."

"I know, honey, I know. I'm so glad you're safe."

"I got lost. I didn't know where I was."

"I'm sorry. I'm sorry. I'll never let you go out like that again, I promise. It was crazy."

Mark stood apart from them and turned the light of his flashlight off them, beaming it onto the ground at his feet. An ache seized his chest as he watched them cling together, and he didn't like the feeling. It had been a long time since he'd yearned after something he couldn't have, and he didn't want

118

to go back to that. Whatever he had or didn't have in his life now, at least it didn't include disappointment and heartache.

He thought of Rachel, and the way he'd dreamed of her all the way to Manila and for weeks in the hospital as he'd hovered on the edge of death. Then there had been the long, slow recovery, the wearying plane trip to Hawaii and later to California to yet another military hospital. He had hungered for his wife's face and touch. He remembered how, when she came at last, she had walked uncertainly onto the ward, her wide eyes flickering around the room, growing bigger and rounder when she spotted him. But he hadn't caught on to what was inside her then; he was too eager to see her. All he'd wanted was to reach out and hold on to her as Nicole held on to her mother now, soaking up all the love and warmth and reassurance. But it hadn't been long before he realized those things weren't there; Rachel had had barely enough to keep herself going and nothing to give to him.

Mark gripped the head of his cane tightly and shoved down the rising memories. He wasn't about to get sucked back into that quagmire. He curled and uncurled his fingers, squeezing the emotion out of him until he was able to watch Anne's and Nicole's reunion impassively.

Finally Anne's arms loosened around her daughter and she lifted her head and looked toward Mark. Nicole slid down to the ground and turned to him, too, her arm still looped around her mother's waist, Anne's around her shoulders. Even in the dim light cast by the downturned flashlight, Anne was lovely. Her eyes were soft and wet and brilliant from her tears, her face flushed, mouth full and trembling slightly. She was unutterably beautiful and vulnerable in a way that made Mark want to seize her and possess her, yet want to protect her from the world, too.

"Mr. Pascal, thank you. I'm so, so glad you found Nicole. I don't know what I—"

He cut ruthlessly through her words. "Don't thank me, lady. Next time, just have a little sense!"

Anne stopped, startled by his tone and words. She stared at him, groping for something to say.

119

His face was dark and harsh in the faint circle of light, his black hair blending into the night. Clipped, brutal words rushed from his mouth. "Goddamn it! What in the hell were you thinking of, to let a kid go out by herself onto the mountain? You're lucky I happened to run into her when I was coming back from the high pasture."

Tears formed again in Anne's eyes, tears of hurt this time, and she had to press her lips together to keep them from wobbling like a child's. After the emotional storm she'd just gone through, she wasn't ready to face a chewing-out with equanimity. "I—I'm sorry. I didn't think. I mean, I figured she'd be okay alone since we weren't in the city. I didn't think anything'd happen to her in the country."

He let out a hiss of contempt, and his mouth twisted. "God save us from greenhorns. City dangers aren't the only ones in the world, you know. A city kid couldn't find her way out of a sack out here. Your daughter doesn't know the first thing about where she is or what to do in the woods. She could have fallen down and broken a leg and not been able to get back, even if she'd known the way to go. She could have been trapped out here all night, and it gets damn cold. She could have died of exposure and dehydration. There are snakes and animals and all kinds of places to fall off of in the dark. You must be crazy to let her loose like that!"

His words were like fingers prodding at the sores already made by her own guilt, and Anne's defensive instincts rose against the new lashing. She wanted to hit him with all her force, and at the same time she wanted to burst into tears. She was filled with a rushing hatred for him, and she would have liked to fling back hateful, angry words in his face. But she could think of nothing to say. He was right, and it made it all the worse. "I'm sorry you were put to the trouble of rescuing my daughter," she spat out. "I'll make sure it doesn't happen again."

"Good!" Mark could see the sparkle of tears in her eyes, the wounded mouth, and he hated himself. And somehow that fed the fire of his anger, made him want to lash out again. "See that you do."

Anne's fingers tightened around her flashlight, and for a

moment he thought she was going to launch herself at him, swinging the light like a club. He tightened almost eagerly. But then she swung around without a word and rushed off down the path, dragging Nicole with her. Nicole twisted her head around to look back at him, and Mark saw her surprise and hurt mingled with a lingering gratitude. He turned and stalked back toward his cabin, moving as fast as his hobbling steps would permit, half hoping he would stumble and fall, as if the punishment might erase his self-hatred.

The long walk back to the house settled Anne's nerves a bit, although she was still alternating between fuming and self-recrimination when she and Nicole reached Heartwood. She took Nicole upstairs immediately and applied antiseptic to the scratches on her arms and legs. On one knee was a huge, purpling bruise centered by a raw patch of skin.

"I fell down," Nicole explained as Anne carefully cleaned the area. "Ouch!"

"Sorry. What happened, Nicole? How did you get lost?" In the past she would have been furious with Nicole for causing her so much worry, but tonight all her anger had been directed at Mark Pascal, and she hadn't given Nicole a single lecture.

Nicole shrugged. "I got lost. I don't know. It was weird. I figured if I was high up I'd be able to see everything below and could tell where the house was. But I kept going up and up, and I still couldn't see anything because of the trees! So finally I decided I better try coming back the way I went up, but somehow or other I got off on a different trail. And I walked and walked and never got to anything. I got so tired and hungry, and it was turning dark. Then I found the creek and followed it. But the mosquitoes nearly ate me up. Anyway, I guess I was following the stream the wrong direction. Finally, I met Mark. Boy, was I ever glad to see him! He took me back to his house and gave me a sandwich, and I got to look at all his stuff. He's got this neat carving of a raccoon; you should see it. He was real nice, and he told me I could come watch him work some time."

Anne gave her a sideways glance. "I wouldn't count on it."

"Why was he so mad at you?"

Anne sighed and raked her hands through her hair, dislodging a few small twigs and leaves. "Because I did a stupid thing, letting you go out into the woods by yourself. I wasn't thinking properly."

"I won't get lost next time, I promise."

"There won't be a next time."

"Ah, Mom!"

"Really, Nicole, do you expect me to let you run wild out there again after what happened today? I'd have to be crazy!"

"It won't happen again. Honest. I'll be more careful. I'll walk beside the creek all the way, and that way I won't get turned around. Besides, I figured out a lot of landmarks and stuff today when I was wandering around. I can do it."

"Sorry, but I'm not willing to experiment."

"Pleeease. It was neat—until I got lost. What if I got some books about nature and stuff and read them? Then could I go?"

"I'm not sure that books about nature will solve your problem."

"I mean, what to do in the woods, what kinds of berries you can eat, stuff like that. How to follow your tracks."

"I think we'll all be better off if you don't pretend to be Daniel Boone this summer. You can explore close to the house and go riding. That ought to be enough."

"You're always telling me that I don't get enough exercise."

"Nicole, please. Let's not talk about this now. Okay? It's time for supper, anyway. Come on, let's go downstairs."

Anne and Nicole spent the next morning riding and again enjoyed it, though Nicole kept pleading for them to go to Iron Creek and find her some books on nature and surviving outdoors. She stubbornly maintained that she would be able to roam the countryside without getting lost after she had absorbed these books, but Anne was determined not to let her out of sight of the house again. One scare like that was enough to last her all summer.

After lunch, Nicole took some of Sophia's books on the

area up to her room to read. Anne put the baby down for a nap, then returned to the comfortable sitting room downstairs. Sophia was there, little half-glasses on her nose, needlepointing a cloth stretched across a small standing frame. She looked up and smiled as Anne entered the room. "Ah, there you are. Baby down all right?"

"Oh, yes. I think he's the easiest baby alive to take care of. He loves to sleep and eat, and he doesn't have a bad-tempered bone in his body."

"He is a sweet baby. Gary wasn't that way at all." A reminiscent smile touched her lips. "He was a heller from the word go. Always running and into mischief. It was a real job keeping up with him. Not that he was bad. Just bubbling over with life and curiosity."

Anne sat down beside her to look at the needlepoint work. "What are you making?"

Sophia shrugged. "Nothing special. I like to have something to do with my hands. I've already redone the cushions of several chairs, and I framed some of the better pieces. Most of them are packed away in a box."

For a moment there was silence as Anne watched Sophia's hand moving slowly through the cloth. Then Sophia spoke again. "I take it the ride was a success this morning?"

"Oh, yes. Nicole loved it; I think she'll want to go there every day."

"It'll be good for her. City kids don't get enough exercise or enough taste of the outdoors. I'm sure Jim gave her a good horse."

"Yes. It was gentle and not stubborn. Usually if we go riding, we get horses that balk at every turn and want to do nothing but chew weeds and trees and everything else."

Sophia chuckled. "Jim has good mounts, and he cares for them well."

"You said that Mark Pascal works for him?" Anne didn't know why she was asking about him; he'd been so rude to her it should have killed all her curiosity. But somehow he kept popping into her mind.

"Yes. He runs a string of horses for Jim up in one of the mountain meadows. He brings down a new string every two or three days and takes the ones in the corral back up to the meadow. He's good with animals. And very solitary. The life suits him, I think."

"With his charm, he'd have to live a solitary life."

Sophia chuckled. "Mark can be rather . . . blunt."

"Blunt! That's hardly the word. He was downright nasty to me. Why is he like that? Just because he's artistic?"

"I don't know that it has anything to do with his being an artist. Or maybe it does. It was his sensitivity, I think, that made it so hard on him, and sensitivity is part and parcel of being creative."

"Made what so hard on him?"

"He was in Vietnam; his leg was shattered. I've never found out many of the details; he doesn't talk about it often. It was late in the war, 1970 or '71, I think. Since then he's spent a lot of time in army and veterans hospitals. They did several operations on his leg, and there was lots of therapy each time. Anyway, the whole experience made him bitter and withdrawn. But he's not a bad person. Actually he's rather kind. That's why he does so much for me. I give him the cabin where he lives in exchange for his work, but he does more than that little house deserves, I'll tell you."

"Oh. I wondered what happened to his leg." Anne leaned her head back against the sofa. That explained his personality somewhat, she thought. It was sad to think that his experiences had so warped him. She wondered what he had been like before the war. Before his face had become lined and grim.

"Not that he's told me all this. Most of it I picked up here and there, from little things he said and what Jim's told me about him. Jim's the closest thing to a friend that he's got."

"He doesn't have any family?"

"None around here." Again Sophia shrugged. "He wandered up here a few years ago; he's not from the area. He used to know Jim Mueller. He's never said anything about parents or a brother or sister. I think he was married earlier, but they divorced long ago. He's a real loner."

Anne could imagine what Bryan would say about Mark Pascal. He had little respect for people who didn't pull themselves out of their difficulties. In Bryan's eyes problems, both mental and physical, should be dealt with quickly and then forgotten. One picked oneself up and went on his way, or else he became part of that huge conglomeration of people that Bryan termed "losers." Anne knew that she had probably been assigned to this scrap heap of humanity by her former husband. She'd had too much trouble with their divorce to qualify as one who knew how to deal with life's blows.

Anne sighed and ran her fingers through her thick, springing hair. Why in the world was she doing this? The only thing stupider than wondering about Mark Pascal was thinking of her ex-husband.

She lifted her head from the back of the couch. "I thought I might run into Iron Creek this afternoon to get a closer look at it. Nicole wants to buy some books about the Rockies."

"That sounds nice." Sophia paused, then turned to her. "Would you mind running a couple of errands for me while you're there? I've gotten to where I can hardly bear riding over that road to the highway. I don't go anywhere except to visit the doctor. But it puts a big load on Linda to run my errands. She's not exactly young anymore."

Anne hid a smile at her white-haired grandmother referring to a woman much younger than she as being old. "Sure. I'd be happy to. What would you like for me to do?"

"Run by the bank and make a deposit. That's the main thing. Oh, and stop by the grocery to get my order. Linda already phoned it in, and they should have it ready to go."

By the time Anne left, Sophia had thought of three more things she needed done. Anne took Nicole with her and left John Peter sleeping upstairs. Nicole was ecstatic to be going to look for the books she wanted, although when they reached the village of Iron Creek, she immediately pronounced it "boring."

"What do you mean?" Anne protested, looking around at the quaint shops lining the up-and-down streets. Built up the side of the hill, parallel streets rose above them, the wooden gingerbread houses in tiers. The streets were uneven; most of the sidewalks were old-fashioned wood plank ones, and some had porches extending over them from the stores, supported on the outside by delicate wrought-iron columns. "I think it's lovely. It's unique."

Nicole cast an encompassing look at the buildings around them. "It's old," she summed up.

"Well, of course it is. That's part of its beauty. Doesn't it give you goosebumps to know that people walked past these same storefronts a hundred years ago?"

Nicole shrugged. "I guess." She perked up suddenly. "Hey, look at this." She crossed to a storefront window with a display of T-shirts, sweat suits, and night shirts, all emblazoned with the wonders of Colorado and the Rockies. Nicole stared down at the array of belts of metal and leather spread across the window's floor. "Can I go in here? They've got books in there, too."

"Okay. But don't leave. I'll run down to the bank and come right back. I don't want to lose you."

"Sure." Nicole hurried into the store, and Anne walked down two buildings to the small bank. It seemed to take forever for the teller to make the deposit, and since she was withdrawing part of the deposit in cash for Sophia, the woman had to call Sophia to make sure it was all right. By the time Anne got the money, she was growing nervous, thinking that Nicole might have disobeyed her and left the store. She hated to think of having to search all up and down the street for her. Anne stuck the money in her purse and hurried out the front door, almost running into a woman passing by.

"Oh! I'm sorry!" Anne gasped as the other woman staggered back a couple of steps. She reached out to grab the woman's arm, but she had already regained her balance.

The other woman held up both hands in a gesture that she was all right. "No problem. Don't worry about it." She leaned forward a little, studying Anne. "Say, are you Mrs. Kerr's granddaughter?"

Anne's jaw dropped. "Yes. How did you know?"

The other woman laughed merrily. "That's life in a small town for you. You'll have to get used to it. Mrs. Kerr told a few people, and Linda Whitton told even more, and pretty soon the word was all over town—as well as a description of you."

"Oh. I see."

"I'm sorry. I didn't introduce myself. I'm Phyllis Cortini. I own one of the shops down the street."

"Hello, Phyllis. It's nice to meet you. Sorry I almost ran you down."

Phyllis grinned. "It wasn't even close. I was just going down to the ice cream shop for my coffee break. Why don't you join me?" Anne's face must have registered surprise, for Phyllis laughed and said, "Life in a small town, again. Sorry. We all live in each other's pockets around here. The addition of a newcomer is the most exciting thing to happen in weeks, so everybody wants to know all about you. It probably seems strange to you, coming from a city, where you can see the same person every day for weeks and barely work up to a nod and a 'hi.'"

Anne smiled. "A little, yeah." Phyllis was a lively looking woman a few years older than herself, with short dark hair and bright hazel eyes. Laugh lines creased the skin around her mouth and eyes, and she radiated energy and good humor. Anne had been taken aback by her invitation to coffee only moments after she'd met her. Phyllis was right; there were lots of women whom she saw every day in the office building or in nearby restaurants and she never went beyond a pleasant smile and a "hello" with them. But she liked Phyllis immediately; she was hard to resist. And it would be nice to sit down for a good chat with a new acquaintance. "I'd love to go, but my daughter's at the Emporium, and I promised her I'd be back in just a little while."

"The Emporium? Why, that's my store. Why don't we just walk back and get her? Bring her along, too."

"Well, if you're sure you don't mind . . ."

"Heavens, no. Why, it'll be quite a feather in my cap among the coffee break crowd to have been the first to talk to you."

Nicole had found at least half a dozen purchases she wanted to make, but Anne managed to tow her away, promising to return later and look at the books and T-shirts she wanted. They walked down a block to an old-fashioned ice cream parlor, complete with white metal chairs with red cushions and a long, cool marble bar across the back. Nicole was entranced and ordered a tall strawberry soda, insisting on sitting on one of the revolving bar stools to drink it.

Anne and Phyllis chatted casually, Anne sketching in her past life for the other woman. Phyllis introduced her to several other store owners and workers who were also taking their afternoon breaks. Every time the door opened and another local citizen came in, they took one look at Phyllis's booth and headed toward it. Anne was amazed and amused by the townspeople's blatant interest in her. Phyllis just laughed and assured her that eventually it would die down.

"Once everybody's met you, their curiosity will be satisfied. Just wait a couple of weeks."

"But I'm only going to be here a few weeks, not longer than the summer. Why, I'm really just a tourist."

"Nah. Tourists aren't the granddaughter of the town's wealthiest and most leading citizen. Almost the oldest, too. Only old Cordy Benson, up on the ridge road, is older than Sophia Kerr. You belong to this town by association. Besides, you're something of a mystery; you have a story behind you. All the natives were trying to remember the facts about your father and mother."

"Natives?"

"Yeah. The people who've lived here all their lives. Some of us who own the shops and stuff have moved in during the past ten or twenty years because we loved the country. Skiers, nature lovers. You know. It's something of a mixture here."

"I see."

"Your grandmother is the most original of the original citizens. Her grandfather was one of the very first settlers. She's practically part of the history of Iron Creek."

"I guess so. I know very little about her. I didn't even know she existed until a few days ago. Probably the 'natives' know more about the 'story behind' me than I do." Anne smiled faintly. "It's hard for me to believe that Gary Kerr was my father or that I really have any connection to Sophia or this town. It seems a little unreal."

"I can imagine."

Anne shrugged off the pensive mood. "Okay, now you've learned all about my life. Now you tell me about the people around here."

"Facts or gossip?"

"Either. Both."

"Well, let's see now. You've probably already met Mrs. Kerr's handsome, brooding tenant."

"Mark Pascal? Yes. I certainly have."

"Gorgeous, isn't he? Well, not gorgeous, exactly. But . . . appealing. Prickly as hell, too."

"I'll agree with that."

"So he barked at you, too, huh?" Phyllis sighed. "Mark's his own worst enemy. But he's very talented. Did you see his work in my store?"

"No. Are you the one who sells it? He mentioned that he sold it at a store here."

"Yeah. My goodness, he must have been talking up a storm to you. Most people around here haven't heard him say more than a sentence or two. In fact, I think he's the local bogeyman to some of the kids. And there's an adult or two who've told me that he's an ex-con."

"An ex-con!"

"He's not. Don't worry. He's perfectly harmless. Well, maybe not harmless. But he's not violent."

"I hope not."

"Let's see. . . . Have you met Jim Mueller? He owns the stables there on Mrs. Kerr's land. Or, rather, he owns the business and rents the stables from Mrs. Kerr."

"Yeah. Nicole and I went riding this morning."

"He's another import. Moved here about five years ago. A super guy. Has a wife and two kids. She works in Ben Coulter's jewelry store on Main." Phyllis went on to give her a nutshell history of most of the people Anne had been introduced to, until Anne was almost reeling from all the facts.

Nicole began to get restive, and Anne decided to leave,

thanking Phyllis for the conversation and the welcome. All three walked back to the Emporium, where Anne dutifully examined Nicole's "finds." She agreed to buy two guides on backpacking and survival in the Rockies. She grumbled a little at the expense, but books were far more worthwhile than many of the things on which Nicole wanted to spend money. At least this was educational.

Then Anne worked her way around the store until she found Mark Pascal's work. There were the bowls and vases of satin-smooth aspen, the boxes in varying shapes and sizes with their intricate mosaics of woods. But there were also figures beautifully carved from wood—animals, people, abstract shapes. And there were square flats of wood on which had been carved pictures of great detail and with a sense of flowing, swirling life. Anne was captivated and examined them at such length that Nicole began tugging at her sleeve, urging her to leave.

Anne moved away with a sigh. They were all far too expensive for her. Except maybe one of the boxes . . . She turned back, much to Nicole's disgust, and selected a small, dark box with a mandala pattern on top.

As they were driving home, Nicole turned toward her mother, her face screwed into a frown. "Is Mama Sophie really dying?"

"Yes, honey, I'm afraid she is."

"She doesn't look like it."

"No. She still looks rather healthy. But that will change before long."

"J.P. really likes her." Anne winced inwardly at hearing Nicole call her brother the same name Bryan did, the name Anne had refused to call him. "He'll probably be real upset when she dies."

Anne glanced at her daughter in surprise and started to assure her that the baby was too young even to understand that Sophia would be gone forever, let alone be upset by it. Then a glimmer of understanding hit her, and she asked softly, "What about you, Nicole? Will you be upset?"

Nicole shrugged and looked out the side window. "I doubt it. I'm used to stuff like that."

"Like what?"

"People leaving."

"Like Daddy?"

"Yeah. And then you."

"Me? What do you mean? I didn't go anywhere."

"You're never home anymore. You started going to work."

"Oh. I see. Did you feel I'd deserted you?"

Nicole cast hard, bright eyes upon her, and her mouth thinned. "No. I just told you. I got used to it. That's why it won't bother me with Mama Sophie. Besides, I won't like her that much."

"I see." And she did see, all too well. It had never occurred to her that Nicole saw herself as being abandoned by not just one, but two parents. While Bryan had always been in and out of her life, Anne had been the rock on which Nicole's existence was built, eternally available to her daughter. No wonder Nicole had turned so much of her anger and fear against her mother when she felt Anne had deserted her. Nicole was already planning not to get hurt by Sophia's leaving, too; she was preparing herself not to grow too close to the woman. Anne understood it; she'd had some of the same feelings herself. Why let yourself in for the grief of liking Sophia, of feeling a kinship to her, when she would be gone before long, and you would be left with nothing but hurt?

Anne had often told herself that Nicole's sudden anger and disagreeableness were nothing but a shell she had constructed to seal herself off from pain. Now she realized that that was truly the case. She had a golden opportunity here to help her daughter, to teach her to risk her emotions despite the possibility of sorrow or betrayal. But she didn't know how to start. How did you bring another person out from hiding behind her barricades? Especially when you suspected that you were pretty busy hiding, too.

Chapter Eight

AFTER SUPPER, NICOLE RUSHED UPSTAIRS TO HER ROOM TO READ her new books. Anne put John Peter to bed and returned to the kitchen to wash the supper dishes. Though Linda prepared supper every evening, she went home as soon as it was ready, and Anne had taken over the job of cleaning up the dinner dishes. It seemed little enough, considering all the work Linda did. Anne couldn't imagine another servant in this day and age working such long hours as Linda.

Anne had scraped off the dishes earlier, when she had carried them to the sink from the table. Now she placed them in the dishwasher, added soap, and turned it on. With the dishwasher humming noisily in the background, she wiped off the table, stove, and counters with a damp cloth. She tossed the rag into the sink and went into the den, where Sophia sat.

They talked a little, but neither felt inclined to say much. Though Anne's nerves had calmed down a great deal, she still felt shaky and drained from her torrent of emotions. Nor could she rid herself of the throb of hurt Mark's harsh words had inflicted on her. He seemed to hate her, an emotion Anne wasn't used to arousing in people.

After a while, Anne returned to the kitchen for a glass of ice water. She flipped on the light and stopped, gasping. The double sink was filled with water, and it poured out steadily onto the floor below. A shallow pool covered half the floor. "Oh, no!" She sagged against the doorjamb and covered her eyes.

But she couldn't remain like that. The water would simply keep on running. Finally she drew herself up and slogged through the water to the dishwasher and turned it off. At least that would stop the steady supply of water. Going back to the door, she slipped off her shoes so as not to track water onto the lovely Persian rugs and went to Sophia. "The water's running over in the kitchen. Where are some old towels I could use to mop it up?"

"What? Oh, dear." Sophia rose and went past Anne to view the damage herself. She sighed. "We'd better have Mark over to look at it. The old towels are in the linen closet at the top of the stairs."

"Mark?" That was the last person she wanted to see.

"Yes. No plumber would come out this late, and, anyway, there aren't any in Iron Creek. We'd have to get one from Fitch."

"Why don't I clean it up and wait until morning to call a plumber in Fitch, then?"

"No point in it. Mark's pretty good at this sort of thing. He doesn't have a phone, though. You'll have to run down to his cabin and fetch him. You don't mind, do you?"

"No, of course not," Anne lied, then stopped. "Well, actually, I saw him the other day, and he was rather rude."

Sophia dismissed this with a wave of her hand. "That's just Mark's way. It doesn't mean anything."

"It's rather late, and I'd hate to get him out."

"Don't worry. He stays up late; I've heard him say so. I don't think he sleeps well. Now's as good a time as any for him."

Anne didn't see how she could get out of it. It would seem absurd to Sophia for a grown woman like herself to be afraid to face Mark again. It wasn't as if he would do her physical harm. She ought to be able to go there like an adult and deliver her message; it didn't require friendliness on either side to tell him the sink needed fixing. If he was accustomed to doing such things for Sophia, surely he wouldn't get mad at her for coming to tell him.

Still . . . she mopped up the floor and tried her hand at unstopping the sink herself before she gave up and went to get him. She wore a sweater and carried a flashlight, but despite that it was still too chilly and dark for her. She didn't like the sigh of the wind in the treetops or the faint scurrying noises and crackling of twigs underfoot. Somehow the beam of light in front of her made the darkness to the side and behind her even worse. Anne felt frightened and very alone. It seemed to take much longer than the other time she'd walked to his cabin. Had she, too, managed to get lost?

When at last she spotted the glow of light from Mark's cabin, she was so relieved she almost ran to the front door. She knocked loudly, and moments later Mark opened the door. His eyebrows went up at seeing her on his doorstep, and Anne's embarrassment swelled anew.

"Hello. Excuse me, I, uh . . . the kitchen sink's stopped up. Sophia sent me here to get you. She said you fixed things like that at her house."

He continued to gaze at her for so long that Anne was afraid he was going to refuse to come. Then he said, "Sure. Let me get some tools."

He didn't invite her in, and she didn't want to step in unasked, so she waited outside. When he came back with a heavy flannel shirt hanging open over his T-shirt and a metal box in one hand, they left the cabin, lights burning, and started down the trail. He moved along surprisingly quickly, even with the heavy toolbox in his hand. His cane made a soft, steady tap upon the ground in counterpoint to the thuds of their footsteps.

They walked in silence. Anne couldn't imagine trying to keep up a friendly chatter after their other hostile exchanges, but neither did she feel comfortable walking together without speaking. It was awkward. She wished he had a telephone in his cabin. How did anyone get along without a phone these days, anyhow?

Mark's gruff voice cut through the night calm, startling Anne. "I shouldn't have jumped down your throat yesterday," he began abruptly. "It wasn't any of my business."

"No, it's all right," Anne responded automatically, then felt irritated with herself. If someone pulled a gun on her, she'd probably reassure them that it was okay. "That is, well, I was kind of upset, but you were right." She sighed. "I shouldn't have let her go out alone like that. It was stupid. I didn't think." It was true, but it tasted bitter as gall to admit it.

Mark glanced at her, but Anne couldn't see him well enough to tell his expression. "Everybody does stupid things sometimes. No sense blaming yourself for it." He smiled, surprising her, and his teeth gleamed whitely in the dark. "When I first came here, I got lost one evening and had to spend half the night out on the mountain. Luckily it was in the summer, so I didn't freeze to death. But I sure felt stupid."

"Really?"

"Yeah. You can't expect a city girl to know all about the outdoors, can you? The thing is to learn from your mistakes, not kick yourself for them."

"But when I think of what could have happened to Nicole . . ."

"It didn't. I'm sorry I got mad at you. I should have known you'd be berating yourself already. It was—well, I haven't got any excuse. Except maybe that it scared me, finding her and thinking what would have happened to her if I hadn't run across her by accident."

Anne swallowed. "I'm very grateful to you for bringing her home."

"Anybody would have done the same."

"Maybe. But it was you who did it, and I can't thank you enough."

They fell silent again as they continued toward the house. He had apologized, and it had soothed her wounded feelings, Anne knew, but still there was an awkward constraint between them. It was hard to forget the two nasty scenes they'd gone through earlier. She watched him carrying the metal toolbox and wished he would let her carry it. It looked terribly heavy and awkward. But she knew he'd bite her head off if she asked. He seemed to be very sensitive about his leg.

Anne tried to think of something to talk about. She didn't like feeling this uncomfortable with him. She cleared her throat. "Have you lived here long?"

He didn't glance at her. "Three years."

His leg was beginning to protest at the hurried pace he was setting, but he couldn't bear to limp along like an old man with Anne beside him. Thank God there were only three steps up onto the porch at Heartwood; he was about as fast as a toddler on stairs. He hated to let her see how hobbled he was; he could imagine the soft pity in her eyes, and it made his gut coil. He didn't want her to think of him as a cripple; he wanted her to think of him as a man. And that was the most foolish thing of all. Hell, she probably just thought of him as an idiot, the way he couldn't ever think of anything to say around her.

Anne felt like grinding her teeth. Mark was the most exasperating man to talk to. She tried again, "Where did you live before?"

"Around. Lots of places. Texas, California."

Anne wondered if he ever volunteered information. She was running out of questions that didn't sound rude or nosy. Again they slipped into silence. It was a relief when they reached the house.

Mark followed her through the side door and into the kitchen. He walked over to the sink and looked down at the dirty water that filled it. "You have a plumber's friend?"

"Yes." Anne retrieved it from the pantry and held it out to him. "But I already tried it. And I put in drain cleaner. It didn't work either."

"What happened, exactly? Why did it stop up?" He stuck the long-handled instrument into the sink and began to push the handle up and down with far more force than Anne could ever have used. His hands were wrapped tightly around the wooden handle, squeezing; the tendons and veins stood out, and the muscles moved in his forearms.

"What? Oh. I don't know why. I'd just put the dishes in the

washer and turned it on. I went into the den for a while, and when I came back, the sink was overflowing."

Mark gave the handle a last, forceful push, but nothing happened. He set the plumber's friend aside and opened the doors beneath the sink. He peered into it for a moment, then straightened. "I'll have to go turn off the water," he said, and left the house.

When he returned, he lowered himself awkwardly to the floor by the sink, his bad leg going out straight in front of him. Taking off his flannel overshirt, he tossed it aside, then pulled the toolbox closer and opened it. He rummaged around in it for a few moments and came up with a few tools. He laid them on the cabinet floor beneath the pipes and stuck his head into the cabinet.

"Could I help you?" Anne volunteered. She felt foolish just standing there watching him, yet she found herself lingering.

"No. I can handle it." The last thing he wanted was Anne looking at him the whole time he worked; it would make him nervous and clumsy.

"Well, all right. I guess I'll be in the den. Call if you need anything."

He nodded shortly, and Anne left the room. She puttered around in the den for a while, but there was little to do. Sophia had already gone up to bed, and both the television and a book bored her. She couldn't keep her mind off Mark's presence in the kitchen, and, though she felt uncomfortable around him, she also felt silly being in here, as if she were hiding from him. Finally she wandered to the kitchen door.

Mark lay on his back on the floor, his head stuck inside the cabinet beneath the sink. Anne looked at his slim, blue-jean-clad legs and the cowboy boots on his feet. As his arms moved, the T-shirt beneath slid up and down, revealing a narrow swath of stomach, tanned and centered by a line of black hair. Anne looked away, strangely nervous. You'd think she'd never seen a man's stomach before, when she routinely saw far more flesh than that revealed on the beach or at the swimming pool.

There was a clank of metal on metal from inside the

cabinet, followed by a vicious curse, and Mark slid out from beneath the sink, slamming down a wrench. He glanced up and saw Anne, and the thunderous look on his face changed to a sheepish grin. "Oh. I didn't know you were out here. Sorry."

"Having trouble?"

"I don't think there's a thing in this house that is really inanimate. They all have personalities, including the lights and the plumbing. And they universally dislike me."

Anne had to grin. He seemed much more human this way, frustrated and irritated, yet joking about it. "Can I do anything to help?"

He shook his head. "I think I'm almost finished, really." He ducked back under the sink. Anne lingered for a moment, watching the muscles of his stomach tighten and relax as he worked.

She stepped a little closer so that she could see his upper torso and face. There was a section of pipe missing and with one hand he was holding something inside the pipe above him. His free hand groped around over the floor beside his hips. "Damn!" He raised his head, looking for something.

Anne went to the sink and knelt down beside him. "What do you need?"

"That elbow." He pointed to a section of pipe lying on the floor.

Anne picked it up and handed it to him. His roughened fingertips grazed her palm, and her skin was suddenly warm and sensitive where he had touched it. She remained kneeling beside his legs as he fitted the pipe into place, so close to him that she could feel his warmth and smell the faint tang of sweat on his body. If she had reached out her hand, she could have touched his jean-clad legs.

She thought about his legs. She wondered if the bad one hurt him. She wondered if it hindered him in making love. Anne sat back on her heels, heat rising in her face. She had a sudden, very clear vision of Mark making love, lying between a woman's legs, his arms bulging from supporting his weight, his face contorted. The woman was herself.

She stood up and moved away. "There!" Mark exclaimed triumphantly, sliding out from beneath the sink. "I've finished. At least for the moment. I'm not guaranteeing it won't happen again. The pipe was put in there kinda screwy."

He rose to one knee and used the edge of the sink to help pull himself up. "Let me turn on the water, and we'll see." He went out the side door. When he returned, he turned on the faucet and water gushed out, falling into the sink and disappearing down the drain. Mark smiled. "You can use the dishwasher now."

"Thank you very much."

"You're welcome. Anything else?" He washed his hands and dried them on a nearby dish towel.

She wished she could think of something for him to do; she found herself wanting to get him to stay. Reluctantly, she said, "Not that I know of. Sophia didn't say anything."

"I guess I'll go, then."

"Would you like a drink?"

"No," he answered swiftly, and jammed his hands in his front pockets. "That's okay. I—no need to go to any trouble." He wanted more than anything to stay. He wanted to look at her, hear her voice, listen to her laugh, watch the sway of her hair, the curve of her mouth, the soft line of breasts and waist and hips. But he was scared to death to stay. He wouldn't be able to think of anything to say to her. He'd look like a fool.

"It's no trouble." She went to the refrigerator and opened it. "What would you like? Beer? A coke? Wine?"

"Beer's fine."

Anne pulled a can from its plastic ring. "Somehow Sophia doesn't seem the type to drink beer."

"She keeps a little around for me."

Anne got down a pilsner glass and popped the tab on the can, then poured the beer slowly into the glass, tilting it. Mark liked watching her hands; it touched some chord within him to see her doing even so slight a thing for him.

"I'm not used to such class," he remarked, smiling a little. "I usually drink it from the can."

Anne smiled back at him. It was nice to hear him offer a sentence without being prodded or questioned. "Mother's training."

She handed him the glass, very aware of the touch of his fingers as he took it. Mark remained standing, leaning against the sink, while Anne took out a bottle of white wine and poured herself a glass.

He had figured her for white wine, Mark thought. It went with the clothes and "mother's training." He wished he could think of something to say. He wondered what she'd do if she had any idea of what he thought about her, of how he imagined her in bed with him. His fingers tightened around the glass. This was insane. He didn't belong here.

"I better get back." He took a gulp of the drink.

Anne gave him a surprised look. "But you've hardly drunk any of your beer."

He took another gulp. "I need to, uh, do some work."

"Your carving?"

"Yeah."

"Oh." Anne couldn't think of anything else to say to delay his departure. She couldn't understand why he had done such an about-face. She wondered if she had somehow offended him, if he thought maybe that she was going to try to work up some kind of romance between them. Rising, she gave him a formal smile, "Of course. Well, thanks again."

"Sure. Good-bye."

" 'Bye."

Mark set down the glass on the counter and plunged out the door. What a fool he'd been! He shouldn't have agreed to the drink. He knew he couldn't talk to her. He'd been alone for too many years, was too accustomed to blunt, brief speech.

He'd lost the art of talking to women. That was obvious from the way he had already insulted Anne on more than one occasion. He was so attracted to her it was scary, and whenever he was around her, there was a tension inside him, waiting to explode. Scared of what he might say or do, dreading humiliation or a glance of pity from her, he had said nothing or had done exactly the opposite of what he would

140

have liked to have done. He wanted to seduce, and instead he pushed her away with caustic remarks. Crazy.

It was better to stay away from her. That way, at least, he wouldn't make an idiot of himself. And he wouldn't have to face the pain of rejection. The only problem was, no matter what he resolved to do, every time he saw Anne Hamilton, he wanted her more.

As the days passed, Anne and the children settled in. Nicole, having read her nature books, was positive she could find her way about and begged to be allowed to go exploring. Anne steadfastly refused. Nicole also continued to ask to visit Mark Pascal's workshop. "Really, Mama, he invited me."

"Sweetheart, lots of times people say things like that to be nice, but they don't really mean it." Although she couldn't imagine that man ever saying anything to be nice. He seemed to work hard at presenting exactly the opposite impression.

"Well, he shouldn't say it if he didn't mean it. It'd teach him a lesson if I went."

"Maybe. But I don't want you to impose. Mr. Pascal works for Sophia and he cares for the stable horses, and I imagine those jobs leave him little time to work on his carvings. It wouldn't be fair for us to use up some of that time."

"He could work while I watched. I wouldn't interfere."

"Just watching can interfere. Creative people are sometimes very sensitive about people watching them work. It might make him nervous."

"He wouldn't get nervous. He didn't say anything about it when he invited me."

"Well, even if it were all right with him, you couldn't walk clear to his cabin by yourself. It's too far."

For once, Nicole didn't follow the red herring. "Then you can go with me."

But Anne dreaded having to face Mark Pascal again. "Nicole, we are not going," Anne told her firmly. "So forget it."

But Nicole didn't forget it, and she had the last say on the matter a few days later. Anne had gone into Iron Creek to shop and had stopped by for a chat with Phyllis Cortini. When she arrived home, Nicole met her at the door, a self-satisfied grin spreading across her face. "Guess what."

"What?" Anne had the distinct feeling she wasn't going to like it.

"Mark was here this morning trimming some of the hedges. So I asked him if I could watch him work."

"Oh, Nicole! You didn't."

"I did. And he said it was all right. I told him you thought he was just being polite and we shouldn't disturb him, but he said you were too concerned about manners."

"That sounds like him."

"I even asked if he minded if you came along, because you didn't want me walking over there by myself. And he said it was fine."

"I really don't like your asking—"

"He said we could come this afternoon."

Anne sighed. They'd boxed her in. "Oh, all right. I guess I don't have much choice, do I?"

After lunch, Anne put John Peter down for his afternoon nap, then she and Nicole set out along the path to Pascal's house. Though she had been irritated with Nicole for forcing the issue, Anne couldn't resist the tranquillity of the trees or their heady scent, and before long she relaxed.

Nicole picked up a tiny pine cone and flipped it idly from one hand to the other. Her brow furrowed a little. "Mom? What did you and Mama Sophie do the other day when you drove over to that other town?"

"Fitch? Why, we went to the doctor."

"I know. But, what I mean is, what did he say? Did he say she's going to die?"

"Yes, I'm afraid so."

"Can't the doctor give her medicine or something?"

"No, honey, I don't think so. At least, well, there is a treatment she could take, but Sophia doesn't want to. It's painful, and she'd have to stay in Denver, and it wouldn't be very successful, anyway. Sophia would rather stay here."

Nicole tossed aside the pine cone. "You know Missy Carleton?"

"Her father owns a construction firm?"

"Yeah. They build highways. He had to go to court 'cause they said he was stealing money from the government. Anyway, after that, he got religion. Least, that's what Missy says. Missy talks about God and stuff all the time now. *She* says that even someone who's dying can get better, if only they believe in the Lord and believe he can heal them. You just have to pray a lot."

"I'm not sure it's quite that simple."

Nicole stuck her hands in her shorts pockets and sighed. "I didn't figure it was. Missy says you can make anything happen by praying about it long and hard enough. So I tried it; I prayed every night that Daddy wouldn't marry Gwen and that he'd come back to live with us. I prayed for two weeks, but it didn't do any good. Missy said I didn't believe hard enough."

"Sweetheart, praying isn't the same thing as wishing. I suspect Missy's a little confused. Just wanting something and asking God for it every night isn't going to make you get it."

Nicole shrugged. "Personally, I don't think she's playing with a full deck. But I thought maybe it'd work better if you were talking about somebody not dying, instead of not getting married."

"Well, if you want to pray for Sophia, it certainly isn't going to hurt."

"But it's not going to help, either." Nicole glanced at her mother, her face shuttered, as it had been so much the past year. An ache started in Anne's chest. Nicole was too young to become cynical. Why couldn't she have retained her innocence and optimism a little longer? Anne wondered if it was another casualty of the divorce or if it was the crowd of kids she ran with at school, who all seemed to have had and done and seen too much for ten-year-olds.

When they reached Mark's cabin, he stepped out the front door and held it open for them, and Anne was amazed to see that there was actually a slight smile on his lips. She hadn't believed that he really didn't mind their coming, only that Nicole had boxed him into a corner as she had Anne. But the face he turned toward Nicole held a certain affection and ease.

"Hey, there, kid, how you doing?"

"Okay." Nicole went inside. "Where's that raccoon? I want to show Mom."

"Out on the porch." He turned toward Anne. As always, she made his insides start quivering and jumping. "Hello. How's the sink?"

"What? Oh. Oh, fine. I'm—uh, sorry about this." Anne linked her hands together a little nervously. She dreaded the thought of upsetting him by their presence, yet she was excited at the prospect of watching him work.

"About what?"

"Barging in on you while you're working. I hope Nicole didn't bug you to death about it."

He shook his head. "She didn't bother me. She just asked. I don't care if you watch while I work."

"I was afraid it might disturb your concentration, or something."

"I don't think I have much artistic temperament." He grinned. "My bad temper is simply bad temper."

"Oh. Well, good, then."

"I hope it doesn't interrupt your day."

"No. Heavens. I think it'd be fascinating."

"Mom! Come on!" Nicole bounded back into the room and waved impatiently to her mother.

"I guess we better stop apologizing to each other and get to it," Mark said, and Anne went inside.

She hadn't seen this room of the house the other time she had been there, only the screened-in porch and small passageway where Mark stored his finished work. There was little to the cabin, just one large main room and a couple of doors opening off it, indicating the presence of a bathroom and closet. A big stone fireplace dominated one wall of the cabin, and there were a couple of gas heaters at the other end. The room was sparsely furnished, containing only two bookcases and an easy chair with a hassock and standing lamp beside the fireplace and a double bed and chest of drawers on the other end of the room. Tucked away in one corner was a tiny kitchen separated from the rest of the room by an eating bar.

Beside the kitchen a door opened into the passageway Anne had seen before. It was through this door that Nicole now ran, and Anne followed, thinking that Mark's cabin could benefit greatly from a bright quilt across the bed and a pretty sofa. She wondered if financial necessity kept the place this barren, or whether he preferred it that way. Surely the pieces Phyllis sold in Iron Creek were popular, and they weren't inexpensive. Plus, he got money from the stables for caring for the horses in the pasture, and his cabin was free in return for the odd jobs he did for Sophia. You'd think he'd have enough to brighten up his surroundings a little.

Mark watched Anne glance around the room. He liked the thought of her in his house. He knew tonight he'd think about her standing there, remember her looking at the furniture and walls. He could imagine her sitting in his chair or touching the table. He could envision her walking to the bed and turning, inviting him. She gave life to the bare room, warmed its chill. Mark found himself wanting to keep her there a little longer.

"How's Sophia?" he asked, surprising them both by starting a conversation.

"She seems to be doing pretty well. I took her to her doctor the other day, though, and he says she'll die soon unless she gets treatment."

"I'm sorry. She's a good woman. She's been very kind to me."

"To me, too."

"I never knew she had a granddaughter. Jim told me she just had one son, who died when he was a kid."

"He was college-age. That was my father. My mother was from Texas, and they met when she was up here vacationing with her family one summer. She was just out of high school." She recounted the sad little story she had learned from her mother.

Mark's eyes darkened with sympathy and he moved a few steps closer to her. He seemed about to speak, but then Nicole called out impatiently from the other room, "Mom! Come look at this."

"I'm coming." Anne gave Mark a tentative little smile and walked through the room into the small chamber where Mark kept his work. Anne held out a carving, and Anne dutifully admired the bright-looking little raccoon seated on a stump. She glanced around, trying to pick out any new pieces. Mark sat down at his table and proceeded to work, almost as if she and Nicole didn't exist. Anne sat down in a folding chair, and Nicole perched beside her on a sturdy box as they watched Mark's hands move surely over the wood. His fingers were long and supple, sprinkled with black, curling hair. The skin was very tanned, and the half-moons of his short nails were pale against it. He gripped the handle of an auger in his right hand, and his knuckles stood out whitely as he dug into the wood. A strip of wood curled up before his auger and fell away, leaving bits of sawdust clinging to the hairs of his hand.

Anne stared, fascinated by the movement of his hand, the steady grip of the other hand around the back of the block of wood. There was a certain grace to his hands, despite their thick knuckles and roughened palms. But there was more than that. Something primitive and inviting. When he set down the auger and ran his fingertips over his work, he seemed almost to caress it. He moved with a competence and slowness that reminded her of a lover's touch. His hands glided and gripped and formed the wood to his command.

Amazed, Anne realized that her insides were growing hot and waxen. An ache she had thought long dead was starting up between her legs. Watching his hands was arousing her. For a moment she couldn't believe it. It had been so long since she had felt even a spark of desire.

Months before the marriage officially ended, her and Bryan's sexual life had ground to a halt, and Anne had felt nothing but relief. For a long time Bryan's lovemaking had aroused only boredom or irritation in her. Bryan had too often critiqued her performance or gazed with a plastic surgeon's eye upon her less-than-perfect naked body for her to feel comfortable during their lovemaking. After she had had John Peter, her interest in the act and in Bryan had nose-dived. She found that she no longer cared when Bryan opined that she didn't caress him enough or didn't enjoy foreplay as much as women were supposed to or urged her to have a tummy-tuck on the slight pot belly she hadn't been able to get rid of after John Peter's birth. Anne had reached the point where Bryan's opinion had ceased to slice her feelings to shreds.

Then, after Bryan left, Anne had continued to look upon men and sex with uninterest. She was too tired, too scared, too hurt, too concerned with her children and new life. After a while, hearing other divorcées talk about their constant hunt for male companionship, she had decided that she had simply grown cold over the years. Perhaps she had had some deep hang-up about sex all these years without knowing it until now. Or maybe the months of pretending to enjoy sex with Bryan when she had really only gritted her teeth and accepted it had taken their toll on her ability to feel. Whatever the reason, she had given up on ever really wanting a man again.

Yet now, here she was, her juices suddenly beginning to thaw and stir. And over such a man! If she was going to get interested in a man again, you'd think her body could have chosen someone better than a prickly, defensive artist who disliked her!

Still, she couldn't suppress the sudden excitement flooding her—or even pretend that she wished it hadn't occurred. There might be little chance of her new-found longing ever reaching fulfillment with Mark Pascal, but it was undeniably wonderful to feel again!

Chapter Nine

THE PORCH WAS SILENT EXCEPT FOR THE SOUNDS OF MARK'S working, but after a while Nicole's curiosity became too much for her and she began to query Mark. "How'd you do that?" she asked. "How do you make it smooth?" Nicole paused. "Why is there that brown streak there?"

"Nicole, don't bother Mr. Pascal while he's working," Anne told her sharply. "He'll be sorry he let you watch."

"Oh." Nicole glanced up worriedly at him. "I'm sorry."

"It's okay." Again the face Mark turned toward the child had little of its usual harshness. "I don't mind. I'm used to a lot of noise and questions. In fact, that's how I learned to do it—by asking questions."

"When you were a kid?"

"No. I didn't do any wood-working until I was in my twenties. When I was a kid, I lived on a farm."

"Where? In Colorado?"

"No. Iowa. When I was older, I worked in construction. I was a carpenter's apprentice before I went to Nam."

"You mean the war?" Nicole asked, eyes widening. "The war in Vietnam?"

"Yeah. You know anything about it?"

"Just stuff I've read in the papers about the monument in Washington. The kind of thing we talk about in school."

"I was wounded over there."

"You got shot?"

Anne tensed, expecting Mark to turn angry. "Nicole . . ."

Mark half-turned toward Anne. "No, it's okay. Really."

"Nicole knows better than to be nosy about personal things." Anne directed a frown at her daughter, who shrugged. "I don't want her to bother you. Or . . . or bring up painful memories, or anything."

"It's okay." Mark rubbed his knee lightly, almost unconsciously, as he turned back to Nicole and said, "Shrapnel. That's lots of little pieces of metal. It tore up my knee and some of my thigh. So I spent a lot of time after Nam in V.A. hospitals. That's where I started working with wood. There was a guy there who carved beautiful stuff. It fascinated me to lie there and watch him work. Man, he was good!"

Anne leaned forward, elbows on her knees, as eager as her daughter to hear what Mark was saying. He rose from his chair and limped back inside the house, returning a moment later with a dark wood cane. The curved handle of the cane was an intricately carved head of a mythical beast, part lion and part dragon. It was so vivid and real it was almost frightening, yet the workmanship was so lovely that she couldn't look away.

"How beautiful," Anne breathed, reaching out to touch it, then drawing back.

"It's all right. Go ahead." Mark held out the cane to her, and Anne ran her fingertips over the curves and ridges of the figure. Each edge and plane and curve was smooth as glass, almost silken to the touch.

"It's lovely. He must be awfully good."

"Oh, he is. Charley Gordon." Mark looked down at the cane, reminiscently running his thumb across it. "Talk about an artist—there is a real artist."

"Does he do this for a living, too?" Anne asked.

Mark stiffened fractionally. "No. He's still in a V.A. hospital."

"Oh. I see. He must have been seriously hurt."

"Yeah." He turned away to hand the cane to Nicole. "He'll never leave, except in a box."

Anne's eyes widened at his blunt words, and she glanced apprehensively at Nicole. However, Nicole seemed to be not at all shocked. She considered Mark's words seriously, leaning her chin on one hand. "You mean when he dies?"

"Yeah."

"Is he that sick?"

"Not physically."

Nicole frowned. "What does that mean?"

"He means mentally," Anne inserted quickly. "That's enough questions, Nicole."

"He's crazy?"

"Nicole!"

The girl's words didn't offend Mark, though. He simply shrugged and set the cane down, leaning it against the wall. "I guess. I don't know exactly what 'crazy' means. Do you?"

Nicole started to answer immediately, then shut her mouth and tilted her head to one side, looking at him. "Weird? Not all there?"

"Well, Charley's weird, all right." Mark smiled a little. "He's definitely weird. I'll tell you all about him some time."

"Why not now?"

Again he shrugged and didn't answer.

"Do you have a picture of him? Can I see him?" Nicole pursued, undaunted.

Mark was still for a moment, then nodded his head once, shortly, and went back into the house.

"Nicole, don't you think you're being rude?" Anne turned to her after Mark left. "He doesn't want to talk about his friend, and you keep pressing."

"I don't think he minds that much. He smiles and answers my questions. That's the thing about Mark; the other night when he found me, I asked him a bunch of questions, like I always do, and when he didn't want to answer he just told me. Then I shut up. So if he doesn't say he minds, I figure he doesn't."

Anne frowned. "I don't know if you can assume that."

"Besides, lots of times I don't want to tell you something, but you keep asking."

"That's different. I'm your mother. I need to know what

150

you're doing. You don't need to know about his friend Charley."

"But sometimes, even when I don't want to tell you, I'm glad afterward that you bugged me until I did. Then I feel better. Maybe it's the same with Mark. I figure he must get awful lonely living way out here by himself all the time. He probably likes talking about anything."

Anne stopped protesting, won by the sharp sense of pleasure she'd felt when Nicole admitted she was glad Anne questioned her at times, no matter what she said. Anne had often feared that she was overstepping the boundaries of privacy, not showing respect for her daughter as a person.

Mark reentered the room, a small square photograph in his hand. He held it out to Nicole, and Anne slipped around in back of her to look at it. It was a color snapshot of a man in a wheelchair. He was balding in front and had a bushy, light brown beard. He was laughing and squinting into the camera. He had no legs below the thighs, only pinned-up trousers over short stumps. The photograph silenced even Nicole, who set the picture down on the table.

They found Sophia waiting for them when they returned home. She seemed excited, and when Anne and Nicole came in the door, she took Anne's hand and led her upstairs, her eyes shining. Intrigued by Sophia's manner, Nicole followed them. "You know what? I had the best idea this afternoon. I went into the baby's room to take him out of the crib when he woke up, and I got to thinking. That room doesn't suit a baby at all. So I decided we ought to redecorate it."

"Redecorate it! But why?"

"I just told you. It doesn't suit a baby. It's not like a nursery at all. I didn't redo most of the bedrooms after Mother and Dad died, just my bedroom and study and the room you're in. So the room needs redoing, anyway. So does Nicole's. Don't you think so, Nicole?"

"Sure!"

"We could put baby-type paper in John Peter's room and build low shelves along one wall for toys. You know, where he could reach them. And we could make Nicole's room more suitable for a young lady. Probably some shelves there, too, and maybe a built-in desk."

"That sounds neat," Nicole agreed, and dashed off to survey her room while Sophia led Anne into the baby's room.

"Sophia, are you sure you want to do this?" Anne asked doubtfully. "I mean, it's very nice of you, but it would be rather expensive, wouldn't it?" She started to point out that they wouldn't be here long, but bit back the words; the reason they wouldn't stay long was because Sophia would soon die.

Sophia lifted her hands in a "so what?" gesture. "I've plenty of money, you know. It won't hurt me. I'd like to do it. It would give me pleasure. Besides, it won't cost much. It just needs painting and maybe wallpaper on one wall. The furniture's okay, don't you think? It was Gary's baby stuff."

"It's lovely. So are the floors."

"Yes. So it's painting, wallpapering, and building the shelves. I'll hire Mark to do it. He's good at that sort of thing. I'll leave word with Jim for Mark to drop by tomorrow morning. Now let's look at Nicole's room."

Nicole was full of plans when they arrived and eagerly dashed about the room, chattering about colors, wallpaper, and paint, pointing out the little window seat with storage space underneath, and noting how perfect it would look with a cushion to match the drapes, wallpaper, and comforter. Finally Anne threw up her hands, laughing, and said, "Stop! Stop. I can't absorb any more. I tell you what. We'll go to Denver and find exactly what you want. Okay?"

"Super!"

The next morning when Anne went down to the kitchen to make coffee, she saw Mark sitting on the porch steps outside. He leaned against the porch column, his weak leg stuck out in front of him. His other leg was firmly planted on the step below and bent at the knee. He wore faded jeans, worn thin with time and usage, and they molded softly against his legs. A denim jacket warded off the early morning chill; it was unsnapped and hung open to reveal the dark T-shirt beneath. The early morning sun lit Mark's face palely, washing out the lines and shadows. His eyes were closed, and the fringe of his lashes was dark against his cheek. He looked tired and vulnerable, and Anne had a brief, compelling urge to take him into her arms and let him rest, pillowed on her breasts.

She glanced down at her old flowered robe, which had two buttons missing and was fastened at the top with a large safety pin, and she immediately turned around and dashed back upstairs to dress. A few minutes later, dressed in jeans and a soft knit top, hair brushed and a bit of lipstick on her mouth, Anne returned to the kitchen and opened the door onto the porch.

"Hi."

Mark turned sharply. His face didn't look as harsh as when she first met him, Anne thought. Or was it that she had grown accustomed to his expression? "Hi. I was starting to wonder if you guys ever get up."

Anne smiled. "Come in and have a cup of coffee. I'm up early today. Usually Linda's here before I get down."

"Must be nice," he teased, a wry grin taking the sting from his words. He gripped the slender pole of the woodwork framing the porch and pulled up as he stood, taking the weight from his weak leg.

"Do you have to get up early to bring the horses down to the stables?"

"Yeah. I usually wake up about five."

"Five!" Anne pivoted and regarded him with mock horror. "Goodness, you must go to bed at nightfall."

He shook his head as they stepped inside the kitchen. "I don't need much sleep. I think I used up my lifetime quota when I was in the hospitals. When I first came back from Nam, I slept practically round the clock."

Escaping, Anne thought, but she didn't say it. "Want some coffee?"

"Sounds good." Mark glanced around the quiet kitchen as he shrugged out of his denim jacket and hung it on the chair back. The T-shirt underneath was black and short-sleeved, and his arms were very brown and muscled below the sleeves. It embarrassed Anne a little that she noticed. "Your kids sleep this late?"

"Sometimes. I heard the baby a minute ago, but Nicole went in to get him."

"I've never seen the baby. Nicole mentioned him."

Anne smiled. "You'll get your chance. But I warn you"—she waved an admonitory finger—"you'll fall for him. Everybody does." Except his father, she added mentally.

Mark smiled and settled into a chair at the table, watching her move about the kitchen, finding the things she needed. She filled the electric coffeepot with water and poured the grounds into the metal container after reading the instructions on the side of the coffee can. Then she set it in place in the pot and plugged in the coffeepot. She turned back to find a slight smile on Mark's lips. Anne grinned sheepishly.

"I'm really not as incompetent as I look. I *have* made coffee before. But I've never used an electric coffeepot. Just drip ones."

He grinned. "You should try making it over an open fire in a tin pot."

"Spare me. I don't think I'm cut out for roughing it."

The phone rang shrilly, interrupting their conversation, and Anne grabbed it. "Hello?"

"Anne?"

"Bryan." Her heart sank to the soles of her feet. He must have returned from his honeymoon.

"Would you care to explain to me what in the hell is going on?"

"Haven't you read my letter?"

"Yes, I read your letter," he mimicked savagely. "You think that's an explanation? That you've gone to Colorado to visit a grandmother you didn't know you had!"

"It's more than that. I told you."

"You've done a lot of harebrained things in your time, but I think this tops the list. Jesus H. Christ. What did you have in your head?"

"It's not a federal crime, Bryan. I simply left Dallas for the summer, or at least part of it."

"You never breathed a word of this to me before."

"I didn't know about it."

154

"Great. And you think that's not harebrained? Not impulsive?"

"I didn't say it wasn't impulsive. But just because something is done quickly doesn't mean it's wrong."

"It makes the odds pretty high. Who is this woman, anyway?"

"Her name is Sophia Kerr, and she's my grandmother. I explained it in the letter. Why do we have to go through it again?"

"Because I'm hoping it'll make more sense this time."

"I don't know why you should think that," Anne retorted. "Nothing I do ever makes sense to you."

He sighed. "Annie, you're flighty. Grant me that."

Anne set her jaw. "I won't. Your opinions are not natural laws, Bryan."

"I have a right to see my daughter every weekend. You're depriving me of that right."

"What about your right to see your son?"

"And John Peter. Why do you think you can whisk them out of the state without even warning me?"

"I didn't kidnap them! I told you, I had to leave quickly; Sophia doesn't have too long. I couldn't twiddle my thumbs in Dallas, waiting for you to get back from your honeymoon."

"Is that why you did this? To punish me for marrying again? To get back at me for taking a honeymoon with my new wife?"

"No! Not everything I do revolves around you! I did it because *I* wanted to. Because I thought it would be good for the kids to see the mountains and breathe some fresh air for a change."

"Oh, yeah. It'll be real swell for them to live with a dying woman."

"It's a fact of life, Bryan. I don't plan to expose them to anything morbid, but I can hardly pretend that there isn't illness or death in the world. I see no reason to."

"And I see no reason for thrusting them into an environment where they have to live with illness and death on a daily basis. How can you do this to your children?"

"I'm not doing anything bad to them! If it gets too depressing, I'll send them back to Dallas to live with you."

There was a heavy silence on the other end, and Anne had the inner satisfaction of knowing she'd landed a blow. She could almost hear Bryan grinding his teeth. "Very funny. You've exceeded the boundaries on this one, Anne. I have regular visitation rights under our divorce agreement. You're violating them. You can't leave the state like that."

"I'm not on parole, Bryan. I can leave the state whenever I want and take my kids with me. In case you didn't notice, I have custody of them. I'm sorry you won't have your weekends with Nicole this summer, but she can come for a week-long visit instead. She could fly down; she's old enough."

"It isn't practical, and you know it. Gwen and I both work. She'd be by herself all day."

"I worked, and she lived with me." Anne paused and drew a calming breath. "Frankly, I thought you might appreciate having a month or two without her visits while you and your bride are settling down."

"Gwen likes Nicole and was looking forward to getting better acquainted with her."

"Then let her get acquainted with her in a week-long visit," Anne retorted. "Send Nicole to a day-care center during the day. Let her stay with Mom or your mother. It can be worked out, if you want to see her."

"I didn't call to argue about whether I want to see my daughter. I think that's fairly obvious. You're in the wrong here, and you know it. I'm going to call my attorney as soon as I hang up. You can't go rocketing off around the country whenever you get the notion, dragging my kids with you."

"*My* kids."

Bryan made an exasperated noise. "I've got to go. I have a patient waiting."

"Of course. That's far more important."

"When did you turn so sarcastic? Listen, Anne, I've got some advice for you. It's time you grew up and stopped playing these childish games."

Stinging tears filled her eyes, and Anne blinked them back angrily. Damn it! How did he always manage to make her cry, even when she knew she was in the right? Even when she hated him.

Anne slammed the receiver down on its wall hook and spun around, clasping her arms tightly around her waist. She walked to the door and stared out its window, her vision obscured by tears. She was seething. Why did she let him get to her? You'd think she'd have gotten tougher over the years.

"Ex-husband?" Mark inquired softly from his seat at the table, and Anne cut her eyes toward him. The movement made the swelling tears plop out of her eyes and roll down her cheeks.

"How'd you guess?" she retorted with heavy irony.

Mark rose clumsily and went to her. He felt impelled to comfort her, to soothe her pain, but he didn't know what to do, what she would accept from him. He raised his hand and awkwardly touched her hair. The fine, curling hairs tickled his skin. His fingers trembled slightly. He wondered how much he felt a desire to help her and how much was simply desire. He jammed his hand in his pocket and moved back a step. "I'm sorry."

Anne slammed her fist into the other palm. "He makes me so mad! To hear him talk, everything I do is because of him. I'm trying to win him back if I act nicely; if I get angry with him, it's because he left me a year ago, not because of the issue at hand; if I take the kids to Colorado to visit my grandmother, it's because I'm trying to keep him apart from his daughter. To punish him because he got married again. As if I cared!"

"Do you care?"

"No! Oh, hell, I don't know. I'm not in love with him. I haven't been for ages. You know what made me angriest when he left? The fact that *he* was walking out, when I'd been the one who had wanted to for almost two years, but I'd stayed for Nicole's sake. It seemed so unfair. Such a waste."

Anne brushed her palms against her jeans and moved to the cabinet. She took out coffee cups and saucers, hoping the mundane movements would settle her nerves. She found a sugar bowl and set it on the table along with a couple of spoons, pulled the milk out of the refrigerator, and poured a small amount into a creamer. The coffee was still perking, and she could do nothing more. She sat down in a chair across the table from Mark.

"Sorry for sounding off," she murmured, not looking at him. "I'm sure it wasn't pleasant to have to listen to a family quarrel."

"Don't worry. I've heard worse."

Anne looked at him. The structure of his face was hard—thrusting cheekbones and a sharp jaw, thick black brows, deeply grooved lines beside his mouth and eyes—but his dark eyes were different from the way they'd looked in the past. Not soft, exactly, but not rejecting or harsh, either. They were somber and tinged with pain, but open, waiting, accepting. Suddenly Anne found herself wanting to spill out the whole story of her marriage. More than that, she found herself wanting to know what pain and sorrow had stamped Mark's face into its present lines.

"Were you ever married?" she asked, surprising them both.

"Yes. Several years ago."

"What happened?"

He shrugged. "We should never have gotten married. We were attracted to each other, and I had just received my draft notice. We knew I'd be going off to Nam; we thought we were in love. So we decided to get married before I was inducted. It seemed romantic at the time. But we really didn't know each other well. We hadn't dated long, and then we spent my training camp apart. After that I was in Nam for eight months, then in the hospital in Manila and Hawaii and California. Anyway, it was a year and a half before we saw each other again. We didn't know each other, didn't belong together. Rachel couldn't handle my wounds or the amount of time I spent in hospitals. Of course, I thought she should be holding my hand and whispering comfort." He twisted his mouth into a wry expression. "It didn't work out that way.

We got a divorce after a year or so. The only thing that kept us together that long was her guilt about divorcing a guy who was practically an invalid."

His words were unemotional and removed, almost as if he were talking about someone else, but from the tightening of his face and the way his eyes turned unreadable, Anne sensed a great depth of pain beneath his matter-of-fact recital. Impulsively she reached over and laid her hand over one of his on the table. He glanced up at her, startled. "I'm sorry. It must have been very hard on you."

Mark paused and drew a short breath. He was intensely aware of her physical presence, had been since she first opened the door and said hello this morning. Her hand on his was deliciously warm and soft; Mark thought he would have liked it to remain there forever. Yet he tightened all over, awkward, unsure. She was just being friendly; he mustn't let her know her touch aroused something far more than friendship in him. He wondered if she felt his flesh tense and begin to quiver under her palm. He pulled his hand away, shaking his head a little. "It's not important. Tell me about you. What happened with you and Bryan?"

Anne pulled back her hand, feeling foolish, her friendship rejected. Mark Pascal was a hard man to figure. Closed up. She rose and moved over to the coffeepot to hide the moment of awkwardness. "The same thing as you," she said, as she poured two cups of coffee. "We probably shouldn't have gotten married. Bryan is a perfectionist, very brilliant and intense, whereas I am sloppy and procrastinating and lazy. I drove him crazy."

Mark studied her back. There was a vulnerability in her stance, head curved down, watching the hot liquid pour into the cups. The white nape of her neck was exposed, fragile and feminine. Mark felt a sudden flash of anger at her former husband. "What about him? Didn't his perfectionism drive you crazy?"

"God, yes!" Anne turned, her eyebrows lifting to emphasize her words. "I could never understand why getting little lines around my eyes mattered. Or why Nicole should wear frilly dresses when they were a pain to take care of. Or why it's so awful to be late anywhere or run around in crummy old blue jeans." Anne crossed the room and set their cups down on the table. "We were really opposites. The problem was, when you look at the subjects we differed on, Bryan was usually right. He knew stuff, you see; I wasn't nearly as smart. How can you say somebody's wrong when they just want you to be on time or keep the house clean or dress the children prettily?"

"So when you clashed, you were always the one in the wrong?"

"Unfortunately, yes. I mean, there's no reason for Bryan to be such a perfectionist; he carried it to an extreme. And he had no right to interfere so with me and my life. Still, on every topic, he was basically right. I *am* slow and lazy and too permissive with the kids. I've had a terrible time since we got divorced; I'm late to work, late to pick the kids up, late to drop them off at school. I forget to pay bills; I can't seem to get everything organized and moving right."

"My sister-in-law swears that she's resigned to never having a moment of peace and order until her children are both grown and out of the house."

Anne smiled a little. Mark seemed almost friendly now. She couldn't figure him out. "Sure, the kids are part of it. But I was too dependent on Bryan to make decisions for me and do things I didn't like to do. I can't manage well on my own."

"Who can? That's why kids need two parents."

"Look, you saw me. I let Nicole wander off in the woods by herself when we'd been here only a couple of days. Was that smart? Or competent?"

"No. But it wasn't criminal, either. You can't expect to make the right decision every time. You didn't know what the mountains are like; you probably made a good decision for a city-dweller."

"Thank you." She took a sip of coffee and tried not to let his compliment make her glow. "I'm probably not being fair to myself. But I hate it when I make mistakes with the kids. I'm afraid it'll damage them irrevocably."

"Not many things are irrevocable."

"Maybe. But sometimes I think I might warp their personalities."

Mark chuckled. "Nicole doesn't seem particularly warped."

"Of course not!"

"So you couldn't have done too poorly."

"I guess not. I wonder why that's so hard for me to admit."

"Maybe you like the idea of being helpless and incompetent."

She shot him a fierce glance. "Sure. Just like I enjoyed Bryan telling me how wrong I looked all the time."

Mark gaped. "How wrong you looked!"

"Yeah. I didn't dress right. Too sloppy and crummy. I'd wear jeans, which accent my worst figure flaw, my hips. I didn't look stylish, sleek, and sophisticated. It wasn't just the clothes; it was me. My hair is too wild to ever look sleek. When it's loose, it curls all over the place and bushes out. My nose is too long, my face too formless. Let's see—oh, yes, then there are the things Bryan always wanted to take his knife to."

"His knife!"

Anne smiled at Mark's stunned expression. "He's a plastic surgeon."

"Oh."

"He wanted to remove the little wrinkles around here." Anne touched the outer corner of one eye. "After I had John Peter, I got this little pot belly. I couldn't get rid of it with exercise or dieting or anything; it was just because the baby was big. So Bryan wanted to do a tummy-tuck on me."

"You've got to be joking! I can't imagine anyone wanting to improve on your looks or telling you that you don't look right. You're beautiful." Mark didn't pause to consider what he said, simply blurted out the truth in his astonishment. But then his words lay there between them, sharp and undeniable, a piece of himself exposed. Suddenly, the kitchen was filled with sexual awareness. It leaped like an arc of electricity from Mark's body to Anne's and quivered inside them. Anne was terribly aware of his lean frame, the blue jeans worn and tight against his skin; she knew exactly how close his hands were to her, how warm his body burned. She saw the involuntary flicker of Mark's eyes to her breasts, and her breasts felt full and yearning. In that instant, she wanted to feel his touch and kiss, and she knew that he wanted the same.

Then Nicole came barreling into the kitchen, John Peter tottering at her heels, and the moment was gone.

Chapter Ten

"Hɪ, Mᴀʀᴋ!" Nɪᴄᴏʟᴇ ɢʀᴇᴇᴛᴇᴅ ᴛʜᴇɪʀ ᴠɪsɪᴛᴏʀ ᴇɴᴛʜᴜsɪᴀsᴛɪ-cally.

"Hello, kid. Who's this?" He nodded toward John Peter.

John Peter, always shy around men, stopped abruptly in the doorway, then sidled up to his mother's leg and leaned against it. Thumb in mouth, he gazed interestedly at Mark. Anne let her hand rest on his head, stroking the fine, blond hair. "This is the baby, John Peter."

Mark smiled at him but didn't speak or make a move toward him. His gaze went back up to Anne's face, a little remote, as if the moment of closeness between them had never happened. "Do you know why Sophia asked me to stop by?"

"Sophia wants to redo Nicole's and John Peter's rooms, and she'd like to hire you to do it."

"Redo them? How?"

"Nothing major. She just wants to repaint them, maybe put up wallpaper. She'd like low shelves along one wall in the baby's room and shelves and a desk in Nicole's room."

Mark regarded her steadily for a moment. "Does that mean you're planning on staying here?"

"What? Oh. You mean, after this summer?"

"Yes."

"No. We'll return to Dallas when the summer's over. Nicole's school and friends are there. My family. The children's father. There's no way we could live here. Sophia knows that. I guess she just wants to see it, to see the rooms redone, see how the kids like them. I'm not sure about the reason. But she wants to. So . . ." Anne shrugged eloquently.

"It's her money."

Nicole pulled a carton of orange juice out of the refrigerator and plopped it down on the table to pour it into a glass. "Wait'll you see what I'm going to do with my room," she told Mark. "It'll be gorgeous. Mom said I could pick out my own wallpaper and paint and everything."

"Within reason, of course," Anne amended quickly.

"Ah, Mom. . . . What does that mean?"

"You know what it means. You can't throw away money."

"So you'll get to veto my choice?" Nicole asked with a tinge of sarcasm.

"Yes." Anne injected as much firmness as she could into the word.

"I get a veto, too," Mark added.

Nicole turned toward him. "You? But why?"

"If I'm painting, wallpapering, and building all this stuff, I demand the right to rule out something impractical."

Nicole frowned, but belligerence didn't take over her features as it so often did in her quarrels with her mother. "Like what?"

"Like foil wallpaper. Too difficult for an amateur like me. In fact, it's too difficult for a lot of professionals. Or a kind of paint that doesn't wear well or go on easily."

"Oh. Well, that's okay."

Anne carefully refrained from showing her surprise at Nicole's easy acquiescence. It was amazing how much nicer she acted with strangers than with her mother. Or maybe not so amazing. Look at the way she and her own mother had never gotten along well. Sometimes she thought mothers and daughters were doomed to misunderstanding and strife.

The baby, feeling more secure now, edged away from Anne, still staring fixedly at Mark. Mark appeared not to notice him, but he reached into his pocket and withdrew a set of keys, which he held carelessly in his hand, letting them sway enough to jingle. John Peter ducked down and crawled under the table to the other side. He surfaced inches away from Mark, glancing up at him apprehensively, then over at the keys. The attraction conquered his uneasiness and he took two sliding steps forward and reached for the silver keys. Mark handed them to him, and John Peter gave them a healthy shake. He began to investigate the variety of sounds they made, while Mark talked softly, aimlessly to him. John Peter gave no sign that he heard a thing, but before long he was leaning against Mark's leg, spreading the keys out on Mark's worn jeans. He slammed the keys down on Mark's thigh, and Anne came up out of her chair.

"Johnny! No! Don't hit."

Mark shook his head. "Don't worry. It didn't hurt. There's so much scar tissue there, I couldn't feel a thing."

He looked down at the baby and held out a finger. John Peter took it and studied it. He pulled one short, curling black hair and was delighted by the grunt of protest Mark made. He pulled again.

"Ouch! You're vicious." Mark grinned, taking out all the bite from his words.

Anne watched, smiling, and thought of Mark's rapport with Nicole. She wondered what it meant if a man got along easily with children. Maybe it showed he had a warm and loving heart beneath his shell. Or maybe it just meant he was immature.

Linda arrived shortly thereafter and began to fix breakfast. Anne took Mark upstairs to show him the rooms Sophia wanted redone, leaving the hungry children below. Mark walked around each room and examined the walls. "Where do you want the shelves?" he asked. "Do you want them all painted or wallpapered or a little of each?"

"I don't know. I don't think Sophia has any specific plan in mind, but she'll be up in a little while and you can ask her."

"I suspect she'll let you make the decision. After all, it'll be yours before long." Anne's brow furrowed, and Mark abandoned the subject. "I might as well measure the rooms while we're waiting for Sophia."

He went downstairs to get the measuring tape. Anne wanted to get it to save Mark the long trip downstairs and back up again, but she clenched her teeth against the words. Mark wouldn't appreciate any favors or reminders of his weakness.

After what seemed like an interminable wait, Anne heard the slow, uneven thump of Mark's tread on the stairs. He entered the room, and together they measured, Anne holding the silver tab and Mark reeling out the metal tape and reading the numbers. Anne had to clamp down on her tongue again to keep from protesting as she watched Mark kneel and squat awkwardly as he measured, his bad leg remaining stiff as his other leg flexed easily, athletically. Every minute Anne hated more the injury that had so slowed him. It was obvious from the movements of his arms and other leg, from the rock-hard set of his muscles, that once he had moved with fluidity and strength. It seemed horribly unfair that he now should have to endure slowness and awkwardness, a betrayal by his own flesh.

There was a noise at the door, and they both turned. Sophia stood in the doorway. Anne thought she looked unusually tired this morning, but she said nothing. "Well, I see you're already on to my pet project."

"Yeah, but I need some details. Like color and wallpaper patterns and where you want the shelves."

Sophia made a dismissive gesture. "Let Anne decide that. She knows better than I what her children will like."

"I wouldn't be so sure about that," Anne put in wryly.

Sophia smiled. "You and Mark can drive to Denver tomorrow and select the paints and wallpapers."

Anne could sense Mark's tightening clear across the room, but he said nothing, only gave a brief nod and went back to his measuring. He didn't like the idea of going with her to choose paints and paper, she thought. Did he still dislike her and view her as a gold digger? The other day at his house she had thought he was beginning to warm up to her, and this morning they had talked in a friendly way.

"Well, uh, I guess you don't need my help any longer. I'll go downstairs." Anne edged toward the door.

"I'll get my tools and start scraping away the old paint and wallpaper from the walls."

Anne nodded and went downstairs to eat breakfast with the children. As she ate she heard Mark leave by the front door. About an hour later he returned and went up to the nursery. As soon as he came in, both the children gravitated to him. Anne tried to keep them from bothering him, especially John Peter, who was apt to stick his fingers into everything he saw, but it was a continual and mostly losing battle. After the fourth time she came in to pull the baby out of the room, Mark waved her back into the room. "Forget it. He's not bothering me. Either one of them. Let 'em stay."

"It's hard to keep Johnny out of your tools and the trash and everything."

He shrugged. "I'll keep an eye on him, and so can Nicole. Can't you, hon?"

"Sure. I'll make sure he doesn't eat any paint chips. I saw a commercial on TV one time about that. Old paint that had lead in it, and a kid would eat it and get lead poisoning."

"Well, as long as you're sure." Anne cast a look at Mark, who had turned back to the wall and was scraping off paint. Frankly, she would have liked to stay, too, and watch Mark work. There was a certain fascination about the slender, jean-clad legs and the lean-muscled arm moving up and down the wall, brown and strong. The fingers curled around the scraper were long and sensitive without any hint of delicacy, just as his arms and chest were strong and muscled without bulk. His thick, black hair was a trifle shaggy, with a slight wave near the bottom, and it swayed fractionally with the movements of his shoulders and arms. Anne knew a funny little curling longing in her stomach to touch it. She wondered if it was as silky as it looked.

She could have stayed and watched the soothing, monotonous chore for hours, just like the kids, but she knew she had no reason to stay, so she walked out of the room.

At lunchtime she came back to force the children downstairs to eat lunch. With a sigh, Nicole left the room, herding

John Peter before her. Anne turned to Mark, whose back was to her as he continued to work. "Mark? Don't you want to come down to lunch?"

"What?" He turned, looking surprised.

"Lunch is ready. Wouldn't you like some? It's ham sandwiches, and I fixed potato salad."

"Uh, that's okay. I'll just work."

"You must be hungry after all that work."

"I'm not very good around a lot of people."

Anne raised her eyebrows. "Sophia, Linda, me, and the kids? That's a lot of people?"

Mark thrust his hands into his back pockets and looked at the floor, then away. He seemed to be trying to think of something to say.

"Did the kids get on your nerves? I'll keep them out this afternoon."

"No, they're fine. Really. They're great kids. Nicole's sharp, and John Peter—" He smiled, his dark eyes warming. "He's a charmer. Funny, full of spirit."

"Then I don't understand." Anne frowned, and Mark shifted a little.

"I—uh, I don't know how to explain it exactly . . ."

"I'm sorry. I didn't mean to pry. How about if I bring you up a sandwich?"

"That's too much trouble."

"You have to eat."

Mark sighed. She looked so earnest and concerned, so reasonable. So utterly desirable. How could he explain to her that he would love to sit that close to her for fifteen minutes, watching her face and movements, the shifting pattern of emotions across her features, the fit of her clothes upon her body, yet it made him nervous as a cat to think of being with her? How did you tell a woman her presence was exciting and scary and filled you with such rushing, conflicting, painful feelings that you felt like a teen-ager? And felt like a fool to be that way at the age of thirty-six. After all these years, he was out of place with the people of the real world, especially women. When one attracted him like Anne Hamilton did, he was tongue-tied, clumsy, and stupid. He could think of nothing to say, and his limbs suddenly became enormous and unresponsive to his commands. His bad leg practically refused to work, making his limp more pronounced, and all the things he usually did to compensate failed. Every time he was around Anne, he trembled inside with excitement and yet was filled with humiliation.

"Okay," he said finally, to rid himself of the dilemma. "I'll get a sandwich and eat it here while I work."

"It's no trouble. I'll run it up."

Anne turned and left before he could object. He could just get proud and hurt because she refused to let him go downstairs to get his food. She was not going to have him marching downstairs and back up just for a sandwich. It was crazy.

Anne fixed him a thick sandwich and added a healthy mound of potato salad to the plate, then poured an iced cola and took the meal up on a small tin tray. She set the tray down on the dresser beside Mark, and he gave her a faint smile. "Thank you. You really didn't need to bother."

"No trouble." She wasn't sure why, but instead of leaving, Anne flopped down in the large padded rocker. Mark looked disconcerted, but he perched on the wooden toy box, set the tray on his lap, and began to eat. "When do you want to leave for Denver tomorrow?" Anne asked.

"What? Oh. Early, I guess. About eight-thirty; that'll get us to the stores around ten, ten-thirty."

"I promised Nicole she could help pick out her paint and wallpaper, so we'll have to take the kids along. Is that all right?"

If she wasn't mistaken, Mark looked distinctly relieved. "Sure. They're no trouble. I like kids."

"You and your wife didn't have any?"

"No. At least that was one mistake we didn't make."

"Divorce is an awfully hard thing on kids," Anne agreed sadly.

Mark looked chagrined. "Wait, I didn't mean to imply that your kids—I mean, that you'd done anything wrong."

Anne shrugged. "There's no right thing to do. If you stay together, they suffer from the unhappiness in the house. If you split up, they miss the other parent. John Peter's too young now to know the difference, but Nicole has been unhappy since Bryan left. She blames me for the divorce—if I'd been a better wife, Daddy wouldn't have left, etc. Nicole and I were once very close, but for the past year, we've been at odds about everything. It's been a terrible time for her."

"And for you, I imagine."

Anne sighed. "Yeah, for me, too." She forced a smile. "But at least I found out I could survive. Before that, I figured I wouldn't last a day on my own, especially with two kids to look after. But I managed to get a job and keep them fed and clothed and sometimes even get Nicole to school on time."

"That's a lot. Sometimes just surviving is the hardest thing in the world."

"You sound as if you know from experience."

He grimaced. "Yeah. I know. I remember lying in bed in that hospital in Manila, my leg feeling like there was a fire in it. I'd think that if I could just get home, it'd be all right. My wife would be there to comfort me; I'd have a home. I'd be safe, like on home base in tag." He shook his head in cynical amusement. "What an idiot I was. I got back to the States, but it was just another hospital. They kept talking about amputating; I was scared to go to sleep for fear I'd wake up and find my leg gone. When I finally got to see my wife, I discovered there wasn't anything between us anymore; it had all been a mistake. I was in and out of hospitals for years. Ten years of having operations, recovering from them, rehabilitation, then tests, and another operation. It was a crazy life. Makes you weird."

"You're not weird."

He glanced up at her from beneath heavy eyebrows, and genuine amusement quirked his mouth. "Oh, yeah?"

Anne chuckled. "Well, maybe you were nasty-tempered a few times."

"Come on, confess. You think I'm unreasonable and moody as hell."

"I don't quite understand you," Anne agreed. "Or why

170

you—I don't know. Sometimes you seem to dislike me, and I don't know exactly why."

He grunted and dug in his shirt pocket. "You got a cigarette?"

"No. You shouldn't smoke."

"Tell me about it." He made a search of all his pockets and found only a crumpled, empty pack. He crushed it and tossed it in the trash. "It's not that I dislike you." He looked down as he spoke, seemingly absorbed in a study of his hands. "There's nothing to dislike. You're a nice lady. But I can be mean as a snake. My leg hurts like hell sometimes; I could blame it on that. But the truth is, I don't operate very well around people anymore."

Anne frowned. "I don't understand."

"Have you ever been in a hospital?"

"When I had Nicole and John Peter. About three days each time."

"No. I mean for a long time. A couple of weeks, at least."

"No."

"Hospitals are strange places. They're dull and nothing like home, but you get real used to them. They're secure. There's a routine, you know. You have breakfast at the same time every day, and you go to the physical therapist at the same time, and the juice lady comes around every afternoon at three o'clock. You get used to talking to doctors and nurses. And in a V.A. hospital, practically everybody in there's like you; they were in the war and got shot up. You all have your horror stories about the times you almost got killed and the buddies that did get killed. You're never alone, and yet you're alone any time you want. Everyone has a shell, and the others respect it."

Mark studied his fingernails. His fingers were trembling, and he wished desperately that he had a cigarette. He couldn't imagine why he was telling Anne this, but he couldn't keep it from tumbling out. She would probably think he was the kind of guy who felt sorry for himself all the time, he thought; at best, this would make her pity him. But he couldn't stop the drive to tell her about himself and his life, to let her understand him. He couldn't stand for her to think he was simply grumpy or disliked her.

"After a while, you get to where you feel secure there. It's your world. It's so different from the outside world that it's scary. Then you don't want to leave. Does that make any sense?"

"Yeah, it makes sense." She knew what it was like to stay in a marriage because it was familiar and secure, even if it was bad.

"The longer you stay there, the scarier it gets to leave. Every time you come out, the world's changed some more; it keeps on passing you by. You don't know anyone; no one knows you. More than that, no one cares. You remember things that the rest of the world can't imagine, and they want to forget what they do know of it. Nam was part of me; I can't forget it. It changed my life forever. I was one person when I went in, and I'm somebody else entirely now. But to most people it's just a shameful thing that they want to put behind them as quickly as possible. They don't like to be reminded of it. Those of us who were over there—well, the world thinks we're all crazy murderers. You know. Time bombs that could go off at any minute. Guys who got their kicks out of slaughtering whole villages.

"Christ! Nobody knows what it was like. Nobody! Creeping through that goddamned jungle, never knowing whether some kid you met was going to throw a grenade at you, if the natives were friends or enemies, or when you were going to step on a mine or into some booby trap the Cong had laid for you. It was going and fighting and waiting and dreading and being bored out of your skull, with nothing to relieve any of it but drugs or a hooker who likely as not would turn out to be fifteen years old. Younger than your kid sister, for Pete's sake."

He shook his head as if to throw off the memories. "I'm sorry. I didn't mean to get into that. What I was trying to say was that people don't want to hear about it, and they don't have any idea what you've been through or what you want. Things . . . people . . . seem against you. You come home, dreaming of being back in the world you knew, only when you get there you find out you don't know it anymore. You don't fit. Every time you're out of the hospital for a few months, you belong even less. You're more and more unsure of yourself. Until finally you begin to not want to leave the hospital at all."

"Oh, Mark." Anne, always easily touched by another's emotions, felt his pain to the core of her being. She crossed the room quickly and sank down on her knees before him, impulsively seizing his knotted hands in her own and squeezing them. "I'm so sorry."

He jerked his hands away, growling, "I'm not asking for your pity."

"I'm not pitying you! I'm just sorry it happened, sorry you feel that way. I wish . . . I wish I could change it, make it disappear." She realized that her hands were now resting on his thighs, and awkwardly she pulled them away and let them fall into her lap as she squatted back on her heels.

Mark shrugged and ran a hand through his hair, then leaned back against the wall, away from her. "I'm a freak. Not as bad as some of the guys; at least I'm able to make it in the outside world. Some of them can't live outside the hospitals. They get released and pretty soon there they are again, doing anything to get back in. Even into the mental ward. It doesn't matter where the V.A. hospital is; they're all alike in the essentials, the things that matter—they're safe."

Anne sat down cross-legged on the floor in front of him, carefully putting a little distance between them. Apparently Mark couldn't accept the nearness; she knew she must not crowd him. "Is that what happened to your friend? The one you said wouldn't leave until he died?"

"Charley? Yeah. He has more raw talent in his little finger than I do in my whole body. But he'll stay in the V.A., whittling away, taking pills, and going to bed, eating, and swimming at the same time every day, his whole life run by a nurse with a watch."

"But you left. You're able to make it out here."

"Better than some," he agreed. He sighed, and his eyes fluttered closed. "But not like a normal person. I told you; I'm a freak. I get along okay as long as I don't have to be around a lot of people, as long as I can live out here and carve and care for Jim's horses. I don't really function well except by myself."

"Why do you think that? You get along great with the kids, and I can't think of anything harder on one's nerves than children."

A faint smile touched his lips, and Mark opened his eyes. "They're okay. This is how we got started, isn't it? Kids—I can talk to kids. They're straightforward. They're blunt, and they don't care if you are, too. They don't mind if you're odd, and they don't know about politeness or social chatter. You know, the first time I met Nicole, it took her about two minutes to say, 'Hey, what's the matter with your leg?' You never asked me; I could see you looking and hear the wheels turning in your head, but you didn't say anything."

"Well, I—I didn't want to embarrass you. I thought you might be sensitive about it, and you were so standoffish."

"So you wondered and thought I was weird."

"I didn't!"

He cocked an eyebrow. "Tell me another one."

"Well, maybe I did at first. But not after I got to know you better. Did I talk to you like I thought you were weird this morning?"

"No." He looked away. "Even at first you didn't talk to me as if you thought I was weird."

"Well?"

"Well, what?"

"Why am I worse than the kids? How come you're comfortable around them and not around me?"

"Because you're a woman. An adult. Hell, I don't know! I just know that around you, around other adults, I feel awkward. Tongue-tied. I don't know what to say or do; I've been out of touch for twelve or thirteen years. I'm light years away from other people. I get all churned up inside. Scared." He snorted. "I got a Purple Heart for getting shot up. They ought to give Purple Hearts to all the guys who managed to come back and get married and live normal lives. They're the ones with real courage."

"You have courage, too."

"Do I?" he asked quizzically.

"Yes. You left the hospital, didn't you?"

"Yeah. I did that. But I'm still out of my element. Crowds make me nervous. You make me nervous."

"Me? Come on. I'm the least threatening person in the world."

"No, you're not. You threaten the hell out of me."

"Why?"

He shook his head. "Never mind. Look, I just wanted to explain to you why I acted weird about going down to lunch. I'd have felt funny sitting down to eat with you. I don't fit, Anne. In social situations, I freeze up. My mind goes numb, and I either sit there like a dummy and say nothing, or I say something stupid and look like an even bigger idiot. I make other people uncomfortable; I make myself uncomfortable."

"Even with people you know?"

"Well, no, not if I know them well."

"If you ate with us a few times and talked to us, pretty soon you'd know us well, wouldn't you?"

"You're trying to back me into a corner."

"That's right. Well, wouldn't you?"

"I suppose."

"Okay, then, if you endure eating with us a few times, you'll be comfortable around us."

"What about the first few times?"

"What about them? You already feel comfortable around the children. So it's just me, Linda, and Sophia, right? Unless you feel you already know Sophia and Linda well enough."

"I get by with them."

"Then it's mostly me."

"Yeah. It's you."

"I'll tell you about me: I'm not a frightening person. I'm not gorgeous or witty or hard to get along with. Even Bryan would admit that. If you're silent, we'll talk enough to make up for it. If you say something stupid, it won't sound strange to the mother of two children. All you have to do is let your stomach churn through a couple of dinners, and then it will be okay. Right? Right."

He smiled. "Right."

"Then it's settled. We'll start tonight. Stay and have supper with us."

"Anne . . ."

She shook her head firmly and rose to her feet. "Nope, I won't hear another word. I'll leave you alone now, and let you finish your sandwich and get back to work. And, I'll set a place for you at the dinner table."

She turned and walked out the door without giving him a chance to protest. Mark gazed after her for a long time. Finally he brought his eyes down to the lunch before him, staring at it as if he'd never seen it before. His stomach was already beginning to knot up. But he knew he wouldn't pass up supper at Heartwood tonight for anything in the world.

Chapter Eleven

MARK ATE SUPPER WITH THEM THAT EVENING AND WAS AS QUIET as he had warned Anne he would be. However, Sophia and Anne kept the conversation running so smoothly that his silence wasn't noticeable. He relaxed in the undemanding atmosphere and even began to enjoy the evening. No one urged him to talk or looked at him expectantly, so that he was able to listen and smile at funny remarks or watch Anne's face without feeling that he was failing in his social duties.

The next morning he picked up Anne and her children in his four-wheel-drive car, which thrilled Nicole, and she besieged him with questions and chatter all the way to Denver, so that once again Mark didn't have a chance to feel uncomfortable. When they reached the paint store in Denver, John Peter led them a merry chase, grabbing rolls of wallpaper and sheets of paint samples, climbing onto the carpet rolls, and investigating the various items of painting equipment. But he was so humorous and inventive in his pursuits that they couldn't help but laugh at his antics instead of scold him.

Finally, to keep the baby entertained, Mark paraded him around the store on his shoulders, periodically tossing him up in the air, while Anne and Nicole quickly flipped through the wallpaper books and paint samples. John Peter's room was easy; there were only a few wallpapers appropriate for a baby boy. They soon purchased the paint and paper for the baby's room, as well as the other supplies Mark needed. But it was a much lengthier process to decorate Nicole's room. Eventually they decided to go to a department store where it would be easier to select wallpaper to match curtains and a bedspread.

They paused for a brief lunch, then attacked the larger stores. Although it was a tiring afternoon, it wasn't unpleasant. Nicole was in the best mood Anne had seen in a long time, and John Peter was delighted by Mark's attention. Mark appeared to be having almost as good a time as the boy. He smiled at John Peter's laughter and babbling excitement and burst into laughter at some of the things he did. John Peter was a born clown, and Mark's enjoyment of his antics encouraged him. It saddened Anne a little to see them, for it was obvious how much her son missed an adult male's companionship and interest. Yet she knew that he would never get it from his own father. Anne had given the child all she could in time and attention, but it wasn't enough. She couldn't supply the masculine model he needed. For the millionth time she seethed over Bryan's lack of interest in—even dislike for—his own son.

She would have to have it out with Bryan when they returned to Dallas, she thought. It wasn't fair to John Peter for Bryan to continue the way he had so far. Of course, Bryan wouldn't be pleased to have Anne point out a fault in him, but this time she couldn't dodge the issue in order to avoid conflict. Anne sighed inwardly. She certainly didn't look forward to a confrontation. Bryan's response to criticism was usually a defensive, sarcastic recital of her own deficiencies, both mental and physical. That had always been his major weapon against her.

Bryan had never told her that she wasn't attractive, but his continual criticisms of her dress and looks had been like drips of water gradually wearing away the core of her confidence. Many times she had wondered why Bryan had been attracted to her to begin with, for he usually disapproved of her looks after they married. Yet she realized that from the beginning

Bryan's feeling for her had been primarily one of physical attraction. They hadn't talked and laughed together and enjoyed good times. Real dates, such as dinner or the movies, had been rare. Instead they had sneaked moments away from Bryan's intensive medical studies, moments which they spent in hurried grappling and kisses. At the time she had thought his passion was love and had loved him as much for his love of her as for any other reason.

It hadn't made sense to her later when Bryan started trying to mold her looks into a different style. Then she realized that throughout their period of dating, she must not have looked as good to Bryan as she had thought, that he hadn't desired her as much, and she was embarrassed and ashamed. He must have seen in her merely raw material that needed refining to look its best. She had done her best to change, but it had never been successful. At times she had striven to appear cool and lovely; at other times she had lashed back with a defiantly loose and free hair style or sloppy clothes. But throughout it all, she had carried inside her the weary knowledge that reddish-brown, curling hair, a full mouth, and a sprinkling of freckles across her cheek and nose could never achieve cool loveliness. She was doomed to failure.

Bit had upbraided her for trying to change for Bryan, contending that it was Bryan's problem, not Anne's. If he preferred a cool blond beauty, that was his loss. Anne, she insisted, didn't need to change a thing, nor to feel guilty for not changing. Since the divorce, Anne had grown more and more to believe her sister, though she still lacked the ability to shrug off Bryan's criticisms. Away from Bryan, she was more confident of her looks. From time to time she was sure that men had looked at her admiringly as she walked by. But Mark's impulsive remark yesterday that Bryan was crazy and she was lovely had done more to reassure her that her looks were appealing than anything else had.

Anne sneaked a sideways glance at Mark. He must have meant what he said. It had obviously come out without thinking; he had been too tense and awkward afterward for the words to have been a line. It had given her ego a much-needed boost, and the feeling lingered.

Mark turned and caught her watching him, and he smiled. Anne felt a hot, unfamiliar surge within her. She realized that she wanted him to kiss her. She wondered if he had any interest in her. There had been an unmistakable sizzle of desire between them yesterday, but Anne didn't know what that meant for today or tomorrow or the rest of her stay here. Mark was no longer antagonistic toward her, as he had been at first, but he was still remote most of the time—at least with her. He spoke more with John Peter and Nicole than with her, and even when they were laughing together and having fun, like today, Mark never came close to her in any physical way. He didn't take her arm, touch her, wink, or exhibit any other masculine gesture of friendliness or liking.

After they managed to find what Nicole wanted, Mark whimsically suggested that they take in a movie. They found an old Walt Disney cartoon feature at one of the malls and spent the rest of the afternoon happily munching popcorn and laughing at the antics of the characters on the screen. Fortunately for them all, John Peter fell asleep not long after it started and snoozed through most of the movie.

They topped the day off by visiting a hamburger place, where Mark tirelessly helped John Peter try out all the restaurant's playground equipment. At last they drove home, tired and satisfied. John Peter dozed in his seat in the back, and even Nicole was too tired to chatter. Anne leaned her head back against the seat and let the dark monotony of the road soothe her into dozing.

Mark glanced at her, then back at the road. Anne's image stayed in his mind, soft and vulnerable. Her eyelashes cast shadows on her cheeks; her translucent skin was soft and relaxed. Her lips, slightly parted in sleep, beckoned him sensually. He would have liked to gaze at her for a long time. Even more he wished she was his and he could contemplate their slow, lazy lovemaking when they reached home and put the children to bed.

He clenched the steering wheel. It was crazy to dream things like that. Yet he couldn't stop himself.

* * *

Mark left soon after he brought them home. Anne whisked the children into bed and went to Sophia's sitting room to regale her with descriptions of the things they had bought or ordered.

Afterward they settled down to the game of gin rummy that had become their almost nightly routine. Anne had never been an enthusiastic card player, but the second evening they were at Heartwood, Sophia had suggested a game and Anne had been happy to oblige her. After that they had played a game almost every evening after the children went to bed. Sophia looked forward to the games, and Anne suspected that they took her mind off her illness. They talked as they played; Sophia seemed to converse more easily while her hands were busy.

"I forgot to tell you," Sophia commented, as she shuffled and dealt the cards. "Your real estate agent called while you were gone. She said the closing's set for next Friday and can you make it?"

"I guess I'll have to. I can fly in and out the same day."

"Why don't you leave the children here? Linda and I can keep an eye on them. Nicole's very helpful with the baby."

"Yes. That'd make it an easier trip." Anne paused and frowned. "No, I suppose I'd better take Nicole with me so that she can see her father. I'll spend the weekend with my sister, and Nicole can have a couple of days with Bryan."

Sophia cocked her head to one side. "You haven't been married twice, have you?"

"Good heavens, no! What gave you that idea?"

"It's the way you talk about Nicole and her father, almost as if the baby had a different father." Sophia stopped and her eyes widened at the implication of her words. "Oh, dear."

Anne laughed. "Don't worry. You haven't stumbled onto a dark secret. Bryan is John Peter's father." She sighed, and the laughter fell away from her face. "The thing is, Bryan's never really . . . well, he doesn't like John Peter. He doesn't take him with them when he gets Nicole. His excuse is that John Peter's too young to be taken away from his mother. But if he really thought that and wanted to see him, Bryan would take him for a few hours in the afternoon, at least. Bryan's not a man who likes babies; he prefers older children he can talk to and reason with. But he paid Nicole more attention when she was a baby than he does John Peter.''

"How odd. Most men are so proud of their sons."

"Not Bryan." Anne frowned. "Sometimes it worries me. Whenever Bryan comes over, John Peter makes pathetic little attempts to get Bryan to pick him up or notice him. Imagine what it'll be like when he gets older, when he needs to have a male figure around to talk to and emulate. I hate to think how he'll react when he's old enough to understand who Bryan is and how Bryan ought to love him—just think how rejected he'll feel, knowing that his own father hasn't wanted anything to do with him since he was a baby!''

"Why does Bryan do it? Have you asked him?"

Anne shook her head. "No. It wouldn't be any use. I've made a comment once or twice, and Bryan pretended he didn't know what I was talking about. He'd say, 'It's just that I can't take him now because he'd be so out of control.' Or he'd give me the line about the baby needing to be with his mother. He would deny it if I asked him point-blank.''

Sophia shrugged. "You never know. It might be bothering him, too. He might like to talk about it."

Anne grimaced. "Bryan's not big on expressing his feelings. It used to drive him crazy that I'd cry when he got angry with me. That was one of our problems. He hated emotions and weakness. And I was so emotional and weak!''

"The two aren't the same thing, you know," Sophia replied tartly, and fixed her with a stern gaze. "Something I've noticed about you—you're always deprecating yourself, implying that you're weak or not intelligent or not pretty. It's silly.''

Anne had to smile at her choice of words. "Silly?"

"Yes, silly. I won't dignify it by saying it's wrong. That's obvious. The fact that you don't realize that it's wrong is silly. I wish you'd stop that nonsense.''

"If only it were that easy. I know you'd like to think I was strong. Everyone wants me to be stronger. They always have. Mother, Bit, Bryan. They couldn't understand how I turned out so weak. They had no trouble making decisions or standing up for themselves or doing hard things. But I can't summon up those qualities in myself. I've tried. I really have. But I always fold. Whenever Mother and I argued, I was the one who buckled and gave in. Bit's three years younger than I, and she was the one who protected me! Once when I was about six and Bit was three, we were playing with a neighbor. The girl said something that hurt me, and I started to cry. Bit jumped up and shoved the kid down and told her to get out of our yard and not come back because she was mean to me. At three—can you imagine?" Anne smiled a little wistfully. "Everyone else is so sure of themselves! But not me. I always see the other person's side of the argument; then I wonder if I'm right or wrong. I can't make decisions. I end up flailing around until somebody forces me to move. I'm not firm with Nicole and John Peter. I never take anything back to a store because it embarrasses me or I'm scared they won't believe me, or something. People talk me into things. I'm a real patsy."

"And you think that constitutes a weak person? Not arguing with a store clerk or not knowing what to do all the time?" Sophia shook her head. "That's not strength at all. Maybe your sister was braver than you. Some people can make decisions faster. Maybe you aren't as thick-skinned as some folks. But those things are positive qualities as well. You're more sensitive than other people. Sometimes that's what people need: sensitivity, understanding, sympathy. When you're feeling low, what use is a person who doesn't feel hurt or pain, but just forges ahead like a bull in a china shop? Nor is it necessarily good to make decisions quickly. Impulsive decisions are more likely to be wrong. You're slower, but maybe you reach a better decision in the end. You're a person who sees all the options. And seeing another person's side of an argument—that's empathy, a very valuable quality. Try living with someone who doesn't have it."

"I have," Anne put in wryly.

"Then you know what I mean. You ought to have realized that being overbearing and having to win every argument is not an admirable quality, either. Bravery, my dear, is often foolhardiness, or lack of thought. Perhaps your sister jumped in to protect you simply because she *was* younger than you and didn't have the maturity to understand the situation. Surely you don't believe that the answer to a problem with a friend is to knock her down and order her out of your life."

"No, not really—although I've been tempted to, sometimes."

"Why do you believe those characteristics mean strength? Why do you assume you don't have any?"

Anne stared, unable to think of an answer. "I don't know. I guess, well, I'm always scared . . . you know, afraid to argue or stand up for myself. Scared to ask Bryan why he treats John Peter the way he does."

"Well, let me tell you something. Strength isn't a lack of fear. It's not bravery or a domineering personality or always making the right decisions. It's being able to take life's blows and survive. It's making the best out of what you're given. You've done that, in spades. You took a marriage that was basically poor and tried like hell to make it work, didn't you? When it was finally over, you didn't fall apart."

"I came close."

"So you cried and suffered. Everyone does. I wanted to give up when Gary died, but I didn't. Someone without strength would have. They'd have committed suicide or gone crazy or something. You could have done those things, too, but you didn't."

"I thought about it sometimes," Anne confessed quietly. "Not killing myself, so much. Bryan wasn't worth that. But I thought lots of times about giving up and just dissolving into tears. Going home to Mother and asking her to help me. Walking out the front door and never coming back. Admitting myself to the mental ward."

"But you didn't."

"I couldn't. I had the baby and Nicole. I knew I couldn't leave them alone or with Mother. I *had* to keep going."

"And that's strength." Sophia jabbed a forefinger at Anne to make her point.

"Yes'm." Smiling and pulling herself up straight, Anne gave her grandmother a mock salute.

Later, alone, she thought about what Sophia had said, and she wondered if her grandmother had been right. Had she allowed Bryan and others to convince her that she was weak when she wasn't? Had she been wrong about herself all these years?

The following morning Mark started to work again on the walls of the children's rooms. He was at Heartwood nearly every day for the next two weeks, and soon his presence became a normal part of their lives. The children visited him often, and he was invariably kind and patient with them, even when John Peter was determined to stick his hands into all Mark's materials and tools. Anne often heard them laughing together as Mark worked, and more than once she found Mark roughhousing with the baby, tossing him up in the air, tickling him, or blowing on his stomach while John Peter giggled and shrieked in glee. Once she came upstairs to find Mark attempting to change John Peter's diapers, with Nicole standing by giving instructions and advice.

At the sound of Anne's footsteps, Mark turned and grinned a little sheepishly. "Hi. I, uh, thought I'd try my hand at it. Save you the trouble." He looked back at the disposable diaper, the tapes fastened crookedly and the top sticking out far above the tapes and looking rather like a scoop. "Somehow I don't think it came out exactly right."

Anne had to grin. John Peter was smiling, quite pleased with himself, and she knew that he loved the attention from Mark. Her chest flooded with warmth, and it was hard for her to resist the desire to go to Mark. She wanted to be close to him, to touch him. But she knew she must not violate the defenses Mark had built around himself, so she stayed where she was. "Thank you. It's fine."

"I used to play with my brother's kids, but I rarely changed their diapers. Anyway, that was a long time ago, when they still used cloth diapers." Mark swooped the baby up in the air high above his head, and set him down gently onto the floor.

Mark returned to his work, and Anne lingered for a moment. There was no reason for her to stay, but she was as drawn to Mark as the children were. Two or three times a day she would come up to check on the children or ask Mark if he wanted a drink or food. Sometimes she didn't even bother to have an excuse, just came to stand or sit in the old rocker and watch him work.

Sometimes they talked and other times Anne sat in silence, soothed by the steady, hypnotic movements of his arm and shoulders. As the days passed, Mark grew more comfortable in her presence, until even if the children weren't there as a buffer, he didn't tighten up when she entered the room. He could talk to her without wondering if what he said was stupid. He had found that, strange as it seemed, Anne was truly interested in whatever he had to say. Once he had asked her why, and she had looked surprised.

"I don't know," she had replied. "I like to hear about things. People and places I don't know. Events. I'm fascinated by people, by what they've done and seen." She gave a deprecating little smile. "I don't mean to pry, so if I do, just tell me, and . . ."

"No, no. Don't apologize for it. It's a terrific quality. I just asked because I couldn't believe you really wanted to hear about the town where I grew up or my family or any of those things. I didn't want to bore you."

"I'm not bored, really. Please tell me."

So Mark had continued to talk, growing freer in his conversation all the time. His mind no longer went blank when she was there. He enjoyed her presence without the churning uncertainty he had known before. He also found that he could be quiet around her without the silence seeming a huge, spreading shadow between them. In short, he had grown to feel normal, even comfortable, with Anne, and her visits, freed from his insecurity and nerves, were the highlights of his day. He listened for the sound of her steps on the stairs or her voice in the hall. When he arrived each day, he came in through the kitchen because it was there he was most likely to see her. Whenever she stepped into the room where he was working, Mark felt her presence like a physical touch. He would turn to smile at her, and the sight of her standing there filled him with warmth.

He ate lunch with them every day as a matter of course,

and quite frequently he ate supper with them, too. He felt at ease with them now. It was almost as if he had a family. He realized that his life had had a huge, gaping hole in it, which Anne had filled. Before there had been cold loneliness, an emptiness with nothing to fill it except his art. There had been satisfaction in proving that he could live a life away from the hospital, but there had been little joy. But there was joy in Anne and her children, a happiness that overshadowed the ache in his leg or the dark nights when he couldn't sleep.

The only thing that marred his enjoyment was his persistent, ever-growing desire for Anne. The first time he saw her, desire had stirred in his loins, and the longing had never subsided. Instead, it became steadily larger and more intense. The warm, almost earthy quality in Anne entranced him; she was a fire at which he could warm his long-cold flesh. Every time he saw her added a new dimension to her sensual appeal. Her laughter, a sidelong, teasing glance from her eyes, the shape of her mouth, the play of her buttocks beneath her shorts—there was nothing about the way she looked or acted that didn't stoke the fire of his yearning.

Mark daydreamed about her when he was at home alone, imagining the silk of her hair sliding through his fingers, her soft, giving body beneath him, her mouth opening under his lips, hot and inviting. He pictured her coming to his bed and sliding between the sheets, her hands reaching out to stroke his arms and chest, sliding down to his legs, her velvety lips nibbling at his skin. At those times he would become so hard and hot for her that Mark thought he would die from wanting and not having, knowing he could never have her.

For it would be crazy to hope Anne might desire him in return, to believe that something could come of his feeling for her. Anne was simply a warm person who felt sorry for a crippled veteran, he reminded himself. Her friendliness didn't mean she had any real feeling for him or that she would look upon intimacy with him with anything other than horror. Mark didn't kid himself about what he had to offer a woman; it was flat nothing. He had little money and a lonely life style up here in the mountains. He couldn't imagine any woman, especially one from a bustling city, wanting to share that life.

He personally was no enticement—moody, isolated, practically a hermit, with a bum leg that would make a woman sick to see in its naked rawness. A long time ago he had faced up to the fact that he wouldn't be sharing the rest of his life with a woman. Especially not a woman like Anne Hamilton, who had so much to give any man.

Had Anne had any inkling of Mark's thoughts or his desire for her, she would have been astounded. They had become much friendlier, and he was clearly fond of Nicole and John Peter, but he still had an almost tangible barrier of aloofness around him that Anne conjectured he carried to ward off personal entanglements. Even as he laughed with her, dark eyes sparkling, she sensed that he held himself away from her. He avoided relationships, she thought, or at least ones that might prove to be long term. He enjoyed her as a friend, but she didn't dream he could want anything more from her. But there were times, as Anne watched the smooth play of muscles across Mark's back and arms as he scraped the paint from the walls, that she knew she wanted something from him that was definitely not friendship. She hadn't felt this much sexual interest in a man for a long, long time . . . if ever. She couldn't remember her chest ever before tightening until she could hardly breathe as it had the day she walked into Nicole's room and found Mark working there, his shirt off in the heat of his exertions. Swallowing, she had sat down and stared at his back. His shoulders were padded with muscle, his backbone a line of knobby outcroppings where the skin stretched tautly across. A light film of perspiration had covered his shoulders, and Anne had watched, fascinated, as a bead of sweat slid out from beneath Mark's damp hair and rolled down his neck and over his shoulder. She had known a wild urge to trace the course of the drop with her tongue and taste the salty tang of his skin.

Her insides had turned to hot wax, and she had pressed her legs together in an attempt to stop the sudden, hungry ache there. She wanted much to touch Mark's damp skin, to slide her hands around him and tangle her fingers in the curling black hairs of his chest. She wanted to kiss and caress him and to feel his hands on her body in return. She thought of his strong, browned hands cupping her breasts, his mouth coming down to take her nipple. Her nipples had turned tight and pebbly at the thought, and her palms had dampened. She wondered what it would be like to see Mark's aloofness melt in white-hot lovemaking. How would it feel to lie in the arms of a man who wasn't always in control, as Bryan had been, but who was emotional and sensitive?

Anne imagined Mark would be shocked if he knew the kind of thoughts she had about him. They even shocked her, they were so unusual and unexpected. Still, she couldn't stop imagining what would happen if Mark knew, or how it would feel if he took her in his arms and kissed her. There were times when she was tempted to touch him or let him know she would not be averse to his touch, but Anne had never been an aggressive person in any aspect of life, least of all sexually, and she couldn't bring herself to start. After all, Mark had shown little interest in her; it was likely he would reject any advance she made, and then she would feel humiliated and unable to face him again. It was too nice having his friendship to risk that.

So they continued to talk to each other as friends, spending bits and pieces of time together as he worked, often with Nicole and John Peter around, telling themselves that it was the best they could hope for. Yet neither could shake the physical hunger that lurked about their friendship.

The next time Anne took her grandmother to the doctor, he beamed at Anne and announced that Sophia was doing very well. "I think it's your influence," he said to Anne. "She has more interest in life now. Isn't that right, Mrs. Kerr?"

"Of course I have. I'm redoing my great-grandchildren's rooms, and I've got to see that finished, haven't I?"

"Sure," Dr. Kressel agreed heartily. "Keep up the good work. You're doing better than I had hoped for."

When they returned from Fitch, Anne related the happy news to Linda and went upstairs to Nicole's room, where the children were playing as Mark worked. "Guess what!"

Nicole looked up at her with great disinterest. John Peter flung himself at her knees and began the little dance that meant he wanted to be picked up. Mark turned around, smiling slowly as he looked at her. She was dressed up to visit the doctor, wearing a pale yellow suit that was one of her expensive, too-sophisticated outfits. Mark thought about peeling it from her bit by bit to expose the heat beneath, and the familiar hunger flooded his groin.

"What?" he asked, his voice a little hoarse.

"The doctor said Sophia is making good progress. There's been hardly any deterioration in her condition in the past two weeks."

"Great!"

"He was very pleased about it and said it was better than what he'd expected." Anne beamed and gave John Peter a squeeze.

Nicole gave her mother a sour look. "It doesn't mean anything."

Anne frowned. "What?"

"I said it doesn't mean anything. I looked up what Mama Sophie has in one of those big medical books in her library. It said that can happen for a brief period, but it doesn't mean it's in remission."

"Well, no, I suppose not. But it means she'll live a little longer." Anne cast an uncertain look at Mark. "Doesn't it?"

He shrugged. Nicole stood up from the floor where she had been playing blocks with the baby. "No, it doesn't," she said harshly. "She's still going to die, no matter what."

"Nicole . . ."

"I don't want to talk about it. I don't know why you get so excited about something like that. She's going to die." Nicole's nostrils flared, and Anne glimpsed the sparkle of tears in her eyes.

"Nicki, honey, I'm sorry." Anne went toward her daughter, an arm outstretched to take her in. "I know it hurts to think of Sophia dying."

Nicole jerked out of her reach. "No, it doesn't. I knew she would. I knew it when we came here. I don't fool myself like you do."

"Nicole, you can admit that it hurts to think of Sophia dying. There's nothing wrong with feeling pain at that idea."

"I don't feel it!" Nicole insisted angrily. "I don't! I just wish I could go home."

Anne stared at her, astonished at the sudden change in subject. "Sweetheart, we planned to stay the whole summer. You know that. I thought you liked it here."

Nicole shot a contemptuous look around. "There's nothing to do. I'm bored. Let's go home."

"There's riding. You like that. And I thought you got a kick out of redecorating your room."

Nicole shrugged. "It's okay. But I don't know anybody here. I want to go home."

"Well, we aren't," Anne snapped, irritated and hurt. "Why are you acting so selfish?"

"It's not me that's selfish!" Nicole lashed back. "It's you. I never wanted to come up here in the first place. But you dragged me up because *you* wanted to go. You didn't care about what I wanted to do. Just like you didn't care about Daddy. Just you! And John Peter. He's the only one you love!"

"Nicole, that's not true! Though, goodness knows, you make it very hard to—"

"It is true! It is! You don't care about me at all!" Nicole whirled and ran from the room, leaving Anne staring at the empty doorway, open-mouthed.

Chapter Twelve

AFTER NICOLE'S STORMY DEPARTURE, JOHN PETER STUCK HIS thumb into his mouth and looked up worriedly at his mother, his forehead beginning to pucker into a frown, mouth drawing down.

"It's okay, baby," Anne reassured him shakily. "It's okay." She patted him on the leg and set him down on the floor. "You go play with your blocks."

But the baby hurried to the door and down the hall in search of his sister. Anne sank down on a straight-backed, embroidered chair. "I thought that was ending. Nicole has been so much friendlier since we came here." Anne ran her fingers back through her hair, then covered her face with her hands. "That's the way we were at home. A fight every time you turned around. But I thought she liked it here. She's so interested in you and what you're doing. She likes the house and Sophia. I just know she does!"

"She probably does," Mark agreed. He came closer and sank down on his good knee to look into Anne's face. "You know, you're taking this too much to heart. Your first guess was probably right—Nicole hates to face the fact that Sophia's dying. She doesn't want to get involved with Sophia and have Sophia leave her. It's a natural reaction, particularly since Nicole's father left her a year ago. So she wills herself not to like Sophia nor to be sad that she's dying. But her very effort confirms the fact that she does care."

"Do you think so?" Anne looked at him hopefully. "She used to be such a sweet girl, so loving and caring. Sometimes I think I've ruined her."

"You haven't ruined anything. Look, Nicole's almost a teen-ager, and she's gone through some bad emotional experiences. People often lash out at the person they love most. My guess is that Nicole takes her worries and fears out on you because she feels secure in your love. She's not afraid you'll leave her if she yells at you. I'd say it's a positive sign about your relationship."

"How do you know all this?"

Mark smiled. "You'll read anything when you're flat on your back in the hospital month after month. I've read all kinds of books and magazines, including a bunch of pop psychology and classic psychology. Plus, I've been around a lot of people who were hurting."

Anne frowned, thinking about what Mark had said. "Do you really think she doesn't hate me?"

"I'm sure she doesn't hate you. When people are hurt or scared, they often express it in anger." Mark's expression turned wry. "I'm an example. I'm uneasy around people, so I act rude and antagonistic. That frightens them away, and I don't have to deal with them. It also allows me to pretend that I'm not scared, to concentrate on another emotion. You understand what I'm saying?"

"Yeah."

"I think that's what Nicole's doing. She's lost one parent, for all intents and purposes, and at the same time she's entering the insecure world of adolescence. That fact alone turns most kids into strangers. Everything is unsettled, uncertain. Nicole herself is changing, and I doubt she understands what she's doing any better than you do. She's scared, so she lashes out. You're handy and safe, so she takes it out on you."

"But what should I do? My sister tells me I shouldn't let her talk to me that way, that I ought to be stricter. Bit could do it; but I can't seem to."

"You know what I think? You ought to do what *you* think is

best. Not what some book or another person thinks is right. You know yourself and your daughter better than anyone. In the past you've had a good relationship, so you must have handled it well then. I'm sure what you'll do now will be just as right."

Anne cocked an eyebrow at him. "But I can't think of anything to do!"

"Then do nothing. Maybe that's the answer. Don't make a big deal of it. Remain as calm and normal as possible. That will help calm Nicole and reassure her that not everything will change. You'll provide her with a sense of stability."

Anne gazed at him, amazed by his perception. But, then, as he said, he knew about pain. "Thank you. You've made me feel much better."

"Good." Mark smiled. "Something else you might try— why not put Nicole in a situation where there are girls her age? Here, I mean. Maybe there's a lady who keeps kids in her house, or something. Nicole's probably lonely and misses her friends back home."

"Yes, that's true." Anne began to chew absentmindedly at her thumbnail. "But she hated being in a day-care center; she told me so regularly."

"She might feel different about it here. In Dallas she didn't need to make friends; here she does. Other kids are important to children her age."

"I guess you're right. She wouldn't have to stay there all day like she did at home. Maybe just in the mornings." She paused. "Do you know anybody who does that?"

He shook his head. "No. I'm not exactly gregarious, though. Ask Phyllis Cortini. Do you know her? She owns a store in Iron Creek."

"Yeah, we've visited some. She's a nice lady."

"She also knows everything about everyone around here. If such a place exists in Iron Creek, she'll know about it."

"Okay. I'll ask her." Anne rose. "Thank you again."

Mark made a dismissive gesture. "I've been thinking. Why don't I take you and Nicole out for a walk? We can explore; I could teach you a little about finding your way around. What to do when you're lost, stuff like that."

"You mean, so we wouldn't be such greenhorns?" Anne teased lightly.

"Yeah. I was pretty hard on you that day for letting Nicole go out into the woods when she didn't know anything. So I thought, well, I could teach you and her. That way Nicole could go out by herself sometimes."

"I'd appreciate that."

"Good. Saturday?"

"Okay, if you're sure you want to spend your day off that way. No, wait, we have to go to Dallas this weekend. I'm closing on the sale of our house, and I'm taking Nicole with me to visit Bryan."

His face fell a little. Mark realized he didn't like the prospect of Anne's being gone two days, particularly not when it involved seeing her ex-husband again. "Oh. Well, no problem. We'll make it for the next Monday. How's that?"

"Sure. Thanks."

He shrugged and turned back to his work.

True to Mark's prediction, Phyllis Cortini knew exactly whom Anne should see about child care. "Oh, sure," she replied quickly when Anne explained that she was interested in putting Nicole in day-care where she could make friends. "There's Cindy Upshaw, up on the end of Wolf Point Road. Or, no wait, I know. Deidre Bailey. She lives out on your side of town, on Ross Street. She takes in three or four kids, I think, and she has a daughter about Nicole's age. She's a sweet kid, too; her name's Sherry. I think Nicole would like her. More important, so would you."

"Great. Thank you."

"No trouble. Let me find her address." Phyllis reached beneath the counter and pulled out the Iron Creek phone directory. She thumbed through it until she found the right name. "Here it is. 811 Ross. You know where Ross is?" Anne shook her head. "You ought to get around more. Well, take the side street here by the store and go up two blocks. That's Ross. Then turn right and go down, oh, about four blocks, I guess. Something like that. Her house is a cute little doll-house kind of place with a fenced-in yard."

Anne wrote down the address and slung her purse over her shoulder. "Mark was right. You know everything and everyone in Iron Creek."

Phyllis grinned, lines crinkling in her leathery face. "Sure. The town gossip, that's me. My ex always told me I was the nosiest person alive." She leaned forward as though conveying a great secret. "But he never turned down a chance to hear what I knew."

Anne chuckled and went out the door. She found Deidre Bailey's house easily from Phyllis's directions, and she parked and went inside. There were four children playing inside the house, ranging in age from two to about eight, and another two kids outside. The din was horrendous, but Deidre Bailey sat smiling in the midst of it, helping one little girl with her toy. The front door had been opened by a young girl about Nicole's age, whom Anne guessed to be Sherry. She had a pleasant face, with twinkly brown eyes, as if she were aware of some joke no one else knew. She guided Anne to her mother, and Deidre, much like her daughter in looks—short and slight, with merry brown eyes that gave life to her whole face—came forward and led Anne into the kitchen, where she firmly shut the door against the noise.

When Anne explained her situation, Deidre was enthusiastic about Nicole's staying at her house part-time. "That would be lovely. Sherry really doesn't have much of anyone to play with. She winds up spending most of her time helping me with the kids. She'd love to have a girl her own age here. Most of her friends at school and church live too far away to visit often."

So it was arranged that Nicole and John Peter would stay with Deidre three days a week. Anne took the children to Deidre the following morning, and she was delighted when she picked them up later to find Nicole bubbling with enthusiasm. Nicole had liked Sherry right off and was pleased that Sherry had invited her to come to church with her sometime to meet her friends.

"Can I go, Mom? Can I?"

"Not this Sunday."

"Aw, Mom!"

"We're going to Dallas, remember? I'm going to close on the house, and you're spending the weekend with your father."

Nicole was silent for a moment. "Maybe I could stay here."

"After all the griping you and Bryan have done about me taking you away from him this summer? Not on your life! You're going to spend the weekend with him."

"Then can I go with Sherry the next Sunday?"

"I don't see why not." It surprised her that Nicole seemed so uninterested in the trip to Dallas. She had expected her daughter to be jumping with anticipation. Of course, Anne herself had little interest in going there. She found herself reluctant to leave Heartwood and the mountains. It was only for a couple of days, and it meant a large amount of money to her to close the deal on the house, but, as the time grew closer to their departure, Anne grew more and more depressed by the thought. By the time she left Heartwood late Thursday afternoon, she was dreading going home. She supposed she was uncertain about selling the house, with all its memories, even though many were bad. She knew Nicole was very attached to the house and would hate to lose it, but she hadn't realized until now that she had any lurking sadness at selling it.

The flight was harried, with John Peter climbing all over her and Nicole, and Anne's nerves were on edge by the time they finally landed, thirty minutes late. Bit was waiting for them and whisked them out of the airport and onto the expressway leading into Dallas. They dropped by Bryan's new townhouse to leave Nicole with him. Bit stopped the car at the front sidewalk, and Anne turned toward Nicole in the back seat. Nicole made no move toward the door.

"Here we are, honey," Anne prompted. "Go on up to the door. Don't forget your suitcase."

Nicole cast her a strangely beseeching look and leaned down to pick up her small case. "Mom, could you walk up there with me?"

"What?" Anne was astonished. "But why? What's the matter?"

"I don't know. I'm scared," Nicole confessed in a whisper.

"Of what? Heavens, you've gone to your father's house lots of times before."

"I know, but I—he wasn't—Gwen didn't live there then."

"I see." Anne curled her fingers into her palm. The idea of escorting Nicole to the door and having to face Bryan or, heaven forbid, his new wife, was not an appealing one. Still, she couldn't deny the unaccustomed appeal in Nicole's voice. "Okay. I'll walk up there with you."

Nicole kept her head lowered, ashamed by her display of cowardice. She hated having to depend on anyone, Anne knew, including her mother. Still, she needed Anne, and that touched her deeply. So often nowadays it seemed that Nicole neither needed nor wanted her.

Anne stepped out of the car, and Nicole followed, case in hand. They walked up the sidewalk, Nicole slightly behind Anne. Anne would have liked to hold her daughter's hand or put a hand on Nicole's shoulder in a gesture of support, but she suspected Nicole would have felt further shamed by it. Anne rang the doorbell and waited; her hands were sweating. What if it was Gwen who opened the door? It was a very real possibility—and one Anne didn't want to face. She had never actually met Gwen, only seen her a time or two sitting in the car when Bryan picked up Nicole. Once Anne had thought she had seen Gwen in a grocery store, but Anne had fled immediately and gone down the street to another store to avoid running into her.

The door opened, and the light framed a woman's figure. She switched on the porchlight, and her face was clearer. It was Gwen. Up close, she was shorter than she had seemed at a distance. Or perhaps it was that Anne hadn't seen her before without high heels. Her blond hair was pulled back and held with a black comb on either side. She wore designer jeans and a black-and-white blouse with full sleeves, immaculate and stylish, but casual. Gwen was a few years younger than herself, Anne guessed. Her make-up was fresh and perfectly applied, and her figure was slim, with narrow hips and small, high breasts. She looked very good in clothes, Anne thought, even if she was short.

Her eyes went to Anne questioningly, then down to Nicole, and Anne saw Gwen's features tighten even as she smiled. "Hello, Nicole. How are you? Your dad and I weren't expecting you this early."

Nicole frowned. "Our plane was thirty minutes late."

"Oh, well." Gwen looked a little rattled and checked her slim-cased gold watch. "Yes, I see. My, it *is* later than I thought. We let the time get away from us." She wet her lips and looked at Anne. She formed a careful smile. "You must be Anne."

Gwen extended a hand, and Anne shook it. "Yes, I am." Curiously, she didn't feel the rush of emotions she had expected to experience when she finally met Gwen. Jealousy, fear, rage, embarrassment, jangling nerves—none of them popped up in her.

"Come in, honey," Gwen said to Nicole. Was that a trace of anxiety Anne detected in the other woman's voice? She glanced down at her daughter's mulishly set face, and unexpectedly she felt a twinge of pity for Gwen. Nicole would never make it easy for her. "Bryan's—your dad's in the den. Anne, uh, would you care to come in?"

"No. I have to run. I just wanted to see Nicole safely to the door." She leaned down to kiss Nicole on the top of the head. Not so far to lean anymore. "'Bye, sweetheart. I'll see you Sunday morning."

To Anne's surprise, Nicole flung her arms around her and gave her a hug. "Okay. 'Bye, Mom." Nicole hurried inside, head tucked down to avoid both Gwen's and Anne's eyes. Anne gave Gwen a mechanical smile and walked back to Bit's car.

"Well, well," Bit said as Anne settled in and closed the door. "So you got to meet the dragon lady."

Anne smiled. "Yeah. It wasn't much of an event, though. I almost felt sorry for her. She's got a tough row to hoe with Nicole."

Bit chuckled. "I'll say one thing for our Nicole; she's not an easy mark."

"No. She's not. I've found one adult she seems to like, though."

"Oh, yeah? Who? Your grandmother?"

"No. Oh, I think she likes her well enough, but I meant a man who lives near there. He rents a cabin from Sophia and does odd jobs for her in return. He's an artist. He does things in wood—all kinds of stuff, figures, practical things. His work looks very good to me. Nicole is fascinated by him. She loves to watch him work and plagues him with questions. He's very good-natured about it. No, that's not true. I think he really likes her. And the baby, too." She glanced back to smile at John Peter in the back seat, squirming in his never-ending attempt to break loose from the seat belt.

"That's not hard."

"Except for Bryan."

Bit shrugged. "Well, you know my opinion of Bryan. This guy sounds interesting. What's his name? It sounds as if you find him interesting, too."

"His name's Mark Pascal." Anne paused. "And, yeah, I do. I find him interesting." She stared out the window. "This sounds crazy, I guess, but . . . I think I'm falling for the guy."

Anne had expected to feel a nostalgic pull at the closing on the sale of the house, but she found she felt almost nothing at all. The meeting, conducted at the title company's office, was so full of papers, signings, and jargon that it was difficult to connect it with the house they had lived in. Afterward, she and Bit went out to an elegant restaurant to celebrate. On their way, she asked Bit to drive by the house one last time. But seeing it again produced not even a tear or a faint taste of regret. She had never been happy in that house, and she didn't regret selling it, but it had been where they lived when John Peter was born and where all his life had taken place. She had expected a tug at the heartstrings simply because of the memories it held.

In fact, her whole lack of feeling at being home in Dallas was rather surprising. She and Bit drove past a few condominiums and townhouses, and she scanned the Sunday real estate section, but she couldn't work up any interest in finding a new house. There'd be time enough for that when they returned to Dallas later in the summer. Anne suspected that after

Sophia's death she would probably welcome the opportunity to keep herself busy. But now her mind and heart were still in Colorado, and this visit was merely an annoying interruption. She was anxious to get back to Iron Creek, and if it hadn't been for Nicole's visit with Bryan, she would have flown back immediately after the closing.

Anne saw her mother only briefly, when she dropped the baby off at Beverly's house before the closing and later when she returned to pick him up. There was a constraint between them, each full of questions, yet unsure of the other's reaction. It was a relief to leave Beverly's house.

Their plane left Sunday afternoon at 2:30. Bryan returned Nicole to Bit's townhouse promptly at twelve. It was another surprise for Anne to open the door to him and feel none of the usual churning nerves in her stomach, none of the instinctive hostility and resentment. There was little there, she thought, except indifference. How could her emotions have changed so much in a matter of a few weeks?

"Hi, sweetheart," Anne said to Nicole, hugging her. Nicole endured the embrace without protest. "How are you? Hello, Bryan. Would you like to come in?" She stepped back. He cast her an odd look and walked through the door. Anne realized that she had never asked him that before, never treated him as a stranger, but had always simply assumed he would enter the house.

"Where's Bit?" Nicole asked, heading for the stairs. "I want to ask her something."

"Up in her office, I think."

Nicole took the stairs two at a time, leaving Bryan and Anne standing awkwardly together in the entry. Bryan's mouth twisted slightly. "Bit is Nicole's resident expert. She and I were arguing about an historical event, and she said she'd ask Bit which of us was right."

Anne suppressed a smile. Bryan wouldn't appreciate his daughter not accepting him as the final authority on everything. "History was Bit's minor in college. She and Nicole have always shared that interest." Which Bryan would have known if he had paid more attention to his daughter, she added silently.

Bryan shrugged. "Uh, Anne, Nicole talked a lot about some man that lives near this place where you're staying."

"Mark Pascal?"

"Yeah, that's the guy. You dating him?"

"No. He lives close by, and he works for Sophia sometimes. He's been at the house a lot lately because he's redoing the children's rooms."

Bryan crossed his arms, frowning. "What's he like? He sounded kind of strange."

"He's not strange." Anne straightened defensively. "He's an artist who likes to live close to nature."

Bryan made a derisive noise. "Nicole told me he whittled for a living."

"It's hardly whittling, Bryan. He's an artist who works in wood, like a sculptor in metal or marble. His work is very good."

"But he's got some sort of physical problem?"

"He limps," Anne said tightly. "He was wounded in Vietnam, and he's had a lot of operations on his left leg. He uses a cane. Why all these questions about Mark Pascal?"

"Some of those Vietnam vets have mental problems. Flashbacks and all that."

"Oh, Bryan, for God's sake. He's perfectly normal. He doesn't lapse into moments of violence or anything. What's wrong with you?"

Bryan stared. "What's wrong with me? I happen to care about my children; I'm concerned about the people they're around. I'm sure you won't believe this, but I actually care about you, too. I don't want any of you to get into a situation where you could get hurt."

"Mark is not violent. Believe me." Anne turned and walked away.

"Come on, don't get huffy. I'm sorry if I offended you. I'm worried about you, that's all. Anne, I'll always care for you in a way. We grew apart, but I still want what's best for you."

Anne cast him a look of disbelief. "Oh?"

"Yeah! I know you like to think I'm callous and don't give a damn, but I do. I'm sorry our marriage turned out the way it did. And I don't want you to get involved with some weird character who might hurt you. Naturally, I'm concerned about the children. You apparently think I just like to nag you, but I've always acted out of a concern for you and your health and . . . and well-being. I admit I urged you to improve frequently, but, Anne, can't you see that I did it because you were important to me? Because I cared what happened to you? Because I wanted you to be as much as you could be?"

Anne turned around to face him. She shook her head slowly. "Maybe that's what you believed, Bryan. But I think it was more that you wanted me to be what *you* wanted, not what I was capable of being."

He grimaced. "Oh, Anne . . ."

"Please. Let's not fight. What's the point?"

He paused, then said reluctantly, "Yes, I suppose you're right. I, uh, I'll be going now. Tell Nicole I gave her my love."

"You haven't asked about the baby."

Guilt flickered across his face. "Oh. Yes. How is he?"

"Fine. He's taking an early nap right now so he'll be rested for the plane trip."

"That's good. Well, give him my love, too."

"Bryan, would you answer a question for me?" Anne moved closer to him, her eyes intent on his face. She'd never had the nerve to ask him before, too afraid of the answer or his anger, but somehow this afternoon she felt little fear of Bryan.

He eyed her warily. "I guess. What?"

"You've always had something against John Peter."

"Now, Anne, that's not—"

"It *is* true, and we both know it. I'm not trying to make you feel guilty or anything. I'd just like to know why. Why do you dislike him?"

"I don't dislike him," Bryan protested. "I—oh, hell. I had decided to leave you and then you told me you were pregnant with him."

"Oh. You mean, you already wanted a divorce back then?"

"Yeah. I, uh—Anne, you know we weren't good together. Hadn't been for a long time. I had been thinking about leaving for a while. Weighing the pros and cons. I wanted to go, but there was the practice and all the mess of getting a divorce. With community property that can be a real bitch. Even though divorce isn't the stigma that it used to be, it reflects badly on you. I didn't want, you know, to get any bad publicity about it, particularly with the circle of people we knew."

Anne stared, speechless. She couldn't imagine even Bryan being so pragmatic and cool about an emotional issue like divorce. He stirred restlessly under her gaze. "Anyway, I was about ready to go when you found out you were pregnant. It ruined my plans. I couldn't leave you when you were pregnant."

"Bad press?"

"Give me some credit, Anne. I'm not without feelings. I was responsible for you. I couldn't walk out at a time like that, leaving you to face the pregnancy and labor and all that alone. But . . . I admit that I resented John Peter. I tried not to, but I couldn't help it. It was like he was the ball and chain that kept me there."

"He's not keeping you there anymore." Anne could understand Bryan's resentment, but she was flooded with irritation, too. Surely an adult ought to be able to work out that feeling. Firmly, she suppressed her irritation. It wouldn't do John Peter any good. She and Bryan hadn't talked about anything without bickering and hostility in ages; this was too important an opportunity to sour it by getting angry. She clasped her hands together and looked at Bryan almost pleadingly. "It doesn't make much difference to him now. He wants you to notice him, but it doesn't hurt him when you don't. In a few years, though, he'll need his father. If you ignore him or push him away, it could affect him badly. I mean, you *are* his father. It's all in the past; you're free and happy now. So couldn't you try to look at him in a new light? Forget about the past and think of him as just a boy, just your son, not something that kept you in the marriage when you didn't want to be?"

"I've thought about that a lot. You'll marry, I'm sure. Maybe it would be better if he gets his fathering from your second husband. After all, he'll be the one John Peter will have to live with; he'd only see me on the weekends."

"Bryan, he'll know you're his father. Besides, what makes you think I'll remarry? I doubt I ever will, certainly not in the next year or two. I'm not even dating anyone."

Bryan smoothed his hands down his pants legs. "You're projecting too far ahead. Let's worry about it when the time comes. Okay? Right now he's a baby, and he needs you, not me. In a year or two, we'll—"

"He's still your child!" Anne flared, her hands planted on her hips.

"Look!" Bryan snapped back. "I don't want him to be my child. I don't want to drag him into my new family. Nicole's different. She's almost grown; she's a person. But J.P.—well, he'd be a disruption. Gwen doesn't know anything about babies. Neither do I, frankly. Having him around would upset everything."

"I can't believe you're that callous."

"I'm not callous. Simply realistic."

Anne glared at him. She would have liked to pick up something and smash him with it. How could he talk that way about his own son? John Peter always wanted Bryan to like him, to notice him. She thought of the way he'd dance at Bryan's feet, begging to be picked up, and Bryan would ignore him. "You're a real son-of-a-bitch, you know that?"

"Anne, must you always be so emotional? Can't you look at this logically? Realistically? You'll see that—"

"I *see* that you're a selfish, immature man, that's what I see!" Anne retorted heatedly. "You hurt me a lot in the past, criticizing me, trying to make me different. I felt so low, so unworthy because I couldn't be what you wanted. I gave you that power over me. I thought you knew it all; I presumed you were right and I was wrong. I failed because I couldn't live up to your standards. I wasn't bright enough or beautiful enough or cool and logical enough! It's incredible that I believed you, that I thought you had such knowledge of right and wrong. All that time you weren't any kind of superior being! You were just a selfish, grasping boy who never grew up. I doubt you knew what was right for yourself, and you sure as hell didn't know what was right for me!"

Bryan stiffened and cast Anne a cold, contemptuous look. "There's no point talking to you when you get like this. I'll see you in a few weeks when you return to Dallas."

Anne clenched her fists, seething. That was always Bryan's reaction to her anger. He cut her off, told her she was immature or emotional or impulsive and then fled. Anne watched him exit, holding open the door for him, and she slammed it shut behind him. Damn him!

Upstairs John Peter began to cry, awakened prematurely from his nap. Anne started up the stairs, teeth grinding in exasperation. Thank heavens she didn't have to live with Bryan anymore or even deal with him much. Let him see Nicole on the weekends and try to establish some sort of relationship with her. She and John Peter would keep out of his way. It was infuriating to think that she had meekly accepted his rules all these years, blaming herself for not being a good wife. She'd known Bryan had faults and problems; she hadn't thought of him as a saint or superman. But she had given him the power to hurt her, and she had accepted his standards as the norm. It was idiotic. She had been unhappy, had often railed at his complaints or commands, but she hadn't questioned their validity or his authority.

Well, at least she was through with that. She could deal with Bryan; she wasn't afraid or unsure. She marched up the stairs, new-found confidence soaring in her. She rescued John Peter from his bed and walked down the hall to the tiny study adjacent to Bit's bedroom. Nicole lounged in the doorway, talking to her aunt.

"Hi. How was your weekend?" she asked Nicole.

Nicole shrugged. "Okay, I guess."

Anne's eyebrows went up. "Only okay?"

"Gross Gwen was around all the time. Daddy dropped me off at Michelle's Friday."

"I thought you wanted to see Michelle."

"Yeah, but he left me there all day. I mean, I liked it,

but . . . oh, I don't know. I thought I'd do something with him, you know."

"Yeah, I know." Anne paused. "Are you set to return to Colorado?"

Nicole nodded. "I'm glad we're going back."

"Me, too." Anne smiled. There was a sense of anticipation in her that she hadn't known in a long time. "Me, too."

Chapter Thirteen

HE COULD HARDLY WAIT TO SEE HER. THE THREE DAYS ANNE and the children were away had been so empty it scared him. He had worked over at Sophia's house a little, but he and Sophia had just rattled around in the big old house. It had been too quiet without the kids, and there had been no pulse-quickening awareness that at any moment Anne might come into the room, or that he might run into her on his way down the stairs. So he had stopped working there and had returned to his cottage, but even his wood seemed dull and lifeless. He kept thinking about her.

Mark took a fresh string of horses to the stable early Monday morning, then made himself wait there until nine before he went to the main house. After all, he couldn't barge into Heartwood at the crack of dawn. No doubt they were tired from their trip and wanted to sleep. Finally, when he couldn't wait any longer, he saddled three horses and led them to the house. He hoped Anne hadn't forgotten about his invitation to a nature trip or decided that she didn't want to go.

He looped the reins through the old iron horse-head hitching posts in front of the house and went up the porch steps. Anne answered his knock on the front door, and the sight of her took his breath away. It was crazy, but she looked even lovelier than he remembered. There was a hint of sparkle to her eyes, a glow that hadn't been there before.

His stomach tightened. She was beautiful. He wanted to pull her to him and kiss her until he couldn't think anymore. His smile was stiff. "Hello."

"Mark! Hi. Come on in."

He wondered what could have added the glow to her face. Had seeing her ex-husband again put it there? Mark cleared his throat and stepped inside. "Nice weekend?"

Anne shrugged. "I guess. It was nice to get the check. I'm afraid Nicole and I aren't quite ready. I wasn't sure when you were coming."

"Doesn't matter. I'll wait. You, uh, you still want to go?"

"Sure. Why not?"

"I don't know. I thought you might be too tired or something."

"No. Heavens, Nicole would have my head. She's been looking forward to this ever since you suggested it. She talked about it all the way back on the plane."

Nicole. It wasn't the answer he longed for, but Mark reminded himself that his rule of life was to settle for reality, not cling to dreams.

The baby stepped into the doorway at the end of the hall, thumb in his mouth and a small blanket trailing from one hand. When he saw Mark, the thumb popped out, and he shrieked Mark's name. He came running, blanket rippling behind him. Mark grinned and bent to catch him. He tossed him high in the air, and John Peter squealed with delight. Again and again he threw him up in the air, and when Mark stopped, John Peter demanded, "More. More."

"More!" Mark repeated with a pretense of outrage. "You want more? How about more of this?" He began to tickle him, and John Peter squirmed to the floor, giggling and thrashing around.

Anne looked on, smiling. Mark had no inhibitions where the baby was concerned. She wished she could have even a fraction of that warmth turned on her. When the doorbell had rung, she had guessed it was Mark, and excitement had begun to fizz inside her. By the time she reached the door and opened it, she knew she was smiling idiotically. She wondered if he had noticed. She wondered if he had felt anything like that, too.

She watched as he picked up the baby and nuzzled its neck, his black hair tangling with the corn-silk blond strands of John Peter's hair. Anne was very aware of Mark physically—the strength of his hands and arms, the texture of his skin, the sharp blackness of his eyebrows and lashes. She turned away abruptly.

"I'll get Nicole. We'll be ready in a minute." Anne ran up the stairs.

It was a slow, pleasant sort of day. They followed the creek back into the mountains, and as the horses plodded along, Mark pointed out the dangers of the creek as well as the fact that the direction of its flow could be used as a constant if you were lost. They left Iron Creek and wandered farther into the trees. Sometimes they stopped and dismounted so that Mark could lead them deeper into the undergrowth. He pointed out the different kinds of trees and bushes, warning which ones were poisonous. He took them past his house, where Anne had never been before.

They rode in sun-dappled serenity, the sun a lazy warmth on their heads and shoulders, muted by the shelter of tall pines. The air was wonderfully laden with the smell of pine, and the only sounds were the crunch of pine cones and needles beneath the horses' feet and an occasional blown-out breath. They rode single file most of the time, with Mark in front and Anne bringing up the rear. Anne was content to breathe in the peaceful atmosphere and watch Mark's back. Nicole hung upon his words and asked eager questions, but most of the time Anne hardly heard what he said, simply listened to his voice.

They returned long before Nicole wanted to, but Mark insisted that he had to work on her room and promised that he would take them out into the woods again soon. Mark went home to clean up and change clothes and returned to Heartwood not long after Anne put the baby down for his nap. Nicole had wheedled her mother into letting her play outside, now that Mark had shown them around, promising to stay with the creek. For once, neither of the children were in the room with Mark, so Anne seized the opportunity to sit down and watch him work.

"How was Dallas?" he asked.

Anne shrugged. "The same. Busy. I've gotten unused to it. I was amazed at how noisy it was. How rushed."

"I couldn't live in a city," he agreed. He paused, then went on cautiously, "Did you see the kids' father?"

"Bryan?" Anne chuckled at the memory. "Yes. I certainly did. We had one of our usual friendly meetings."

"Meaning?"

"Meaning we were at each other's throats."

Mark's hand relaxed around the handle of the scraper, and he realized how tightly he had clenched his fingers on it. "Is he still mad about your coming up here?"

"Actually, we didn't have time to get into that. We argued about you."

"Me?" Mark swung around, amazed. "Why in the world would you argue about me?"

"I think he's a little jealous of you."

"Jealous?" The breath caught in Mark's lungs, and again he clutched the scraper like a life preserver.

"Because Nicole talked about you so much while she was with him."

"Oh. I see."

"He wanted to know who you were and what you were like, and he wasn't sure I should let Nicole associate with you."

"Why? Does he think I'm a pervert or something?"

Anne shrugged. "Who knows what Bryan thinks? He's a very suspicious person. He made some vague warnings about Vietnam vets."

Mark grimaced. "Did he say anything like that to Nicole?"

"Not that I know of. She didn't mention it. Probably not, knowing Bryan. He doesn't talk to kids; I mean, not like you'd talk to a person. Anyway, I told him you were nice, and we argued. Then I asked him why he acts the way he does toward John Peter. Amazingly enough, he told me."

"How does he act?"

"He doesn't like him."

"Doesn't like him? How could you not like him?"

"Thank you. That's how I feel about him. But to Bryan, John Peter is just a baby he didn't want. The pregnancy that kept Bryan from leaving me when he wanted to. So he ignores him."

"He's crazy." Mark went back to the wall.

Anne smiled. "I've thought the same thing myself." She paused. She wondered if Mark had missed her. "Anything happen here while we were gone?"

"Same old stuff." Except that he'd been unbearably lonely. He wondered if she had given him even a thought while she was gone.

"Will you stay for supper tonight?"

"Sure, if you want me to."

"Of course. You're always welcome."

Welcome. Mark guessed he was. But "welcome" wasn't at all the same thing as "wanted."

Mark kept looking at Anne throughout supper. She had changed clothes before the meal and now wore a shimmery blue blouse with big puffed sleeves. Her skin glowed, and her eyes seemed twice as blue as usual. Mark had trouble remembering there was anyone else at the table.

When they finished, John Peter pulled Sophia to the den to finish the intriguing search of a closet that they had begun before supper. Nicole cleared the table quickly. It was a task she had undertaken after Mark began eating with them regularly. He had suggested in a firm tone that she ought to do it to help her mother. Nicole had gazed at him, horrified, for a moment, but then she had gotten up and done it without a murmur of protest. She had continued to do it, too, with only an occasional reminder. Usually she dawdled over the job, but tonight she rushed. Her favorite program was on TV, and she hurried into the den to watch it as soon as the last plate was stacked on the counter.

"Well, I guess it's my baby now," Anne sighed and stood up. "Want another cup of coffee?"

"Sure. I'll get it." Mark went to the coffeemaker on the counter and filled his cup. "One for you?"

"Well . . . why not? The dishes can wait a while." Anne sat back down. She and Mark had gotten into the habit of lingering at the table after the others, chatting and often sharing a cup of coffee before they tackled the dishes. Anne enjoyed this slice of time more than any other in the day; she was quite happy to stretch it out.

Mark put her cup on the table and sat down across from her. They sipped their coffee quietly, neither wanting to break the tranquil companionship of the moment. Mark knew he shouldn't have taken the drink and the extra time with Anne. He'd been around her too much today already. It was dangerous; it made him want to forget the boundaries.

"I was happy to get back," Anne said, sitting forward and leaning her elbows on the table. "It's so beautiful here. Sometimes in the evening I sit on the front porch and listen to the creek and the evening sounds. Do you ever do that?"

"Yeah. Lots of times." He would sit and listen and think about her. Dangerous again, but it sure beat the things he used to sit and think about.

"Why did you move to Iron Creek?"

He looked startled. "I thought I'd told you. I don't get along well with people. I'm better suited for the mountains."

"No. I mean, why Iron Creek in particular? Why not some other place?"

"Oh. Jim Mueller told me about it. He offered me the job and suggested I rent from Sophia."

"Then he was already a friend of yours."

"Sort of. He worked at one of the hospitals where I was a patient. He knew I liked horses and was raised around them. We used to talk about horses a lot. When he left the hospital to come here, he told me where he was going and invited me up here when I got out. I didn't come right away; I was an outpatient for a long time. But the idea appealed to me more every day I was in the city. So eventually I moved here."

"I see. Was Jim a doctor?"

He shook his head. "No. A physical therapist. He worked

with me a lot. He'd done it for fifteen years, and finally he burned out."

Anne smiled faintly. "Heartwood seems to be a kind of refuge for everyone."

"Not you."

"Yes. Me, too. I came here to help Sophia, granted, but as much as anything I was running from my life in Dallas. You know, a time-out from reality."

"Taking care of a dying woman? That's not reality?"

"That scared me, believe me. Still scares me—I don't think I'm cut out to be a person to lean on. But even so, it was a kind of reprieve."

"You know, I think you're wrong. I think you're very much a woman people can lean on."

"Me?" Anne laughed shortly. "Are you kidding?"

"No, I'm not. You have the kind of warmth that . . . draws people. You give comfort just by being near." He stopped, aware that he was again skirting close to trouble. Another minute and he'd be pouring out his guts to her, practically begging for sympathy and love. Mark stood up abruptly. "I guess we better get to those dishes."

Anne blinked, startled by the sudden change in topic. She wanted to reach out and pull him back down, to tell him that she wanted to hear more. What he had said had been tantalizing—not just the words, but the tone of his voice, the softness in his dark eyes. He had sounded as if he was talking about himself, not people in general. As if she warmed *him*. Anne started to speak, to protest his leaving, but then she stopped. What could she say? Ask him to tell her more about how wonderful she was? She pressed her lips together and followed Mark to the sink.

Rolling up the voluminous sleeves of her blouse, she began to scrape the dishes and hand them to Mark, who set them in the dishwasher. It was the easy routine they had fallen into over the past couple of weeks whenever he ate with them. He insisted on helping with the dishes, and they worked well together. But tonight Anne sensed a restlessness in him, an unusual brooding. He moved jerkily, and his eyes quickly slid away whenever they rested on her. Now and then their fingers touched as she handed him a dish, and each time he whipped the dish away, moving his whole body from her.

Anne wasn't sure what the problem was. She began to lightly tease him as she used to tease Nicole when she was in a fit of glooms. She joked about the job they were doing and swore she'd write him a recommendation as a housewife and pulled a long face when he didn't respond. Anne kept teasing Mark until at last she won a reluctant smile from him. He closed the dishwasher and walked behind her, rolling down his sleeves. As he passed, he bumped her arm a little, so that the bottom of her sleeve touched the water. Anne turned and he flashed a grin at her, then turned away and headed for the table.

"Oh!" Anne exclaimed in mock rage and grabbed a dish towel. Mark's back was to her, and without his seeing her, she whipped the thin towel around and around between her hands as she had when she and Bit were young and had indulged in kitchen spats. When the towel was twisted like a rope, she whipped it out with a loud snap and popped Mark lightly on the rear of his jeans.

Surprised, laughing, he whirled around and grabbed the other end of the offending towel. Twisting his sinewy hand, he wrapped it around and around his hand, reeling the towel in. But instead of letting go of the rag, Anne came with it. With each slow twist of his hand, Mark pulled her closer. The laughter left his face; there was no expression except in his eyes, and they were hard and bright. Anne gazed into his face, lips parting slightly, excitement fizzing in her stomach. Then his hand reached the end of the towel and met her own hand. He took it and pulled her one step closer. He bent his head and kissed her.

It was a soft, undemanding kiss, a tasting. Anne felt his hand tremble on hers, and then his hand slid up her arm, and his arms encircled her, pressing her into him. His kiss deepened, his lips sinking into hers, his tongue entering her mouth. His mouth was hot and urgent. He ground her against his bones and flesh. It was a hungry, almost desperate kiss, an eager, primitive seeking. Anne grasped the front of his shirt, shaken by the emotion he conveyed and unsure how to respond. Instincts, long tamped-down in her, surged upward, and she trembled, confused and eager.

Abruptly Mark broke away from her, stepping back. Color blazed beneath his tanned cheeks, and his black eyes crackled. Anne stared, dazed, unable to gather her scattered thoughts.

Mark rapped out an oath. His chest rose and fell unevenly, and his voice was hoarse. "I'm sorry, Anne. I'm sorry."

He lurched from the room, awkward in his haste, grabbing his cane as he rushed out the door and down the porch steps. Anne stood frozen for a moment before she hurried out the door after him. She stopped on the porch and watched Mark as he hastened across the clearing toward the shelter of the trees. She wanted to call him back, to run after him, but she held back, stymied by her own confusion and Mark's obvious reluctance. She leaned against the slender wooden column and looked as he disappeared into the trees.

She remained there for a long time. Then slowly she turned and went inside. She was distant and preoccupied the rest of the evening, going mechanically through the evening routines of putting the kids to bed and playing a round of gin with Sophia. When she went to bed later, she had trouble sleeping. Mark's kiss had left her pent-up and unsatisfied, full of doubts and confusion. She had been surprised when he kissed her, but, given the fact that he had kissed her, it seemed even more astounding that he had left so abruptly, saying he was sorry. Sorry? For what? Why had he stopped? What had sent him rushing like a madman back to his cabin?

The kiss must mean he wanted her. Why else would he kiss her—and with such eager passion? She hadn't exactly been cool to his kiss; he couldn't have thought she rejected it. Could he? Maybe she had shown a terrible lack of expertise—but surely he would try more than one kiss before deciding she was a dud! Then why had he left? Was he scared of commitment? Was he put off by her eager response, rather than the opposite? Did he still love his wife? Did he think of her only as the kids' mother and therefore beyond the realm of sexuality? She couldn't figure it out.

Equally disturbing was her reaction to the kiss. She had flared up like dry tinder. Her passions had been dormant so long Anne had assumed they were largely dead. The whole summer Mark had been making inroads on those beliefs, awakening her deadened feelings. She had begun to look forward to their revival, but she hadn't expected such a sudden thunderburst of passion. His kiss had shaken her to her toes, sent her thoughts flying every which way . . . and left her hungering for more. She had felt a swift upsurge of desire so hot that she still felt jittery and warm inside. She was achy and jumpy and eager, like a young girl in the throes of first love.

Only this time she was a woman, and she had a woman's passion, far more mature and knowledgeable. She knew what she wanted and had less interest in waiting for nature to take its course. She wanted Mark in her arms, inside her. She wanted to feel his mouth on her body, to feel his supple fingers caressing her. She wanted to touch him and taste him and experience the hard, delicious weight of his body upon hers.

Anne closed her eyes as a chill ran down her. She was getting positively lascivious. It was way out of the ordinary for her. And it was terribly exciting.

She rose, turned on the light, and began to pace the room. By one-thirty, she was still awake, and she decided to check on John Peter, just to have something to do. She left her room and padded down the hall. The glossy wooden boards beneath her feet were chilly, and she hurried.

Then she saw the light from beneath Sophia's door, and she stopped. Sophia was still up at one-thirty? She moved closer and leaned her head against the door. There was a click inside and a rustle of material. Anne tapped lightly on the door. "Sophia?"

She heard footsteps, and the door opened. Sophia stood in the doorway, clad in her nightgown with a worn flannel bathrobe over it. In the dim light she looked older and more tired than usual. Her eyes were sunk deep in their sockets, her mouth a grim line. Anne stared.

"Why are you still up? Is something the matter?"

Sophia shook her head. "I often stay up this late. Recently. You're usually asleep by now."

"I didn't realize." Anne frowned. "Do you feel bad? Could I get you something?"

Sophia attempted a smile. "A new body, perhaps." She shook her head. "Sorry. I don't make very good jokes in the middle of the night."

"Would you like to sit and talk for a while?"

"If you aren't sleepy . . ."

"No. I couldn't get to sleep. I was about to check on the baby for want of anything better to do."

"Come in." Sophia led the way through the connecting door into her sitting room. "It's more comfortable to sit in here." She sank into an easy chair and leaned her head back.

"Why are you having trouble sleeping?" Anne asked bluntly. "Are you in pain?"

Sophia nodded. "Some. The pain is worse at night. I suppose it's because nothing's happening to take my mind off it."

"I didn't know . . ."

"Don't look so worried. It's part of the territory. I knew it was coming. The doctor gave me pills for the pain, but I try not to take a lot of them. I don't want to end my life drugged."

"But surely, at night, I mean, if it would help you sleep. . . ."

"Oh, I gave in and started taking them. I'm not a stoic. But the past few nights they haven't been as effective." She grimaced. "That's looking at it backward. I imagine they're as effective as ever; the pain's gotten worse."

"Can you take more?"

"I suspect I'll have to. I just took a second pill. I'll start feeling it in a little while." She pushed a hand through her hair. Anne noticed how frail and thin her hand looked, flesh clinging to the bone.

"Have you lost weight?"

"A little. Ten pounds or so."

Anne frowned and began to chew at a cuticle. A spasm

crossed Sophia's face, and Anne leaped to her feet. "Sophia? What's the matter?"

Sophia shook her head. "A twinge. It's gone. Nothing to get excited about." She motioned Anne back down. "To be quite truthful, I think this is the beginning of the end. Next time we go to Fitch, I don't think the doctor's going to be as pleased. I can feel myself beginning to slide."

Tears burned in Anne's eyes. "Oh, Sophia . . ."

"Don't be sad."

"How can I not be? Do you think—could you be mistaken?"

Sophia shrugged. "It's possible. But it'll come sooner or later. I don't expect any miracles. I'm very happy you came here. It's made a world of difference for me. But I didn't bring you up here to make you unhappy."

"Of course not. I know that. But I don't want you to die."

"And I don't want your pity. I don't want your sorrow. I'm not sorry that I'm dying. That probably sounds strange to you, but it's true. When I first learned about it, it shocked me. I thought of all I'd missed, the things I'd done wrong. I wanted to see you. I wanted to get my life in order. Now I've done that. I'm as prepared as I could possibly be. I'm ready." She closed her eyes, and for a moment Anne thought she had dozed off. Then she raised her lids and looked at Anne. "I don't want the pain, but I'm looking forward to getting it over with. I'll see Gary again."

Tears spilled out of Anne's eyes and down her cheeks. Sophia's eyes were watery, too, now. Her voice trembled. "Do you know how long it's been since I've seen him? Over thirty years. Can you imagine? Thirty-two years without your only child. It's a long time, and I don't think a day's gone by that I haven't missed him. I think to myself: it can't be so very bad, can it? You'll be with Gary again."

Anne made an incoherent noise and clapped her hand to her mouth to hold back the crying inside. Sophia's eyes drifted closed, then opened again. She pointed a stern forefinger at her granddaughter. "Now don't you go all sobby on me, you hear? You hardly know me, remember that. My death won't ruin your life nor make you lonely. If I thought I

219

left you more unhappy than before you came, I wouldn't have asked you here. I'm glad I met you, and I want you to be glad you met me."

"I am, I am."

"Good. Then remember what I said—there's no need to mourn me. I'm expecting to get back a piece of me that's been missing for a long time." She paused. "I think the medicine's starting to work now. I'm getting sleepy. If you don't mind, I'll go to bed."

"Of course. Can I help you?"

Sophia shook her head. "No. I'm fine. Go ahead; check on the baby and get to bed." She rose and walked to the connecting door. She stopped and turned back toward Anne. "You know what?"

"What?"

"I watched Mark Pascal looking at you tonight at the dinner table. I think he's got a thing for you."

Laughter bubbled up Anne's throat, mingling with the raw taste of tears. "Oh, Sophia. Sophia. You're something else."

Chapter Fourteen

IT WAS THREE DAYS BEFORE MARK CAME TO WORK AGAIN. ANNE remained confused and simmering with curiosity about his kiss, and the feelings grew with each day that passed. Why did he stay away? What was going on?

Sometimes she thought about walking over to his cottage and boldly confronting him, but she couldn't work up the courage. Once she went so far as to start along the path to his house, but she stopped, riddled with self-doubt. Maybe she had misinterpreted everything; maybe he didn't really want her. Or he might be appalled at her forwardness. Anne could smile at her thoughts—she sounded like a woman from decades ago, worrying about being thought "forward." But she couldn't shake her ingrained lack of confidence. The thought of taking such a step only to discover that Mark didn't really want her froze her.

So Anne didn't go to the cabin. Instead she followed her usual routines, taking the kids to day-care, playing gin with Sophia, helping Linda around the house. She and Nicole rode out on horses several times, and each time Nicole begged her to ask Mark to go with them. Anne found it difficult to explain why they could not. Nicole missed Mark and frequently asked where he was and why he didn't come to see them. Even John Peter, usually blissfully unconcerned about anything or anyone that was not with him at the moment, leaned against his mother's leg and plaintively said "Mawuk, Mawuk." Anne didn't know how to answer either of them. Somewhat mendaciously, she told Nicole she didn't know why Mark hadn't come to the house as he usually did. Nicole immediately wanted to go to his cabin and ask him. At first Anne refused to let her, but after a couple of days, Anne mentally shrugged and thought, why not? Maybe it would spur him to return, or at least to make some sort of explanation.

So she let Nicole run over to his cabin to visit. The girl came back several hours later, and Anne went out eagerly to meet her. "Hi, sweetheart. Did you find Mark?"

"Yeah." Nicole smiled. "He's not mad. He told me I hadn't done anything wrong."

"Of course not. Did you think you had?"

Nicole shrugged. "I thought I must have done something. But he was just working on the shelves for our rooms. He said it was easier to do it at his house, where he has sawhorses and an electric saw and all that stuff. So I stayed and watched him. They're really pretty. He's got them sanded, he says he'll paint them or stain them next and then attach them to the walls. He said he was sorry he hadn't told us he'd be gone a few days."

"I see. Did he say when he'd come back?"

Nicole shook her head. "Hunh-uh. He said he'd come when he finished the shelves. He asked me if you'd said anything about him being gone."

"What did you tell him?"

Nicole frowned. "Nothing much. I said you told me you didn't know why he hadn't come back but that he probably had a good reason. He acted kinda weird."

"What do you mean?"

"I don't know, exactly. He asked me strange questions, like how you looked when you said that and if you seemed glad he hadn't come. Did you all have a fight or something?"

"No. No, of course not."

222

"Then why do you keep asking about each other and what you said and everything?"

"'Cause we're silly, I suppose." Anne smiled down at her daughter. "Like you, I was afraid maybe I'd offended him."

"He didn't say anything about being mad at you. Maybe he thinks you're mad at him."

Anne almost walked over to his house that evening, but every time she thought of it, the tension in her stomach would start up again, and she kept putting it off until it was too late. The next day, she told herself. After she took the kids to their sitter she would go.

When Anne returned from Iron Creek the next morning, she dressed in her best-fitting pair of denim shorts and a thin pastel blouse that did flattering things for her skin and her figure. She curled her hair and put on a little bit of make-up. She checked her image in the bathroom mirror at least three times. Anne knew she looked as good as she was going to, but she dreaded the thought of putting those looks to the test. She wet her lips and left her bedroom, slowly trailing down the steps. Halfway down, she saw Mark round the corner newel post and start up the stairs. She stopped abruptly. Mark lifted his head at the small sound she made, and he, too, stopped.

His hand tightened around the handle of his toolbox. He started to speak, then stopped and cleared his throat. "Anne."

"Hello, Mark." Anne laced her fingers together behind her back so he couldn't see their trembling. "How are you?"

"Fine. And you?"

"Fine."

"Good. Uh—I've been working on the shelving."

"Nicole told me."

"She said her wallpaper had come in."

"Yeah. The store's shipping it on to us. They said it would get here today or tomorrow. Nicole's really excited about it."

"I bet. I'll finish the walls today. Then I can put up Nicole's paper as soon as it gets here."

"She'll love that." Anne continued slowly down the steps until she stood beside him in the hall. Mark had glanced at her almost furtively once or twice as they talked, but the rest of the time he had kept his gaze determinedly away from her, looking at the floor, the steps, above her head or just beside it—anywhere except her face.

Standing this close, Mark was forced to look at her, and he did. His jaw was rigid, and there was a raw emotion in his eyes, something Anne couldn't identify, almost fear, almost anger. A kind of—disgust? Anne's stomach quivered at the thought; he *had* been turned off by her the other night. "Anne? I—" Again he looked away, concentrating on the large knob atop the newel. "I want to apologize for the other night. I haven't come by the past couple of days because I was . . . too ashamed, I guess. I felt like a real heel, and I was afraid you were so mad you wouldn't want to even see me."

Anne couldn't think of anything to say. She stared at him, trying to make sense out of his words. "Why?"

He frowned. "Why?" He glanced up at her, then away again. He shrugged. "Well, you know, because I—well, I mean, after you've been so nice to me, it was a crummy thing to do. You've been great: inviting me to stay for supper all the time; treating me like I was part of the family. It's meant a lot. It made me feel—hell, I can't explain it. It just made me feel good. Normal. Then I had to go and mess it up."

Mark's voice had gotten softer and softer as he talked, until Anne had to strain to hear his last few words. She stepped closer, and Mark braced himself as though it was an effort not to move away. Anne grimaced. "I don't understand what you're talking about. Why are you apologizing? For kissing me?"

"Yes. I don't usually go around mauling women. It won't happen again. I promise."

"Why not?" Anne asked boldly.

"Why not?" His head snapped up and he stared at her with narrowed eyes. "What do you mean? I won't let it, that's why. I normally have a lot of control over myself."

"Mark, I'm really confused. Didn't you want to kiss me?"

"Yes, of course." He glared, almost hating her for asking these questions and prolonging his agony, forcing him to strip bare his soul.

"And didn't I kiss you back?" He was silent, just staring at her, and Anne hurried on. "I'm sorry. You'll have to explain to me. I don't understand. This isn't usually what happens after two people kiss each other. I thought you wanted to kiss me; I thought you enjoyed it. Then you ran off like I'd sprouted horns or something, and I didn't see you for three days. Now you come back telling me you're sorry for kissing me, and I honestly don't understand why."

"I'm sorry because I didn't want to upset you or make you angry. I don't want you to tell me to never come back."

"Well, if you didn't want to make me angry, why'd you leave and not say a word to me for three days?" Anne stepped back, crossing her arms defensively. "I'm a grown woman, Mark. I can take it if you tell me you regretted kissing me. I can accept it if you wanted to kiss me, but didn't like it and wished you hadn't." That was a lie, of course; it would hurt like anything if that was his problem. But she had to pretend to accept it if that was what it would take to put their relationship back on an even course. They simply couldn't remain awkward with each other when they would be together so much while he finished the children's rooms. "It's been a long time since I was in the social arena as a single woman. My kissing technique is doubtless dated . . ." She tried to keep her tone light and twist her lips upward in a smile.

"Good God, Anne, it wasn't that I didn't like it!" Mark hissed. "It's all I've thought about for three days! But I—aren't you angry? Aren't you offended?"

"Because you kissed me? No. I, well . . ." Anne blushed and glanced away. "I enjoyed it."

He set the toolbox down with a crash, and Anne jumped at the noise. Her head whipped back up. She was sure her face was red as fire, and she felt like a naïve fool. You wouldn't think a woman who'd been married for ten years would act like such a blushing virgin.

Mark moved forward and grasped Anne's upper arms. His eyes were glittering now, and his fingers dug into her. "What? What are you saying? You didn't mind?"

Anne shook her head. "I liked it. Didn't you?"

"God, yes. Couldn't you feel how much I wanted you?"

He was staring down at her intently, so close to her that she felt the warmth of his body. "I thought you did. That's why I couldn't understand when you left so suddenly—and didn't come back for three days. Why did you?"

His fingers moved a little on her arms, loosening their hold and beginning a slow, caressing, circular movement. Still his black eyes searched her face, as if he would find there some proof that her words were real. "I didn't think—I never dreamed you might have enjoyed it. I figured you were disgusted with me, hated me."

"For kissing me?" Anne asked in astonishment. "It's not as if you raped me. You kissed me, and I kissed you back."

"I wanted you," he said huskily. "I've wanted you for a long, long time. But—how could you want me? You've been kind, but you're a sweet woman. You'd be nice to any stray. I didn't figure it meant you had any particular interest in me."

He bent slowly, as if to give Anne ample time to pull away, and brushed his lips against her forehead. Anne leaned into him, her hands coming up to rest on his chest. He slid his hands up her arms and onto her shoulders, spreading them out to hold the back of her neck and head. His voice was shaky as he whispered, "You're beautiful." He pressed his lips to her forehead again. "Beautiful. Oh, Anne, tell me you're not joking."

"I'm not joking," she replied with some asperity. Anne tilted back her head to look into his eyes. "You certainly are a doubting Thomas."

There was hunger and a dazed joy in his eyes. "I must have replayed that kiss in my mind a million times."

"Me, too."

His fingertips trembled slightly against her scalp. His mouth drifted down to hers, and he kissed her tentatively. When she didn't move, his soft kiss deepened, and he pulled her into him, wrapping his arms around her tightly. At last he pulled away and rested his head against her hair. Anne snuggled into the warm comfort of his T-shirt. The faint smell of wood shavings clung to his clothes as it always did, mingling with his own male scent, and it was both comforting and enticing. Mark rubbed his cheek against her hair. "I want you," he murmured. "I'm inept as hell about this."

He released her and stepped back, glancing around. "This isn't the time or place, I guess," he said and crossed his arms across his chest. He held himself stiffly, and his face was set.

Anne's hands knotted in frustration. It was true that Linda or Sophia might appear at any moment, but she hated to let this moment slip away from her. "The kids are at day-care this morning."

Mark glanced at her, eagerness warring with doubt and surprise in his face. "Do you—would you like to go back to my place?"

"Yes." Her voice was low, and her cheeks were stained with color again, but Anne was too anxious to be alone with him to allow modesty to stand in her way.

Mark swallowed and held out his hand. She took it. His skin was searing. He gripped her hand tightly, and they slipped out the front door and walked across the clearing to the path through the trees. Anne could think of nothing to say. Her mind was too full of uncertainty and hope and excitement. She was a little afraid and very eager.

The walk took forever. Mark slipped his fingers between hers, and after a moment his thumb began a light, rhythmic caress on the back of her hand. Anne glanced up to find him watching her. His face was a tight mask, his eyes burning, and she knew that he wanted to stop and kiss her. Anne leaned against him. He took his hand from hers and slid his arm around her shoulders. They were closer now, their bodies touching at hip and chest; his hard ribs pressed into the side of her breast.

They walked along, touching but not talking, intensely aware of each other, so that by the time they arrived at Mark's cabin, they were alive with anticipation, skin tingling wherever they touched. Yet at the same time, the long silence and the very intensity of their desires made them awkward. Anne was unused to casual sex; she hadn't slept with any man but her ex-husband, and it had been a long time since she had been with him. Mark, on the other hand, had for years been used to nothing but casual sex. He had felt no emotion for any woman he slept with and had never seen them more than once. It was his way of protecting himself against hurt or ridicule or pity. But now he realized that he had done it for so long that he hardly knew how to act with a woman he cared for. He was afraid he would rush Anne, might frighten or hurt her. He was terrified she would turn from him in disgust if she saw his naked, wounded leg.

Anne, on the other hand, feared Mark would lose interest when he saw her unclothed body. She was, after all, 31 years old and the mother of two children. Would he see the faint white stretch marks at the base of her abdomen? Would he care? Would he think her belly too rounded, as Bryan had? Her legs too heavy? She didn't know how to act or what to do. She had never been in this position before. The closest thing to it had been her wedding night, for she had been a virgin when she married. But even that had been different, for she had been younger then and more assured of her beauty, yet more fearful and less eager for what was to come.

When they entered the cabin, they stopped awkwardly near the door. Mark stepped away from her and jammed his hands into his back pockets. Anne swallowed and attempted a smile.

"Are you as nervous as I am?" Mark asked suddenly.

Anne nodded, a giggle escaping to betray her tension. "If so, you must be awfully nervous."

"I am."

Anne looked at him. "Would you—could you just hold me a minute?"

He came to her quickly and engulfed her in his arms, and Anne slid her own arms around his waist and leaned gratefully against his hard chest. Anne lay quiescently in his arms, letting the comfort of his nearness seep through her. Mark began to stroke her hair and back soothingly, and Anne relaxed. She felt hazy and drifting, suspended in time, yet every sense was vibrantly alive. The heat of his body warmed her flesh; she heard the steady thrum of his heart beneath her ear; his breath ruffled her hair. She was acutely aware of every inch of flesh upon her body and just as aware of his.

Gradually the gentle rhythm of his hand altered, and he

began to roam down her side, brushing the edge of her breast and curving over the line of her buttocks and thighs. The soft roundness of her derrière seemed to fascinate him, and his hand returned to it again and again, following its shape with ever slower strokes. Under her head, Anne felt his heart pick up its beat and his breathing quicken.

She didn't move, afraid he might stop if she showed the slightest cognizance of his sensual explorations. She waited, almost trembling, until finally Mark bent his head to hers and nuzzled into her hair, sighing her name. "Anne. Oh, Anne."

His lips touched the tender skin where her neck and shoulders joined. It was the barest brushing of flesh on flesh, and it made her shiver. She snuggled into him, sighing with pleasure. He continued to nibble and kiss the sensitive skin while his hands moved over her body. He maneuvered their linked bodies over to the bed and sat down on it, pulling Anne into his lap. She could feel the hard, insistent bulge beneath his jeans pressing into her buttocks. He continued to nuzzle her neck as his hand slid down her front and insinuated itself between her legs. His palm was hard against the fleshy mound of her femininity, and his fingers stroked the denim seam of her shorts between her legs, pressing it up against her. Rubbing, caressing, searching out the tiny tongue of pleasure hidden by folds of flesh and coarse material.

Mark's movements peeled away his reason stroke by stroke until he was nothing but hunger and need, hot animal force seeking its goal. Her name was a groan on his lips, a surrender to selfish, blatant want. Anne leaned back, arching up to thrust her pelvis against the pressure of his hand. Her hair slithered over his arm, and her head fell back to expose the long, curved line of her throat. It was as if she entrusted herself to him, offered up her most vulnerable parts to his need. Mark was filled with a deep, primitive longing to take her, use her, and yet hold her from all hurt, even that of his own strength.

He slid his lips along the satiny skin of her throat and traced the indentation at the base with his tongue. Anne dug her fingers into his hair and pressed her legs together around his hand. Then, at last, his mouth moved up to hers, and he kissed her as he had yearned to for so long. He tasted again the sweetness that had been a vivid, indelible memory for days and found it even more delicious.

He shuddered, and his passion broke its bounds. Suddenly he was wild and fierce, his arms and legs twining around her and squeezing her against him, his mouth avid and bruising. His lips twisted on hers, as if he must consume her from every direction, and his fingers came up to tangle in her hair, slightly moving her head from side to side with the movements of his mouth. He kissed her mouth, her face, her ears, trailing down her neck to the restrictive cloth of her blouse. His fingers fumbled with the buttons, clumsy with haste, and when at last he unfastened them, he let out a tormented growl at finding her brassiere still blocking him.

He snapped it apart and pushed the garments off her body, and her breasts were exposed to him, fleshy, pink-tipped mounds, quivering and succulent. Twisting, he lowered her to the bed and covered her with his body. His jeans were rough against Anne's shorts-clad legs; his shirt teased the sensitive nipples of her breasts. Crudely his pelvis rotated upon hers, and Anne moved, wrapping her legs around him. Mark groaned, his face contorted, and sweat shone on his face and neck.

His mouth was all over her, devouring and desperate, wild in his yearning, and Anne gave herself to him freely. His breath rasped in his throat; his hands trembled on her skin. For weeks he had suffered hot, tormenting dreams of Anne's naked body, and now he could not get enough of the reality. Yet neither could he linger to savor it because of the pounding need within him. Only the sheath of her body could ease the sweet agony in his loins. He rose to his knees, straddling her, and popped the snaps of her denim shorts, lust flooding him anew at the suggestive sound. Anne lifted her hips to enable him to pull down her clothes. He tore at his shirt impatiently, and Anne's hands moved to the fastenings of his jeans. Her movement sent desire surging through Mark, but he retained enough sense to leave the bed and remove his clothes, turning to block her view of his bad leg as he pulled off shoes and jeans and underwear. He whipped down the covers, and they slipped beneath them.

Anne turned to him, opening her arms, and he covered her with his body, sinking into the delicious softness. Her fingers caressed his arms and back, exploring the curve of musculature that bunched to hold his weight on his arms. Her legs moved apart, inviting him, and he came into her, filling her so that she cried out with satisfaction. Mark was unsure whether it was a cry of joy or pain, but he was past caring, unable to stop. He knew only the surge of raw instinct that drove his aching, distended maleness into her. She took him, gripping and moving in a way that drove his frenzy higher.

Anne had never felt such eager yearning for the joys of the body, such intensity of passion. Mark's ramming thrusts shook her again and again, filling her emptiness, yet stoking the ache of her desire so that it grew ever larger, ever more eager for satisfaction. At last the knot of desire tightened and exploded within her and above her, and Mark groaned and shook under the force of his own coming.

Anne looked at the face lying only inches from her own. Mark's black hair was tousled, tumbling loosely over his forehead. His eyes were closed, and thick, black lashes fanned his cheeks. The deep lines of his face were relaxed and he looked at peace for the first time since she had met him. Anne smiled and reached over to brush a lock of hair back from his eyes. He had fallen asleep almost immediately after their lovemaking, and Anne had enjoyed watching him sleep and thinking about what had just happened.

She had never experienced a lovemaking like that, even in the early days of her marriage. She had been too nervous and inexperienced then, and Bryan at his most passionate had never exhibited the kind of desire Mark had. Mark had been eager and hungry for her, as if he wanted to consume her. He had feasted on her, adoring her body, possessing her as if it were the pinnacle of his life. Anne smiled. No woman could resist that. But there had been more—a gentleness and a vulnerability in him that captured her heart. She had felt a magic in his touch that Bryan had never given her. His caresses had electrified her; she had wanted him with every fiber of her being, yearning to explore him with all her senses, aching to feel the full force of his passion. She had discovered a deep force within herself that heretofore had been a void. No matter what happened with Mark, Anne thought, she would never be the same.

Mark's eyes fluttered opened and closed, then opened wide. Shock was followed by remembrance, and he grinned slowly. "Hello. Did I fall asleep?"

Anne nodded, smiling. "You've slept for ages."

"You must have worn me out." She was there; he could see her, Mark thought. Yet he still could not quite believe it. It had happened too suddenly. His world had been turned upside down in the course of the morning. He had gone from miserable and aching with an unrequited love to blissful passion in her arms. It astounded him that she had told him she had enjoyed his kiss, that she had wanted to make love with him. He couldn't imagine what she could see in him. She had been divorced for a year and never had a man. Why rush into this with him?

Anne ran her forefinger along the lines of Mark's face, tracing nose and forehead, cheekbones and chin. He closed his eyes, luxuriating in the caress. "You look very peaceful when you sleep."

"When I sleep after making love with you," he corrected.

"Meaning I bore you?" she teased.

He raised up and slid his arm under her neck. "Meaning you released weeks of tension. Tension, I might add, built up by you."

"Not on purpose!" she protested.

"No, not on purpose. You did it entirely naturally." He gazed down at her for a moment, then bent to kiss her eyes and the tip of her nose. "You're very beautiful. Better than my dreams, even."

"Come on."

"I'm serious. Why should I joke?"

"Do you really think I'm pretty? Even with my clothes off?"

"Especially with your clothes off."

"No, really. I mean it."

"Of course. You're more than pretty. You're lovely and very, very desirable."

"Stretch marks and all?"

"I didn't notice them. Let me see." He peeled back the sheet and examined her naked body with a mockingly studious frown. "These little things?" He ran a finger over a mark, and she felt a shiver of excitement. She nodded. "I can hardly see them."

"And my pot belly? Bryan was always after me to let him take it off."

"This?" He spread his long, supple fingers across her abdomen. "This is not a pot belly." He bent and kissed her navel and the area just below. "This is pure beauty. Almost as beautiful as these." His mouth slid up to kiss each breast. When he looked up at her again, his face was flushed and his voice a trifle unsteady. "You're beautiful and feminine, the kind of woman every man dreams of."

Anne laughed delightedly, pinkening a little under the compliments. "I think that might be a bit of an exaggeration, but thank you anyway."

Mark gazed at her seriously. "Haven't other men wanted you?"

She shrugged. "Several guys have asked me out since I got divorced. When I was married there was always someone around who was willing to have an affair. But I never trusted what they said because they just wanted to get me into bed."

"Then trust me. You're very desirable. You're the first woman in years whom I've wanted like this. Wanted to have in my bed, wanted to make love to over and over, wanted to feel and know in every way." He broke off, aware of how much he revealed about himself, and ended his words with a fierce kiss.

Anne smiled to herself, basking in his words of praise. She felt warm and content and happier than she had in years. Suddenly a whole new world was opening up for her, bright and gleaming. She would have liked to talk about it. She wanted to tell him she loved him. But she knew better than that. Mark Pascal was a loner, and he would probably run like a scared rabbit if she mentioned the word love. So she contented herself with running her hand along the side of his face and down the sinews of his neck, letting her touch speak for her.

Mark rolled his head in the direction of her hand, then took her hand in his and brought it to his lips. He kissed her palm, tasting the faint trace of salt on her skin, and closed his eyes as desire washed through him again. He pressed her palm closer against his mouth, then began a slow trail of kisses up her arm until he reached her neck and shoulders. Anne arched her neck, giving herself up to the pleasures of his mouth. And slowly, leisurely, they made love once again.

Chapter Fifteen

ANNE WAS LATE PICKING UP THE CHILDREN FROM DAY-CARE, BUT she was too happy to feel even a twinge of guilt. Mark went with her to get them, and his presence so delighted the children that Nicole didn't utter a word of reproach at Anne's lateness.

They ate lunch together in town, and though Anne tried to be circumspect in front of Nicole and John Peter, she and Mark couldn't refrain from touching each other in little ways or looking at each other. Mark took her hand as they walked from the car to the restaurant. Anne saw that Nicole cast a sidelong glance at their clasped hands, but her daughter made no comment.

Afterward they drove back to Heartwood, and Mark went upstairs to work on Nicole's room while Anne puttered around trying to find something to keep her occupied. Nothing appealed to her, and she couldn't keep her mind on one subject long enough to accomplish anything. She and Sophia played a game or two of cards, but she had trouble concentrating and played so poorly that Sophia sent her a sharp look of surprise and curiosity.

Anne felt drawn to wherever Mark was. Every so often she ran up to Nicole's room to check on how he or the kids were doing or to offer to bring refreshments up. Whenever she entered, Mark couldn't keep his eyes off her, and his gaze turned her shivery inside. Anne knew she was inclined to giggle, but she couldn't work up any embarrassment over the way she acted. She simply couldn't hold in the delight she was feeling; it had to slip out somehow.

Mark stayed for supper, and after they cleaned the dishes, he and Anne sat on the porch watching the evening sky. His arm was around her shoulders and now and then he leaned over to kiss her lightly or nuzzle her hair. "Will you come home with me?" he asked huskily.

Anne swallowed. It was what she wanted to do more than anything. "I have to put the kids to bed."

"I'll wait."

"Then I usually play gin with Sophia." She glanced up at him, her eyes transmitting a little plea. She wanted badly to be with him, but she couldn't cut out her card games with Sophia. Not when Sophia had such a short time to live and enjoyed them so much. "I—could I come over after that? We usually finish about ten or ten-thirty."

He nodded. "I'll wait. I'll look at the tube while you're playing."

"You don't have to wait. I could walk over later."

He shook his head. "I don't mind. No point in your walking over by yourself." He found he didn't like the idea of her going along that path alone in the dark. Besides, he knew he'd be as useless at home by himself as he was here. All he could think of, all he wanted to do was touch Anne and kiss her.

He waited for her to finish the game, and afterward they strolled through the crisp, quiet night to his cabin and again made slow, sweet love. Anne noticed that Mark did not undress until he had turned off the light, and she remembered his efforts this morning to hide his lame leg from her as he undressed and dressed. She wanted to tell him that he didn't need to, but she held back. It was too early, she thought, to press him on any point.

Over the next few days they spent every available moment together, and instead of decreasing, it seemed as if their desire for each other's company grew. They made love often, but they also discovered the joys of lying together in bed and talking, revealing their lives and beliefs, softly laughing or exclaiming with outrage or listening quietly. Anne knew she was falling ever more deeply in love with Mark. Each day added to her understanding of him, her pleasure in his company, her longing to be with him.

Though it was obvious to everyone around them that there was a new, special feeling between them, they were careful not to advertise their physical relationship. They never made love in Anne's room at Heartwood, but always returned to Mark's cabin in the woods. They rarely went to the cabin at night, as they had that first evening, and their lovemaking was usually confined to the morning hours when the children were away and Sophia kept to her room. It was never enough time for Anne, and she wished, with a deep ache, that she could be with Mark any time they wanted. Still, she refused to make Sophia uncomfortable by openly acknowledging their intimate relationship, and she dreaded the effect it might have on the children. Much as they liked Mark, she wasn't sure they would accept a romantic relationship between them.

However, the restraint couldn't spoil their happiness. They were together so much when they weren't making love that it seemed ungrateful and selfish to wish for more.

Their lovemaking was sometimes wildly passionate, as it had been the first time, sometimes teasing and slow, at other times brimming with laughter and good humor. But it was always exciting and satisfying. The only thing that caused Anne distress was Mark's continued attempts to conceal his wounded leg. He undressed with the lights out if it was night, and in the daytime he was careful to turn so that she couldn't see the front of his bad leg. He would hop quickly into bed and pull up the sheet, never letting it slip off to reveal his leg unless they were in the midst of lovemaking.

His actions irritated Anne even as she felt pity for his obvious embarrassment. She wished he felt close enough to let her see the leg, that he trusted her enough. But she continued not to make an issue of it, knowing that such trust would come only with time and love.

One morning when Anne went to the cabin she found Mark surly and preoccupied. He was working on the back porch, and as Anne approached, she heard him utter an oath and slam down a tool onto the table. When he saw her, he forced a smile and offered her some coffee, but Anne could tell there was no real joy in his greeting. She was taken aback, but she tried to make small talk. When she got nothing but silence or short responses from Mark, she stopped talking. She sipped her coffee and watched Mark move restlessly about the room.

"Are you feeling okay?" she asked worriedly.

He turned and frowned at her. "Of course. There's nothing wrong. I'm having trouble with my work. Haven't you ever heard of artistic temperament?"

"I thought you didn't have any. You told me that your bad temper was just plain old bad temper."

He smiled briefly and shrugged. "You caught me there. You're right." He limped over to the far side of the porch and stared out at the trees. "I'm afraid I'm not very good company this morning."

Anne drew a deep breath. "Would you rather I left?"

"It's up to you. Go if you want to."

Tears burned her eyes, but Anne struggled to keep her voice calm and reasonable. "I don't want to go. I'd much rather be with you, even when you're grumpy as an old bear. I offered because I thought you might prefer that I not be here."

He sighed and walked back to her. "Ah, hell, I'm sorry, honey. I'm worse than an old bear." He took her into his arms and held her close. Anne cuddled against him, closing her eyes in relief. "It's not you. It's nothing to do with you. My leg's acting up. I kept putting too much weight on it yesterday while I was papering, and this morning it was sore as hell. The weather didn't help any." It had rained the night before and the day had dawned chilly and damp.

Anne squeezed him. "I'm sorry. Can I do anything?"

He shook his head. "Nah. It'll go away eventually. I'll try not to alienate you in the meantime."

"Would it help if I massaged it? My father, I mean, Bill,

had an old football injury, and when it ached I used to rub it for him. He said it made it feel better."

"It might. The physical therapists massaged it at the hospital."

"Why don't I try it? If it hurts, I'll stop."

"No. That's okay. It's too much trouble."

Anne leaned away from him to look up into his face. "It's no trouble. It won't take long, really. Come on."

"No." The word was clipped. Mark released her and moved away. "I don't need it."

"It won't hurt to at least try it."

He shook his head. "I don't want to."

"Why not?"

"Let's drop it. Okay?"

Anne raised one eyebrow. "You just don't want me to see your leg." He looked toward the wall and said nothing, but Anne persisted, "That's it, isn't it? It's the same reason you turn away when you undress or take your clothes off in the dark. You're hiding it from me."

Mark shifted his vision to a point on the floor. His voice was so low she had to strain to hear it. "Yes. It is. I don't want you to see it. Now could we drop the subject?"

"No!" She had tried not to press the issue, but the opportunity had dropped right into her lap, and she wasn't about to let it slide by. It wasn't healthy for Mark or their relationship. "I don't want to drop it. I think it's important. Not just for this moment. I don't like your hiding your leg from me."

He crossed his arms and took a step backward. His face assumed a set, emotionless expression. "Believe me, you wouldn't want to see it. It's ugly."

"I'm not a squeamish person. I could handle it."

"Anne, you don't realize . . . it's sickening. Why do you want to see it?"

"It's not that I get my kicks out of looking at wounds," Anne retorted sharply. "But it's part of you. I like all of you; I want to know all of you. I feel—I feel as if you're hiding something from me, and I don't like it. Please, Mark, I don't want you to treat me like a stranger. I don't want to be someone you have to hide things from or pretend to. I'd like for you to be comfortable with me. I want you to give me the chance to accept you, all of you."

Mark ground his teeth together in frustration. She didn't understand; she had no idea what she was asking. Anne didn't realize how gruesome his scars looked, how much he hated and was shamed by them. Every mark on his leg had scarred his soul as well, leaving a legacy of pain and humiliation. He remembered those endless dark nights in the ward and the ghostly wanderings of the other men who could not sleep but were more mobile than he. He remembered the doctors cutting away the bandages and examining his leg, often calling in colleagues to study his leg as if it were an object, not a part of a living man. He remembered the impersonal touch of the nurses. The agony and grim doubts of physical therapy. To show Anne his leg would be like opening all those years for her view, letting her see him weak and helpless and hurting.

He could imagine the horror on her face when she looked at it, the instinctive revulsion. He remembered his ex-wife's expression when she first saw the scars. Rachel had paled and turned away, sickened. After that she was careful not to come near his leg, and she looked away whenever he unthinkingly exposed it. As much as anything, his wounds had driven Rachel away from him.

Mark hated the thought of Anne's pity, but even more he hated the thought of her rejection. That would be more than he could bear, Mark thought. He couldn't let her see his leg. He couldn't stand it.

Yet how could he refuse her request? To turn her down would be to say that he didn't believe her loving words, that he couldn't trust her. She would be hurt, and it would drive a wedge between them. She didn't understand what she was asking; she thought it something far less than it was. There was no way she could understand until she saw the leg—and then it would be too late.

"Anne, please don't." His words were low and tormented.

Anne released a little sigh of defeat and sat down. Why did

he keep erecting this wall between them? Why couldn't he let her close? It was as if he didn't want her to share and soothe his past pain. He wanted to keep her out of his inner life.

"All right," she said quietly. "I won't talk about it anymore. I'm sorry. I didn't mean to stick my nose in." Tears glimmered in her eyes, and she turned her head away quickly so he wouldn't see them. It was the same problem she had had with Bryan when they were first married; she had always wanted to know about him, to share his hurts and joys and desires, but he had held her away, never inviting her into her mind or heart. It hadn't been long before she no longer cared about reaching him. With Bryan it had been a disappointment, a rejection, but now, with Mark, it was an open, pulsing wound, a deep slash into her love for him.

Mark saw the pain in her eyes, the hurt way her face fell before she turned her head aside, and her pain bit into him. He groaned, feeling trapped. If he didn't let her see his leg, she would be hurt and alienated; she would take it as a refusal of her loving concern. But if he let her see it, she would recoil from him; he might very well lose her. "Anne, you don't understand. It's not that I—I mean, I believe that you want to help me and that you think it won't bother you. But you don't know what it's like."

"How can I when you don't let me find out?" Anne retorted sharply. "I'm sorry. I shouldn't have said that. It's none of my business." She moved a little away from him.

Mark was chilled to the bone. She was withdrawing from him. She had offered him her healing warmth, as she always did, and now that he had rejected it, she might not give it again so freely. "No, don't say that." His hands went to his belt and unfastened the buckle, moving jerkily, as if they were not part of his body, but a separate, mechanical entity. "I'll show you."

Better to lose her now, he thought, as he moved to the bed and sat to remove his boots and socks. It wouldn't hurt as much as losing her later. Someday she was bound to see it; you couldn't hide something like his scars forever. A quick cut would be better than her moving gradually, slowly away from him, closing up bit by bit as she was starting to now. He could take it, he reminded himself, although he was careful not to glance her way. It was only a few moments of humiliation, and he'd borne that hundreds of times in the hospitals. But then it hadn't been Anne, a little voice cried inside him. They had been strangers, people he didn't care about. But Anne—Anne was everything to him. If she looked at him as Rachel had, if she turned away in disgust . . .

He unzipped his jeans and peeled them down, keeping his eyes averted from Anne. He didn't want to see her face when she saw the mass of scars. Yet when he pulled his left leg out of the jeans, he couldn't help but look into her eyes. It would be even worse not to know, always to wonder what her immediate reaction had been. And, crazily, there was the tiny hope deep inside that he couldn't dampen, the little yearning dream that she would not be repulsed.

Anne's palms began to sweat as she watched Mark undress. She felt guilty for having forced him into something he didn't want to do. What if he was right and she couldn't take the sight of his scarred flesh? What if it looked so awful that her stomach turned? What if the fact that it was Mark's flesh that had been hurt made her shudder? She couldn't show it; she must not hurt Mark. Anne wished she hadn't pushed the issue.

Then Mark pulled off his jeans and tossed them aside, and Anne looked at his leg. Jagged scars crisscrossed his thigh and clustered around the knee, trailing down onto his calf. Most were pale, a few pink, some wide, others thin. All were raised and fleshy. The scars at his knee were so numerous they ran together, and no hair grew there. Deep pits were sunk here and there into his flesh, as if chunks had been gouged out. The injured leg was thinner than the other one, and his knee and thigh came together at an odd angle.

"Oh, Mark." Anne found she wasn't sick at all. She felt only a deep wave of pity and empathy for Mark's pain. The tears that had hovered behind her eyes rushed out, spilling down her cheeks. It was only skin, nothing so terrible, but she knew Mark must have suffered unbearably. She thought of him wounded, his leg torn and bleeding; she thought of the agony of numerous operations and months of painful therapy. The searing pain, the throbbing ache, the endless hurt as he lay waiting for it to heal. It had cost him so much in time and emotional and physical pain.

Mark's breath stopped for a moment as he watched her. Instead of the amazed revulsion he had expected, Anne's face filled with sorrow until the sadness seeped out in tears. She walked toward him, and Mark waited, not daring to move or speak, not daring to hope. She gazed up into his face, her eyes huge and velvet with tears, then her eyes moved downward to his leg. She knelt before him and placed her hands gently on either side of his knee. She bent and pressed her lips to the center of the scars.

For a long time Mark stood, stunned. Anne's lips were feather-light, barely brushing his skin, and through the thick scars he could feel little except the sensation of pressure. But the realization of what she did seared into his brain. She had kissed the most repulsive part of him, then laid her soft cheek against it, bathing his wounds in her tears and her silken fall of hair. Anne's warmth crept into his leg, healing and soothing, absorbing the pain. The warmth spread upward into his chest, wrapping him around with light and heat, closing a deep, gaping wound in his soul. She gave her love to the most unlovable part of him, and he felt whole again, a complete man. Mark was filled with a bittersweet poignancy, and hot tears leaked from his eyes to trickle down his cheeks.

Mark reached down and pulled Anne up, wrapping his arms around her and squeezing her into his body. He wanted to be closer to her than it was humanly possible to be, to melt into her, consume her. He kissed her hair again and again, and his hands began to move over her body, pressing into her with slow, hard strokes. There was a deep, demanding desire within him, a desire which sprang not from physical need, but from an emotional yearning. It was a hunger of his soul, of his heart, which nothing except their complete joining could fill.

Anne tilted back her head, and his hands moved up to hold her head still, fingertips pressing into her scalp. He kissed her, a long, slow kiss. There was not the hot, insistent need that had been there in his first kisses, but a slow, lingering search. He did not want her quickly, but completely. His fingertips massaged her scalp and his tongue and lips explored her mouth; Anne went limp under the combined pleasures. They parted reluctantly to remove their clothes. Anne wore no brassiere under her blouse, as she often did when she came to visit him, and the omission stirred Mark. His hand sought her mound of Venus, his fingers slipping between her legs and lifting her up slightly. He rubbed and pressed while his mouth trailed down Anne's throat and took one hard, pointing nipple into his mouth. He suckled and caressed her endlessly, until Anne twisted and whimpered beneath his ministrations, murmuring inarticulately for satisfaction.

Finally they lay down on the bed, and Mark entered her. He began to stroke with infinite slowness, savoring each pleasure, each surge of desire that pushed them higher and higher. At last he exploded into a shattering climax, hurtling Anne into her own, and they clung together, stunned by the depth and glory of their lovemaking. Anne felt as if for a moment she truly had become part of him, joined indistinguishably, as if their souls had touched and linked.

It was a long time later that they released each other and slowly moved apart. The ache in his leg had been driven from Mark's head long since, but Anne had not forgotten. She moved down the bed to massage his leg. Quietly she stroked and rubbed his thigh and knee, pressing in gently with her thumbs. Before long even that throb of pain had stopped. Mark drifted into sleep, exhausted and soothed.

Anne's love for Mark and their time alone together were the bright spots in her world, made all the more precious by the pain and death that were now encircling Heartwood. Sophia's condition gradually deteriorated over the weeks following Anne's return from Dallas. She slept poorly and was often in pain, though the doctor prescribed more potent painkillers for her. Sophia rose later and later in the morning, and often Anne would take breakfast to her on a tray because Sophia didn't feel up to leaving her bed. It would be afternoon before she managed to dress and go downstairs. Soon she no longer made the effort to go downstairs.

Anne visited her every afternoon and evening in Sophia's sitting room. It saddened her to see her grandmother growing paler and thinner with every day that passed. At first they talked and played cards when Anne was there, but before long Sophia lost interest in the card games. Her conversation turned more and more to the past, and she recalled her husband and Gary, relating the little stories of their daily lives over the years.

Often when she left Sophia, Anne was on the verge of tears. Sophia had seemed so well at first that Anne had been able to push the thought of her dying out of her mind, but now the knowledge intruded in full force. Death hung in the air at Heartwood. Each morning Anne rushed to meet Mark in his cabin, where his love would wipe out the bitter gloom surrounding her. Only there did she feel free or happy or alive.

Mark finished the children's rooms, and after that she saw him only in the mornings after she took the children to day-care and at supper. He began to take Nicole and John Peter on outings in the afternoon, riding them up to a picnic in the alpine meadow where he kept the horses or walking through the woods or simply taking them back to his cabin. Anne was deeply grateful to him for taking the children out of the house and its sad atmosphere and for occupying their time, since she could spare them little. More and more she spent her time doing things for Sophia or simply sitting with her.

One evening late in July, Anne awoke in the middle of the night and was padding down the hall to the bathroom when she heard a groan from Sophia's room. She stopped short, frowning, and crossed the hall, easing the door open. Sophia lay tangled in her bedsheets, her hands clutching at a pillow, and her face was contorted with pain. She groaned again. Anne's heart flew into her throat and she hurried across the room.

"Sophia! What's the matter?"

Sophia's eyelids fluttered open. Her eyes were sunken and shadowed with blue. "It hurts," she whimpered, her voice almost that of a child's. "Can you stop it? Please?"

Anne rushed to the dresser and pulled out the bottle of painkillers. "Have you taken a pill?"

"Before I went to bed. But it hasn't helped."

Anne glanced at the illuminated face of the clock. That had been three hours ago. It wasn't yet time for a pill, but she wasn't going to wait. She got a glass of water from the bathroom and handed Sophia two pills instead of one. One hadn't done any good. And what harm could it do? There was no point in worrying about addiction or harming Sophia's organs now. The only thing that was important was ending this dreadful pain.

Sophia swallowed the pills and sank back on her pillows. She gritted her teeth, waiting, hoping for the pain to recede. Anne took Sophia's hand in hers, and Sophia clutched her gratefully. It seemed hours before Sophia's hold began to loosen and the tight lines of her face melted. Her hand slid from Anne's, and her eyes closed. She slept.

Anne leaned her forehead against the tall corner post of Sophia's bed. Her arm trembled, and she felt weak. It was a long time before she left Sophia's room.

After that she put a small rollaway bed in Sophia's sitting room and slept on it, so she could hear Sophia when the pain got worse in the night.

Anne was horrified at how quickly Sophia was going. Her illness had been hardly visible at first, and its development had seemed gradual over the last few weeks. But now it was hurtling along like a freight train, crushing Sophia. Over the next three days, she seemed to grow weaker by the hour.

Anne was by her side almost constantly. She didn't see Mark except when he came into the sickroom or when she went down for a meal with the family. He stayed with the children almost all the time now, and she blessed him for relieving her of that burden. Though she rarely saw him, she could feel his presence in the house, and it gave her strength.

The doctor prescribed an even stronger pain medication, but by the third night, it, too, could no longer negate Sophia's pain. Anne was up all night, giving Sophia her medicine and holding her hands as Sophia fought the pain. Sophia dozed off a time or two, but the pain always brought her awake again.

"I dreamed about my mama and papa," she told Anne once when she awoke. A faint smile curved her lips. "I dreamed they were here taking care of me like they did when I was a little girl. Mama would hold my hand, and Papa would sing to me. He had the most beautiful, light, tenor voice." Tears rolled out of her eyes. "I thought I would see them when I woke up."

Empathetic tears trickled from Anne's eyes. Sophia's words had an eerie quality that scared her, but there was also a deep misery and unhappiness that touched her own well of feelings. Even as they lay dying, people still searched for their parents.

About five o'clock in the morning, Sophia fell into a deeper sleep, and Anne knew she would rest for two or three hours at least. She had once again given Sophia more painkiller than prescribed. She couldn't bear to watch Sophia in pain. Anne walked to the window and looked out. There was no sun outside yet, but there was a faint lightening of the night sky, a graying of the blackness.

Anne flexed her hands. They were red and cramped, even bruised, from Sophia's clutching them in the throes of her pain. Anne ran a shaky hand through her hair. She could understand now the impulse to kill a loved one who was terminally ill, to put them out of their misery. The agony was almost unendurable to watch. Tears poured out of Anne's eyes. She felt lost and alone, facing an obstacle she couldn't deal with.

She glanced over at Sophia, noting her even breathing. She had to get out of here; Sophia would sleep all right without her for a while. Anne slipped out the door and down the hall to her bedroom, where she exchanged her soft bedroom slippers for shoes and pulled on jeans and a long-sleeved sweat shirt. She moved quietly, for Nicole had taken to sleeping in Anne's bed since Anne had started using the cot in Sophia's sitting room. Anne paused before she left the room and gazed for a moment at her sleeping daughter. Nicole looked innocent and vulnerable and very much like she had when she was younger. Anne thought of the many times over the years that she had checked on Nicole in her sleep and had found her like this, her face soft and slack, eyelashes shadowing her cheeks, forehead smooth. There was nothing so beautiful, so heart-tugging as a sleeping child, she thought, and once again her eyes misted with tears. But now, as she left the room, she felt curiously lighter.

Anne went downstairs, intending to sit on the porch for a short time. She didn't dare leave Sophia alone for long. As she walked down the hall, however, she glimpsed a low light in the den, and, frowning, she went toward it. Had the kids left a light on when they went to bed? She stopped in the doorway.

A dim lamp burned on the end table beside the couch. Mark lay stretched out on the couch, a paperback book lying open on his chest. At the sound of her step, his eyes flew open, and he sat up. "What is it?"

Anne shook her head. "Nothing. Sophia's finally gone to sleep. I didn't know you were here."

"Yeah. I've stayed the past couple of nights, in case you needed me."

"Thank you." Anne came in, drawn by his presence, and he swung his legs to the floor so she could sit beside him. Looping an arm around her shoulders, he pulled her against his body. Anne realized how chilled she felt inside; his body heat warmed her to the core. But she felt as if she had absorbed the misery, illness, and death of the sickroom, so that her body was contaminated. She wondered if anything or anyone could really cleanse her again; she was afraid she would infect Mark with the emotional dirt of the death watch.

"Sophia should sleep for an hour or two. I wanted to sit on the porch and get a breath of fresh air."

Mark's hand rubbed her arm up and down in a comforting motion. "Why don't you take a walk in the woods? Or a drive? Get away for a couple of hours, where you can't even see the house. It would help get rid of it."

Anne didn't have to ask what *it* was; she knew the miasma of death and pain she carried around was almost visible to someone like Mark. Her heart leaped at the thought of getting away, but she tamped down the hope. "What if Sophia wakes up? I'm afraid to leave the house."

"Don't worry. I'll be here. I'll sleep in the sitting room, so I can hear her if she calls. Sophia will accept help from me, I think."

Anne looked at him, hope lighting in her eyes. "Would you? Oh, Mark, that's too much to ask."

He shook his head. "I'm more used to it than you. You've given me so much. Let me give you this."

"Thank you." Anne stretched up to kiss him, and he wrapped her in a tight hug. "I love you."

Mark buried his face in the crook of her neck. "I love you, too. I love you more than anything in the world. I hate to see you going through this."

"Thank you for being here. Thank you for helping."

"I wish I could do more."

She smiled up at him, her eyes sparkling with tears. It seemed to her as if she had cried for days; her supply of tears must be unending. She cried in sadness, in empathy, in happiness. Everything seemed bittersweet and fraught with a kind of tender irony. She kissed Mark again and left the house.

Anne grabbed a sweater on her way out, for it was chilly outside, and when she put her hands in the pockets, she discovered her car keys there. She glanced toward the trees. Though the sky was lightening more and more, adding a golden glow to the grayness, the heavy growth of trees looked somber and dark. Anne knew she didn't want to go walking there. The thought of driving was much more appealing. She pulled the set of keys out of her pocket and walked to her car.

The car coughed slowly to life. It had been days since it had been started. Anne drove down to the highway and turned toward Iron Creek. She drove aimlessly, climbing and descending the narrow streets of the town without really seeing anything. At the end of one street she saw a cemetery, and she started to turn right onto the next side street. But she stopped, staring at the open cemetery gates before her. It was a pretty little area, built in a relatively flat space of land and sheltered by pine trees. The gateposts were square pillars of stone. Arching across the top, connecting the posts, was a sign made of wrought iron which spelled out the words "Iron Creek Cemetery."

It was peaceful looking, and Anne was drawn to it. She had never seen her father's grave. She hadn't been curious before, but now she wondered where it was and wanted to see it. She parked the car outside the gates and walked inside. It would be nice to walk a bit, and it seemed somehow a desecration to drive through the old-fashioned graveyard, even though the graveled roads attested to the fact that others did so.

The tombstones closest to the gates were old, many encrusted with moss. She wandered among them, noting the old dates and the sentiments, often flowery, sometimes blunt, and frequently poignant. She looked for the name Kerr, but couldn't find it. Then she remembered that Sophia's husband was not from this area. It would be Sophia's family who would lie here. What was Sophia's maiden name? Anne thought Sophia had mentioned it once, but she wasn't sure. Was it Randall? She saw a large granite stone a short distance away on which the name Reynolds was carved, and the name clicked in her mind. That was it. Reynolds. She walked toward the massive stone. It stood in the center of several plots, and smaller stones lay at each grave around it.

Anne circled the family plot slowly. There was a tiny grave, a child's grave, no doubt. The name on the stone was Charlotte Reynolds; she had died at two months. Her birth and death dates were in 1905. Anne wondered if she had been Sophia's sister. There were two graves with a double headstone labeled Father and Mother, and their given names. Another double tombstone caught her eye, and she walked around to it. Across the top, it read Kerr, and excitement seized Anne's chest. One half read Wendall P., Beloved Husband, and gave the dates of his birth and death. The other half read Sophia Reynolds and gave only a birth date. A shiver ran through Anne; it seemed an eerie thing to have your tombstone waiting for you. But, then, Sophia had had no family to do it for her after her death; it struck Anne how very alone Sophia had been before she and the children came.

Beside the empty space where Sophia would lie, there was another grave with a carved red granite tombstone at its head. The stone was simple and stated only the name and dates: Gary W. Kerr, May 31, 1932—August 9, 1952. It was her father's grave.

Anne squatted down beside the stone. There was nothing there to tell her of the boy/man who had given her life. The man her mother had loved before Bill Mitchell. The son Sophia had mourned for so long and looked forward to being reunited with.

It seemed strange that she knew so little about him, felt so little for him. Anne ran a finger across the glass-smooth surface of the granite. She knew much of her came from him—the reddish hair, the blue eyes, the smile. Sophia had said as much. No doubt there were other things about her that were like him, perhaps her feet or hands or the turn of her head. It was because of him that she was in this time and place. He was what had brought her to Sophia. To Mark. She didn't know him at all, yet he had given her life. And now he had changed her life.

She stood up and jammed her hands in the pockets of her jeans. Her throat was raw. Before long Sophia would be lying here beside her son. Anne knew there was no hope of anything else. She hoped Sophia was right and that she would find Gary waiting for her. Anne gazed out across the shady graveyard. A slight breeze lifted tendrils of her hair and brushed them across her forehead. She pushed them back and thought of Sophia and Gary. She thought of her life, of her mother and Bit and Bill, of Bryan and the children, of Sophia, of Mark. She stood for a long time. It seemed as if the breeze were blowing away the heavy atmosphere which had clung to her, sweeping it off in layer after layer, until finally it reached inside her and cleansed her there, too.

Anne sighed and turned away. She had to return to the house soon. As she started walking, she realized that she was cold, but it wasn't an unpleasant cold. She felt sad and tired, but curiously refreshed—and accepting. It was time to give up the fight, she thought. Time to let Sophia go, as Sophia wanted to. She would call the doctor in Fitch this morning and have him come see Sophia. She hadn't called him the past few days for fear of what he would tell her. But now she knew it was over. She had to let the ending start.

Chapter Sixteen

ANNE CALLED DR. KRESSEL AS SOON AS HIS OFFICE OPENED, and he drove to Heartwood during his lunch hour. When he entered Sophia's room, she looked up at him with weary resignation. He gave her a cursory examination. One look at her and Anne's description of the past few days told him enough. He cleared his throat and looked her in the eye. "Mrs. Kerr, I'm afraid you need to go to the hospital. I'm going to start you on stronger pain medication, and you'll need care round the clock."

"Yes. I know Linda and Anne are having to do too much." Sophia's face was creased with lines of pain, and now she frowned severely, pulling her face into a harsh mask. "But don't you dare put me on one of those machines. No respirator or anything."

"I won't."

"Promise me."

"I promise."

"I have that written down in a document in my desk. Anne, go over there and get it. Top right-hand drawer. Take it with you, and don't let them do anything."

"I will." Anne went to the desk in the sitting room and found the document, more to busy herself than anything else.

"I'll send an ambulance for you," Dr. Kressel went on.

"No! Absolutely not. I won't go in an ambulance."

"Mrs. Kerr, be reasonable. You're in no shape to get down those stairs."

Sophia struggled to a sitting position, her eyes flaming. "Damn it, nobody's carrying me out of my house on a stretcher! I won't allow it! I'll walk down the stairs. Anne and Mark will help me, and Mark will drive us to the hospital."

"I can't let you. It's too exhausting."

"Let me tell you something." Despite her pain and weakness, Sophia assumed her grande dame face, frozen and intimidating. "*You* can't 'let' or not 'let' me do anything. You send an ambulance for me, and I won't be here. Mark and Anne will take me. I'll be there this afternoon." She sent him an imperious nod, dismissing him.

Dr. Kressel grimaced and turned. "Mrs. Hamilton? Could I speak to you?"

Anne cast a smile toward Sophia and followed the doctor into the hall. He turned, crossing his arms. "She can't possibly walk down those stairs. She'll fall."

"We'll support her."

"She'll probably take both of you down with her. It's ridiculous—all for a point of pride. If she does manage it, it will sap all her strength."

"Does that really matter?" Anne asked softly. "Is it preferable that she have the strength to struggle with her pain for another day or two? At this point, pride is all she has left. It's important to her to leave Heartwood on her own, and she will."

Dr. Kressel glanced at the small out-thrust chin and smiled suddenly. "I can tell that you two are related." He sighed. "All right. I guess it doesn't make much difference. Bring her in to the hospital as soon as you can. I'll see you there this afternoon."

Anne showed the doctor out of the house and went back upstairs to Sophia's room. Sophia's eyes were closed when Anne entered, but her lids flew open at the sound of the door opening. "Well?"

"Well, what? Mark and I will take you into Fitch, just like you said."

Sophia smiled faintly. "I thought so. Look in my closet. There's a gown and robe hanging there. Kind of a dusty pink color. That's what I want to wear."

Anne took them out of the closet. They seemed brand new; Anne wondered if Sophia had ever worn them before. She helped Sophia dress and put pink leather house slippers on her feet. Finally, she combed Sophia's hair, and then Sophia lay back down on top of the covers. "Pack me a little bag," Sophia told her. "You know what to take. Not a lot of stuff. Then you go eat lunch. I think I'll rest a bit before I tackle those stairs."

Anne went downstairs. The others were in the kitchen eating, but she couldn't force herself to take a bite. "We're taking Sophia into Fitch today, Mark. Can you bring your car around?"

"Sure." He watched her, concern pressing two little grooves between his eyebrows. "You okay?"

Anne nodded, but her throat closed up, and she couldn't speak. Linda was standing by the sink, sniffing noisily, tears streaming down her face. Anne glanced at her and then away. Her eyes fell on Nicole, who watched her steadily. "Is Mama Sophie going to die now?"

Anne cleared her throat. "Yes, I'm afraid so."

Nicole looked back down at her plate and said nothing.

"Why don't you go upstairs and see her before she goes?" Anne suggested.

Nicole's head jerked up. Her eyes were bright and hard. "No! I don't want to. I don't want to see her. She'll look—she'll look—"

"She does look sick and weak," Anne admitted quietly. "You don't have to see her if you don't want to."

Nicole stuck out her lower lip mulishly. "Well, I don't want to."

"Okay."

Mark left the house to get his truck while Anne arranged with Linda to keep the children while they were gone. Nicole disappeared, and Anne picked up John Peter and took him upstairs to Sophia's room.

Sophia opened her eyes and smiled when she saw the baby.

She watched as John Peter explored the room for a few minutes. Then he allowed her to give him a hug and kiss before Anne took him to his room to nap. By the time Anne had John Peter in his bed, Mark had arrived. He climbed the stairs, and Sophia sat up in bed, swinging her legs around to the side. Mark came into the room, leaving the door wide open for their exit.

"Hello, Sophia."

"Hello, Mark. Haven't seen you in a few days."

"No. I've been keeping the kids out of Anne's hair, mostly." He smiled. "You ready to go?"

"As ready as I'll ever be. I'm afraid you'll have to help me."

"I just wish I could carry you. But I'd probably send us both tumbling down the stairs." He was strong enough to carry Sophia, but his leg couldn't support it. Anne knew that that fact ate at him.

"We'll manage with one of us on either side of you," Anne put in quickly.

They helped Sophia out of bed and made their slow, shuffling way out of the room and down the hall to the stairs. With Sophia's arms around their shoulders and their arms around her waist, Anne and Mark half carried her. But on the stairs, Sophia was forced to take more of her own weight in order to maintain their balance. She hadn't left bed in several days nor eaten well for a long time; those things, coupled with her voracious disease, left her terribly weak. When the trio reached the landing, they were forced to pause for a few minutes and let Sophia sit down on the top step to rest, leaning her head against the banister. When at last they made it to the bottom of the stairs, Sophia sank down in one of the stiff, antique chairs that adorned the hallway. Anne ran back upstairs to get Sophia's suitcase and her own purse and carried them out to Mark's car while Sophia closed her eyes and rested. Finally Sophia signaled that she was ready, and Anne and Mark placed her between them once again, bearing nearly all her weight, and took her out of the house and helped her into the back seat of the car.

As they were settling Sophia in her seat, Anne heard

Nicole's voice calling, and she turned. Nicole was running across the field toward them, waving her arms. Anne nodded and waved to her. Nicole pelted up to the open car door and hesitated, peering in at Sophia. She held one hand behind her back. "Mama Sophie?"

"Hello, Nicole. I'm glad you came to say good-bye."

"It's not good-bye," Nicole corrected fiercely. "You'll come back."

Sophia smiled. "I'm afraid not, sweetheart. What's that in your hand?"

Nicole stretched out her right hand to Sophia. In it was a cluster of mountain daisies, iris, and several of the tiny, bright flowers that decorated the low bushes at this high altitude. "I picked you some flowers. That's why I was almost late."

"Why, thank you. They're beautiful." Sophia took the bouquet and smiled down at the colorful blooms. "I'll have a nurse put them in water as soon as I get there. It'll make a nice bright spot in the room. If I know hospitals, it'll be as dull as ditchwater."

Nicole hung back for a moment, then crawled inside the car and put her arms around Sophia. She kissed her on the cheek. "I love you," Nicole whispered, and backed out of the car. She whirled and ran into the house before Anne could say anything to her. Anne swallowed and closed the door. She looked at Mark across the top of the car, and they climbed into the front seat.

He started the car and drove carefully down the uneven drive. Anne glanced back at Sophia to see how she was taking the rough road. Sophia's head was turned, looking out the back window. She was gazing at Heartwood. They reached the highway and turned onto it, and in a moment Heartwood was hidden by the trees. Sophia turned around and settled into the corner. She looked tired beyond belief, and her eyes closed quickly.

She slept most of the way into Fitch. When they arrived at the hospital, she awoke and glanced around, disoriented. "Where are we?"

"Fitch. At the hospital."

Sophia frowned at Anne, puzzled. "Beverly?" Then she

moved her head a little from side to side in negation. "No. What am I thinking of? Anne. And Mark's here, too, isn't he?"

"Yes. He went inside to get an attendant with a wheelchair."

Sophia straightened and set her legs on the floor. "I hate hospitals." Her voice was faint and whispery, and Anne had to lean into the back seat to catch her words. "Gary died here. Not this hospital; it's too new. The old one in the center of town. I think of him every time I go into a hospital. Hate them."

A white-coated orderly came out of the emergency entrance, pushing an empty wheelchair. He and Anne helped Sophia into the chair, and the attendant wheeled her inside. He took Sophia up to her room while Mark and Anne remained downstairs checking her in. Finally they were through with the red tape and followed Sophia to the second floor. Anne asked for her grandmother's room number at the nurses' station, and one of the nurses pointed the way. Anne started down the hall, but Mark hung back, and Anne turned to him questioningly.

"Wouldn't you rather see her by yourself?"

Anne reached out a hand impulsively and grabbed his. "No, please. Please come with me."

He squeezed Anne's hand and they walked down the hall to the end room. He pushed open the door, and Anne went inside, Mark behind her. Sophia turned her head toward the door. "There you are. They've given me a shot of something, said I'd sleep in a bit." Her voice was already a little slurred.

Anne walked around to the side of the bed and took her grandmother's hand. It was tiny and frail, the skin wasted over the bones. Sophia's eyes were cloudy. "This is the place they brought Gary. Did I tell you?"

Anne nodded.

Sophia sighed. "They had his body in one of the examination rooms, and they let me in to see him. There wasn't a scratch on him, hardly. Just a little cut on his cheek where some glass hit him. But they said he hit the ground so hard it broke all his bones." She raised a hand waveringly and pressed it to the side of her head. "His face was . . . lopsided, sort of. Like a giant took his hand and pressed real hard, here." She closed her eyes and tears seeped beneath her lids.

Anne patted her hand. "Sophia, please, maybe you shouldn't think about it."

Sophia went on as if Anne hadn't spoken. "I was cruel, you know. I wouldn't let Beverly see his body. I told the doctor no one but family, and she wasn't family. I hated her. Hated her." She hissed out the words. "Poor girl. I sat beside the table and held his hand. I sat there for a long, long time, until somebody came and pulled me away. His hand was cold, but it was all I had of him." She sighed and turned her head away, closing her eyes. Anne thought she had fallen asleep, but then she spoke again.

"I shouldn't have done what I did. I should have taken her to me. We could have given each other comfort. She had all that there would ever be of Gary. We should have helped each other. I wouldn't even look at her." She opened her eyes and looked hazily at Anne. "Funny, all the pain we inflict in the name of love."

Sophia died two days later. Anne was sitting in a chair beside her, staring blankly at the floor, when she noticed there was something different in the room. She glanced up, puzzled, and realized that the faint, whispery sound of Sophia's breathing was gone. She jumped up and rang the bell for the nurse, rushing to bend over Sophia.

"Sophia! Sophia!"

The nurse pushed her aside, and Anne stumbled back to the chair, sinking into it numbly. It was over.

Mark, who had been down the hall at the coffee machine, saw the nurse rush into Sophia's room, and he set down the cup of coffee he'd just purchased and hurried after her. He pulled Anne into the crook of his arm and led her down the hall to the waiting room. He propelled her to a seat on the couch and sat down beside her, his arm around her shoulders. Anne clasped her hands together on her knees. She felt lacerated and numb.

"I don't know what to do," she said finally.

"Don't worry. I'll take care of it."

Anne smiled faintly and leaned her head against his shoulder. "Thank you. You're so good to me."

"It's easy to be good to you."

She snuggled closer, feeling gradually returning to her. "I guess I never really believed this moment would come. One of those things that remain perpetually in the future."

Mark leaned back and pulled Anne onto his lap, wrapping both arms around her. She curled up tightly against him, and his chest swelled with the joy of her love and her need for him. He rubbed her back with one hand, in slow, soothing strokes. "You've been wonderful through all this," he told her softly. "No one could have handled it better. You're a strong, strong lady, did you know that?"

Anne moved her head a little in negation. "I don't feel strong at all."

"You are. You gave Sophia what she needed. You didn't turn away or try to avoid the grief."

"Oh, Mark." Anne drew a shuddering breath. "I wish I could have!" She began to cry, hard, deep sobs that shook her body, and her fingers curled into his shirt, holding on desperately.

He held her even tighter, rocking her, while her numbness gave way to realization and sorrow. She poured out her grief, and he accepted it, until at last she lay quietly in his arms.

For a long time after she stopped crying they remained that way, unwilling to break the contact. Anne had never felt so warm and loved. Even in her sorrow, she knew a peace and joy she had never before even guessed existed. She was encircled with love. She was at home.

Mark felt the same love enfolding them, but his feelings were bittersweet. He clung to her with the fervor of a man grasping the last few precious moments of life. Soon, he knew, Anne would be leaving. Sophia's death had been more than the loss of a friend; it meant the end of his brief time of happiness with Anne. She would return to Dallas now, and he would lose the warmth and brightness that had visited his world this summer. It was callous, he thought, to worry about his own happiness with Sophia just dead and Anne sorrowing, but Mark couldn't hold back his fear and aching despair.

He had tried to keep his mind off the way this summer would end and simply enjoy the time he had with Anne. He had tried to ignore the thought of the eventual death and loss and grief, but except when he was with Anne, the effort had been largely unsuccessful. There were times when Mark didn't think he could bear it. Before Anne came, he had convinced himself that he was relatively happy with his life. But now, having tasted the sweetness of her love, that life would be empty and dark. Her memory would haunt him the rest of his life.

He would have liked to keep Anne with him, to bind her to him with the chains of her love, but he refused to give into that selfish wish. She had fallen in love with him because she was lonely and her ex-husband had made her feel unloved and unlovable. Moreover, the situation with Sophia had thrown her into an emotional turmoil. She loved him because she wasn't one to give herself where her love wasn't engaged. But it couldn't be a lasting love. He had to let her go.

It would be far worse to take advantage of her emotional state now and ask her to marry him. Then he would have to watch her lose her love for him and grow discontented. She would realize in time that he wasn't enough for her, that she deserved far more. She would get lonely and bored in the mountains. He could offer her nothing of the life she was used to. She would discover that and she might realize, too, how he had bound her, taking advantage of her sorrow and her gratitude. Then she would despise him, and that was the worst thing that could happen.

It would be better to let her go now, to send her away freely. He loved her. He couldn't ask her to share anything but the best of lives. She must go back where she belonged and find someone better, someone who could give her the life she deserved. He had to let her go. He *had* to.

But that knowledge didn't make it any easier to bear. Mark squeezed her closer with the hunger of desperation.

* * *

Anne awoke slowly, pulled to consciousness by the low rumble of a male voice and the higher-pitched ones of children. She glanced around her, trying to collect her thoughts, unsure for a moment where she was. There was a clatter below her and a girl's laughter, then again the man's voice. She smiled slightly. Mark was here, downstairs in the kitchen with Nicole and John Peter.

She sat up, rolling her head to stretch her neck. She had slept most of the time since Mark brought her home from the hospital yesterday. He had sent her straight up to bed while he went to fetch the kids from their sitter, and she had gone willingly. In the last week she had lost a great deal of sleep. She had slept through dinner, but Mark had awakened her later and insisted that she eat. She had eaten and played a little while with John Peter. Nicole had seemed both sullen and frightened, saying little, but sticking close to her mother's side.

When the children were both tucked into bed, Anne had gone back to sleep. This time Mark had stayed with her, sleeping in her bed and enfolding her in the blissful warmth of his arms. She had slept like a rock throughout the night, exhausted and secure.

She yawned and stretched and pulled herself out of bed, filled with the lassitude of one who had slept far longer than normal. She thought she could simply have lain in bed staring at the ceiling for the rest of the day, but she had a much stronger yearning to be with Mark and the children. Besides, there were things to do. She would have to see about Sophia's funeral and select the dress she would be buried in, and there were doubtless people who would have to be notified— Sophia's lawyers and whatever outlying family there was. Anne sighed. She dreaded the thought of doing it.

After she dressed Anne left her room and started toward the stairs, then stopped and went to Sophia's bedroom. She opened the door and stepped inside. The smell of death still lingered there, mixed with the scent of the sachet Sophia used in her drawers. Anne stopped. It was too much. She couldn't bear to enter just yet. But after a moment, she made herself walk to Sophia's closet. She opened the door and began to look through Sophia's clothes. There must be one dress that was right. She hadn't known Sophia long enough to know which dresses were her favorites.

The smell of Sophia's perfume wafted up from her dresses, and Anne's eyes began to tear. She leaned against the door frame, hit by a sudden wave of longing. She wanted . . . she wasn't quite sure what. Then Beverly's voice sounded in her head, and Anne knew: she wanted her mother. She paused, examining the thought, rather startled by it. She and Beverly were not close; they never had been. She hadn't even run to her mother for comfort when Bryan left her. But right now she wished very much that Beverly were here.

Anne glanced through the connecting door to the phone in the sitting room. She could call Beverly and ask. She couldn't imagine Beverly being willing to come. She had disliked Sophia as heartily as Sophia had disliked her, and she wasn't the kind of mother who would drop everything to fly to her child to comfort her. Was she? Anne wasn't sure. She couldn't remember ever asking her to before.

Still, it seemed somehow appropriate that Beverly be there for the funeral. She was, after all, the link between Sophia and Anne. At the end of her life, Sophia had expressed deep regret for the chasm between her and Beverly. Perhaps she ought to ask her. Anne wandered into the next room and paused, then picked up the phone. She dialed her mother's number.

"Hello?"

"Mother?"

"Anne? How are you, dear?"

"I—Sophia died yesterday."

There was a moment of silence on the other end, then Beverly said, "Oh, sweetheart, I'm sorry. How are you doing?"

"All right, I guess. The reason I called was—this sounds kind of strange, but—I was wondering if you could come up here."

"Yes, of course," Beverly answered promptly. "I'll catch the first plane. Don't bother coming to meet me. I'll rent a car."

"Will you be able to find the house?"

"Yes. Oh, yes. I remember Iron Creek well."

Downstairs the air was filled with the aroma of cooking bacon. Anne entered the kitchen to find Nicole standing at the stove like a sentry, meat fork in hand, watching the bacon sputter, and Mark seated on the floor with John Peter, a large bowl of batter between them, which the baby was stirring with delight. "Well, hello, what have we here?"

All three turned toward her, different shades of smiles on their faces, and spoke at once: "We're cooking breakfast." "How'd you sleep?" "Pannycake!"

"Very well. Thank you for getting up with John Peter and letting me sleep." She answered Mark first, going to where they sat and lightly touching his hair. She bent down and ruffled the baby's hair and went on to the stove. "Mmm. That smells delicious. Where'd you learn to cook bacon?"

"Just now. Mark showed me how."

Anne put her arm around Nicole's shoulders and gave her a little hug, bending down to kiss the top of her head. For once, Nicole didn't shrug off her embrace. "Gee-Gee's coming up here today."

"Honest?" Nicole glanced up at her, then returned her gaze to the all-important bacon. "How come?"

"Who's Gee-Gee?" Mark asked.

"My mother," Anne answered him first, then went back to Nicole's questions. "And she's coming because I called and asked her to."

"Oh. Are we going to get her at the airport?"

"No. She said she'd rent a car and drive up. She used to live here in the summers and knows the way."

Mark levered himself off the floor and picked up the large bowl of batter, despite John Peter's protestations. He set it down on the counter beside Anne and began to prepare the griddle. "That'll be good, having your mother here."

"I hope so." She watched him grease and heat the griddle, then drop the first batch of pancakes onto it. John Peter tugged at her trouser legs, demanding to be held up where he could see the pancake making, and Anne swung him up onto her hip. It was a cozy scene, Anne thought, so homey and natural, the four of them making breakfast together. They seemed like a family. A lump formed in Anne's chest. Did they have any chance of becoming one?

She had avoided the subject as long as possible, telling herself that she would face the issue after Sophia died, hoping that something would happen that would make it all work out. But now Sophia was dead, and nothing had happened to change the situation. It was almost August. She could linger here a couple of more weeks, but no longer than that. Nicole's school started the third week in August, and she had to buy her new clothes and get the kids back in day-care. Look for a job. Buy a new house. If she was reasonable, she'd admit that she needed to leave as soon as the funeral was over and she'd turned over Heartwood to a real estate agent.

Anne didn't want to go. She loved the mountains and this house. She loved Mark. She would have liked very much to stay in Heartwood and raise the kids here, to continue the closeness with Mark. But Nicole would throw a fit if they didn't return to Dallas; she would want to go back to her friends and school and Bryan. And Mark hadn't given any indication that he wanted her to stay. He had said he loved her, but that wasn't the same as telling her he wanted her with him, needed her with him. Why didn't he ask her not to go? If only he would, she knew she'd risk Nicole's anger—and Bryan's. She kept waiting, hoping; that was the "something" she'd kept hoping would come along.

But the time was getting short. If Mark didn't say something soon, circumstances would force her to move on. She couldn't remain here long without a reason. Nicole would be screaming to return, and she had to sell Heartwood. She had thought of getting a job in the village and living in Heartwood, but that was virtually impossible. There would be few, if any, jobs in the village, and she was sure they wouldn't pay much. Though she wouldn't have to make house payments, she was sure the taxes and insurance on a house like Heartwood would be enormous. Plus there was the upkeep; it was too valuable a house not to maintain it in the best condition. If she invested the money from the sale of the house in

Dallas, that extra income might enable her to swing it, but she had the sneaking suspicion she would soon be dipping into the principal and before long that would be gone, too.

Anne frowned and turned away, setting John Peter down and going to the cabinet to take out the dishes for the table. There was another possibility. Heartwood would be a beautiful place for a bed-and-breakfast inn. The rooms on the second floor were in good, livable condition. She wouldn't have to make any renovations, and that meant that she would need little capital to get started. It was something she knew she could do, having both office and household skills. And she could earn money without being away from home all day. She could be there when Nicole got out of school. She could take John Peter to day-care or keep him home, whichever she wished. If one of the children got sick, she wouldn't have to worry about putting her child before her job. In many ways it would be ideal. Of course, there was no guarantee that an inn would be a success, and Anne was sure there must be pitfalls—there were in any undertaking. But it fit most of her needs. The area was a tourist place both summer and winter, and Heartwood would appeal to many people.

The idea had occurred to her almost two weeks before when she had read an article on a bed-and-breakfast inn in Vermont. She had more or less stored it away in the back of her mind, but it had been germinating there, and every day or so, some new thought would pop into her head. Now, putting it all together as she laid the table, Anne decided it would be a perfect thing for her, the children, and the house.

But what good was the idea if Mark didn't want her to stay? Anne glanced over at Mark, stacking another set of pancakes on a plate. Why didn't he ask her? Was he afraid of the commitment? Too used to being alone? Or was it too soon for him to be sure? She frowned, considering. She could work such things out. She could live here without actually living with Mark, without marriage. That would give them time to make sure this was really what they wanted—or, rather, give him time, for she was sure of what she wanted. But how could she tell Mark that when he hadn't given her any indication that he wanted her to stay at all?

She stopped abruptly and dropped into one of the chairs. Why, she asked herself, why did she have to wait for Mark to ask her to stay? She was thirty-one years old, mother of two children, and dependent on no one. Surely she was capable of deciding where she wanted to live. All her life she'd let others make her decisions—first her mother and then Bryan. Even after her divorce, she had put up with Bryan's instructions and Nicole's demands, struggling to please them. She'd despised herself for her weakness and railed against the way she lived her life, always waiting for fate to shove her in a new direction. She hated her passivity, her acceptance of others' directions; hated the aimless, reactive way her life ran. Yet here she was again, preparing to give someone else the power to direct her life!

It was absurd. *She* should be the one who decided whether she remained in Iron Creek. Not Mark, not Nicole. She would stay here, and Mark could make of that what he would. Their relationship could run in the way either or both of them wanted. It was astonishing that she hadn't decided to do that earlier.

Mark and Nicole put the food on the table, and Mark stuck the baby in his high chair. They began to eat, but Anne's attention wasn't on the meal. She ate mechanically, her mind running on its own course. The others noticed her silence, but made no mention of it. What little conversation there was, was provided by Mark and Nicole. Toward the end of the meal, Anne laid down her fork and cleared her throat. Her voice was soft and a trifle hesitant as she began, "I've been thinking about something."

Mark glanced up at her. He had a queasy feeling in his stomach that the moment he'd feared was upon them. Anne was about to announce when she and the children would leave Iron Creek. He waited, one hand unconsciously clenched around his fork handle.

"I, uh, I've been thinking about staying in Iron Creek."

Her words were so far from what he had expected that Mark simply stared at her. Nicole, too, gaped in silence. John Peter, sensing that something was amiss, ceased his repetitive kicking of the high chair's foot rest and looked from one person to another. His thumb went into his mouth, and he waited.

Anne felt the full force of everyone's stare, and her courage began to seep away. "I love Heartwood, and I thought we might be able to live here."

"How?" The word was out before Mark thought. Everything in him had leaped up in hope when Anne's words sank in, and he couldn't help but respond with an eager question. Maybe she really meant it. Maybe it could be done.

"I have the money from the sale of our house in Dallas. I could invest that and get a little income from it. And I thought I'd turn the house into a bed-and-breakfast inn. You know, take in a few guests. Tourists. It would bring in money, and it would be an ideal job for me." She stumbled over her words, forgetting most of her careful reasoning. Oh, why couldn't she lay it forth calmly and logically, so they would see what an excellent idea it was for everyone?

"You've got to be kidding." Nicole finally found her voice. Her face twisted anxiously. "Mom! Aren't you?"

"No."

"But I have to go back! We can't live here all the time! What about school?"

"There's one in Iron Creek."

"A little hick school," Nicole agreed contemptuously. "I don't want to go there. I don't want to move a million miles away from my friends. From Daddy. I want to go home!"

Anne clenched her hands. Nicole's words tore at her heart, touching every chord of guilt within her, and Mark's lack of words unnerved her. He hadn't even smiled. "It's not a million miles." She tried to squelch the tremor in her voice and infuse it with false courage. "You'll be able to go back and see your daddy often. I thought—I thought you had friends here now. I thought you liked Iron Creek."

"It's not the same. I like Sherry and Jennifer, but—I haven't known them long. Michelle and Cathy have been my friends for years! I don't want to move. I won't do it!"

"Nicole." Mark's voice cut across Nicole's increasingly hysterical words. He wasn't loud, but the tone was so firm that Nicole stopped talking immediately and looked at him.

"Take John Peter and go play with him. I want to talk to your mother."

Nicole's chin jutted forward, and for a moment Anne thought she would refuse, but then she jumped up and hauled the baby out of his chair. "Okay. But I hope you convince her she's wrong."

Mark's mouth tightened, but he made no comment. Anne pushed her plate back and clasped her hands on top of the table. She stared down at them, waiting for Mark to speak, her stomach tumbling. He didn't like it; she could tell. He was too still, too quiet, too expressionless.

She didn't see Mark look at her or rub his forehead. Nor did she see the bright pain in his eyes. Mark hadn't expected it to come quite this soon. Not this morning. His defenses were down. Her words had gone straight through him and made jelly out of his insides. He wanted her to stay. But this was where he had to play the hero. He must tell her to go with his blessing, without guilt. If he really loved her, he reminded himself, he would want her to find the right man and the right life for herself.

"Anne, I—" He hesitated, then continued harshly, "You ought to go back to Dallas."

Anne didn't raise her head. His words had pinned her to her chair. "You don't want me to stay," she said dully.

"It's not a question of wanting or not wanting. I'm talking about what's best for you. Honey, it could never work out for us. I've known that from the beginning. Haven't you?"

"No. I guess I'm stupider than you. I thought—why did you say you loved me?" She looked up then, straight into his eyes, and Mark sucked in his breath. Her eyes swam with tears; they were the most vivid, most beautiful blue he'd ever seen.

"I do," he rasped. "I do love you. But I'm not right. I'm no good for you."

"How can you say that? That's crazy. Don't I know better than you what's right for me? *Who's* right for me?"

He smiled faintly. "I don't know. You married Bryan, didn't you?"

"Yes, but . . . it's not the same. You know it's not the same."

Mark sighed and rose. "I don't know much of anything, except that I'm not going to make your life miserable. I'm bitter; I'm moody. I've got nothing to offer a woman. Any woman, but especially one as beautiful and—and as good as you. I'm a loser."

"You're not!" Anne flushed and jumped up to face him. "You're a good artist and a fine human being. I won't let you say things like that about yourself. You're kind and caring. You're great with kids. You've done more for me than I could ever hope to repay. How can you say you have nothing to offer?"

"I do all right with my work," Mark conceded. "But that doesn't make me good for a woman. Just the opposite. It makes me self-centered and isolated. Anne, listen to me! What we have is a temporary thing. I knew it wouldn't last beyond the summer, and so did you. It's over. So forget it! Forget me, and go home."

Pain seared Anne, flooding her mouth and throat with a bitter, rusty taste. He didn't want her. Her hopes, her sudden determination crumbled before her. What good was directing her own life if Mark didn't want her? What good were this quaint town or the beautiful scenery or Heartwood itself if she couldn't be with Mark? She felt utterly desolated. Sophia was gone. Mark was tearing himself out of her life. She was back to nothing. Square one, except with a much bigger hole in her heart. She turned away to hide her face from him. "All right, then. Go on. Go back to your hide-out." Suddenly she blazed up and whirled to face him, tears streaming down her face, voice choking, her eyes shooting fire. "I hope you're happy all alone. No doubt it's all you need. You're very well suited—just you and your wood!"

Anne turned and fled out of the room.

Chapter Seventeen

As soon as she left the room, Anne regretted the bitter words she'd thrown at him, but there was nothing she could do about it. He wanted out of her life. She went to her room and sat for a few minutes, trying to calm her jumbled thoughts and emotions. No matter what had happened between her and Mark, there were many things she had to do today. She couldn't allow herself time to mope and cry. After a while, she rose and rounded up the children to take them to their sitter. Then she set about doing the hundreds of things that must be done when someone dies. By the time she finished with the funeral home, the newspapers, and notifying Sophia's distant kin, she was exhausted.

Still, she had to let Sophia's attorney know, so while she was downtown in Iron Creek, she went by his office. His secretary announced her to him, and he came out to greet her, his expression grave. He was a tall, slender man in his late fifties who looked like Anne's mental image of a judge. He went to Anne, extending his hand to shake hers. "Mrs. Hamilton? I'm sorry we haven't met before. Has—is Sophia all right?"

Anne shook her head. "She died yesterday afternoon."

He sighed. "I was afraid that was why you were here.

Won't you come into my office?" He stepped back and let her precede him into the inner office. It was a large room, but very cluttered and chock full of furniture, bookcases, and files. Charles Dawson took a set of files off a leather chair, and motioned for her to sit down. Then he sat behind his massive desk, leaned his elbows on the surface, and sighed. "Poor Sophia. A true original. I'm afraid she'll be sadly missed in this town."

"Yes, I'm sure." Anne was tired, and she wished she were home. "Mr. Dawson, I don't know what else I'm supposed to do. I just wanted to let you know that she had died. I guess you'll do all the stuff about her will and everything. Is there anything you need me to do?"

"Let me see. I'd like to go over the will with you, but I'm sure this afternoon isn't a very good time. How about Monday? Would that be suitable?"

Anne frowned. "Yes, I suppose so. But I don't see what the will has to do with me. I mean, I'll be happy to help you with sorting through all the personal effects and furniture or whatever you have to do. But I don't see why I'd need to see the will."

"But you are one of the beneficiaries, Mrs. Hamilton."

"I beg your pardon."

"Sophia gave you the house by outright deed before she died, but she also left you the furniture and her personal, tangible property in the will."

"Oh. Yes, that's right. I remember her saying something about it when I first met her."

"She also left you a bequest of $200,000."

"What?" Anne's voice vaulted upward. He repeated his words, and Anne gaped, stunned. Finally she murmured, "But I never. I mean, she never said. I didn't realize . . ."

"I understand. Mrs. Kerr was full of little secrets, I'm afraid. She took a certain joy in giving people something unexpected—as she bequeathed that cabin and a sum of money to the young man who rented from her."

"Mark Pascal?"

"Yes, that's the one. She left Linda Whitton a bequest also, and of course her husband's property went to his cousins. The bulk of her monetary estate is going to charity. But she told me that she didn't want Heartwood to become an albatross around your neck. She wanted you to have some money as well, in the hopes it would enable you not to have to sell the house."

"I—I had thought about keeping it." (Until Mark pushed her out of his life.) This money would have made her scheme to turn the house into an inn much easier. She might even have renovated the servants' quarters behind the house and turned it into rooms to rent, also. But that was a moot issue now, of course.

"Well, good, I'm glad to hear it. Then may I expect you to come back to my office on Monday?"

"Yes. Of course. What time?"

"In the morning? Say, ten o'clock?"

"Yes, that's fine." Anne's mind was blank. She was so stunned by what Sophia had done for her that she answered Mr. Dawson more out of instinct than thought.

"Excellent. I'll look forward to seeing you."

Anne rose and shook hands with him and let him escort her out the door, still somewhat in shock. She had never suspected that Sophia had left her money as well. But it was just like Sophia to take into account every aspect of the situation. It was also just like her not to have told her, Anne acknowledged with a wry inner smile.

Tears stung her eyes, not for the first or the last time that day.

Mechanically, she drove to the sitter's house to pick up the children and then drove home. Nicole ostentatiously avoided speaking to her, but Anne couldn't bring herself to worry about it. Just as the news Sophia's attorney had given couldn't really penetrate her sorrow, Nicole's little pricks couldn't measure up to the great wound inside her now.

When she reached Heartwood, Anne went into the formal parlor and dropped onto a chair. She tried to think, but it was too difficult, her mind too jumbled. She found herself merely staring out the front bay window.

When a car pulled up in front of the house, and Beverly Mitchell stepped out, Anne flew out the front door and threw herself into her mother's arms. Beverly looked surprised but quickly returned the embrace. Finally Anne released her and led her inside the house. Beverly walked through Heartwood slowly, her eyes misting over now and then.

"It's so lovely," she murmured. "I'd forgotten quite how much—it's been so long."

They sat and talked a little, but Beverly didn't press for explanations or an outpouring of Anne's emotions. Anne couldn't remember ever having such easy companionship with her mother before.

Later that evening, after the children were in bed, Beverly turned to Anne and said in a soft voice, "There's something troubling you besides Mrs. Kerr's death, isn't there?"

Anne glanced up in surprise. "Well, yes. I mean, I'd become very fond of Sophia, but . . . there's more." Slowly she began to relate what had taken place between her and Mark this summer, ending with their parting earlier that morning.

When Anne finished, Beverly was quiet for a long time. Then she wet her lips and said, "You know, sweetheart, you shouldn't ever let love get away."

"I can't hogtie him. I can't make him love me."

"You said he loved you."

"That's what he said, but—well, how could he send me away like that if he did?"

Beverly shrugged. "I don't know. People do strange things. They make decisions for all the wrong reasons, and then they regret them the rest of their lives. Believe me, the regret's a lot worse than trying again."

"What are you talking about?"

"Your father, I guess. Ever since he died, I've regretted not telling him about you. I wanted to marry him for only the right reasons, you see, so I held back that knowledge. I should have told him. Maybe it would have saved his life. At least he would have died knowing about you."

"Did you—love him very much?"

"More than anything in the world," Beverly replied simply. "I never stopped loving him. I still miss him." She bit her lower lip to stop its slight quivering. "I've thought about him and missed him every day since he died. I love Bill; I don't mean that. And I got to where I wasn't one big walking emotional sore. But the love I feel for Bill is pale compared to what I felt for Gary. With Bill it's *friendly*. But I loved Gary with everything I had, every single part of me. That's different; special."

"Then why didn't—" Anne cut off her words suddenly.

"What? Why didn't what?"

For a moment Anne started not to answer, but then the words burst out of her with all the force of years long suppressed, "Why didn't you love me? If you loved my father so much, why didn't you welcome me? Love me?"

Beverly gaped. "Why didn't I love you?" She repeated dazedly. "Are you crazy? Anne—I've always loved you. Always. You were the most precious thing in the world to me. You still are."

"How can you say that? You've never been close to me, not like you are with Bit. You always thought I was incompetent, couldn't do anything. Yet you trusted Bit completely. You joked and laughed with her. You didn't keep her from doing things."

Beverly stared at Anne, her brows contracted in thought and her eyes filling with misery. "Sweetheart, I never meant for you to think that. I—oh, the situation was so different when Bit came along. I didn't worry about Bit. You don't worry so much with the second child. You know that. And she was always able to take care of herself. She's like Bill, full of energy and drive and love. There's no holding her back. I treated you differently, it's true, but it wasn't out of lack of love! If anything, it was because I loved you too much."

Beverly rose and came forward to take Anne's hands, sitting down beside her on the couch. She gazed earnestly into Anne's eyes, willing her daughter to understand and believe her words. "*You* were what kept me alive after Gary died. If I hadn't been carrying you, I would have killed myself. I swear it. I was so miserable that I just wanted to die and join him. I couldn't bear it. But I knew I was carrying you, his child, and I couldn't snuff out your life to satisfy my own selfish grief. I loved you too much even then to hurt you. I married Bill because I loved you, because I didn't want you to have the shame of illegitimacy to bear all your life. Can you imagine how it hurt to marry a man you didn't love while you grieved over the man who had been your whole world? Nothing but deep, deep love could have made me do that. Nothing else could have made me try my best to make that marriage work. I wanted to be a good wife; I wanted us to be a good family for your sake. I loved you terribly, desperately. I was scared to death something might happen to you, that you would be taken from me, too. That's why I overprotected you. I see now that it was wrong. When Bit came along, I realized I had kept you down, made you fearful and unsure of yourself. It wasn't what I had meant to do. I just wanted to keep you safe from harm. I didn't want you to try anything where you might get hurt. I always wanted you to wait until you were older and stronger. The reason was because you were so dear to me. I couldn't stand to lose you or see you hurt. It was an excess of love, not too little. Don't you see?"

Anne digested what her mother had said, looking back on the events of her childhood with new eyes. She could see how her mother's words and actions could have sprung from a fear of losing something infinitely precious to her instead of from a belief in Anne's incompetence and failure. "Yes," she answered slowly. "I guess so."

"When I finally began to wake up to how wrong it was, it was too late. I didn't know how to change what I'd already done to you, and I was so in the habit of worrying about you that I couldn't stop. That's why I wanted you to marry Bryan. I thought he would take care of you."

"But what about the closeness between you and Bit? Why didn't you and I have that? Why have we always been so distant?"

Beverly sighed and released Anne's hands. "I'm not sure. I felt it, too. It's frustrated me so, yet I was unable to do anything to change it. It wasn't lack of love, believe me. But I felt a barrier between us from the moment you were born. I think it was because I was grieving over Gary. I loved you, but I couldn't delight in you. Do you understand what I mean? I had nothing to give. Emotionally, I mean. My heart had died with Gary. I was empty inside. A shell. That's how I saw myself. All my energies were directed first at giving you life and then at making everything around you as nice and secure and happy as I could. I worked hard at being a good wife and mother. But my love had been so blasted—well, it's hard to give what you don't have. My love for you was a basic, primitive, driving force. Because I loved you, I got up every morning and went about my tasks. I did everything I could for you, bought you everything we could afford. But my grief was there like a wall between us. I couldn't get through it, and it made me cold and distant at the very time you most needed my love and security."

Beverly sighed. "I don't know how much you love this Mark of yours. But—when you love very deeply and then lose that love, it kills something inside of you." She rose and began to pace, rubbing her palms up and down across each other. "You can't ever get it back. It's gone from you." She turned, and Anne was amazed to see that tears sparkled in her mother's eyes. "After thirty-two years, I still miss Gary. I've lost forever the joy and youthfulness and spontaneity I once had. I've been walking around without a vital part of me for the biggest portion of my life. That's what losing your love does to you. Don't let anyone tell you that there isn't such a thing as a one, true love or that you can recover from the loss of anyone. It's not true! There are some people whom you'll never stop missing and wanting and needing. That's the real truth, though it's too harsh for most people to want to believe."

Anne went to her mother and put her arms around her. "Oh, Mama, I never knew! I never realized. All that time when I thought you were cold, you were unhappy. You were grieving."

"Yes. But I can see that it made me appear cold. No matter how much I loved you, I found it hard to show it. It was as if there were ice encasing my heart, and not even my love for you and Bit could melt it." Beverly squeezed her and stepped back, holding Anne away from her so she could look into her eyes. "That's why I told you not to give up on Mark if you really love him. Don't leave here because of pride or hurt feelings. If you love him, stay. Be here for him; seduce him back to you. Whatever you have to do. It's worth it."

"But he doesn't want me. And Nicole is so bitterly against it. How can I fight them both?"

"Easily. Nicole's only ten years old. Don't give her the right to run everyone's lives. There's no reason to slavishly follow her wishes. She'll adjust. If you can create something with the man you love, you'll give her a good family and a good example of what a man and woman can have. That's worth far more to her in the long run. It's like giving her a nutritious meal instead of the candy she's crying for. From what you said about Mark, I don't think it's that he doesn't love you. He's simply stubborn and wrong-headed and thinks he isn't good enough for you. Even if he didn't love you, it'd be worth the effort if you love him that much. The worst thing that could happen is that you'd lose him, and that's already occurred, right?"

"Yes."

"What would happen if you stayed here, yet didn't get him back?"

Anne frowned. "It would be painful to be around and see him every now and then. I'd hate to have him think I'm pushy and . . . selfish."

"Baloney," Beverly said with inelegant bluntness. "You're scared of looking like a fool if you stay and he refuses you again."

"I guess that's part of it."

"That's *most* of it. You won't have to see him a lot if he refuses you again; you told me he's practically a hermit. So the prospect of feeling pain whenever you see him isn't all that great because you'll hardly ever see him. It's not realistic. It's a rationalization for your fear of getting rejected by him."

Anne sighed. "I suppose so."

"Listen, I'll tell you just like I would tell Bit. Go out there and try. Strive. Risk yourself. Don't hang around and take whatever's dealt to you."

Anne thought about her mother's words for a long time after she went to bed that night, and when she awoke her eyes were dark-circled from lack of sleep. She continued to go over her mother's arguments. She thought of her fears and the possibilities of whichever course she chose. She considered her pride and her pain and the consequences if she tried again and found out Mark really didn't love her. She also thought about risking the life she'd led, the strengths she'd discovered within herself over the summer.

Then, trembling inside, she went into her daughter's room and sat down on the edge of the bed. "Nicole, I want to talk to you."

Nicole, who had been reading, lowered her book. Her eyes were wary. "I have to get dressed for Mama Sophie's funeral."

"It's two hours away. You have plenty of time."

"What do you want?"

"I've come to tell you that I'm not changing my mind about what I said yesterday. We're going to stay at Heartwood. You can go back to Dallas frequently to see your father and friends. But we'll live here. I'll return to Dallas only to ship our things in storage and to settle a few things with Bryan. The only choice—" She paused, suddenly breathless with fear, then cleared her throat and went on, "The only choice you have is whether you want to live with me or live in Dallas with your father full-time."

"What kind of choice is that?" Nicole yelped. "Gwen doesn't want me. Daddy doesn't really want me!" Her eyes filled with tears.

"Darling, that's not true." Anne took her daughter's hand. "He does want you. I know your father pretty well, and I'll be the first to admit that he doesn't know how to express his emotions. He rarely shows anyone affection. And it would be difficult for him if you lived with him; a stepchild can put a strain on a new marriage. But none of that means he doesn't love you. He does."

Nicole gripped her mother's hand tightly. "I don't know. I think—I think Mark likes me better than Daddy does!"

"Mark is very fond of you. He does love you, I think, both you and John Peter."

"Does he love you?" Nicole asked suddenly.

Anne looked at her, startled. "What makes you ask that?"

"I've seen him kiss you sometimes or put his arm around you. And he looks at you . . . funny. I don't know. He just—I wondered. That's all."

"If he did," Anne began carefully, "how would you feel about it?"

"You mean if he moved in? Married you?"

"Yeah, something like that."

"I think—I think I'd like it." She lowered her head and her voice was low and torn. "Oh, Mama, sometimes I like him better than Daddy."

"Sweetheart." Anne pulled her daughter close. "Don't feel bad about it. Or guilty. Your father is your father, and nothing will ever change that. No other man can be that to you. But you don't have to have a storybook relationship with him. You have with Bryan whatever you and Bryan work out, whatever suits the two of you. You don't have to be a television series kind of father and daughter. You don't have to close yourself off from feeling respect or friendship or love for another man. You can love Mark without taking anything away from your father, just as you can love John Peter without stopping loving Bryan or me. Just as I can love John Peter or Mark without stopping loving you."

"Do you really?"

"What?"

"Still love me the same?"

"Of course I do. Honey, I know we haven't gotten along well lately, but I still love you. I love you very much."

Nicole sighed. "Sometimes I feel rotten. I get mad at you, and then I get scared that you don't love me. That makes me madder than ever."

"I know how difficult this time of your life is. I was once your age, and I was always in a turmoil, too. I know that doesn't help you much. But . . . no matter how we struggle, please, please believe that I love you very much."

Nicole rested quietly against Anne's shoulder for a moment, then said. "What about Mark? *Is* he going to move in?"

"I don't know. I'd like for him to, but he's reluctant. He

thinks we ought to go back to Dallas. I can't promise you that if we stay he'll be here with us. But I'll try to convince him to."

"I'm scared, Mama."

"Of what?"

"Of starting school here. Of going away from home. Leaving all my friends. Being new in school here. I don't want to do it."

"I know it's scary. But I'm sure you can overcome that. You have to face new and sometimes scary things or you'll never grow."

Nicole groaned and stood up. "Now you sound like a teacher."

Anne chuckled. She could see that Nicole was past the worst of it. "Sorry. But it's the truth. You'll see; you'll do well here. I have a lot of confidence in you."

Nicole plucked at her bedspread. "Maybe." She looked up and grimaced. "Maybe it'll be okay. Living here, I mean."

Anne smiled, her chest suddenly swelling with a feeling of success and courage. "I'm so glad." She leaned forward and kissed Nicole on the forehead, and Nicole didn't flinch away. "I love you, honey."

"I love you, too."

Anne saw Mark at the funeral. His eyes flickered toward her once and then away. He was at the graveside, too, but he left quickly, not even stopping to express his sympathy to Anne, as the other townspeople did. Anne's heart twisted a little, but she made no move toward him. This was neither the time nor the place.

After most of the people had left, Beverly left Anne's side and drifted over to the simple stone that marked Gary Kerr's grave. She squatted down beside it and ran a loving hand over the earth. Anne ached to see the pain that still lay within her mother, and she was filled with a rush of determination to make a happier life for herself. It was growing late, but she would go to Mark's cabin when she got home. Beverly would be there to look after the children. She would confront him again with her love and her decision to stay. She would strip her pride before him, if that's what it took. Anything, as long as there was a chance to live in his love.

When they got home, Anne changed clothes and left the house, setting out along the path leading to Mark's cabin. She walked slowly, needing a little time to build up her courage, which was rapidly slipping the nearer she came to Mark's home. When she entered the clearing in which the cabin lay, she walked around to the rear, expecting him to be on the porch with his creations. When she stepped up to the screen door, she saw that he was indeed there, but he wasn't working. His tools lay in his hands, but he sat staring into space.

Anne opened the screen door, and Mark's head snapped around at the noise. His eyes widened when he saw her, and a strange mixture of emotions passed across his face before he froze it into blankness. "What do you want?" he asked gruffly, rising.

Anne linked her hands behind her, steeling herself not to retreat before his rough tone. "I want to talk to you."

"About what?"

"Us."

"There isn't such a thing anymore."

"Denying something doesn't make it go away, Mark," she retorted sharply, and was surprised to find that her muscles were relaxing. She could do it, she thought in surprise. No matter what happened, at least she was going to be able to fight without running.

Mark glowered, but she faced him calmly. "I came to tell you I'm staying at Heartwood."

"We've been over that," he grated out, jaw clenched. When she had stepped onto the porch, Mark had wanted to jump up and go to her, just as he'd wanted to go to her today at the funeral. At the funeral he had wanted to hold and comfort her. Now he wanted to beg her not to leave him. The past day had been hellish, and knowing he'd done the right and honorable thing didn't diminish the pain. Selfishly, against all logic, he wanted Anne. That's all his heart and body understood.

"I know. You say you don't want me to stay. But, you

know, Mark, it really isn't your decision whether I stay or go. It's mine, and I'm staying. I've talked to Nicole, and she understands. She's scared, but she'll work it out. She's hoping you'll live with us."

"Anne, please . . ."

"I'm hoping so, too," Anne plowed on, not daring to pause, for fear she would lose her courage. "I won't push you. If you don't love me, I'll have to learn to accept it. But I love you, and I love this place, and I'm staying here. I'm not asking you for a commitment, if that scares you. I'm not asking you to marry me or even to move in." She tried a little smile, but it failed. She wet her lips nervously. "I—I just want to live here and have a chance to love you. These have been the craziest months of my life. Sad because of Sophia's dying, yet the happiest because I found you. Mark, I love you. I can't tell you how much I love you. My mother suffered all her life because she lost the man she loved. I don't want that to happen to me! Please, please, give us another chance. Don't turn me away. I promise I won't make demands on you or—"

"Damn it! You think I care about your making demands on me? Christ, I'd love it. You could demand anything of me, and I'd kill myself trying to do it. I love you. I love you! You think I don't want to marry you? To sleep with you? To fill my life up with your warmth and joy? You're everything to me."

"Then why are you sending me away! Was it what I said about the inn idea? Would having guests around bother you? I don't have to do it. I found out yesterday that Sophia left me some money; I could swing living here without opening an inn."

"It's not that. I don't care about the people. If I had you, there could be a hundred guests through there every day and it wouldn't bother me. But, Anne, don't you see? I'm no good for you. You'll regret it if you stay. I don't want to see you unhappy. I couldn't bear it when you realized how trapped and miserable you were."

"I won't be trapped and miserable. How dare you tell me what I'll think and feel and do? I love you. I'll marry you; I'll be your mistress; I'll be your occasional one-night stand, if that's what you want. I just want you any way I can have you."

"Anne. Anne." Mark crossed the porch and seized her by the arms, pulling her to him. He kissed her again and again, until they were both breathless and laughing and crying all at the same time. "I love you. Stay with me. Marry me. God, I love you. It scares me to think of having such happiness."

Anne kissed him again. "It scares me, too, but not as bad as being without you scares me."

Mark smiled, his dark eyes alive and bright. "You know, this is where a really noble guy would make the ultimate sacrifice. He'd lie and tell you he didn't love you so you wouldn't waste yourself on him." He ran his forefinger along the line of her cheek and caressed her lips. "Thank God I'm not a very noble guy."

Anne trembled with the release of nerves and the sudden joy she had feared wouldn't materialize. It seemed unfair, unkind, in a way, to have such happiness, knowing that it had been brought about by Sophia's illness and death. She would never have known Mark otherwise.

But there was a certain rightness to it, too, a completion. It was fitting that all the tangled, pained, unhappy threads left from the tragedy of Sophia's and Beverly's love for Anne's father should at last be pulled together and knotted up in love.